The Traveler

Book I

Peter Krausche

Published by

MusterionPress

Inspirational Fiction

a division of VMI Publishers
Sisters, Oregon
www.vmipublishers.com

ISBN 0-9747190-7-2
Library of Congress Control Number: 2005926295

Author Contact:
http://www.PeterKrausche.com

Printed and bound in the United States of America

Acknowledgements

Author's Note

Preamble

Prologue

Prelude: The Rose

Part 1: The Traveler

1. Arrival

2. The Vision

3. The Proprietor

4. Dead Drop

5. Chimes of Destiny

6. The Dispatch

7. View from a Window

8. Catyana

9. Gold of the Heavens

10. The Guest

11. Conversation with a Lady

12. The Rendezvous

13. The Sinaven

14. Vicious Revenge

15. The One Law

16. Sincerity and Hypocrisy

17. The Artifact

18. Tracks in the Forest

19. Eastern Technology

20. The Games of the Noble

21. An Evening in the Tavern

22. The Way Station

23. Prophecy

24. Meeting in Skull Alley

25. The Second Shot

26. The Message

27. Practice

28. Aftermath

29. The Bow

30. The Market

31. Confessions

32. The Debt

33. Waiting

34. The Grave

35. Moment of Truth

36. Dispute in the Navaren

37. The Audition

38. A Tinavar's Choice

39. Empty Assurances

40. The Sacrifice

41. Golden Gifts

42. A Goblet Together

43. Mina's Lesson

44. The Operative

45. The Ballad

46. An Approaching Storm

47. Taking Leave

The Traveler: Appendices

Acknowledgements

Many people have assisted me in the compilation of this manuscript and I would like to give thanks where credit is due. I apologize to anyone that has been of help and isn't mentioned here, but the list of supporters would be longer than this short acknowledgement would allow. Sorry guys!

Thanks to my wife, Rita, and my boys, Conrad and Caleb, for your love and patience.

Thanks to Bill and Nancie Carmichael, Tom Horn and the other great people at VMI, for your support and faith in this project.

Thanks to Lisa Bowden. You've done a wonderful job editing this manuscript and taught me more about writing than I ever thought I'd know.

Thanks to Gillian White, for a wonderful lamb filet dinner. By the way, it was your sculpture, *Sphere V / The Globe*, which inspired the Artifact and the Selanian principles of Sensation and Induction.

Thanks to Beatrice, Erika, Eva, Julianne, Lou Ann, Maria and Regula for being such enduring victims and for your constant enthusiasm and encouragement.

Thanks to John Clements, Director of the Association for Renaissance Martial Arts (www.TheARMA.org) for taking a look at the relevant sections regarding swords and swordsmanship.

And last, thanks to all the terrific members of the Critters Online Writer's Workshop (www.Critters.org), for helping to make *The Traveler* what it has become today.

Author's Note

I first met Philip Brannon in a small, run-down bar in Bend during the summer of 1990 while I was staying in Central Oregon with my family. As he told me later, his friends Bill and Carol Marten were in New York City at the time, so he was working the circuit by himself. He impressed me by the casual way in which he mixed with the regulars, relating, encouraging, or discreetly stashing a few dollars into someone's pocket if he felt they could use it. I was familiar and often discouraged with the way members of religious groups canvassed the populace in search of new proponents, and was therefore favorably surprised to find someone that actually had such a caring and unobtrusive influence on the people around him. We got to talking and my impression deepened. By the time I returned to Switzerland with my family in the spring of 1991, Philip and I had become fast friends.

Just before we left, Philip entrusted me with a manuscript, which he had titled *The Rose*, and asked me to see what I could do with it. As it turned out, the document was an account of his experiences leading to the formation of the Selanian Society. I was at first overwhelmed by the prospect of compiling any form of narration on such a delicate subject, and my personal situation at the time also compelled me to lay the manuscript aside for over a decade. But Philip's incessant yet subtle coaxing and my own increasing awareness of the significance of the ensuing events finally led me to seriously contemplate the necessity of such a bold venture.

I originally envisioned *The Traveler* as a four-part novel. It soon became evident, though, that the tale's length and complexity went far beyond the scope of what could effectively be published in a single volume. Having gained a momentum all its own, the story would no longer allow me to contain it in only four parts.

The principal narration is set approximately 4500 years in the past on the planet Piral; it is recounted in the main parts of this and any subsequent installment of the *Traveler* series. This chronicle is interspersed with a secondary plot—set in approximately our time—that begins with Philip's account of *The Rose* and will also be continued in the form of interludes to the following installments. Although the two plots—past and present—are directly related, I fear the structure I have chosen for this series veils the connection. I am certain, though, that observant readers will have discovered the relationship for themselves long before the series is concluded, when the two plots converge and the mystery surrounding the Traveler's identity and background is finally resolved.

The Rose is therefore to be taken, not as the prelude to this novel, but as the overture to an entire series. I felt that Philip's account was significant enough to warrant such a prominent position, and I hope the outcome will justify my anticipation. I am aware that this literary structure is uncommon and might possibly lead to some confusion. I also admit that the saga itself will frequently offer more mysteries than solutions and may therefore be the cause of additional perplexity. I solemnly pledge that everything will be resolved by the end of the series. In the meantime, I hope that this tale will give my readers as much pleasure as it has given me in relating it.

Preamble

Ah, the vexatious enigma of chronology and consequence! Although it is one of the most intriguing dilemmas of the chronological sciences and poses many questions regarding the interpretation and classification of historical data, the main difficulty seems to lie in a simple character fault: arrogance. It is our attitude which, in the end, will determine the importance we assign to our research.

Alright then, where do we begin? How do we proceed? What do we include and when do we omit? Are we more interested in the subjective viewpoint of an individual that we have placed under scrutiny, or do we consider the objective angle of an impartial observer? Is it the impact of an instant that captures our imagination, or the unfolding drama in a course of events?

Have we come so far that, in our condescension, we attempt to adapt the divine perspective of omniscience, by which authority we may reveal all aspects of eternity from everlasting to everlasting? Or do we prefer the power of perpetual omnipresence, in which promise and fulfillment become inseparable manifestations of the sinuate currents of time and space?

No, dear friend, remember: no matter how significant we believe our opinion to be and regardless of the confidence we place in the extent and excellence of our examinations, in the end the trivial farces we have compiled—which we dare call historic chronicles—will always remain mere and feeble glimpses of the infinite moments that constitute our unfathomable existence. Believe me; in the overall scheme of things, we can't even begin to imagine how crucial a gentle breeze on a bright spring morning may turn out to be.

—The Traveler, *Excerpts on History*

Prologue

The Prophet raised his eyes and glanced at the creatures surrounding him. The larger moon shone brightly down upon their somber circle, illuminating the parched earth, rocks, and dried shrubs of the desert that spread out for hundreds of leagues around them. The waning sickle of Luna Minor was setting behind the snow-capped peaks of the Covasin Massive, which was faintly visible to the west in the clear night air. The jagged summits of an outcrop of the eastern Tyenar Range that lay before him glowed ominously in the cold, pale moonlight, silently harboring the wreckage of a long-forgotten splendor in their depths.

The creatures had a wild and ardent beauty about them that was difficult to reconcile to their apparent wisdom and gentleness. The moon's light reflected brilliantly from the flowing, crimson crests that enclosed their heads like manes and adorned their sleek bodies and long, muscular tails like streaming, elegant fins, setting them in stunning contrast to the shimmering blackness of their smooth skin. The threatening fangs that jutted from their short snouts and the vicious claws that impended from each of their huge, webbed paws belied the kind glances they shot him from their dark eyes. If the persistent images and visions that led him here had not prepared him, he would have been devastated at the sight of these ferocious beings. They were evidently creatures of the sea, and it would have seemed strange to find them so far from any body of water if he hadn't known better. The fearsome titles that had been given them in the past came to mind as he looked at them:

Demantar.
Leviathan.
Dragons.

The Prophet sighed. He could still physically feel the creatures' pain. His thick, silvery brows furrowed, his lips converged, and his eyes shone with anguish as he considered their circumstances.

"I'm so sorry, my friends," he said. "I wish I could do more for you."

The creatures around him bowed their heads in consent.

"It is enough, my friend," replied the eldest creature. "You have allowed us to join with you in the Rite of Union. We have sought the will of Anae together, and we know now what to do."

"Yes, although it pains me that it will be over five hundred years before Anae sends His Emissary and you are delivered from this desolate state of affairs."

"That is as it should be. The will of the One must be fulfilled. But we will never forget your kindness, Nevacad. You are the only one of your race that has ever sought us out. We have been so lonely these past five centuries."

"Please, Sutanay, don't be too harsh in your judgment of my people. They were unaware that you were spared. They believe this place is cursed and were therefore afraid to come."

The creature nodded. "Yes, it is cursed, as we are cursed. But you have given us hope, my friend. With the fire that you have rekindled in our hearts, we can patiently await the Traveler and his female companion, the Golden Messenger who will release us from our prisons."

At these words, the creatures' passion erupted anew and they lifted their heads in a drawn-out cry that echoed from the ruins behind them.

The Prophet closed his eyes and listened. It was a beautiful and melancholic song that rose and fell in melodious waves. The sounds the creatures emitted were their natural voices. Their vocal chords were not capable of normal speech, and it had been difficult at first for the Prophet to deduce how to communicate with them. Had anyone been eavesdropping, they would not have perceived a word of their mute conversation.

The Prophet opened his eyes again as the last yearning tones of their song faded into the night. Although he was touched by the creatures' longing, his heart also ached for his own people, and he could no longer contain the question that burned in his soul.

"What of Nevilan?"

"We have asked you not to speak his name in our presence," the eldest creature growled.

"But you will have to confront your past at some point."

The creature exhaled forcefully, and smoke billowed from its nostrils. "There will be time enough for that when we have been set free. In the meantime, you know that there is nothing we can do. Your people will have to deal with him as best they can."

The Prophet shook his head. "They will not be able to deal with him. They have absolutely no concept of what they will confront. I shudder at the misery and suffering I see ahead."

The creature relented of its harsh words and advanced carefully, its movements lithe and graceful. It placed its webbed paw gently on the Prophet's shoulder, but almost crushed him with its weight. When it saw that it was hurting him, it started. Then it tried again, this time attempting to better assess its own strength.

"I understand, my friend, and I am sorry," it said. "You have shared in our pain, and we wish to share in yours."

This produced a sad smile on the Prophet's lips. "You are most kind, Sutanay. I understand your reluctance to recall the terrible sins of our parents. We shall speak of them no more."

The creature bowed its head.

"Do you believe that we can master the errand that has been set before us?" the Prophet asked.

The creature looked at him. "Yes, we possess the knowledge to design the instrument that will lead the Traveler to us, but we lack the necessary agility."

"Good, then you will lend me your wisdom and guide my hands, just as Anae has instructed."

"And my comrades and I will ensure that the Traveler finds a safe passage through the wastelands when his time has come to seek us out."

"So be it. My friends, let us begin the sacred task with which we have been entrusted."

The Prophet stood, and the solemn group disappeared into the remains of what had once been the creatures' home.

Prelude: The Rose

I.

The rose strives upward towards the light of the sky in the garden behind the cabin, its shades of cream and pale rose in solemn contrast to the plain headstone behind it. The blossom keeps a solitary vigil, patiently guarding the memory of a lost beauty, her true nature disregarded and unrecognized during her lifetime, now gone like a feather on a breath of air.

I don't remember where she got the rose, probably from my father. She planted the cane sometime in late fall, a bare stem with thorns, hardly something you would notice on passing by. But perceiving latent beauty seemed to be her way. Her heart-felt compassion and gentle hands would coax wilting flowers into full bloom. So many small miracles I never chose to notice. How is it that I can see her so much clearer now, like a warm light in the cold dark?

I remember her affection for candles. She was always lighting them: at the dinner table, on the little shelf above our bed before we drifted off to sleep or in the reading room on winter evenings with a fire crackling in the fireplace. I kept teasing her about that. No, it wasn't just teasing. There was always that subtle touch of sarcasm, just enough bite to cause the slightest margin of pain.

All there is now is the rose. During those nights in which my restless memories hold sleep at bay, I can sometimes see the single blossom silhouetted in the moon's light, just that one, pale, delicate flower, as pale and as delicate as she appeared to me on that first evening almost four years ago.

II.

Twilight was once again settling over the high desert plateau east of the Cascades on that clear and warm midsummer evening in 1982. There had been a brief drizzle that morning, a rarity at that time of year, so I kept my window rolled down to enjoy the thick fragrance of juniper, alder, and manzanita so prominent in the mild night air. The geological analysis I had completed in the Deschutes National Forest that day had been quite demanding, and since I had been itching to give my brand-new Cherokee Chief a thorough tryout, I thought I'd treat myself to a little spin on some of the rarely traveled service roads of the area before starting home.

There was a bend in the road ahead, so I slammed the shift back into second and gradually released the clutch. Despite the gravel scattering in all directions, the vehicle's four-wheel drive clung firmly to the loose, dusty surface. I kicked down the gas midway into the curve and shot out from among the trees onto a clear stretch of road.

There was still barely enough light to see the squirrel vanish beneath my car.

I hit the brakes, and the SUV skidded to an irritatingly slow halt. I switched off the engine and just sat there in shocked surprise, staring out at the road with the sickening, dull little thumps I had heard below me still echoing in my mind. When I finally looked in my rearview mirror, the dust had cleared enough that I could see the small, lifeless form lying there.

Normally, if I had run over some animal careless enough to get in my way, I would have shrugged and kept my foot on the pedal. I couldn't say what influenced me, but I started the engine, pulled back a few yards, and parked at the edge of the road. When I walked over to examine the damage, I could see that the small creature was fortunately still in one piece but undoubtedly no longer alive. I looked around, maybe feeling guilt, perhaps sensing something more.

That was when I saw her. She was standing motionless at the edge of the wood just a few feet away, regarding the squirrel, her expression pale and sorrowful. Her thick, dark hair fell smoothly about her shoulders and cascaded down to her waist in an endless stream. She stepped out onto the road with tears in her eyes, her gown waving lightly in the breeze as she stooped to mourn her little companion.

"I'm really sorry, miss. It wasn't yours, was it?"

She looked up at me but didn't reply. She stroked the soft, grayish fur, then untied a scarf from around her shoulders and enfolded the once lively animal.

"We must bury her," she said, the tone of her voice sad but at the same time pleasant and soothing.

She didn't wait for me to follow. She just turned and walked back into the forest without another glance in my direction.

But I did follow. Without thinking I stepped into the darkness between the trees where she had disappeared. I felt anxious about the swiftly waning light but I soon realized that my worry was unfounded, for it seemed as if a soft radiance surrounded her wherever she walked.

Spellbound, I watched as she dropped down on one knee in a clearing bordered by pine and hemlock. She dug a shallow grave in the soft forest soil with her hands, then reverently laid the squirrel inside and placed the earth back on the small, broken body. She spread her arms to the wind where she kneeled.

"*Anae pirae, Anae milantarae. Alicosar vonala s'Anae. Camar tesiranu anam se pirala, enaviranu alin a pirala. Piral a piral, teman a teman, anemar al anemar.* Sleep well, dear little friend."

She recited the invocation in a low voice, like a gentle breeze whispering in the trees. Then she stood and turned towards me in one sweeping motion.

I still see her before me as if it were today. Her large eyes were dark brown and set in a beautiful, oval face. She seemed fragile and small, barely rising to my chin, yet she emanated a quiet authority that made me feel awkward and out of place. It was as if she belonged, as if the woods around us were a part of her. I felt at a loss under that calm gaze.

"I'm really sorry, miss, about your...your friend. Is there anything I can do?"

"No, she's at peace now."

I shrugged, keeping my hands in my pockets, not really knowing what to do or what to say.

"May I invite you to a cup of tea?" she asked. "I live only a short distance from here."

Despite her unfamiliar accent, she conveyed a sense of genuine sincerity yet cautious deliberation. The sound of her voice and the natural flow of her words had a mesmerizing effect on me.

I was lost. I never had a chance.

I didn't remember her cabin afterwards, but I could imagine how it must have been on that first evening. Just one small, cozy little room filled with plants and herbs, drawings on the walls and a fire in the hearth. We sat at the table, and she talked about the fields and the woods. She explained how each little plant had its own individual significance and described the animals and their ways.

But I guess I just wasn't paying attention. I saw only her face, her hair, her slender figure as she glided about the room, filling a kettle with water, crushing herbs in a mortar, filing jars away in cabinets. I watched her as she sat across from me, sipping her tea, searching my eyes, and listening as I told her about myself. And I heard her name, Silana, a magical sound, like the faint murmuring of a stream or the sighing of trees in the wind.

She closed her eyes for a moment as if from exhaustion.

"My friend, you are not...well." Her voice was filled with concern but remained soft.

"I feel fine."

"No, in here." She placed her hands over her heart.

I didn't understand her then. It was not until much later that I came to appreciate the intuitive perception with which she could penetrate the essence of my being, exposing the little masquerades I employed to keep my true colors so well hidden, sometimes even from myself.

I realized that it was getting late and I needed to leave soon.

"May I come again?" I asked on impulse.

My question seemed to trouble her. But then she smiled as if to apologize for some impropriety.

"Yes. I think that would be alright."

She walked me back to the car, the stars shining down on her hair. The sky was filled with their silent brilliance, and she raised her head for a moment to consider them—a sad, yearning expression—then turned to face me.

"Good-bye, Philip. Come again whenever you can."

I hardly knew what to answer, so I climbed into my Jeep without another word and closed the door. The odious noise of a revving V8 engine intruded upon the peaceful sounds of the night. I eased my vehicle back onto the road and watched her in the rearview mirror until she was lost from sight: a pale and delicate figure gazing up into the night sky with her arms around herself against the evening chill.

III.

I visited her each weekend and sometimes, as my profession of freelance civil engineering consultant would allow, even during the week. The weather in Central Oregon was usually marvelous all year-round, which allowed us to explore her world every time I called on her. She showed me the woods and the streams, the flowers and the trees. But as before, I just didn't listen, being too infatuated by the mere reality of her presence.

One day we came upon a part of the forest that had been destroyed by a fire. Burned ponderosa lay scattered everywhere, and the ground was scorched black. The havoc caused by the fire looked more like the path of a tornado: a long, broad trail of destruction. Silana stood silently. She seemed confused and on the verge of tears. She grabbed my arm and pulled me away, walking as quickly as she could without breaking into a run. Only after we had put quite a distance between us and the devastating scene did she relax and finally loosen her grip.

Physical contact came naturally to her. She was always touching me to get my attention or taking my arm to pull me along in her enthusiasm to show me something new, her flowing movements resembling a graceful dance. But there seemed to be a subtle boundary which she maintained and which I couldn't—wouldn't—cross without further commitment. It would have been like defiling something altogether pure and innocent.

After my initial disorientation, I believed that her exotic manners and her unfamiliar and gentle ways had simply overwhelmed me. I thought that if I just gave myself some time, my feelings might subside. But as the weeks went by and my astonishment grew, I came to realize that this wonderful creature had somehow captured my heart and was swiftly becoming an essential part of my life. I yearned for her and desired her with my entire being, or so I imagined. I therefore watched for an occasion to reveal my feelings to her.

My opportunity came one Sunday afternoon in early fall. We had taken a long walk and were sitting comfortably in a field not too far from her cabin, surrounded by tall, yellow grass, the aspen golden in the warm sunlight and everything so peaceful. Silana took a deep breath of the clear, mountain air and sighed contentedly. Then she smiled at me, her face radiant from the exercise and her eyes shining with a soft glow. I felt that it was now or never and gently took her delicate hand in mine.

"Silana, will you marry me?"

Her smile faded and the troubled look from that first evening in her cabin returned. "Marry you? Do you mean, stay with you, always?"

"Yes, Silana, please stay with me, always."

She glanced out across the field, and her eyes followed a flock of geese flying in formation above the trees, their silhouettes black against the blue late-afternoon sky. Then she eased her hand away from mine, shaking her head.

"I don't know if that would be wise."

Her words hit me like a forty-ton truck. The force of the impact thrust me into a world of cold and darkness, as if I had been dropped to the bottom of the sea with an ocean of water crushing down upon me. For a moment I just struggled to catch my breath. I couldn't say a word.

Silana stared at me, shocked at my reaction, tears filling her eyes.

"Oh, Philip, I...I'm so sorry, I didn't realize..." She shook her head, tossing her long locks. "I should have known.... Oh, how could I have been so selfish?"

"Silana, please, I...I love you, and I just don't know if I could live without you."

She tried to smile through her tears at my confession but failed. Instead, she reached for my hand and lifted my palm to her wet face, then tenderly kissed my fingers.

"My poor Philip, you don't understand. There is so much you don't know, so much you would hardly believe."

"What's wrong? Please tell me what the problem is."

She gazed out across the field again, silent. After a while she looked back at me, her expression pained. "Please try to understand and be patient with me. I...I need time to think."

"I'll give you all the time you want."

Silana brushed a tear away. "Please believe me, I have enjoyed your visits so very much. Until you came I hardly realized how lonely I was. But I wasn't aware of how important it had all become to...to you." She glanced at me, her distress plainly marked in her face.

"When can I see you again?"

She shook her head. "I don't know."

I studied the ground for a moment, hardly daring to look at her. "May I come back next weekend?"

She looked up at me, into my eyes, probing. Then she nodded.

"Alright," she whispered, wiping a tear from under her eye. "But please excuse me now, I...I really need to be alone for a while."

She kissed me on the cheek, then stood and disappeared into the forest. I sat there for a while longer, contemplating her reaction, shocked at what had happened and trembling with anxiety. In the end I somehow managed to get up and haul my numbed body back to the car.

The following week dragged by. Fear and anticipation seemed to be the primary characteristics of my existence. My stomach felt as if it had ingested a jar full of swallowtails, and I could hardly eat. The projects I was working on were delayed because I couldn't concentrate. My thoughts continually revolved around what her answer would be and why she had reacted so mysteriously.

At last the weekend arrived. The drive up Highway 97 was the culmination of all the strain I had endured and seemed to take forever. Every last twig, blade of grass and bump in the road was engraved in my memory. I turned onto Century Drive, then snaked about less traveled lanes until I came down the little road where I had that fateful encounter only a couple of months ago. I parked the car near the wood and walked down the path to her cabin with the warm autumn sun shining down on my face, but my hands remained cold and clammy.

She was sitting in a chair on the veranda knitting a shawl as I approached. When she saw me, she took a deep breath. Then she stood to meet me and placed her work on the table with deliberation. I stepped onto the porch and took her hands in mine, looking deeply into her eyes and searching for an answer. She gently clasped my hands against her stomach and laid her head against my heart.

"Silana, does that mean yes? Will you marry me?" I held my breath.

She nodded. "Yes." An almost inaudible whisper.

Overwhelming joy flooded my thoughts, shattering all the anxiety of the past week like ice cracking on a river in the spring warmth. I embraced her and held her tight, her fragrance, like summer blossoms, heightening my senses.

"Oh, Silana, you can't believe what this means to me. I love you so much."

She looked up at me, and I could see concern in her eyes.

"Yes, dearest Philip, I know," she replied. "But there is so much that you don't know about me, so many questions you would probably like to ask. Please, I beseech you. If you truly love me, then trust me and take me as I am. Allow me to leave behind what is gone and past."

I held her close. "Of course, Silana, I'll do anything you want. Don't worry, everything will be fine."

I was wrong.

IV.

My parents and several of my relatives had lived all their lives in a small town near Medford, Oregon, where I had been born some twenty-seven years earlier. Unfortunately, the inhabitants stubbornly clung to a rather old-fashioned way of thinking. Silana's obscure past therefore triggered mixed feelings in the Brannon family. *Who is this girl,* they wanted to know. *Where does she come from? Who are her parents?* Didn't they realize that the only important thing in the world was our happiness?

But in her own gentle way she won their hearts. It was mainly her natural and almost naive wonder at the beauty she saw in everything around her. She could spend hours marveling over the figurines in my mother's showcase or take an afternoon to revel in the beauty of my father's roses. Her innocent simplicity soon dispelled any doubts concerning her sincere nature.

What tended to be slightly frustrating was her ignorance of the Christian religion. I had a hard time understanding what she did believe, although she was very patient with me and attempted to explain everything carefully. I came to the conclusion that I just didn't have the necessary background since I had never been a very religious person. We therefore made an appointment to meet with the pastor of the church I belonged to, the same church my parents had been married in almost thirty years before.

We were sitting in Pastor Gregg's office around a pine coffee table, relaxing in cushioned chairs with sunlight streaming in through large windows that looked out upon a clear, autumn day.

"Okay, let's try to sort things out," the pastor suggested. "Since you don't have an official birth certificate, I'll just take this down right quick for the record. Your name is Silana Tolares. Is that correct?"

"Yes."

"And your age is…"

"Forty-eight," she replied calmly.

The pastor and I both gaped at her.

"Excuse me?"

"I'm very sorry. I thought you might be startled. I…I suppose it has much to do with the way I've lived up to now."

"Good Lord, you don't look a day over twenty-five."

She blushed. "Yes, I know, but thank you for the compliment."

The pastor turned to me. "Philip, were you aware of this?"

I swallowed. "No, I wasn't," I answered hoarsely.

It must have been apparent that I was having a difficult time digesting this new piece of information because Pastor Gregg watched me intently.

"Will it have a bearing on your decision?" he asked.

Silana was staring at me with a forlorn expression on her face. "I'm so sorry, Philip. I didn't realize it would be so important to you, or I would have told you sooner."

I looked into her large, dark eyes and realized that it somehow just didn't matter.

I shook my head. "No, Silana, I would always want only you, even if you were a thousand years old."

The smile that lighted her eyes was worth the perplexity of the past few moments.

"Oh, darling, what a wonderful thing to say," she replied in a soft voice.

"Would you rather talk about this some more and come back some other time?" Pastor Gregg asked us both.

"No, that's fine," I said. "My mind is made up."

"Okay, I'm glad that's settled," Pastor Gregg said. The topic seemed to embarrass him, and he quickly changed the subject. He turned back to Silana. "I've talked with Philip's parents, and I think it would make them very happy if you were married in our church."

"Yes, they would probably be very pleased," Silana responded cautiously.

"Well, would you be pleased?"

"I don't know. Would a church wedding require the ceremony to take place inside of a building?"

"No, not necessarily. If the weather remains as fair as it has been, we could hold it outside somewhere."

"In that case, I suppose it might be alright."

"Okay, now the next item is very important. Silana, this has nothing to do with you personally; you seem to be a good kind of girl...uh, woman. But I need you to understand that, as an ordained minister, I can only marry you if I have established that your beliefs do not contradict the basic principles of our faith."

"No, that's alright. Please believe me, I do understand."

"Okay, then let me ask you a few questions. Do you already belong to any certain Christian denomination?"

She shook her head in confusion. "I'm sorry, denomination?"

"Okay, let's leave that and take a step back. Would you describe yourself as a Christian?" He gave her a moment to ponder the question.

At first she stared at him blankly, but then she swallowed. "I'm afraid I don't know what being a Christian implies," she answered.

"Okay, let's take another step back. Do you believe in God?"

"Yes, of course."

"Well, that's a good place to start. Now, could you tell me in simple words who God is for you?"

She stared into space, her eyes unfocused and contemplating. "*Sirae cena sirae,* He is who He is. There is no other. It is He who has brought everything into existence. *Anavae i Ulanavae,* the First and the Last, the Beginning and the End, from eternity to eternity."

"That does agree quite accurately with what the Bible says. Now, do you believe in Christ?"

She shook her head. "I'm sorry. I have heard the name, but my knowledge ends there."

"In that case we can skip the Hypostatic Union, the Resurrection, and Salvation by Grace," he stated resignedly. "That implies that you've probably never read the Bible."

"The Bible?"

The pastor and I looked at each other. I shrugged.

"I see that this isn't going to be quite as easy as I expected," he said.

He let his fingers glide though his graying hair, considering what to do next. Then he held up a black, leather-bound volume.

"We call this book the Bible. We believe it is the inspired Word of God, similar to the holy writings of other religions. I think it might be best if I just gave you a copy and you try to read in it. It'll probably be easiest if you start with the Gospel of John in the New Testament and we'll set up another appointment for next week. Does that sound fair?"

Silana nodded and accepted the volume with shining eyes. She held on to it with the deference she might have shown for some very valuable relic.

I visited her several times that week. Whenever I saw her, she was absorbed in its pages, sometimes even in tears, or wandering in her garden in deep reflection with the book clutched to her heart. By the time we returned for our scheduled appointment a week later, she had read the volume from cover to cover, a feat I had never accomplished, let alone in such a short time.

The light of another beautiful autumn day shone into the pastor's warm and cozy office.

"So how far did you get? Were you able to read the Gospel of John?" the pastor inquired.

"Excuse me, Pastor Gregg," I intervened, "but I think she read the whole thing from front to back."

The pastor gaped at her. "What? Is that true?"

She nodded shyly. "Yes, it is."

"That's amazing. Did you take a course in speed reading?"

"No, I just read very quickly. It really wasn't so difficult," she answered modestly.

"Okay, what did you think?"

"I was deeply stirred. Your Bible has many similarities to our *Selani s'Ulavan.*"

"Are those your Holy Scriptures?"

She nodded.

"Well, I have studied the Koran, the four Hindu Vedas and some of the Buddhist scriptures, such as the Tripitaka. But I'm afraid I've never heard of your scriptures before," the pastor confessed.

"That's alright. I'm just so sorry that I didn't get to know the extent and beauty of what Anae has done elsewhere sooner," she said. "I could have learned so much. I do wish, though, that I had studied the Traveler's *Excerpts* in more detail while I was still at home. I would have been so much better prepared, but it just didn't seem important to me at the time." Her voice dropped as she spoke, as if she were talking to herself, not to us.

"The Traveler?"

"Yes, the Traveler, the Covatal. He is an important religious emissary in our society."

"Okay, I understand. But if you actually did read the whole Bible, you probably also read the account of the Prophet Jonah being swallowed by the whale."

Silana seemed confused. "Yes, but it doesn't say 'whale,' it says 'great fish.' From what I have heard, a whale's throat would be too small to actually swallow a whole person."

"Yes, sorry, it was a trick question. My, but you are an observant reader."

"Thank you for saying so, although the story really does remind me of…of an acquaintance of mine."

"An acquaintance?"

"Yes. His name is Talas. I have the feeling that, like the Prophet Jonah, he, too, is running from his destiny. I can only hope he won't be consumed by events beyond his control."

"Oh, I see. But to get back on track, do you know now who Christ is?"

"Yes," she whispered, her eyes far away. "I never would have believed that Anae would do something so wonderful."

"Anae?"

"Yes, Anae, the One, the Almighty."

"Why do you call Him that?"

"For the same reason that you call Him 'Yahweh.' Just as He revealed Himself to your Prophet Moses in a flame of fire from the midst of a bush, He revealed Himself to our Prophet Cades in a brilliant light that blazed from within a cold stone.

Since then my people have called Him 'Anae.'"

"Well, could you tell us who your people are and where you come from?"

"My people call themselves the Selani, and I am from Chyoradan."

"Hmmm...At the risk of seeming completely ignorant, I'm afraid I must admit that I've never heard of that particular country before, either."

"I can imagine. It is very far away."

"Okay, personally, I'm satisfied that you know enough about the Bible now to come to your own conclusions. I guess I am a bit liberal. As a matter of fact, some people in our community even believe me to be sacrilegious. But I think you're mature enough to decide for yourself if your beliefs contradict any of the essential doctrines of our faith. Since I don't want to take up any more of your time, I'll just skip directly to the most important question. Do you think you could consent to a Christian wedding?"

"Yes," she whispered.

"Well, I guess that's all we need to know."

During the conversation he had been toying with a large, wooden cross which he now placed back on the table. It was the same one he usually employed during many of his services.

"Is that a cross?" Silana asked.

"Why, yes it is."

"What do you use it for?"

"Oh, I don't really use it for anything. It's just a symbol, a kind of...reminder."

"A symbol?"

"Well, yes. I believe symbols are very important. They help us to concentrate and focus our attention towards the real values of our faith."

"Nothing more?"

"No." He hesitated. "Do you think there's more to it than that?"

"Yes, I believe so. Doesn't every symbol possess its own ethereal pattern, inseparable from the reality and substance associated with the embodied event?"

"I'm afraid I don't quite understand what you mean."

Silana considered for a moment. "Let me put it this way: I don't believe that love is just an abstract or theoretical idea, bare of emotion or reality. For that reason, I believe that the symbol of the cross, which you use to represent God's love and sacrifice, must also contain the substance and reality associated with that love."

"You believe a symbol contains its own reality? Isn't that almost paganism?"

"Well, of what real worth would such a symbol be if its only value was abstract and its use therefore stripped of any prospect of inductive expression?"

As if to demonstrate what she meant, she reached out with her left hand and lightly grasped the cross at its stem.

Suddenly a pure, white light radiated from the cross. The light spread outwards and filled the room with its luminance until the bright sunshine outside appeared negligible in comparison. Its warmth and brilliance entered my soul, and I sensed for the very first time that wonderful and formidable presence I could never quite recall afterwards: that all-embracing fire before which the darkness of my innermost being was completely exposed. I felt as if I were being torn apart, encompassed in unconditional acceptance yet horrified by the malicious obscurity of my own existence. I desired to stay there throughout eternity, floating in that protecting warmth, oblivious to anything else, but also felt compelled to crawl into some deep, dark hole, to hide my sordid being from that pure, revealing radiance.

Then she let go and the light subsided, returning us to the cold reality of the pastor's sunlit study. The pastor and I stared at the cross, shaken and embarrassed at our emotional upset. I remembered enough to shut my mouth. Pastor Gregg just kept gaping.

"How...How did you do that?" he finally choked out.

"Is it not your duty as a minister of God to always be one with your Creator and His creation?" she asked, gentle reproach in her voice. She regarded him, her eyes unwavering, and he averted his gaze.

Somehow we were able to finish our conversation and coordinate the important details of the wedding, but the pastor kept shooting uneasy glances in Silana's direction. In the end we decided to hold the ceremony in the open if the weather allowed. Knowing Silana, I couldn't have imagined it otherwise.

Afterwards Pastor Gregg took me aside. "I don't know who she is, but I would advise you not to let her out of your sight," he whispered. His farewell was marked by thoughtful trepidation.

While I drove her home we talked about the strange incident.

"I still don't understand how you did it. If I didn't know better, I would say it was sorcery."

She stared at me, aghast. "Are you accusing me of deception?"

"Deception? Now how did you get that idea? No, it was just a very extraordinary experience. You had Pastor Gregg pretty shocked. Not to mention me."

Her expression was pensive. "Philip, there was no sorcery involved in what I did. But sometimes things we do not understand may appear as such. Believe me, my intention was not to delude or upset you, but I just wouldn't know how to explain the principles of Sensation and Induction to you right now. Please forgive me." She lowered her eyes.

"Hey, that's okay. But for a moment there I thought I might be marrying a witch." I smiled at her.

"Well, maybe not quite a witch," she amended with a timid smile.

V.

The wedding day dawned clear and warm, one of the last beautiful and sunny days of that wonderful Indian summer. Silana wore a lovely gown of cream and pale rose. We had found that none of the traditional white wedding gowns agreed with her. Even my mother spontaneously consented to that fact. Silana herself didn't seem to be very interested in what she would be wearing. She amiably let my mother make all the necessary arrangements. When it came to the surroundings, though, Silana was uncompromising. We spent many days driving around the Medford area until we found just the right spot.

Pastor Gregg was quietly radiant during the ceremony. He appeared more composed and somehow at peace compared to his old self. It was as if he had exchanged his former ego for this unfamiliar being now standing before us. I wondered if the incident in his office had anything to do with this sudden transformation.

Silana and I gave each other our holy vow under a giant willow tree. Then I held her in my arms and kissed her tenderly. The scent of her hair was like the perfume of flowers in an open meadow. Silana looked up at the willow raining golden leaves upon us.

"She is bidding us her last, fond farewell," she said, awe

and a strange sadness in her voice. "Good-bye, fair friend, and fear not. We will soon meet again in a gentler world than this."

She smiled at me, a mild glow lighting her eyes. She took my hand and pulled me away from the noise and the crowd and led me into the woods. We silently walked for a while until we came to the edge of a deep but narrow stream. Then she took both my hands and pressed them against her heart. Her eyes were like dark pools, deep and inscrutable as she looked into mine.

"*Siran esarae,* I am yours."

She dropped down on one knee at the waterside and dipped her hands deftly into the water so that her gown framed her graceful figure like the petals of a rose. Then she turned to kneel directly before me, almost touching me, her arms spread wide. Her movements resembled the smooth and elegant dance of aspen in the wind as she drew two sweeping half-circles in the air around us. She rotated only her shoulders from the waist, first to her left, then to her right, while letting the water sift gradually through her lightly closed fingers.

Next she picked up a small piece of wood. She exhaled upon it and placed it in my left hand, closing my fingers over it. She cupped my right hand in hers and brought it up to her parted lips, filling it with her warm breath. Again she gently closed my fingers. Then she drew up a handful of the clear stream water with her left hand and enclosed some of the black, forest soil in her right. At last she stood and faced me with the palms of her hands held just below mine. I opened my hands to mirror hers—and gazed at them in awe. The piece of wood in my left hand was glowing red as if with some intense, inner fire. My right hand contained a little orb of golden light. There was no heat but only a faint tingling sensation on my skin. The material in her hands was also glowing, but her tender glance drew my eyes back to hers before I could examine it more closely.

"*Siran osal esar,* I am your water. *Sires selan anar,* you are my wind. *Siran piral esar,* I am your earth. *Sires pilan anar,* you are my fire. You may fill this cup, or drain it. The stream, the water, is our witness. The air, the wind, is our witness. We make this vow today with earth and with fire. *Siran esarae,* I am yours."

Our hands locked and the materials in our palms were joined. Then she stretched out her arms to the side, taking mine with her, pulling us together.

"We are one with Anae; now let us be one with each other," she whispered.

In one agile motion her gown came off, gliding to the ground on a cushion of air as she slipped into the cool stream. I stood there with my mouth agape and stared at her. She laughed gently when she saw my astonishment, and her eyes twinkled merrily. Then she held out her arms, her ivory figure highlighted under the water's dark surface.

"Come, my love, come to me," she called softly.

I pulled off my clothes, not nearly as effortlessly as she, and stumbled into the water after her. She met me in midstream and embraced me tenderly. Her unresisting softness and warmth pulsated through me like the throbbing of a heart aflame. Then she let herself glide backwards into the lazily flowing waves. Together we went down and my world exploded in bright light and ecstasy.

When I came to, we were lying together in the grass near the stream. Silana stroked my hair and smiled at me.

"Good Lord, what time is it?" I asked, looking around for my clothes.

"Hush, my darling. It's not as late as you might believe."

"But we need to be getting back. What will the guests think?"

"Is that so important? Today is our day."

She gently pushed me back into the grass. I gave up my resistance, and we lay together, enjoying each other's warmth and presence. Staring up into the leaves of the trees above us, I dozed off again.

When I woke up, the texture of the light had clearly changed. It was late afternoon. Silana was down at the stream. She had her gown on and was wading in the shallow near the bank, lifting her skirts to keep them dry and humming an unfamiliar, melancholic tune. She heard me stirring and looked up. Her eyes were deep and sad, but she smiled.

"It's time to go back," she said.

VI.

The first few months passed quickly. Silana declined a honeymoon and chose rather to stay with me in her cabin for a week before moving into our small but comfortable ranch-style house. I had bought an acreage on the outskirts of my hometown, which gave her enough room to work with her plants come spring. The trees lost their colorful foliage, and the world turned cold and gray. I caught up on my delayed projects, and Silana kept busy discovering and organizing the new household.

Was it then that the shadow crept into our lives? Did the darkness of the longer late-autumn nights finally arouse the dark specter dormant in my soul? At night I would often dream that I was running away from something obscure and sinister that was chasing me. In the dream I would come to a large mirror, but instead of myself I saw only Silana on the other side, calling silently and holding out her arms to me. And then I saw it. A faint image, vaguely familiar, reflected in the mirror behind Silana. I turned to face it and woke up drenched in sweat with Silana breathing quietly beside me.

A month after the wedding, I invited Bill Marten, an important client of mine, and his wife to dinner. Silana was busy in the kitchen all afternoon while I prepared several papers to go over with Bill after dinner. The doorbell rang shortly after seven. Silana and I met our guests at the door together.

"Hey Bill! How are you doing? This is my wife, Silana."

"Hi, Philip. Hello, uh, I'm afraid I didn't quite catch that name."

She repeated her name, a timid smile on her lips. "Glad to meet you," she added.

"Silana. Pretty name. This is my wife, Carol."

He introduced an inconspicuous and shy woman of roughly Silana's height with shoulder-length dark blond hair and an insecure smile. Hands were shaken all around. Silana stared at Carol's sweater in hushed amazement.

"Oh, how beautiful!" she remarked quietly. "What a lovely and intense blue. It reminds me of Devil's Lake in the evening. Did you crochet it yourself?"

She linked arms with an overwhelmed Carol and gently led her away. Bill, seemingly amused at having his wife swept off like that, followed me into the parlor where the ladies were already sitting comfortably on the sofa and conversing amicably. Soon thereafter, dinner was served. The meal was excellent and Silana the perfect hostess.

During dessert Carol furtively touched Silana's arm to gain her attention. "Silana, I just don't know how you do it. I have such a hard time getting a dinner organized. Could you give me a few hints?"

"Yes, of course," she answered. "Why don't you come into the kitchen with me after I clear the table? We'll need to leave our husbands to their business anyway."

The red tape Bill and I had to go through was immense

The Traveler

and rather tedious. Assessing the subtle intricacies between the various laws of geological survey, civil engineering, and the state of Oregon was always such a balancing act. After about an hour of paper warfare, we both decided we needed a short break. I went to the kitchen to get us some refreshments. Carol and Silana were sitting at the kitchen table, Silana holding one of Carol's hands in both of hers. As I came through the door, Carol turned quickly to appraise the darkness outside the window, but not before I had seen that her eyes were red and swollen, wet with tears. She was holding a tissue in her free hand and had an ample supply nearby. I shot Silana a questioning glance, but she shook her head. I got a couple of beers from the refrigerator and left as quickly as possible.

The ladies joined us about an hour later after Bill and I had pretty well wrapped things up. We were both astonished when they entered the parlor. For an instant we couldn't recognize the woman that came in with Silana. It was Carol, but what a contrast to the shy and inconspicuous woman I had met just several hours before. She had her hair styled differently and was wearing a dark blue skirt that blended perfectly with her sweater, instead of the gray and unassuming slacks she had worn when she arrived. But the main difference was her casual attitude. She seemed so much more relaxed. Her smile was open and natural, and she joined our conversation in a manner completely devoid of the reserve she had displayed at dinner. Bill could hardly take his eyes off of her.

After they left, sauntering towards their car with their arms tightly around each other's waists, I turned to Silana.

"What was that all about?"

Silana let her fingers glide through a strand of my hair and looked into my eyes.

"I'm sorry, dearest, but it would be an indiscretion for me to talk about it. Please trust me."

She put her arms around me and hugged me tightly.

"Such pain," she remarked, more to herself. "How could anyone bear it?"

Several days later Bill called me on the phone. After a few pleasantries Bill got to the point.

"Philip, what on earth did your wife do to Carol?"

"Why? Is something wrong?"

"No, on the contrary, it's like I was married to a different woman. Our relationship's never been this good."

"Well, I'm really glad to hear that, Bill," I replied carefully.

"Oh, and by the way, I've got some clients that might really appreciate your services, that is, if you're interested."

"Hey, that's...fantastic. You bet I'm interested," I said, attempting to sound more enthusiastic than I felt.

"Great! Why don't you come over for dinner tomorrow evening and we'll discuss the details. And bring your wife."

"All right, does seven-thirty sound okay?"

"That sounds fine. See you then. Bye, Philip."

"Good-bye, Bill."

I put down the receiver and just sat there for a moment, lost in thought. I should have felt excited about the new business opportunity. Instead I felt confused by my own emotions. I had a beautiful wife who loved me and did whatever she could to make me happy and show interest in my endeavors. Why didn't I appreciate the extraordinary effect she had on everyone she met? Why did I feel that I had to compete?

The next day we went over to Bill's place. Carol and Silana embraced like old friends and scooted off to the kitchen together, already chatting companionably. Bill and I took a look at the new contracts. We were still thrashing out some of the more subtle details when dinner was served, so we continued our discussion at the table. There was one item we especially weren't able to come to terms with.

"Excuse me, I know I shouldn't be interrupting and it's probably none of my business, but in this situation, wouldn't it be more honest to allow the concerned party to participate in working towards a solution rather than trying to eliminate the problem yourselves?"

Everybody looked at Silana in surprise.

"What exactly do you mean, Silana?" Bill asked.

"Well, maybe I wasn't listening very well and I certainly don't mean to be rude, but it seemed to me that you were having a difficult time finding a satisfactory solution to your problem. Given the circumstances, wouldn't it be preferable to get the client involved? You could present various alternatives that you had worked out in advance and let him decide for himself. Or maybe even help him to come up with an idea of his own. You wouldn't be taking too much of his time since you went well prepared. And if I were the client, I think I would appreciate your honesty more than your effort to produce a solution that might not even meet my needs."

Bill stared at her. "Well I'll be...Now why didn't I think of that? Philip, wherever did you get a hold of this young lady?"

Silana's natural humility wouldn't allow any pride, but she was obviously glad that she had been of some help. She smiled, her eyes shining softly. Her smile disappeared when she saw me glaring at her. She remained quiet and thoughtful for the rest of the evening.

VII.

Late that fall she planted the rose. It was a gray morning, a cool wind blowing from the north but no frost on the ground. She dipped the roots in a pasty loam and enclosed them with burlap to protect them from the cold. Then she planted the cane, binding it to a wooden pole for support. Every day she would tend to it and cut away dead growth. When spring came, she made sure the rose had enough water, took out wild sprouts, and broke off buds below the main stem to strengthen the single blossom she was raising.

The tension at home grew. I criticized her every deed, voicing sarcastic opinions regarding her customs. It is indeed possible to find fault with perfection if you look hard enough. I even took offence at the fact that she seemed to be left-handed. Silana never replied but waited silently until the mood passed. I was probably hurting myself more than Silana because my friends and neighbors darted indignant glances at me whenever I dropped another cynical remark.

In the late afternoons and early evenings, if my workload allowed, we would often go for a walk back into the wood at the end of the street or just around the block. She linked arms with me and never let her calm and attentive eye miss an iota of her surroundings.

On one such afternoon, we came across the little daughter of a neighbor that Silana was friendly with. The girl was sitting on the sidewalk dissolved in tears, a doll lying next to her with its arm torn off. Silana stopped and looked down at the wretched bundle of misery. I tried to pull her away, not being in a very charitable mood, but she stood her ground. She dropped down on one knee next to the girl and stroked her blond locks.

"Hello, Theresa. You're not very happy today. What's the matter?" she asked.

"Dana's hurt," the girl sobbed, picking up the doll's arm.

"Oh, the poor thing. Shall we make her well again?"

Theresa's head bobbed up and down while a few final tears slid down her face. Silana raised the doll and maneuvered the arm back into its shoulder. Then she unfastened a small ivory brooch carved in the shape of a rose blossom from her sweater and pinned it to the doll's dress. Theresa stared at her toy in awe as Silana returned the doll. She flung her arms around Silana's neck and planted a soggy kiss on her cheek. Silana waved to the child's mother who had just come to the door to see what was going on. The mother waved back, smiling. Theresa ran to her, eager to show her mother the doll's new adornment. We continued our walk.

"Do you know how much a brooch like that costs?" I hissed at her.

She glanced up at me with her large eyes. "What is all the money in the world compared to the delight of a little child?"

I brooded the rest of the way back to the house.

One day I came home after visiting with a client and found Silana on her knees in the den performing some type of ritual. Several candles were lit in different places on the floor around her. Her skirt was tucked in under her knees, and her arms were spread wide. She had her eyes closed and her face raised slightly upward towards unseen celestial spheres. Her countenance was calm and radiant as if it had been washed clean by a warm spring rain, and her lips moved silently as they formed unheard words. The scene projected a peace and beauty I had seldom seen in such intensity.

I threw my briefcase on the table.

Silana drew her arms towards her heart and bowed her head. "Hello, my love," she said in a low voice. Then she blew out the candles, turned around where she sat on the floor, and regarded me evenly. "You've had a hard day. Would you like some tea, or coffee maybe?"

"That would be great, if you could spare the time."

Again that biting sarcasm. Why was I so angry? Was I jealous of her composure?

She walked over to me and laid her hands on my arm. "Philip, what do you want me to do? You know that I belong to you."

One look into her deep, dark eyes, and my anger subsided. In its place I could feel my conscience gnawing at me.

"Yes, I...I know. I'm sorry," I stuttered.

I followed her into the kitchen.

"Would you like coffee or tea?" she asked pleasantly.

"Coffee'll do fine."

I didn't want to feel guilty. What right did she have to make me feel guilty? I felt the anger coming back like some big, black freight train looming in the distance. I sat down at the kitchen table and opened the newspaper, not really reading. Silana fixed the coffee and set it in front of me with a tender smile. Then she turned back to the counter to clean up. I sipped the coffee but then looked at the cup in angry indignation. The freight train thundered through the crossing.

"Silana, how many times have I told you to make the coffee stronger? This is nothing but hot water! Damn it, can't you do anything I tell you?"

She turned towards me. "I'm sorry, Philip." She was on the verge of tears. "I know I'm not a perfect housewife, but I do the best I can."

"Well, that just isn't good enough! Instead of talking to your plants all day, maybe you should listen to what I have to say for a change. Try using your head instead of your worthless feminine intuition and think!"

This time the tears came. I could see shock and confusion as well as pain in her eyes as she turned and walked out of the kitchen. I sat there feeling triumph and guilt battling inside of me, but also a peculiar satisfaction at finally having accomplished the impossible. With such a victory to show for it, what did it matter that the coffee Silana had made was actually perfect? In the end, though, guilt won the upper hand, and I left the kitchen in search of her.

I found her sitting on our bed in the bedroom with her arms around herself and her head bent down. She looked up when I came in, a handkerchief in one hand and tears still streaming down her face.

I was shocked when I saw her. Her usual composure had broken down; her face was pale, and she appeared to be worn out.

"Why, Philip?"

"I...I don't know. It won't happen again."

She didn't answer but looked at her hands, then carefully wiped her eyes and nose with her handkerchief. My heart broke when I saw her sitting there like that, somehow so beautiful but also so vulnerable, and all the anger washed out of me. I went over and sat down beside her.

"Silana, I'm so sorry. Can you forgive me?"

"Yes, I can forgive you."

"Is everything okay?"

She shook her head, her eyes unfocused and full of tears. "No." She turned towards me. "Oh, Philip, I was hoping so much that you would open your heart. I knew it would be difficult, but I never realized..."

"What, honey?"

She shook her head again. "I'm so tired. Could you please just hold me for a moment?"

She leaned her head against my breast and seemed to be listening to the beat of my heart. I put my arms around her and embraced her tightly.

She took a deep, shuddering breath. "I'm so homesick. I

miss my people. I miss my best friend, Tamenisa. And I miss my...my sister so much."

More tears streamed down her face, which she wiped away again.

"Your sister?" I asked, astonished at the revelation.

She nodded.

"Why don't you go visit her?"

She straightened and looked up at me. "Oh, Philip, don't you understand? I can't ever go back."

"No, I'm sorry, but I really don't understand."

She took another deep breath and wiped her eyes. "It's my own fault. I shouldn't have run off like that," she said, more to herself.

I stared at her. "You ran away?"

She nodded and glanced up at me again. "You deserve to hear the truth, my darling, at least as much as I can tell you." She caressed my cheek. "But it's such a mess."

"I'm listening."

I was going to release her from my arms so that she could sit up, but she pleaded with her eyes. "No, my love, please hold me while I'm telling you this. I wouldn't know how to get through it if you didn't."

She cuddled closer to me, like a child seeking protection, and I tightened my hold.

She was quiet for a moment, collecting her thoughts. "There was a young man where I lived who fell in love with me."

I groaned.

"Please don't," she said. "It's difficult enough for me as it is."

"I'm sorry. Go ahead."

"Anyway, I felt how intense his need for me was, and I grew very frightened because I sensed such an imbalance in him. I just didn't know if I had the strength to see him through his crisis. I felt as if I couldn't breathe anymore, and I was afraid I would be trapped forever. But most of all, dearest, I just wasn't sure of my feelings towards him."

Something inside of me clicked. "That situation sounds familiar."

"Yes. I suppose running away is never a solution. The problem always catches up with you."

"So I guess to you I'm just a problem that needs to be solved, huh?"

"Oh, Philip, please stop it."

I studied the wall for a moment. "Silana, am I really so unbalanced?"

She nodded again. "Yes, my love. I'm sorry, but it is so."

I took a deep breath. "Okay, how does the story go on?"

She sighed. "Yes, poor Talas. That was his name, by the way."

"Yeah, I figured as much."

"Darling, there's no need to be so angry. It's not him I love."

"Sorry."

She stared at me in awe. "Philip, if you could only see the wonders inside of yourself that I can see. Then you might be able to understand why I love you as I do. Sometimes, I fear that's the only thing that keeps me going." Her last words were almost inaudible.

I swallowed dryly as she caressed my cheek again.

"It all becomes even more complicated, though," she continued. "You see, it was my sister, Melina, who actually loved Talas, not me."

"You're kidding."

"No, I'm afraid not. Melina was always such a dear and had a heart of gold. She never would have obtruded upon

Talas's intentions towards me. But his heart was focused in the wrong direction. He never looked at her, hardly even realized that she existed, let alone perceived how much she loved him. I felt so sorry for her. Oh, Philip, I miss her so much."

Tears again streamed down her face. I held her tight and gently rocked her back and forth. When she had calmed down a little, I stroked her hair. "What happened then?"

She took another deep breath. "I left. *Escaped* might be a better word. I was hoping to come to terms with myself—wanted some time to think about everything and find a way to resolve the situation without hurting anyone. Instead, I've hurt everyone. I can only hope that my rash actions weren't too painful for them. But who knows? With me gone, maybe Talas finally woke up to the truth. I would be so happy for Melina if he did."

"Why can't you go back, Silana?"

She looked up at me again. "I'm so sorry, dearest. Maybe I should tell you, but somehow I just can't bring myself to do it."

"Why not? Don't you trust me?"

"I do trust you, my love, at least as far as you can trust yourself."

"I trust myself."

"Can you trust yourself to open your heart and let me love you? Can you trust yourself not to let your anger or your sarcasm control you?"

I knew that she was right but couldn't bring myself to admit it, so I remained silent.

"What do you want, my darling?" she asked.

I shrugged. "I don't know. I really don't know."

VIII.

Silana grew very pale. She often felt cold and was never without her knitted shawl about her shoulders. By the time spring arrived, she had lost several pounds. I asked her to see a doctor, but she only shook her head. Spring itself, though, seemed to be cure enough, at least for a while. She had already planted various bulbs in the fall and was now busy sowing seeds and making room for plants and flowers of different sorts.

Although our heart-to-heart talks were helping me to understand Silana better, I still couldn't always control my anger and sarcasm. I found it difficult to break the tenacious habit so deeply rooted in my character, but I did try not to let it get quite so out of hand. Even so, it seemed to drain her, depleting her strength and exhausting the very essence of her being.

On the first Sunday in May we had my parents over for lunch. Visiting the first Sunday of every month had become a custom of sorts, and my parents enjoyed the meals and our company. We were sitting around the table, talking casually. Silana rose to get the dessert but suddenly slumped over and slid to the ground. We all stood in surprise and shock. My mother, who was sitting next to her, reached her first.

"My goodness! Dear child, are you all right?"

Silana tried to prop herself up on one arm, her other hand covering her eyes. She was white as a sheet, a dazed expression on her face. My mother kneeled down beside her and supported her. A thought occurred to her and she smiled.

"You're not pregnant by any chance, are you?" she whispered conspiringly.

But Silana shook her head. "No. Not...not possible. Just need to rest. Philip, could you...could you help me to the bedroom, please?"

With my mother's assistance I eased her up off the floor. Then I supported her to the bedroom and helped her lie down. I sat down next to her, holding her hand and gently stroking her thick black hair. She turned her head and looked up at me. Her face was void of color and her expression one of utter exhaustion.

"Oh, Philip, I'm so sorry," she whispered. Just saying the words seemed to tax her immensely.

"Hey, that's okay. Why don't you get some rest? I'll take care of Ma and Pa."

I tried to get up, but she held on to me.

"Dearest, my heart aches so. I wish so much that I...that I could have been the mother of our child. I'm so sorry that it wasn't possible."

A single tear slipped down her cheek, and I gently brushed it off.

"Honey, that's not important right now. Please just get better."

She shook her head, straining at the effort. "I'm sorry," she whispered.

My heart was tied up in a knot. "Silana, why are you suffering like this?"

"My immune system...it can't cope...talk later...need to rest," she whispered.

She weakly squeezed my hand, turned her head, and closed her eyes. Inside of minutes her breathing had taken on the steady cadence of deep sleep. I caressed her cheek once more while looking down upon her pale but peaceful face. Then I left the bedroom, closing the door quietly behind me.

When I returned to the dining room, my mother said, "Philip, you just have to get that girl to a doctor. She hasn't seemed well for months."

I shrugged. I knew Silana didn't want to see a physician,

but I was becoming more and more troubled myself.

Several days later Silana asked me if we could visit her old cabin. I was surprised but consented, hoping it would benefit her health. On the following weekend we made the long drive to her wood. It was a beautiful, clear day and we reached the cabin in the late morning. It was amazing to see the change that came over her as we strolled through the forest she knew so well. She was silent for the most part and just enjoyed the warm sun filtering through the branches above. It was like seeing her again for the first time: her natural radiance, her composure, and the way she seemed to feel in tune with everything around her.

We spent the night in the cabin. The fresh air must have done me good, for I slept soundly all night and didn't awake until late the next morning. Silana wasn't there. Anxious, I dressed quickly and stepped outside in time to see her coming around the corner of the cabin. She seemed tired but smiled at me. She caught my arm, leaning on me, and we just kept walking. After a while we came to a large, old oak.

Silana stopped and turned towards it. "Thank you, oldest and wisest of friends, for your silence and your understanding. I must say good-bye now, for it is time for me to go, but our hearts remain as one. Greet my friend, the willow, and tell her that I will be meeting her soon, as I will be meeting you again, someday, in that most wonderful of places."

She stepped up to the massive trunk and kissed it gently. The oak seemed to sigh inaudibly while a light breeze swayed its gnarled branches. Silana stepped away, and I thought I saw something glistening in her eyes. She turned and walked away without looking back. I followed her, confusion and alarm growing in my heart. When I caught up with her, I stopped her and gently turned her around to face me.

"Honey, I know I promised not to badger you about your

past, and I think I've been very patient. But I just can't stand it any longer. Please, tell me who you are."

She tenderly looked into my eyes. "I was Silana of the House of Tolares, the High Priestess of my people, Guardian of the Rites of Malentisa and Protectoress of the Woods. I know you can't understand what that means, although I hope that someday you will. But that period of my life is gone and past. Now, my dearest husband, I want only to be your wife with all my heart, although I fear that even that time is waning swiftly."

I felt a lump rise in my throat. "Silana, please don't say that."

But it seemed as if her last words had drained her because she suddenly clutched at me to keep from falling. I put my arm around her, and supported her back to her cabin.

That night, as we lay in bed at home once more, I woke up and realized that she wasn't asleep.

"What's wrong, honey?" I murmured.

She turned towards me and stroked my hair.

"Don't forget me, Philip. Remember," she whispered.

"What do you mean, Silana?" I was still half asleep.

"Don't worry, you'll understand. Go back to sleep."

She continued to let her fingers glide through my hair, and I soon drifted off again.

I had to get up early the next morning and stayed away on important business until fairly late. When I arrived home I couldn't find Silana anywhere. I called around the house, but everything was so dreadfully quiet that I grew anxious. I stepped into the garden and called her but received no answer.

I finally found her lying next to the rose in the growing dusk. Her head was resting on one arm, her hair partly covering her serene face, and her eyes were closed as if she were taking a nap. Filled with dread I bent down and shook her gently. The arm I touched was warm, but there was no reaction.

"Silana," I called, shaking her more vigorously. "Silana, wake up. Please, wake up."

There was no answer, not even the soft sound of her breathing to comfort my growing despair. I sat there, insensitive to my surroundings, letting realization sink in, letting the pain trickle into my soul like some burning poison. I took her lifeless form in my arms and cradled her, her face— her beautiful, placid face—swimming before my eyes.

I don't know how long I stayed there like that, but when I came to myself it was already fully dark. I somehow gathered the strength to lift her up and carry her inside where I laid her as gently as I could on our bed. The following hours were a nightmare, and I only remember them as if through some misty veil. The paramedics, the police, my parents, the coroner, all seemed to swirl before my eyes in an unreal mosaic until my deranged spirit finally fled to the oblivion of dreamless sleep.

IX.

Despite their own intense grief, my parents lovingly attended to all the arrangements of the funeral. Although it was unusual in a case like this, they firmly resisted an autopsy, using their influence in town to attain their objective. Everybody who had known Silana recognized instinctively that she would never have wished it. The violation of her remains would have seemed like an act of desecration.

In the days and weeks after the burial, I found myself wandering aimlessly from place to place, not capable of coming to terms with reality. I let my work slip, not caring, not eating, living off my savings. All I sensed was pain, guilt, and emptiness while endless questions kept spinning in my mind.

At some point, I visited the spot where we had been married. It wasn't a conscious act. Somehow in my disoriented wanderings the location seemed to draw me like a bizarre magnet.

Shock set in immediately. The beautiful park had been demolished. What remained looked like a bludgeoned battlefield. Where there had once been a lush meadow, vibrant with colorful autumn leaves and soft, green grass, there was now only a muddy, torn-up construction area. Instead of sweeping the sky above in golden splendor, the gray mutilated stump of Silana's friend, the willow, was condemned to crouch near the ground, like a cold, severed limb attempting in vain to point towards the heavens, without hope, an image frozen in perpetual despair. A large sign announcing some new business complex stood over it, resembling a heartless prison warden that sternly guarded the mute stump and forever silenced the willow's anguished cry for mercy.

I looked over at the wood behind the building zone, where the true marriage ritual had been performed. I could still remember the elegant laburnum, magnolia, and rhododendron bushes that had once adorned the line of stately trees. The shrubs had been replaced by black, gaping holes filled with refuse. The ground under the trees that had once boasted lovely ferns and moss-covered rocks was trampled and littered with trash. The forest looked dreary and forlorn on this rainy and overcast summer day.

I sloshed through the mud and into the wood. Roaming along, I discovered the stream and little clearing where Silana and I had shared a short moment of blissful harmony on that afternoon so long ago. I stared into the dark water trying desperately to recall that precious instant in time. I imagined a shape outlined in the water next to mine, an ivory figure with long, dark hair, but when I turned there were only leaves and branches waving in the wind.

That night I dreamed that she came to me. She sat down next to me on the bed and stroked my hair.

Remember, Philip, remember, she called to me.

I woke up and tried to hold her but my arms closed on thin air. I got out of bed and moved over to the window, like a person walking in his sleep. When I gazed outside, my memory of her seemed like a veil before the moon, its beams reflecting the pale color of the rose, while tears streamed down my cheeks.

The next day I moved to the cabin that had played such an important role in her life, to the place where her spirit surrounded me day and night. I took the rose with me and planted it in her garden behind the cabin, carefully, as she had done. I rambled about the fields and the woods searching for peace and seeking an answer to the questions that ravaged my soul.

One day I came upon the site in the woods that had been destroyed by the fire. It was the same spot that had caused Silana such grief soon after we had met: a huge scar desecrating the beauty of the surrounding forest. I followed the curve of the black, ugly wound as it became steadily narrower until I found what must have been a rather sizeable object at its apex. Its original form was not distinguishable. Its greater part had probably been buried during the impact, and the wind and leaves had completed the task through several changing seasons, forming a small mound in the landscape. Only a faint, metallic glimmer revealed that the knoll was not just part of the scenery. I could imagine how it must have been as it came down, raking the trees like the talons of some large, wounded bird, intruding abruptly into the silence of the quiet forest.

I walked around the right side of the object. My heart was pounding wildly.

Remember, a soft voice called inside of me. *Remember*.

Near the front of the object I encountered something that might have been an entrance: a small passageway dug into the earth leading downwards at a slight angle. I couldn't see what was in there because of the bright sunlight, so I stepped cautiously inside, drawn forward by some inner force, not fully conscious of my actions.

The tunnel was approximately three times my width and high enough for me to stand upright comfortably. It ended after several feet, and I felt something that might have been metal. I stopped for a moment to let my eyes adjust to what little light fell from the entrance. What I saw was a small section of the object, a perfectly smooth surface. I closed my eyes.

Remember. A distant echo in my soul.

Using my left hand, as Silana might have done, I tenderly caressed the blank facade. It wasn't cold, didn't feel quite like metal.

Like a ghostly specter materializing in the fog, the outline of a hand-sized square with rounded corners appeared on the surface where I had touched it. Inside the square were two smaller, horizontal rectangles, one above the other, both likewise with rounded çorners. The bottom rectangle was light blue, as was the outline of the square around it. The top rectangle was blinking red. Both rectangles had some type of inscription on them, but the characters were foreign to me. Still there was neither recess nor elevation to the surface. The patterns seemed to be a part of it, like the picture on a television screen.

Just as suddenly as they had appeared, the phantom motifs vanished. Bemused, I lightly touched the surface where they had been just seconds before. They reappeared. Without realizing my own intent, I pressed the surface highlighted by the red, blinking rectangle. It stopped blinking and turned dark yellow.

But something else was happening. I couldn't quite make out what. It may have been some type of subliminal vibration starting somewhere in the depths of the object. The bottom rectangle began to blink red.

I hesitated. For an instant, reason governed my thoughts. What was I doing?

But my need to know, my longing to find an answer, was greater than my fear. I pressed the second rectangle. It stopped blinking, and both rectangles turned dark green, then disappeared. The outline of a much larger rectangle appeared on the surface to the right of where the square had been, again with rounded corners, only this one the size of a door. Silently the door slid to the side, leaving an opening about two heads higher than myself and twice my width. Beyond the entrance, subdued light illuminated a corridor, inviting me in.

This time there was no hesitation. I stepped across the threshold and into the corridor before me. The floor was soft, like a carpet, my footsteps soundless. The walls were blank and moderately luminescent. The corridor turned to the right and led to a dead end where another door slid silently open. As if in a trance I entered a large chamber.

"Hello, Philip."

A gentle, familiar voice. Silana stood at the far end of the room, a majestic figure wearing a cream-colored robe which draped to the floor, while her shining, dark hair spilled down her back.

X.

"What you are seeing is only a holographic image of me. I would so much rather be here myself, but at least I can tell you once more how much I love you. I also hope that, in this final message, I might be able to answer a few of the questions which must have been tormenting you after I was forced to depart.

"Please, dearest husband, forgive the induced memory that I planted inside of you before I left. I hope it didn't cause you too much pain or confusion. Under normal circumstances, I never would have resorted to such methods. But if it has led you here, as I intended, then it has fulfilled its purpose and the effects should wear off almost immediately.

"You will already have deduced for yourself by the ship you are standing in that I am not from your world. I truly regret that I couldn't bring myself to tell you the whole truth, but I hope you will understand. The knowledge that is accessible aboard this ship is just too dangerous for anyone whose heart and spirit has not been sufficiently exposed to the healing that only love may bring. But I am confident that you will allow the healing process which has begun in your heart to continue and that you will ensure that the knowledge on this ship is used as it was intended. The consequences would be devastating if it should fall into the wrong hands.

"The ship itself will probably never fly again since there is no one here who could repair the damage. If you should wish to attempt it anyway, you will discover that the telatian field was breached during the attack and a large section of the ship's left rear hull has been fused. But there should be enough of the external matrix left to power the internal facilities almost indefinitely. I have set the console in front of you so that, when you activate it, it will bring up the ship's information facilities in English. They are very easy to use, and I am sure that with your background, you will have no problems with them.

"I'm so sorry, my dearest, but it seems that the High Priestess of Selanae didn't know quite so much about the language of love as she believed. I should have realized sooner that it was not the composure of my training but my vulnerability which was the key to your heart. All I can say in my defense is that, before we married, nobody ever taught me what it really means to be a wife, and I had to learn step by step as I went along.

"Oh, Philip, it would have made me so happy to be here with you today. But I'm afraid that my immune system is under terrible stress on this illicit world of yours. I've known for quite some time that I wouldn't be able to hold up under the strain much longer. It was just becoming too difficult, constantly attempting to restore the languishing ethereal pattern of my physiology, a pattern that was simply not compatible with your world.

"Although I have been away from my home world, Chyoradan, for almost three years now, I somehow still feel shocked by what I have done. I don't believe that anything like this has ever happened in the history of our race. I can hardly believe it myself, that I should be the first High Priestess to just run off the way I did, abandoning my responsibility to the Advisory Council and my people.

"I didn't mean for things to turn out as they did. As I have already told you, I just wanted some time to myself, to think and to sort things out. When I left Melina and Talas and my best friend and protégée, Tamenisa, on Chyoradan, I decided to go to the only place where I believed that no one would follow. That was your world, my dearest, Halena Yazoral, the Forbidden Planet. I didn't realize, though, that a splinter group of my people had established an extensive surveillance network around your solar system. I suppose that, in their religious bigotry, they must think of themselves as some kind of divine enforcers of the ban upon your planet. After what I have experienced here, I believe that the Prophets told us to stay away from your planet as a means to protect your people and ours. But every rule has its exception, particularly when the Law of Love compels us.

"I wish I could tell you that the history of my people has been one long tale of love, peace, and prosperity, but it has not. On Chyoradan we do live in peace: one small, sheltered island in an ocean of conflict. On so many other worlds, though, there is only fear, grief, and misery. Please, my darling, I beg of you to read for yourself the Traveler's *Excerpts on History*. They contain a very accurate account of how our mother planet, Piral, was forever destroyed two thousand years ago; how my people were then scattered amongst the stars in the Galactic Diaspora; and how the Council of Selanae has wrought at least a semblance of peace through the Alliance of Chyoradan.

"Dearest, I feel so much that I should have been there to help them and to love them, working towards a lasting peace for my afflicted and tormented people. They chose me as their High Priestess because they trusted me and believed in me. How I wish that I could have done more for them. But it wasn't possible, and I must let it go.

"Although I sometimes feel as if I have failed utterly, I also realize that Anae had other plans for my life. It was my destiny to meet you, to love you, and to become your wife. I sense that what I was will continue in some form through you. For this reason I wanted you to see me this one last time in my robes of office, as a servant of the life that was once so dear and holy to me.

"And now, my dearest and most beloved husband, I must

leave you. Please remember that I will always love you. My thoughts, my blessings, my dearest wishes belong to you forever. *Siran esarae.* Good-bye, my love."

XI.

The image vanished silently. I reached out and tried to hold on to her, but she was gone. I blinked and tried to restrain tears that were already streaming down my face while her last fading words echoed like a stabbing pain in my soul.

During the following months I spent most of my time on the ship, learning her language; discovering the history, culture and technology of that beautiful race; partaking of the wisdom they had accumulated through the ages. My studies kept me busy and helped me to keep my mind off the constant anguish that sometimes threatened to overwhelm me.

Then I began to listen. I deliberately laid open my heart and listened to the wind in the trees, to the breeze blowing across the fields, and to the sound of the streams rippling softly in the woods. Often I would wander to the old oak and spend hours at its base just learning and listening. Slowly the change I felt in my heart took root in my wounded soul and I discovered that I could live among the plants and herbs of the forests and fields, eliciting their secrets.

At last I could understand how she must have felt in that week before she gave me her answer, conversing with the old oak, struggling with herself, knowing I could not understand. But ultimately overcoming her fear by love, a love so deep I could still not comprehend it. I could look up at the stars as she must have done, aware of her pain and sorrow, her longing for a world she would never see again. I imagined the days when she realized that her strength was waning and she needed to act. And I remembered how she asked me to take her to the cabin, while she held on for as long as she could.

Word spread of my seclusion and the change in my life. In these uncertain times in which so many people are searching for truth and meaning, my experience seemed to draw them like a magnet. Bill and Carol were the first to call on me. They had planned to stay for only a short visit, but the days turned into weeks and the weeks into months. Others followed. They came gradually, first in little trickles, then in tiny streams. Today I can better understand the need that brought all those people to this lonely part of the country, their craving for peace, for healing, for understanding. Most left again, a newfound joy and calling in their hearts. But some stayed, sensing somehow that they had finally come home.

My parents also joined me for several months, but were led to return to their hometown. They did insist, though, that Silana's final resting place be relocated to the site where so much was now growing that was a fruit of her life and passing. As with the funeral, they again tended to whatever was necessary, quietly coordinating the release, exhumation, and transfer so that there would be no stir, aware of the delicacy of the situation and the need for secrecy.

The second burial was sincere and peaceful, a small ceremony held according to Selanian customs and attended by a few good friends. My father personally transplanted the rose so that it would stand as a sentinel above the seed that had surrendered its existence and fallen into the ground, allowing new life to emerge from that which had passed.

Yet even so, I still sometimes feel the pain and loss severely. There are times when I wake up in the middle of the night and feel as if Silana has been calling to me in the darkness, her voice leading me away from the cold and the dark to the warmth and light that had been her life, the beauty I had never really seen while she was with me. Although she devotedly assured me of her love, it seems so difficult to let go of the pain and the guilt. Should it be easier, knowing there was nothing anybody could have done and that I must somehow come to terms with my fate?

But then, not long ago, there came a bright spring morning when I heard a horned lark calling to its mate. I was working in front of the cabin and looking out across the fields when the song reached my ears. In that instant I knew that life was possible, that it didn't need to be just an attempt at deliberately breathing in and out and somehow getting through the day. I knew it because, for the first time, I felt joy again, a simple joy, untarnished by any pain or thought of loss. And although the tears might still come and my heart sometimes aches, I have found the strength to once again look upon that fragile blossom in the garden behind the cabin which guards a simple, warm inscription upon a cold, hard stone:

In Loving Memory Of
The Rose
Silana Tolares Brannon
1934 – 1983

Part 1: The Traveler

When confronting the issue of the Great Houses, Piral, the mother planet, must always constitute the basis of any investigation, if we are to take the hermeneutical principles of the historical sciences at all seriously. At the time in which we will therefore commence our examinations, the end of an era had dawned: an era in which the Elinar had long since fallen victim to their own crisis and disappeared into the void of myth and legend, while the Demantar were but a tale told to children on cold winter nights when families sat together about their warm and cozy hearths.

But it was not until the spring of 1524 TC, almost two and a half millennia before the Galactic Diaspora, that an episode in the little town of Nadil triggered a chain of events which finally led the Council of Selanae to comprehend the magnitude and impact that this first significant struggle between the Great Houses would have on the future of the entire planet.

—The Traveler, *Excerpts on History*

1. *Arrival*

The stranger emerged from the wood near the paved road to Nadil early in the morning of what promised to be a beautiful late spring day. The road was already well traveled because of the approaching conference and—with all the traffic—nobody took particular notice of the solitary figure standing at the edge of the road. If it hadn't been for his foreign, light gray uniform, the stately, dark-haired and clean-shaven wanderer wouldn't have received a second glance. He seemed to be distracted and confused but joined the flow of carriages and wagons traveling west towards the little town.

After a short walk he arrived at the outskirts of the village, but in his perplexed state, he didn't really perceive his environment until he had almost reached the center of town. Then he stopped for a moment to get his bearings and examined the various buildings around him. He could see tables and chairs through the tall windows of a fairly large structure on his right, which appeared to be a tavern. Both wings of the massive and artfully designed wooden door stood open, inviting him in, so he stepped inside.

2. *The Vision*

Dark shapes converged upon her against a vague backdrop of crackling flames. On the ground, thick black smoke crept ominously forwards and curled around her legs, rising in stinging wisps that confounded her senses. From somewhere far away she could hear a faint melody, but in the cold echo of such a song there could be no comfort. Trembling, she looked around, searching for a place to hide, but finding no shelter against the malevolent powers that threatened to engulf her, she fled into herself.

In the sudden stillness that occupied her innermost being, she opened the eyes of her heart and saw eternity stretching out before her. As if across no distance at all, her spirit discerned the glowing, translucent horns of her friends concealed in the emerald dusk of the forests that spread out across the entire Suviltan Plateau and far north into the vast expanses of the Navaren. For just an instant, their familiar presence had a soothing effect on the shaken girl.

You have been chosen, Golden Keeper, the horns sighed.

Her heart almost stopped, and she cringed in despair.

"No, please, don't do this to me," she cried.

You must be strong, Golden Keeper, and hold them together, for the time is near.

"No, please, I cannot."

There was no answer.

"Please, have mercy."

But there was only silence.

"I'm so frightened." Almost a whisper.

When she finally dared to glance about, the ardent light of the fire blinked dully on the blades of countless swords as the black army closed in. The melody she had heard before ascended into a song that filled the air with its vibrant force, pounding her mind until she could hardly breathe. Although she was already paralyzed with fear, her eyes bulged at the sinister shadow that rose up behind the converging silhouettes. The shapes turned towards the dark specter, and their enshrouded faces reflected hopeless terror. The apparition bore down on them, and darkness opened its jaws to release a crimson torrent of fiery violence that swept everything away in its path. Then the shadow engulfed her, and she sat up in bed, a scream stifled on her lips.

Breathing heavily, she looked around. Although the terrifying darkness had passed and her room was gradually being filled with the comforting brightness of the day, she couldn't shake the dreadful images from her mind.

Her eldest sister, already sitting at the dressing table brushing her long, golden hair, turned to face her.

"What's wrong, my little poroda?"

"Oh Caty, please hold me," the girl whispered.

Her sister walked over to the girl's bed. She took the helpless bundle into her arms and embraced her tightly.

"Sinara, you're trembling all over," she said, stroking the girl's golden locks. "Was it the nightmare again?"

The girl nodded. A silent tear rolled down her cheek.

"Can you tell me about it?"

Sinara shook her head. "I can't see it clearly. I smell smoke, and all I see is black, and fire. I hear the siren's song and there's blood, blood everywhere. Oh Caty, don't wake her up. Please, don't let him wake her up."

"Wake who up, dearest?"

Sinara closed her eyes and huddled closer to her sister's reassuring warmth. A shudder went through her as she parted her lips, whispering the three words she feared above all others:

"Tevasala se Nemata."

The Goddess of Death.

3. *The Proprietor*

Since it was still very early in the day, the proprietor was not expecting any customers. He looked up from his task of polishing the tables in surprise when the stranger stumbled in.

"Setavelan mada, vil'anar, good morning, my friend. What can I do for you?"

"Latilares ana, votal, coni siran? Could you please tell me where I am?"

"Sires a Nadil!"

"Ah, Nadil." The stranger's eyes seemed out of focus and far away, as if he was walking in a dream.

"Friend, are you not well? Please, be seated!"

The stranger emerged from his daze and smiled at the owner. "Thank you, my friend, I believe I will."

"If you will excuse me for a moment, I will get you some refreshments."

The proprietor bustled off into the adjoining room, from which his little round wife had been eavesdropping.

"Who is he?" she asked in a whisper.

"I have no idea," he whispered back, "but he must be some very important official, for he speaks in the voice of the Selani."

His wife's eyes became round as saucers. "Whatever could he want from us?"

He shrugged. "What everyone else wants: a goblet of wine and the latest news," he whispered with a wink. "But, for this one, I don't think I can dish up the regular fare."

He rushed off to the cellar and could be heard rummaging through his supplies. When he returned several minutes later, he saw that the stranger had chosen a seat in a secluded corner from which he could survey the entire hall. He made a mental note of the fact, another item that confirmed his notion regarding the newcomer. The owner set down a goblet before the stranger and began pouring the wine.

"Oh, dear friend," said the stranger, raising a hand in apology. "I'm certain that your wine is excellent. But would it be possible to have a simple cup of clear water? Please forgive me for making so much trouble."

The proprietor looked up at his guest in surprise. "Oh, it's no trouble, I assure you." He whisked the goblet and carafe away again. In the next room he and his wife exchanged a short, questioning glance, but then he shook his head and shrugged as he rushed by. There was no need for an explanation, as he was certain that his wife would be listening in on every word for herself. He soon returned with a pitcher from which he poured fresh, cold water into the mug he had placed before his guest.

"Now, my friend, what else can I do for you?"

"Well, if I may be so presuming, it would be very kind if you would just sit with me for a moment. It's been a while since I've had a good conversation."

"Ah, then your journey has been a far and lonely one," the proprietor stated, taking in the visitor's unaccustomed attire, while maneuvering his short but stout frame into the chair opposite his guest.

The stranger smiled faintly. "Yes, you may safely assume as much. But would you first be so kind as to give me today's date? I fear my reckoning may be off, and I'm not quite sure that my calendar is of the same measure as yours."

The proprietor again stared at his visitor in awe. "Why, I've always been led to believe that our calendar has been in common use for ages."

"That may well be, but please, humor me. Speak to me as if I were a child in need of instruction."

"Well, this is Velanetav, the 37th day of the month Ulanaseta, in the year 1524. That is, 1524 *Tena Corasetal,* After Creation," he added, slightly flustered when he perceived the stranger's inquiring glance.

"Ah, yes, I remember. Piral has a thirty-two hour day, and I believe a month is reckoned by the cycle of the larger moon, Velanevos, which is forty days. Is that correct?"

"Yes, absolutely."

The stranger smiled. "You seem to be very knowledgeable."

The proprietor returned his smile. "Well, as for that, please understand that I do have a tavern to run. You wouldn't believe the variety of people that turn in here, and most of my customers expect any and all kinds of information from me." He lowered his voice and winked at the stranger conspiringly. "To tell you the truth, I receive most of my intelligence just by listening to gossip."

"Then it seems that I've come to the right place. But tell me, my friend: how do you come by the unit of measure for one hour?"

"An hour? Let me see. An hour is the time it takes the shadow of the sundial's gnomon at Travis to progress a measure of one hand."

"Ah, Travis. The Council of Selanae."

"I see you are informed, my friend. Yes, that is where the temporal synchronization of the calendar takes place and units of measure are regulated. But you needn't travel quite so far. We have a very accurate replica of the sundial in the town square."

The proprietor became aware of the stranger's gaze and gave him a moment to take a quick glance about his guest hall. It was very spacious, sunny and comfortably furnished. His tavern was quite popular and he expected many of the townspeople in the evenings and on the weekends when they had time to socialize. A proud smile curled up his lips. He knew that, to anyone looking around, it was immediately apparent that he had excellent taste.

The windows were tall, rising from slightly above the floor to just under the ceiling. Each windowpane measured about four square cubits and was set in whitely glazed wood, three panes to a row and four rows to a window. The wooden casing was exquisitely designed and carved. There were four such windows facing the road, with enough wall space between them to allow for subtle decorations and drapery. The entrance was set precisely midway between the windows with two on each side. Since the tavern was on the north side of a road traveling east to west, the sunlight of a perfect morning was now radiating splendidly through the glass.

The hall was adorned with numerous works of art in various forms, the floor of the hall beautifully tiled. The rounded corners of the room contained elaborate but elegant abstract sculptures chiseled from a variety of rocks and stones, rounded and polished until their surfaces were as smooth as the skin of a newborn child. The walls were decorated with an astonishing variety of beautiful paintings, which were also mostly abstract and depicted various compositions of light and color. One side of the hall was elevated like a stage, and resting on the platform were several chairs, note stands, and a few musical instruments. Everything expressed a marvelous harmony: a celebration of the joy and essence of life.

Interestingly enough, there were also several weapons decorating the hall. It may have seemed strange, displaying instruments of death alongside so many portrayals of life, but each and every one was itself a magnificent work of art. The two-handed swords, for instance, were solidly formed and their hilts generously adorned. The deadly metal of their broad and slightly tapered, double-edged blades was polished to mirrorlike perfection on the flat but exhibited a soft metallic sheen towards the razor-sharp edges. The swords were well cared for and oiled, brilliantly reflecting the light streaming abundantly into the hall.

One weapon hanging on the wall behind the stranger especially caught his attention. It was a very compact and powerfully designed archer's bow, which shone like silver in the sunlight. The bowstring was redirected by an exotic mechanism mounted on the top and bottom of the upper and lower limb. The beautifully molded quiver hanging beneath it contained roughly two dozen arrows, their shafts shorter and thicker than normal recurve or longbow arrows. The nocks protruding from the quiver were carved from something similar to ivory, but the fletching vanes were made of a material unfamiliar even to the proprietor.

"Does the Prophet's Bow awake your curiosity?" he asked.

"Yes, it's absolutely fascinating!"

"It's been reported that only the prophet himself was able to wield this particular weapon. Nobody else could draw its weight. It's over five hundred years old."

The stranger glanced at the proprietor in amazement. "Five hundred years? Of what material is it made then?"

"Most likely some crystalline alloy. Completely indestructible, it is said."

"Amazing! How do you come by such priceless wonders?"

The proprietor's answer consisted of a modest smile.

"There is one more question that I need to ask you, my friend," the stranger said. "What kind of payment will you accept for your services?"

"For a cup of water and the pleasant company of a new patron? Don't be ridiculous! Do you wish to insult me?"

"No, my friend, but I do hope that this won't be the last time I require your services," he said with a smile.

The proprietor smiled back. "Well, if that's how the matter stands." He gave the stranger a wink, but then again turned serious. "From the townspeople or the inhabitants of the surrounding farms I'll take most anything. Some pay me with corn or meat. Others bring what they can and when they can. But I hope you understand that I cannot give credit to foreigners who may never return."

"Yes, I understand perfectly. But I still don't know how I could repay you, and I certainly don't wish to offend you. Will you take gold?"

The owner gaped. "Gold? Why yes, of course!"

The stranger breathed a sigh of relief. "Anae be thanked for that!"

"But, sir, what other services might you be wanting if you wish to pay in gold?"

"Oh, please, don't call me 'sir.' And I'm really sorry that I have nothing else to offer. After my long journey, I just don't have any other way to reimburse you. Believe me, my needs are not particular, just the simple ones of a lonesome and weary traveler."

At these words, the two men heard a loud gasp from the adjoining room, followed immediately by the sound of earthenware shattering on the tiled floor.

The proprietor looked upon the stranger with renewed awe and swallowed. It was almost impossible for him to contain the emotions—the hopes and expectations—that welled up inside of him at the stranger's simple remark.

"A Traveler…" he whispered.

4. *Dead Drop*

Bejad stepped over the indistinct shape of a sleeping vagabond who had managed to curl up in an isolated corner among the debris littering the passageway. The sun had risen over an hour ago, but the side street was so narrow that it remained in shadow for the better part of the day. He was already late, so he quickened his pace and reached into the left front pocket of his trousers to take out the instructions he had picked up at the dead drop yesterday.

They weren't there.

He anxiously searched his other pockets but found nothing.

A cold wave of panic washed over him. Was it possible that he had misplaced the information again? Whatever had he done with it? Fortunately he had a good memory and therefore knew where to go. Angry with himself, he kicked a gedashol that had scampered across his path. The effort shifted his attention back to his surroundings; his thoughts wandered and he shook his head.

Divestelan had once been called the "Jewel of the Covasins." If he glanced up at the buildings around him, it was still possible to imagine the stately impression the city must once have made upon astonished visitors. Situated only several leagues east of the Covasin Range, the city had been built completely from stones that had been hauled in from Mt. Toradeh, the highest peak of the "Impassables." When seen from a distance, the capital of the western Suviltan provinces shimmered whitely against the imposing backdrop of the towering summits in the west, and would even glow brilliantly when the sun struck the polished stones' surfaces. But the vision of grandeur faded as soon as the unsuspecting pilgrim came within range of the city's dreadful stench. Any remaining illusions vanished completely when he entered the city's gates and saw the filth and soot that choked its streets.

When Her Eminence had engaged his services some five years ago, she had attempted to explain the situation to him, but he was hardly capable of believing what he heard. How could anyone expect him to comprehend such terror and misery while sitting in a comfortable and peaceful office of the Capitol Building in Travis? It was not until he arrived in Divestelan that the undeniable facts had hit him square in the face.

Conditions in the city had been deteriorating for over thirty years. The metropolis was hopelessly overpopulated, now harboring almost one hundred thousand inhabitants.

Many of them were refugees that had fled in fear from the surrounding areas, hoping to find protection from the unpredictable and shocking acts of violence that ravaged the countryside.

Bejad could only shake his head again as he turned right into another narrow passage lined with the foulness of utter poverty. When confronted with the reality surrounding him, it was difficult to understand why the Council in Travis had waited so long. But when rumors of the declining state of affairs in the western provinces reached Travis some thirty years ago, Bejad had been just as much in denial as everyone else, and he therefore found it difficult to censure the elders for diligently ignoring what others were telling them. People were afraid, and no one wanted to accept that the Millennial Peace was coming to an end. Only after the darkness had spread to the eastern provinces some twenty years back did the elders respond—with more conferences. It had taken the late High Priestess Halita Penates's death here in the city five years ago to bring them to their senses. They finally realized that there might be other forces at work, forces that required drastic measures if they were to be abated.

And so they had chosen Her Eminence as the new High Priestess. Bejad trusted her judgment implicitly. Despite her young age, she had shown courage and competence, even before she was elected, by uncovering the true circumstances surrounding Halita's "accident." Then she had taken over Halita's weak intelligence network and gone into seclusion, spinning her webs, strengthening her contacts with the Resistance, and biding her time until she could reveal herself. In the past five years, she had probably accomplished more than any High Priestess in the hundred years before her.

Bejad had been one of her first liaison officers and had volunteered for the position in Divestelan. Although he had been here for almost five years now, he still couldn't get used to the reek and filth. He missed the warm luminance, the green gardens, and the fresh mountain air of Travis, the "City of Light," which was located five hundred leagues away on the eastern edge of the Suviltan Plateau.

As he made a last turn to his left, he had to press up against the wall to let a patrol pass. With the menace of the Black Guard always imminent, the guards in the dark brown, black, and golden attire of the western houses patrolled the many streets and passages at all hours. Not that it did anyone any good. None of the patrols had ever survived an encounter with their adversaries.

This passage was a bit broader than the back streets he had been taking. He stopped in front of a small tavern huddled up between two craftsmen's shops and glanced left and right. Then he stepped inside and let his eyes grow accustomed to the darkness. The proprietor eyed him suspiciously, and Bejad nodded casually in his direction. In a dismal corner he located his contact, who had a mug resting between his hands. Bejad steered unobtrusively towards him.

"Would you please bring me a strong mug of deventas?" he called over to the proprietor. "This had better be good, Sheletas, for you to call me over here at this ungodly hour," he whispered as he slipped into a chair next to his accomplice.

Sheletas was a tall, muscular man with well-groomed but graying hair and a closely trimmed full beard. His dark skin designated him an inhabitant of the Northern Covasins, and his face was marked by the solid track record of an experienced agent of the Resistance. His high brow gave him an intellectual appearance, and his grave demeanor made it clear that he wasn't the kind of man that would put up with nonsense. Bejad often felt his own mediocrity when in the man's formidable presence, although Sheletas never deliberately attempted to demonstrate any superiority.

In comparison, Bejad possessed only a moderate stature. But the hard work on his parent's farm had produced a strong and sturdy physique, and his often rough life had spawned the dubious virtue of being able to drink most of his friends under the table. Bejad had made several attempts to emulate the trend and grow a beard or moustache, but the fashion didn't become him, so he now propped a meticulously shaven, hardy chin on his left hand and scratched his untamable black hair with his right as he warily observed his companion.

"I think you have more important things to worry about than losing a little sleep," the man answered, and pushed a crumpled piece of paper in Bejad's direction.

Bejad stared at the note for a moment and then diverted his gaze in embarrassment.

Sheletas shook his head. "Bejad, what on earth could have induced you to throw away the contents of a dead drop just twenty steps from where you picked them up? No, don't answer that. Knowing you, I assume she was attractive enough."

Bejad grinned shamefacedly.

Sheletas grimaced in return. "In addition to the negligible fact that your behavior endangers us all, I hope you realize that the dead-letter box has become useless." Bejad didn't miss the cold sarcasm in his voice.

"I'm really sorry," Bejad replied weakly as he let the note disappear into a pocket.

Sheletas made no attempt to answer since the proprietor had just come over. He slammed down a mug of some dark, smelly broth in front of Bejad and immediately moved off again.

"Let's get down to business," Sheletas said when the proprietor was out of earshot.

"I'm listening," Bejad replied, taking a sip of the hot liquid and forcing himself to swallow.

"You know that His Excellency's family is leaving for Tolares in the early afternoon?"

"Yes, although I doubt that they can travel that distance in such a short time. The conference begins in four days, and it's over two hundred leagues. That's cutting it pretty close."

"They have enough resources. Our informants have told us that they'll be traveling day and night and changing their teams every sixteen hours."

"What does that have to do with me?"

Sheletas moved his head closer to his companion. "A person very close to the family has asked to arrange a rendezvous with you. Bejad, listen carefully, whoever it is asked for you by name." The two men exchanged a significant glance. "My contact says that it is very urgent. You must meet with them at noon."

"It could be a trap."

"You'll have to risk that."

"And where is this rendezvous to take place?"

"On the west side of the stables of His Excellency's residence."

"His Excellency's residence? Are you out of your mind?" Bejad hissed. "They're already suspicious enough as it is. If I get caught within a league of the estate, they'll have me executed on the spot."

"Then don't get caught."

"Very funny. Is there no other place we can arrange this meeting?"

Sheletas shook his head. "Sorry, but in this case it just won't be possible. There's not enough time. Look, Bejad, you're the one that's always been pressing for an opportunity like this. And things are getting tight for you, anyway. From what my contact told me, this person must be some very high official. I have been instructed that after the rendezvous, your mission will be to personally get any information back to Her Eminence in Tolares at once. Get your personal belongings cleaned out or destroyed and arrive at the meeting place prepared to leave immediately. I suppose that you'll be on your way back to Travis after that, so we won't be seeing you anymore."

"Sheletas, I can't just leave you and the others here with the pressure building up as it is."

"That's a kind thought, Bejad, but this is our home. The Resistance wants to see those who are destroying the western provinces driven out and Divestelan returned to its former beauty, even if that's not your highest priority," Sheletas said, shooting Bejad a sidelong glance. "And don't think that you're irreplaceable, my friend. Her Eminence will find someone in your stead. When you see her, please tell her that, as long as she is sympathetic to our cause, she can always count on us."

He sighed. "She'll be very happy to hear that."

"Alright, noon on the west side of the stables. The code word will be 'Yanita.' I'll inform my contact that the meeting has been arranged. Don't let me down this time, Bejad."

"I'll do my best. Code word 'Yanita,'" he echoed wearily.

Sheletas placed a coin on the table and rose. As he passed he put his hand on Bejad's shoulder and squeezed firmly, then departed without another word.

Bejad remained seated and stared into his mug, pondering his professedly last mission after five years as intermediary between Her Eminence and the Resistance in this city. Had he ever really been of any help to these people? He wanted to believe it. He would think of a way to get onto the estate.

He threw a coin on the table and left.

5. *Chimes of Destiny*

The stranger in the sunny tavern in Nadil could hardly suppress his amazement at the proprietor's reaction.

"I don't understand," he said. "Did I say something wrong? I assume that many travelers must stop at your tavern."

"Yes, my friend, but none such as you," the proprietor answered. "Please forgive me, but times are not quite as simple as they once were, what with the squabbling between the houses and all. Listen, there is a Lady in town that is a high official and will therefore be participating in the conference, although she does not shout it from the rooftops. I think it might be wise if you meet with her."

The stranger nodded slowly. "Yes, that might be profitable."

"Her handmaiden will most likely be coming into town about midmorning. I will try to intercept her and see if she will take you to see her mistress. In the meantime, please have some breakfast."

"That would be very kind of you. I do believe that I'm beginning to feel hungry."

The owner bustled away again and soon had set the table. He wasn't stingy with the victuals, and the stranger received everything he could have desired to satisfy his hunger or quench his thirst. After attending to the stranger's needs, the proprietor asked to be excused in order to deal with various matters that required his attention, leaving the stranger to contemplate his own thoughts.

The stranger clenched his teeth. Why did he have to be caught in this place and this time? If he remembered correctly, this society could be described as pseudo-Victorian. He would have to exert himself immensely if he wanted to imitate the flamboyant etiquette and exaggerated courtesy predominant in this culture. Why couldn't his fate have led him to some simpler world or time, where he could say what he felt and didn't need to be so sensible of his words and actions? He didn't even know what he had done to provoke such an effect in the proprietor and his wife. It made him feel like a bull in a china shop.

Well, the first thing to do was attempt to suppress his emotions, as everyone else here seemed to be doing. That would probably account for much of the current decorum. He knew some of the phrases in use at this time and would have to rely on his perception to fall in line with what others around him were doing. He had always been good at picking up signals regarding what was expected of him. In this way, he might even get through this episode without causing too much of a stir.

He balled his fist, and his nails bit into the palm of his hand. Why did this have to happen to him? The Temporal Displacement Directive issued by the Alliance was mandatory reading for all citizens in the stellar age. He was therefore aware of the required behavior while he was here, although he had never seriously considered that he would one day fall under the restrictions of the Directive. He took a deep breath. He would just have to steel himself to the task ahead and attempt to get through it as well as possible.

With such thoughts on his mind, the hours crept slowly by. At the time of the habitual midmorning break, other customers entered the establishment, were waited upon amiably by the proprietor and his spouse, and left again. But in the four hours between midmorning and noon, business in the tavern almost came to a complete stop and he found that the proprietor was again able to pass some time with him.

The stranger's eyes were resting upon a ghosted outline on

the wall near the Prophet's Bow. The contour could have represented a cross, but the extended and tapered stem made it more likely that it belonged to a sword.

The proprietor, who was polishing a silvery chalice, must have noticed his gaze. He set down the chalice, walked over, and stood, looking respectfully up at the icon.

He turned to the stranger. "That, my friend, is but a silent admonition."

"An admonition? May I inquire as to the nature of the admonition?"

The proprietor drew a deep breath. "It reminds us of an artifact that was lost to us long ago. It has been foretold, though, that it will be returned to us by…a certain person at the beginning of a new era," he said with a meaningful glance at the stranger, "foretold, actually, by the same prophet that constructed the bow behind you, among others. Many people therefore give up a prominent location in their homes to display such an admonition as you see there behind you. To us it signifies loss, but also hope, and reminds us of the consequences of complacency."

"I assume you speak of the Sword of Selanae?"

The proprietor's smile was filled with anticipation. "There seems to be no need to enlighten you."

"On the contrary, although I've heard of the sword, I'm sorry to say that I couldn't recall the complete tale. I take it that it is most intriguing."

The proprietor seemed disappointed. "Oh, well, yes. But the retelling would be the task of an entire evening, if it were to be done properly. I have no doubt, though, that you'll be hearing it soon enough. Most anybody here would jump at the opportunity to tell it once more."

"Well, I look forward to it. But tell me, my friend, what's that fascinating device in the center of the hall?"

The stranger gestured towards an object that rested upon an elegant, wooden podium slightly lower than the tables around it. The article consisted of a solid, tapered base from which half of a crystalline sphere protruded.

The proprietor's face lit up in pride as he beamed at his guest. "Ah! I see you've discovered my most prized possession. You may not believe this, but the light sculpture was a gift from Elder Yonatan himself."

He went over to the sculpture and deftly touched its base. The effect was instantaneous and completely silent. The stranger had never seen anything that was simultaneously so beautiful, yet somehow so unsettling. The sculpture's movements were slow and well-balanced as fountains of colored light erupted from its base and blossomed almost as high as the ceiling of the hall, then cascaded and melted away again, always in accord.

The proprietor smiled. "Here, listen to this."

His fingers reached through one of the newly emerging blossoms and several bell-like tones flowed from the sculpture, filling the room with harmonious chords that ranged through the entire audible spectrum. Then his hand stroked a delicate shower of light below the fading bloom and the nuance of the harmony changed ever so slightly.

The stranger unconsciously clutched at the edge of the table. The chords unnerved him with an irrevocable sense of foreboding, penetrating his already bewildered mind like ominous chimes heralding his destiny, pounding into him the reality of his current circumstances like nothing else since his arrival. As he watched, almost hypnotized, the sculpture continued to flow and change, and so the diminishing bells which still filled the room flowed with it until they faded away and only the silent sculpture engaged his senses.

The stranger gaped in trepidation. "I...I've never seen anything like it."

"Yes, it is most inspired, isn't it?" the owner agreed as he once more touched the base of the sculpture, allowing the lights and colors to collapse upon themselves and disappear back into the crystal orb. "But you mustn't forget, it was created by Elder Yonatan," he added as he returned to the stranger's table, as if the name was explanation enough. He sat down in the chair he had already occupied once that morning.

The stranger remained silent for a moment and then looked back at his host. "I've heard the name, but I had no idea…"

The proprietor gazed at the stranger with a soft glow in his eyes. "It's always a pleasure to meet a kindred spirit that can appreciate the value of a true work of art."

The stranger drew in a deep breath of air and exhaled slowly through his mouth, attempting to shake off the disturbing premonition that had befallen him.

"Well," he said, "there do seem to be quite a few people on the road today."

"Yes, of course. The Conference of Tolares will begin four days from now, let me see, that is next Velamayav, the first day of the month Anamadani, which is the summer solstice, so it is to be expected."

"The Conference of Tolares? Oh." Something in the stranger clicked and for an instant he was far away again.

"You weren't aware of it?"

"No," he replied slowly, "but now that you mention it, I should have remembered." He sighed. "My friend, don't you think it's time that I cleared my debt?"

The proprietor seemed embarrassed. The stranger assumed that his host had deliberately been delaying the moment when it became necessary for him to settle his account.

"Alright, my friend, what is it that you wish to give me?"

the proprietor asked cautiously.

The stranger reached across the table and handed him a foreign yet skillfully worked piece of gold.

The proprietor took it warily, almost with reverence. He weighed it in his hand, examined it and turned back to the stranger. "My friend, this is too much. How could I accept it?"

"Please, my friend, don't embarrass me. I have nothing else to give you."

The proprietor hesitated. "Well, if it must be. But at least accept my hospitality for the remainder of your stay with us. We have very comfortable and quiet quarters in the back which face the courtyard and gardens. You will not be disturbed there."

The stranger smiled. "Yes, gladly."

They shook hands heartily to complete the transaction.

"Your quarters will be ready for you in the evening. I will show you to them then, but for now I must be getting on again. Please excuse me."

The proprietor rose and quickly retreated to the adjoining room. The stranger heard a muffled gasp and assumed that another pair of eyes was marveling over the seemingly precious object that he had given the proprietor.

6. *The Dispatch*

Zetara had just finished directing the packing of the last of Gevinesa's chests for the Lady's journey to Tolares when her mistress rushed into the room, completely out of breath. Zetara felt an icy hand clutch her heart when she saw the pale and apprehensive expression on Gevinesa's face.

"Vinesa, what's wrong?" she cried in dismay.

Gevinesa stood silently before her for a moment with her

eyes closed, catching her breath and desperately attempting to regain her composure. Zetara unobtrusively motioned for Midena and the other two maids, who had been helping her pack, to leave the room. When the door was closed, Gevinesa opened her eyes and silently handed Zetara a piece of paper that she retrieved from a hidden pocket in the folds of her dress.

Zetara took the single sheet with trembling hands. She could feel the blood draining from her face as she browsed quickly through its contents.

"*A'mada*, Vinesa, where did you get this?" she whispered.

"Yanita was playing in my brother's room while the servants were packing and found it on his desk." Her voice was now quite calm, with a tinge of sarcasm, and Zetara could see the color returning to her cheeks. A slight flush of anger replaced her friend's previous pale fright. "I'm astonished at Yanita's presence of mind for taking it, but not quite so astonished at Corsen's foolish pride for leaving it so openly where anyone could see it. It's fortunate for us that he keeps a copy of such dispatches for his records."

Zetara took another glance at the document. It was a copy of an official dispatch to the captain of the Black Guard with instructions to terminate the designated members of the Resistance in Divestelan identified in the attached list. The operation was to begin precisely at noon. She felt herself growing faint and placed the paper carefully on the Lady's desk before clutching at the furniture to steady herself. Gevinesa reached over to support her.

"Are you alright?" Gevinesa asked.

"Yes, I'm fine." Zetara turned back to her. "Were you able to acquire the list of targets?"

Gevinesa shook her head. "No, just the dispatch."

"Oh, Vinesa, whatever shall we do?"

"There's only one thing to do. You must get this information to your contact in the Resistance at once. It's already past midmorning, and there's no time to lose."

"I can try. My preliminary contact has a cover to maintain and might therefore still be at the market, and if not, I have an auxiliary plan."

"Good. Take my chyeves. The mare is much faster than yours."

"Will I see you again when I return?"

"No, Zetara, I forbid you to return here; it's just too dangerous. Besides, we'll either already be gone by the time you get back, or at the least my father and brother won't let me out of their sight after I return from my rendezvous at the stables. I can't doubt that it will arouse their suspicion, being at the same time that their precious operation is to commence. As a matter of fact, I must devise a way to slip out early, or they will most likely detain me."

"Oh, Vinesa, I was hoping we would have more time to say our farewells."

Gevinesa looked at her and smiled. "Dearest, kindest Zetara, you've been such a comfort to me these past five years. What would I have done without you?"

They fell into each other's arms, and Zetara felt Gevinesa's lips on her cheek. She tried to restrain her tears as they released each other from their tender, parting embrace.

Gevinesa glanced at her. "Don't cry, my gentle little handmaiden. There shall be no tears for us. I have all hope that we will soon see each other again in Travis."

Zetara nodded, but could find no words to get past the lump in her throat.

"Come," her mistress said, "I must return to Yanita's chambers to supervise the servants, and you must leave."

Zetara felt Gevinesa's hand at her elbow, guiding her out the door. In the hall, Zetara turned towards her friend.

"I'll tell the servants to bring down your luggage."

"Yes, but go quickly," Gevinesa whispered. "Farewell, Zetara."

"Farewell, Vinesa," Zetara whispered back.

The two women parted reluctantly, and Zetara walked briskly to the auxiliary chambers, where she found the three maids that had been assigned to attend to her Lady's belongings for the journey. After giving Midena some final instructions, she glided down the central staircase of the noble residence. She was crossing the main hall when Lord Divestelan approached her from the east wing with his son.

"Ah, Zetara, I'm glad I've run into you," the Lord called. "Have my daughter's things been prepared?"

She turned towards the two men and curtsied with her head bowed as they walked up to her. "Yes, My Lord, the maids are just completing the task at this moment. They will inform the servants shortly so that the Lady Gevinesa's luggage may be brought down."

She raised her head and glanced at the men. Lord Divestelan was of moderate stature. His shortly cropped, black hair had a slight tinge of gray and his face was adorned by an elegant mustache and goatee. Corsen was slightly taller, but clean-shaven with a somewhat longer and more liberal hairstyle. He looked even more dashing than his father in his house uniform, a fact that was underlined by a prominent scar on his right cheek that ran vertically down from his eye to his jaw.

"And what are Gevinesa's instructions for you at the moment?" the Lord asked.

"I...must supervise the servants that are returning some unneeded luggage to the lower storage rooms. Her Ladyship didn't wish for them to be standing unused in her chambers while she was gone."

"Very well, you may proceed."

"Yes, and don't dawdle, Zetara," Corsen sneered at her. "We need you back here soon. We have a little, uh, surprise for you before we leave."

Zetara paled at these words but kept her head bowed so that the men wouldn't notice. She just barely caught Lord Divestelan's scornful glance in his son's direction by looking up through her lashes.

"As you wish, My Lord," she replied. Then she curtsied and quickly turned towards the entrance leading to the storage rooms.

It took her a little longer to exit the residence by the lower chambers, but it also attracted less attention. She was glad, for she could hardly believe what she had just heard and the insight made her feel weak and shaky. It was almost certain that she was on Corsen's death list. How had they found her out?

She didn't have any time to engage in such thoughts, though, as she hurried to the stables, where she quickly saddled her mistress's chyeves and left the grounds of the beautiful, parklike estate by inconspicuous trails that she had rehearsed often with Gevinesa for just such occasions. In very little time she had gained the road from Catanin to Divestelan and spurred her mare to utmost speed, with the waters of Lake Divestelan glittering on her right as she flew north.

It was only a little more than five leagues to the city, and she was convinced that Gevinesa's mare would be able to handle the exertion of a quick but short ride. Indeed, she reached the gates of the city in just under half an hour and grimaced at the stench that engulfed her as she passed beneath the magnificent, towering archway. She allowed her chyeves to trot leisurely towards the market and then led the beast by the reins as she approached the pulsating tumult of her destination. She almost fainted with relief when she saw her contact attending to a customer.

The contact caught sight of her and shot her an anxious glance. She was on the verge of completing a transaction with her current customer, and after a few kind words of thanks and parting, she turned immediately towards Zetara.

"*Setavelan mada, vil'anar.* Good morning, my friend. What may I do for you?"

"*Setavelan mada.* My Lady is leaving for Tolares in a few hours and has just discovered that she absolutely requires a new pearl barrette to match her earrings," Zetara replied.

This was the signal for extreme danger, and her contact paled, but adroitly disguised her shock with a shrug at the extravagance of such noble ladies.

"I'm certain that we will find something suitable for the princess. Why don't you step into my pavilion?"

When they were sure of concealment, the young woman immediately turned towards her. "What is it, Zetara?" she whispered.

Zetara quickly explained the situation.

"*Tev'anar!*" the woman whispered when Zetara had finished. "I must relay your message immediately."

She wanted to turn and leave the tent, but Zetara held her arm.

"No, Dena, please wait."

The woman stared at her, astonished. "I didn't realize that you were aware of my identity."

Zetara studied her for a moment, wanting to imprint her image on her memory. Dena was of the same height as she was, but must have been several years younger, certainly no older than thirty-five. She was no particular beauty, but her appearance was pleasant. Instead of the fashionable hairstyle that Zetara was obliged to wear as the personal handmaiden of the Lady Gevinesa, the young woman had her hair simply bound together using a stylish barrette as an advertisement of her products. Her skin was fair, and not the darker texture that marked Zetara as an inhabitant of the Northern Covasins.

"I beg Your Ladyship to forgive me for taking such liberties as to call you by your first name," Zetara finally answered, "but I've always known who you are. I saw you at the ball your father gave for you in Cemasena fifteen years ago to celebrate your coming-out. I was attending to the Lady Gevinesa as her abigail at the time. I recognized you again when we met four years ago."

Dena's astonishment grew. "Never mind the breach of formality. I detest being called Lady Cemasena. It makes me feel so old. Besides, I consider us to be sisters in a mutual cause. How much do you know about me?"

"Enough. Dena, we don't know who has been targeted. And if I was able to discover your identity, it stands to reason that others might also. Besides, my task is now over and I will therefore be heading east. Please, get yourself to safety."

"You're...you're leaving?"

"Yes, I must. I'm almost certain that I've been targeted."

"May I ask where you're going?"

"I'll be going to Tolares first, to see my older brother, then on to Travis."

"Oh, your brother, Eratis. Isn't he steward of Lord Tolares's estate?"

"Yes, I'm very proud of him. He's accomplished much at such a young age. Do you have somewhere to go?"

"Well, yes, I was planning on tracing Tavita. We have just received intelligence that she has gone east, and if you no longer require me as a contact, this would be a good time to follow her."

"What? Tavita?"

"Yes."

"Tavita Marusen? The Captain of Lady Gevinesa's Crimson Brigade?"

"Former captain."

"Dena, do you know what you're doing?"

The young woman raised her head, and her eyes flashed defiantly. "I know what she looks like and am therefore an obvious choice for the mission."

Zetara regarded her with compassion. Dena seemed to have her teeth clenched. If the young woman had tears burning behind her eyes, she suppressed them very well.

"I'm so sorry for your loss, Dena," Zetara said in a soft voice.

Now her eyes were definitely glistening. "I...We need to leave."

"Yes. But if you're also going east, we might see each other again."

"Possibly."

"Farewell, Dena."

"Farewell, Zetara."

They embraced briefly. Then they stepped outside the tent, and, to uphold the charade one last time, Dena courteously bid her alleged customer farewell and expressed her regret that she had found nothing suitable for her mistress. Zetara watched her close shop and hurry away before she took hold of her chyeves. She was just about to mount when a sudden recollection made her stomach turn to ice.

"Oh, Lord, no, the dispatch!" she whispered to herself.

How could she have been so careless? They had even scoffed at Corsen for leaving the document on his desk, and now she had done the same thing, leaving it in the Lady Gevinesa's chambers. If the document were found in her mistress's possession, it would certainly be the Lady's death warrant.

She swung herself up on her mare and raced through the streets, completely disregarding the cursing pedestrians that jumped out of her way. When she finally exited the city, she spurred her chyeves forwards without any consideration for the animal's well-being. She could think only of her friend.

She reached the estate in twenty minutes, hid the wasted and frothing mare in a group of trees, and stole towards the residence, sneaking inside by the back entrance she used when she had left about one and a half hours ago. The main hall was suspiciously quiet. The staircase in the west wing was the one least used, so she eased herself towards that side of the building and climbed the steps to the second floor. When she was almost at the top she encountered one of the maids.

"Zetara!" the maid cried, seemingly shocked at her superior's sudden appearance.

"Midena, have you seen the Lady Gevinesa?"

"Yes, she...she left for the stables just a short while ago."

"Good. I need to inspect her chambers one more time before she departs to see if we've missed anything."

The maid shot her an odd glance, bowed, and hurried past her down the stairs.

Zetara had no time to consider the maid's strange behavior, but rushed forwards. With a pounding heart, she entered Gevinesa's chambers. To her utter relief, the treacherous document was still on the desk. It was the work of a moment to catch it up, light a match, and watch it go up in flames. She performed the task with methodical thoroughness, ensuring that nothing but ashes were left, which she then disposed of in the dustbin.

She had just finished cleaning everything away when she heard heavy steps in the corridor. She turned, but an abrupt surge of terror froze her movements.

Two Black Guards were standing in the doorway with Midena cowering behind them. The men were wearing black uniforms, gloves, and capes, with black masks covering their eyes.

"I'm so sorry, Zetara," the maid whined, "but we were ordered to report you if we saw you, and…"

"Shut up!" one of the guards snarled at her.

Midena cringed, whimpered, and fell silent.

The guard turned back and grinned at Zetara from beneath his mask. He leisurely unsheathed his sword and walked towards her with slow, menacing steps.

Zetara couldn't think. She stared at the approaching demon with her eyes wide open in shock. She wanted to tell Midena that it was alright, that everything would be fine and not to worry, but when she opened her mouth to speak, her breath was forced from her in a silent gasp. Despite the searing pain in her stomach, she couldn't tear her eyes from the grotesque, grinning mask before her. Her hand unconsciously reached down, and she cut her finger on the cold steel protruding from her belly. Dazed, she raised her hand to her face and stared at the trickle of blood running down into her palm. Then her legs gave out beneath her, and she sank to the floor. The last thing she heard was Midena's hysteric shrieks echoing through the building.

7. *View from a Window*

The stranger mused over everything that had happened while dreamily monitoring the activities of the townspeople and foreigners passing by on the road outside. There were simple peasants in overalls and diligent craftsmen in long shirts and trousers quietly and efficiently going about their business. Plain maids in long, serviceable gowns adorned only with unassuming aprons went by on their way to the market. Sometimes pompous lords in stylish tunics and ladies in elegant two- and three-piece dresses drove by in exorbitant carriages.

When the stranger felt the need to relieve himself some time later, he was not directed to the back door of the tavern, as he had expected. Contrary to his fears, the lavatory was not an outhouse, but turned out to be a room inside the tavern, which was well aired, spotless, and fragrant with spring flowers. The tavern had flowing water at its disposal. The proprietor explained that the town possessed a comprehensive water and sewage system. There was a virtually inexhaustible supply of fresh water in subterranean wells around the town, so there was no need for the water to be purified.

The stranger returned to his table, and time again slowed to the pace of a slithering mollusk. The proprietor must have miscalculated, for it was not until an hour before noon that he finally rushed out through the front door.

Since the stranger was alone in the hall, he walked over to one of the windows to get a better view of the events unfolding on the road. Two young women had passed the tavern on their way towards the center of town just before his host had scuttled outside. The women were both carrying empty baskets and chatting amiably. The one on the left must have been the Lady's handmaiden, for her cream-colored robe was draped in an elegant black cloak that appeared to be made of a fine cloth similar to velvet. Because of the pleasant warmth of the day, the hood of the cloak was hanging idly on her back. She had thick, black, unbound hair, most of which disappeared under her mantle. The stranger felt irritated, for the handmaiden's robe seemed familiar, but he just couldn't place it.

Her companion was clothed far more simply in a somewhat worn dress which reached nearly to the ground, as did all the women's attire that he had seen so far. A patched apron was tied about her waist. What came as a surprise was her long golden hair, a true rarity in this black-haired population.

When the two women became aware of the chubby little proprietor shouting and running towards them, they stopped and turned in his direction, smiling and calling some friendly greeting. As soon as he reached them, though, he took the handmaiden's arm and whispered urgently in her ear. Her unaffected smile faded and was replaced by a more solemn and somewhat concerned expression. She glanced cursorily in the direction of the tavern, then back at the proprietor. After several more animated whispers between them, the handmaiden turned to her companion and spoke a few words. The latter nodded with a smile and answered something that seemed to be reassuring, while touching the handmaiden's arm. They embraced affectionately, after which the handmaiden turned with the proprietor towards the tavern, while her companion continued in the direction of the market.

The stranger hurried back to his place and seated himself just as the two entered. The proprietor pointed the handmaiden to his table but didn't join her. Instead, he remained in the background looking busy. She nodded and thanked him, then approached, obliging the stranger to rise again.

He had already assessed her as being very beautiful when he saw her from the window, but reality almost overwhelmed him. Her eyes were dark, like the hair that framed her oval face. Her skin was smooth and perfect. Her features were gentle and friendly, but also composed and thoughtful. There was nothing unnatural or shrewd about this young woman; she seemed completely at ease with herself and her environment. In his experience, it usually took years of intense and specialized training to attain such a state of equanimity. How could the graceful and majestic creature facing him be only a handmaiden? But what startled him even more was her amazing resemblance to his wife.

She must have noticed his perplexed gaze but didn't react to it. Instead, she considered him for a moment and then smiled.

"*Velan mada,* good day." Her voice was mild and pleasant, allowing him to feel instantly at ease. "My friend Folan has informed me that you are new in town and a bit unfamiliar with the surroundings. I'm certain that my mistress, the Lady Utalya, would be glad to offer her assistance, if that would comply with your wishes. May we invite you to our residence for the midday meal?"

"*Velan mada,* My Lady. I thank you for your kind offer and would be delighted to make your mistress's acquaintance."

His words appeared to disturb her. "Please, don't call me 'Lady.' We are naught but simple servants here."

"Oh, I'm sorry. I just thought…"

"No, I understand," she replied with a smile. "My mistress has her whims, and one of them is to dress up her servants like royalty." She made a sweeping gesture at her clothes. "But believe me, beneath the pretentious splendor, I'm no different from my golden-haired friend you saw me with when you were watching from the window."

He almost didn't catch the virtually insignificant change in the tone of her voice and the luster of her eyes. It took a moment for her words to register, but when they did, the stranger shot a quick glance at the proprietor behind the bar, a bit of color rising to his face. Fortunately, the latter hadn't heard but still seemed busy polishing the silverware. The stranger opened his mouth to reply, then thought better of it and closed his mouth again. No, this was no simple handmaiden.

"We are in agreement then?" she asked, without pushing the fact of his impropriety.

He nodded, slowly regaining his composure after his embarrassment.

"I need to buy some things from the market for our meal. Would you like to accompany me?" she asked pleasantly, switching her empty basket to the other hand.

"Yes, that would be very generous. I've been waiting here all morning and some fresh air would do me good."

Besides, he felt it would be best if he just went along with whatever they asked of him for the time being, within reasonable limits, of course.

8. *Catyana*

"*Velan mada, Catyana.* What a pleasant surprise to see you here. Are you going to the market for your mother?"

Catyana almost forgot to smile at Lutrisya's blunt insincerity. Did Lutrisya think she was blind? She had seen Lutrisya overtake them just a few minutes ago, while Catyana was standing near the tavern with her friend, Nova, and Folan, the tavern's proprietor. Lutrisya's greedy stare had been unmistakable as she waddled by, attempting to pass close enough to snatch up a few morsels of Nova and Folan's whispered conversation. Besides, Catyana knew Lutrisya didn't much care for her since she never participated in town gossip. Lutrisya must be very desperate if she was trying it anyway. *Pleasant surprise* indeed!

Catyana's expression was probably more of a pained grimace when she was finally able to fix something like a smile on her lips, but she was too annoyed with Lutrisya to really care. She would at least make an attempt at civility, though. Catyana was as yet several years away from the Age of Maturity, and she wanted Lutrisya to know that she respected her position in the community and her status as Catyana's senior.

"*Velan mada, Lutrisya.* Yes, Mother needs a few provisions to get us through the weekend. Father won't be able to make it into town with the wagon until next Velanav," Catyana replied in a guardedly friendly tone.

"I've just returned from the market myself. Are you and your family doing well?"

Catyana glanced quickly at Lutrisya's basket, which contained a three day's old loaf of bread. She had probably dumped it in to lend her pretext some validity before she rushed away from her spying post at the kitchen window to go fishing for the newest gossip. Catyana wasn't fooled. Lutrisya hadn't gone to the market to buy groceries.

"Thank you for your concern, Lutrisya. We are all doing well."

"And your friend Nova? That was her I saw you with just before, wasn't it?"

Aha! Getting right down to business, wasn't she?

"Yes, your eyes did not deceive you. And from what Nova told me, I did receive the impression that she's also in good health."

"I understand, dear. You didn't have much time to chat, did you?"

"That's true. It's only a short distance from the Lady Utalya's lodge to Folan's tavern."

"Such a shame. I know how fond you two are of each other. But I suppose she had her reasons for leaving you so suddenly."

"I suppose so. She didn't really get around to informing me of them, though."

"That's surprising. I thought you always told each other everything," Lutrisya said, sounding slightly irritated.

"Well, not quite everything. Besides, we'll be seeing each other later this afternoon, and I'm certain we'll have enough time to chat some more then."

"So you didn't hear anything about the stranger that has been in Folan's tavern since early this morning?"

"No, I'm afraid I can't tell you anything about that. Although, if you actually do make a trip to the market to get some bread, I'm sure you could arrange to run into Nova and ask her yourself."

That was the closest Catyana could come to snubbing Lutrisya without actually being rude, and Lutrisya immediately took the hint.

"Well, I never!" Lutrisya lifted her skirts and swept away, holding her head high.

Catyana smiled to herself and continued her walk towards the market. She stopped at a booth with craftily molded brushes and barrettes to see if she could find something suitable for Sinara. She sighed. She had no idea what was happening to her little sister. The dismal visions Sinara was having ever more frequently were very disturbing, and Catyana was worried. She hoped that some pretty little present might cheer her sister up. She would have to mention the nightmares to Nova again in the afternoon. Maybe Nova could do something for Sinara. It seemed to have helped the last time. She chose a wooden barrette that would match nicely with Sinara's golden locks and exchanged a few friendly words while paying the vendor.

Before Catyana turned away from the booth, she glanced back. Lutrisya was whispering with the smith's wife and throwing poisonous glances in Catyana's direction. Well, Catyana had had her fun, but she would probably come to regret it. Lutrisya's husband, who was head of the potter's guild, was also a very important official in the town parliament. Although Mayor Menirel was Lord Tolares's formal representative in Nadil, most business was discussed in parliament meetings in the town hall before any definite decision was reached, and Lutrisya's husband was known to be a very influential person. Mother wouldn't be very happy with her when she told her about the incident.

She turned back towards the market and threw back her thick, golden hair. She immediately regretted the movement. Nadil was currently filled with foreigners passing through in the direction of Tolares for the upcoming conference. She discreetly looked around. It was as she feared. The regular townspeople were accustomed to the sight of the Faeren girls with their unique, golden tresses. There was a mutual understanding between them based on simple courtesy that they would never openly stare at Catyana or her three sisters.

With foreigners, though, it was a different matter. Catyana observed several men who just stopped in the middle of the street and were following her with their eyes, their mouths agape. Her cheeks turned crimson. She diverted her gaze and turned briskly into a road on her left. She decided she would visit the dairy first before continuing on to the market for vegetables.

9. *Gold of the Heavens*

As always, Semanta had been eavesdropping from her listening post in the antechamber. She peeked around the corner in time to see Nova approach her husband with the stranger.

"Folan, I will be abducting your guest for a while, if you don't mind," the handmaiden said.

Folan dropped the pretense of polishing his silverware and joined his two guests. "No, of course not. But please, my friends, you must both come again this evening."

"Don't worry, Folan. Where else would you expect us to go? I will return your guest to you before nightfall."

Semanta felt this was a good opportunity to draw attention to herself, so she cautiously stuck her head out through the doorway.

The handmaiden noticed her immediately. "Oh, hello, Semanta," she called, smiling cheerfully.

Semanta felt no need to suppress her agitation and beckoned for Nova to come. The handmaiden stepped around the bar to join her in the other room, leaving the stranger with Folan in the hall.

"What's the matter, Semanta?" Nova asked with an expression of alarm on her face. "You're not usually this shy."

"Oh, Nova, I'm so sorry to bother you, but it's the stranger. I just don't know what to think. Look," she whispered, "Gold of the Heavens." She held up the piece of gold that the stranger had given to her husband. It was a cube measuring approximately two fingers to an edge, but with rounded edges and corners. Embossed on the sides of the massive nugget were emblems of suns, moons, and stars with the three-leafed symbol for eternity engraved in the background. "Please, we are in such dire need of hope. Do you think he could be…?"

Nova regarded her with concern. "There is always hope." She took the older woman's hands and squeezed them. "Semanta, please promise me not to discuss what happened here today with anyone." At the crestfallen look on her friend's face, she relented. "Alright, at least not with anyone you don't completely trust."

Semanta smiled up at her. "I promise."

They embraced, and Semanta followed the handmaiden into the hall. When Folan saw Nova return, he took the stranger's hands and shook them heartily, entreating him once more to return soon, then released the pair to the bright spring day.

Semanta bit down on her lower lip as she watched them leave. Should she have told Nova everything? Should she, for that matter, tell her husband? She was becoming frightened and confused. If this stranger really was the divine emissary, then all the things she had done behind her husband's back in the past months had been a farce, even if she had believed it to be for the best. She would have to talk to the mayor's wife again soon. Culisa was such a kind and wise friend and could maybe bring some order into the chaos of her emotions. But she had a bad feeling about all this. She had wanted to help set things in motion, just a fresh breeze to bring new life into the land. Instead, she may have helped to release a tempest.

Semanta bit down harder and tasted blood.

10. The Guest

Menirel took a long draw on his pipe, savoring the sweet flavor of the weed on his tongue. Then the mayor gazed over at his guest while leisurely blowing out the smoke.

Talenon Novesta hadn't changed much since he had last seen him, except that he had possibly grown even more condescending. He obviously enjoyed wielding the authority that his function as head of western intelligence had bestowed upon him, and despite his extravagant and often obnoxious tastes, he seemed a capable man. Although Menirel didn't much care for him, he was diplomatic enough not to show it. He knew how powerful the man before him was, a fact that troubled him and often made him wonder what he had gotten himself into.

"We have a problem," he finally said.

"So it seems," replied his guest.

"Then you've already heard about it?"

"News travels quickly in a little town like this."

The two men were sitting in comfortable chairs in the mayor's office, which faced the gardens behind the town hall. Talenon straightened his plain gray robe, the hood of which was down. The robe marked him as a member of the Videsian Order and was adorned only by a burgundy sash around the man's waist, designating him a priest of that Order. Menirel studied the priest's face while his guest's attention was momentarily distracted by some insects buzzing about the bright flowers outside the window. He might have been called handsome, but for the almost unvarying conceited expression engraved on his countenance and the flaming crimson birthmark that blemished his right cheek, a typical characteristic of the male members of the Novesta family.

"My wife came over to inform me about the situation half an hour ago," the mayor stated. "This person, whoever he is, is still in Folan's tavern."

"Yes, I have seen him. He makes for an interesting character study. But where do the proprietor's loyalties lie?"

"I'm afraid he's completely devoted to the Selanian Order, although his wife seems to be alright. Truth be told, I have little taste for the man. I sometimes wished I could run him out of town."

"Maybe you'll get your wish sooner than even you could imagine," his guest replied.

"That would be most pleasing. But what do we do about our current problem?"

"Be patient, my friend. Let's see how the situation develops. If you can use your influence in any way, try to keep the stranger away from the Prophet's Bow."

"I'm sorry, but I don't really have much power over that."

"I understand. Maybe you could have a little chat with the proprietor and express your concern?"

"I could try, but Folan can be pretty stubborn."

"I see. In that case we will have to fall back upon firmer methods of persuasion. I will call in a patrol of western guards to aid in your effort."

"I would be very grateful if you would."

Talenon stood. "Well, Menirel, it was a pleasure seeing you again. I must continue on to Tolares and hope to stop by on my way back to Travis."

Menirel also rose. "That would be very good of you. You know how much we appreciate your expertise."

The two men firmly gripped each others' hands. Then the mayor let his guest out and quietly closed the door of the office behind him.

11. *Conversation with a Lady*

The stranger enjoyed the short walk to the market. It was good to feel the warm sun on his face, while a gentle breeze lazily propelled several feathery cirrus clouds across a cobalt blue sky. The scenery was lovely, for the town was beautifully situated amid gentle hills, forests, meadows and streams, with the peaks of the Tyenar Mountains faintly visible in the east.

Between the buildings there were trees, fountains, gardens, and here or there a little park. The paving stones under his feet were evenly formed and uniformly leveled, not quite smooth so they wouldn't be slippery if it rained, but smooth enough to make the road pleasant to use for pedestrians, beasts, and vehicles alike.

The buildings were amazing architectural structures that contained few proper right angles and blended well into the environment. Most of them were plastered and whitewashed, in many cases with brick or wooden embellishments. The roofs were rounded or tapered and usually decorated with wood, brick, or tiling. The town expressed such creative harmony that he was almost convinced it had been planned and constructed by artists rather than craftsmen.

Every now and then the handmaiden would stop to greet a friend or acquaintance, exchanging a few friendly words or the squeeze of a hand. Although the townspeople greeted the stranger politely, they were reserved, and he noticed their restrained but inquisitive glances in his direction when they thought he wasn't looking.

The marketplace was a cheerful and colorful site, yet well organized and not in the slightest bit noisy. Merchants were calmly offering their products, artists were displaying their work, and everybody seemed to know exactly where to go. What a difference from the markets he had seen in the past!

From where they were standing, the stranger could see the town square. An intriguing fountain adorned its center, but what caught the stranger's eye was the sundial situated near a building, which he supposed was the town hall. He suppressed an urge to walk over and examine it, for he was conscious of the many eyes that were following his every movement.

Just as he was about to turn away, a man in a gray robe with a burgundy sash around his waist stepped out of the town hall. When the man saw the stranger and his companion he checked himself. Their eyes met for an instant. The stranger noted the aversion in the man's expression and eyed him coldly. The man deliberately turned his back on the stranger and walked across the town square and down the road to the western end of town.

The stranger touched his companion's arm. "Do you see that man in the gray robe over there, walking away from us?"

The handmaiden inhaled sharply. "What is he doing here?" she asked almost inaudibly.

"Why? Who is he?"

"His name is Talenon, a priest of the Videsian Order. I must inform my mistress about this."

"The Videsian Order?"

"Yes, it's a religious organization that emphasizes holiness. Actually quite a noble matter, if they weren't so extreme."

Nova had soon completed her purchases, and they returned the way they had come, first passing the tavern, then exiting the town. She stopped several minutes later at a comfortably sized manse on the left side of the road just outside the village. He remembered passing the pretty little lodge in the morning on his way into town. Nova opened one side of the solid wooden, double-winged door and beckoned for him to enter before her.

The corridor they stepped into was quite spacious. It ran most of the front length of the manse, with doors at each end. The opposing wall contained several closed doors, and facing the entrance, an elegant wooden staircase led up to the second floor. Two maidservants, dressed in cream-colored robes similar to the handmaiden's, met her as they entered. They embraced and exchanged a few whispered instructions. Then the handmaiden handed over her cloak and the items she had purchased at the market to one of them, who disappeared to the left, while the second maidservant showed them to a large and comfortable parlor on the right, shutting the door quietly behind them after they had entered.

"Ah, there you are, Nova."

A tall and stately Lady, presumably the Lady Utalya, rose from a desk near the window where she had been writing and turned towards them. Her dark hair was still thick but graying, and fell elegantly around her shoulders. Her robe also was similar to that of the handmaiden, only that she wore an attractive golden brooch above and to the left of her heart. She had an air of quiet authority about her.

Nova dropped down on one knee and bowed her head. "My Lady."

The Lady rushed forward and pulled her up, embracing her affectionately. They whispered together for a moment, after which the Lady turned to the stranger.

"I see my favorite handmaiden has brought a guest. Welcome, my friend."

"Thank you very much for your hospitality. I very much appreciate it."

"Please, don't mention it. The meal will not be ready for a while yet. Shall we sit and have a chat until we are called?"

The Lady showed the stranger to a comfortable sofa and seated herself on a chair facing him. Nova lowered herself onto the soft carpet at the Lady's feet and leaned her head against her mistress's thigh, allowing the latter to stroke her hair.

"So, you are the stranger from the tavern that has caused such a stir."

The handmaiden looked up in surprise.

"Yes," said the Lady, seeing her handmaiden's astonishment, "news travels quickly in such a small town as this. We have already heard it here."

"I really don't understand what all the fuss is about," the stranger replied in distress.

"You must not be too harsh in your judgment. These are simple people living in difficult times. They have come to know fear and therefore cling to any hope that comes their way."

"But what exactly have I done?"

The Lady looked at Nova. "Were you able to test him?"

The handmaiden nodded. "He is sensitive, but not trained."

The stranger's eyes wandered from the one to the other. "May I ask what you are talking about?"

Nova looked up at him. "I'm very sorry that I had to embarrass you in the tavern, but it was necessary."

The stranger's eyes lit up. "Ah, the window."

"Yes. It was not such an impropriety as I led you to believe, but I had to test your perception. You sensed my meaning, namely that it was improper for you to have watched us, and your reaction was one of embarrassment. A sensitive person with little or no training reacts to such an allegation with a slight delay, as you did. Someone with training would have sensed my meaning immediately. Folan, on the other hand, would probably have sensed nothing and would therefore not have reacted at all."

Something inside of the stranger clicked. So that was why Nova had seemed so composed and her robes so familiar! He looked up at the Lady. "I think I understand. Would you be so kind as to inform me of the meaning of the brooch pinned to your robe?"

The Lady smiled. "I see that you are quick. My golden brooch designates a Priestess or Priest of the Selanian Order. I was High Priestess a few years back, and then wore a platinum brooch with a golden border, but I resigned the position when I married."

"I see. And your handmaidens are not just servants, but acolytes, most likely studying to become deaconesses or priestesses."

Again she smiled. "As I said, you are quick."

"I felt that your handmaiden could not be an ordinary servant."

"Your instincts did not deceive you."

"But I am still puzzled. Why did the tavern owner act so strangely? What do they hope of me?"

"As yet they are still afraid to hope, but they hope that there will be reason to hope. Let me attempt to explain." She gently caressed her handmaiden's hair and paused to reflect.

"For the past one thousand years there has been mostly peace, with inconsequential squabbles in between. But a little over thirty years ago, a shadow emerged and began to darken our culture. We heard rumors of acts of violence in the western provinces that were so shocking we could hardly believe them. I'm sorry to say that we didn't take these rumors very seriously. I suppose we were all hoping that the problem would just disappear if we ignored it. Then, about twenty years ago, the terror spilled over into the eastern provinces."

At these words, Nova stiffened almost imperceptibly and closed her eyes. The Lady perceived her handmaiden's distress and paused, looking down at her in concern and deliberately continuing the gentle, caressing movements of her hand. Nova breathed deeply several times, consciously relaxing. After a moment, she opened her eyes again and shot her mistress a grateful glance, then nodded for her to continue.

The Lady looked back at the stranger and sighed. "Anyway, the western houses never were very happy with the way the Advisory Council in Travis handled the situation. I can't really say that I blame them. A few years ago, several of the western houses decided that they would no longer just sit back and watch. They recruited eligible men to strengthen the guard in order to secure their own means of protection. A variety of taxes, tributes, and duties were introduced to finance the guard, but some of the houses rebelled against this idea. Tension developed between the eastern and western provinces, and tempers flared. This finally resulted in skirmishes on some of the borders about six months ago.

"You must understand. We have been a free trade society for so many centuries. Commerce flourished and there was no great hardship for anyone. When there was need, everybody contributed gladly from what they could spare of their own affluence. I suppose it was therefore natural that the idea of duty and taxation should meet with resistance. On the other hand, fear has been growing incessantly since the shadow appeared, and the events of the past months have absolutely terrified many people. Imagine having to live with the threat of civil war in a culture that has only experienced peace for such a long time. The fear of violence has changed much, and our Millennial Peace is now undeniably threatened."

The Lady paused again, and she and her handmaiden looked into each other's eyes. The stranger could see pain and sadness written in them. The Lady turned back to him.

"That was but a short and simplified account of what you are experiencing here. Please believe me, these people are not usually so apprehensive and close. But they are frightened."

"I can understand that," the stranger replied, "and I am truly sorry. But I still don't know what this has to do with me."

"Yes, you are entitled to an explanation." The Lady drew a deep breath. "You see, in our culture, we have had many prophets that have reliably revealed to us the will of Anae, the One. Many of these revelations, along with other divinely inspired writings, have been collected in our Holy Scriptures, the Selani s'Ulavan. These writings predict that there will be great turmoil in our time, but that the turmoil will be ended after the coming of the one who these texts refer to as the Covatal, the Traveler. His coming marks the end of an old and the beginning of a new era. For this reason, if someone were to appear that matched the descriptions of the prophecies, the people would have reason to hope."

The stranger nodded. "That does explain a few things. But why would they believe that I could have anything to do with this person, this…Traveler?"

Nova looked up at him. "It seems that this morning alone you have fulfilled at least nine of the prophecies," she said gently.

He gaped at her. "What?"

The room fell silent while the two women studied him and then looked at each other. The Lady nodded to her handmaiden. The latter was still leaning against her mistress, but now turned completely towards the stranger.

"Before I continue, I must inform you of our responsibilities. As spiritual leaders of our people, or, should I say, prospective leaders," she smiled at her mistress, who smiled back, "we are responsible for the people's spiritual well-being. We must always be wary of imposters and charlatans. It is therefore our duty to test anybody that might lodge a claim, whether knowingly or not, of possessing divine authority. If you were truly to fulfill any of the prophecies regarding the Traveler, then you would be asserting such a claim. Do you understand what I am telling you?"

The stranger nodded slowly. "Yes, I think I understand. Is that the reason why the owner of the tavern asked me to join you here? Did he want you to test me?"

"Yes. But we don't want to do this in secret or behind your back. We want you to know what is happening."

"What is it that you ask of me?"

"At the moment, nothing. If you consent, I will inform you which of the prophecies were involved this morning. We then might ask you some questions, which you may or may not answer. Our main objective is but to observe at this time."

The stranger nodded again. "I'm ready."

"Now," the handmaiden began soothingly, again putting him at ease, "these prophecies were given over a period of approximately eight hundred years and by several different people. The last of these prophecies was made over five hundred years ago. Since every prophet saw a unique view of the events, the prophecies are never chronological. Our scholars have attempted to put the prophecies in order, but that is very difficult and often a question of interpretation."

She paused shortly before continuing.

"One prophecy states that the Traveler will come at a time of beginning turmoil for our people after the Millennial Peace. As you have heard, we believe that this time is at hand. That is why the people are on the lookout for signs that the prophecies regarding the Traveler are being fulfilled.

"Another prophecy states that the Traveler will arrive first in Nadil. We are therefore in the right place.

"The next prophecy describes the Traveler as being a foreigner. His origin will be unknown. These last three prophecies are quite general and could apply to almost anyone here in Nadil that cannot be identified accurately. But now the prophecies become quite precise.

"The Traveler will speak in the voice of the Selani. Your accent is different to that of the townspeople, and it is furthermore obvious that you have had at least some advanced instruction in spiritual matters.

"The Traveler will be 'outside' of time and space. The scholars believe this prophecy to be ambiguous, for there is another prophecy which describes the Traveler as being ignorant or unaware of time and space, in the sense that he will somehow not be quite aware of the exact location of his arrival or of the exact time.

"A further prophecy describes the Traveler as being naturally perceptive. I believe that detail has been verified to our mutual satisfaction.

"The Traveler will have knowledge of the arts.

"He will describe himself as being a lonesome and weary traveler.

"The last point I wish to make is very difficult to refute. One of the most prominent prophecies regarding the Traveler states that he will offer Gold of the Heavens for water."

The stranger sat silently. He was completely dazed and shook his head in confusion. This just couldn't be happening.

"Are you alright, dear friend?" the Lady asked gently.

He looked at her, then again slowly shook his head.

"Would you like some water?"

"No, I just need a moment. This is all so…strange."

They let him sit in silence for a while longer.

He shook his head again. "I just don't know what to say."

"Do you feel well enough to answer a few questions?" Nova inquired, her voice mellow and discrete.

He nodded.

"Is it true that you described yourself as a lonesome and weary traveler to Folan?"

"Yes. I didn't realize at the time why those words should cause such a stir."

"Is it also true that you asked Folan where you were and what the date was?"

Again the stranger nodded

"Could you explain why you did that?" Nova asked.

He shook his head. "I'm sorry."

"You don't seem to be very pleased over this development," she said gently.

"No. To be honest, the concept of being some…religious icon whose life others have foreseen hundreds of years ago…" He shook his head once more.

Again the Lady and the handmaiden exchanged glances.

"Well," the Lady said, "it is…peculiar. I fear that, at the moment, no matter what you do or say, you seem to fulfill one prophecy after the other. I'm very sorry, but there is also a prophecy which anticipates the Traveler's reluctance to accept his fate and destiny."

The stranger leaned forwards, dropping his elbows onto his knees, and let his face sink into his hands with a deep sigh.

Was there no way out of this dilemma?

The Lady regarded him with a tender gaze. "You know, it is a strange thing with prophecies. No matter what you do, they will be fulfilled if the time has come. There is no power on this or any other world that could prevent that. But I doubt just as much that the One who has ordained all this would want somebody to claim a title that only He may bestow. If you are not the person of whom the prophecies speak, you will find a way to prove it. For instance, if you could explain to us where you came from, it would help to lift some of the mystery."

He looked up at her, considering her words, but then sadly shook his head. It was better not to give them too much information. He didn't want to be accused of violating the Directive.

"Listen, my friend," the Lady said. "We can't force you to tell us anything, and we don't want to. We believe that everyone has the right and freedom to choose and must decide for himself what to do, and we respect that right most highly. But you might make things easier if you told us more about yourself."

Again he shook his head. "I'm very sorry, but that is impossible for me at the moment."

She sighed. "Well, we will accept that for the time being. There is another prophecy, though, that might help you shake off this unpleasant burden, if it is unpleasant. The prophecy states that the Traveler will be sent from the heavens as a convergence, a junction in time and space. Would you like to add something to that?" she asked carefully.

The stranger sat in stunned silence and stared at her with his mouth agape. How could they know what had happened to him?

"Oh, I see. I've only made matters worse. I'm very sorry."

It was clear that she could see the pain and confusion in his eyes, and her face expressed compassion, but also concern. "Don't worry, my friend. We won't press the matter further. We sense that you're being sincere, although the mystery itself has deepened. I do believe, though, that the time has come to shed our formality. We have shared in each others pain. Let us therefore now share our names. I am the Lady Utalya of the House of Revan. My husband passed away several years ago, so I will be representing our house at the conference."

The handmaiden took her cue. "I am Novantina, the 'Blossoming Flower,' of the House Satural. But my friends call me Nova."

The stranger smiled sadly at them. He hoped they couldn't detect how much he felt the irony of the situation, but there was no way he was going to give them his name after what he had just heard. "I feel much honored by your trust, but I am also very sorry, for I cannot give you my name. Would you please take a name for me?"

The Lady Utalya regarded him solemnly and nodded. "That is an acceptable custom in our society. How shall we call you?"

"Why not just call me Tavasin, 'Stranger'?"

Nova looked at him and shook her head. "No, for you will hopefully not be a stranger to us for long. I will call you Vilamadan, 'Good Friend,' or Vilam for short, and hope that you will do us the honor of living up to the name. I fear, though, that the townspeople may soon be calling you by a different name."

At that moment one of the maidservants came to the door and announced the meal. Vilam turned towards his hostess.

"Would it be too presumptuous to ask if I could skip the meal and lie down for a while instead? It's been a long night and an even longer morning, and I feel quite fatigued."

"No, that wouldn't be a problem," the Lady replied. "We have a chamber to which you could retire for a few hours. Nova will guide you to it."

They all rose and exited the parlor.

In the hall, the Lady turned and bowed her head respectfully in his direction. "I wish you to rest well," she said sincerely.

"Thank you, My Lady."

She then turned and walked gracefully towards an open door to the left of the staircase, which was undoubtedly the dining room.

The room to which Nova showed him was on the second floor. It faced the garden in the back, was quiet and filled with light, and seemed very comfortable. Nova immediately left him to himself, so he walked over to the window and opened it, leaving it ajar for fresh air. Then he drew the curtains, softening the light. He moved over to the couch and sat down, testing its velvety softness. It completely agreed with him, so he took off his shoes, put up his feet, and had soon floated off into the deep and dreamless sleep of exhaustion.

12. *The Rendezvous*

Bejad unobtrusively approached the stables from the path leading up from the lake. He had taken the narrow trail south from the city along the lake's shore in the hope that nobody would be watching such an insignificant route now that everyone was busy with the royal family's departure. He was relieved that his strategy had paid off. Several frantic stableboys were attempting to prepare the chyevi's harness, but weren't getting on at all. The equerry supervising the procedure was conveniently throwing a fit, and in the general commotion, nobody took notice as Bejad ambled across the stable yard, keeping close to the walls of the building and hopefully well out of anyone's awareness.

Of course his casual attitude was just a sham, and if it hadn't been for the current disorder, he was sure everyone would have heard the furious pounding of his heart. He was dressed in the attire of a simple laborer and had the hood of an old and worn cloak raised over his head. His few worldly possessions were tied up in a dilapidated bag that he had thrown over his shoulder.

The sun stood almost straight above and brightened the lovely environment around him. The city of Divestelan was located on the northern bank of the Suviltan River where it flowed into Lake Divestelan, but His Excellency's residence was situated several leagues south of the river, facing east towards the lake. In this way, the family was distanced from the filth of the city, although the stench was sometimes perceptible when the wind was blowing from the north.

He advanced upon the west wing of the building, unnerved by any sound or movement. He jumped when he discovered a maidservant wearily sweeping the area around the stable where the rendezvous had been arranged. She also had the hood of her simple cloak up against the gleam of the day. The area was well concealed from the main estate by a variety of trees and shrubs. He was conscious of his duty, so he took a deep breath and clenched his teeth, then strode over to her and leaned against the wall with a loud sigh, as if fatigued by some difficult task he had just performed.

When the maidservant came closer, he addressed her. "*Votalaran,* excuse me, my friend," he said in a low voice. "I am looking for Yanita. Have you seen her, by any chance?"

The maid propped her broom up against the wall and turned towards him. "Yes, my friend, you need seek no further."

When Bejad looked into the maid's face, he froze and his

expression paled. He dropped down on one knee and bowed his head. "Please forgive me, My Lady, I didn't recognize you."

The woman grabbed his arm and wrenched him back to his feet. "You fool!" she hissed. "Do you want to get us killed?" She glanced around to see if anyone had seen them, then gazed into his eyes, her lips compressed in anger. "I must admit," she whispered, "I was expecting more from a supposedly experienced operative of Her Eminence's intelligence organization."

"I'm very sorry, My Lady. I didn't anticipate seeing His Excellency's eldest daughter here."

"So it seems. I always thought spies were supposed to be prepared for anything."

He looked at the ground, embarrassed.

"Come, let's move over there, into the shrubs, where we can't be surprised so easily," she said, gripping his arm and pulling him into the bushes.

When the branches and leaves of the underbrush had enclosed them, she pushed him down and they crouched together. She pulled back the hood of her cloak. Her thick, black hair was artfully pinned up on the sides and back of her head in the traditional style of the House Divestelan. Her skin was somewhat darker than his, but he had grown accustomed to the fact that inhabitants of the Northern Covasins generally had darker skin. She was treacherously beautiful, which had been the downfall of numerous unwary suitors. Under her cloak she was wearing a stunning two-piece dress in the house colors of dark brown, black, and gold that highlighted her attractive athletic figure.

She noticed the direction of his gaze and eyed him coolly. "I trust my attire meets with your approval?"

"Yes, of course. Please, excuse me."

They were interrupted by the crack of a whip from the

yard. One of the stableboys cried out in pain. From the sound of things, Bejad thought the equerry would soon either lose his voice or have a heart attack.

"What's going on over there?" he whispered.

There was a mischievous smirk on the Lady's lips. "Nothing particular. The equerry has been with our family for generations, so I took the liberty of informing him that he could either taste my steel or have the coach ready in half an hour. With all due respect, of course. I thought you might be able to use the diversion."

Bejad grinned. Then he remembered why he was there and took a deep breath. "What is it that you want of me, My Lady?"

Her expression turned serious. "My cover has been compromised, and I wish to be extracted."

"Extracted? I don't understand."

"I can see that, but I don't have time to explain. Just know that I've been working for the Resistance and also for Her Eminence for years now."

"That's not how you've been described by my accomplices, My Lady. I'm sorry to say this, but you couldn't imagine the horrific accounts that we've heard of your actions."

She glanced at the ground and swallowed. "Yes, I know," she answered. "I'm very sorry, but I'm afraid many of the accounts are probably true. All I can say in my defense is that everything changed about five years ago. Please believe me and trust me on this."

"How can I trust you?"

She took his arm. "Bejad, we just don't have the time right now for lengthy clarifications." She looked into his eyes and sighed. "Alright, I understand that this is difficult for you, although I wouldn't even know where to begin. I met Her Eminence five years ago at the conference. She wasn't High

Priestess then, but she made such an intense impression on me. She was somehow so gentle and so focused. She accepted me despite the terrible things she must have known I had done. When she was elected a few weeks later, she got in touch with me through her channels in the Resistance. It was a dangerous move on her part, for both of us, but she had assessed my situation correctly. Half a year after that, she came to Divestelan to visit me. Can you imagine that? She put her life in danger to see me personally."

Bejad nodded. "Alright, only someone that knows her well could have been aware that she was here at that time. And it is true that she's always putting others before herself. If you've met her, then I can understand that she may have had that effect on you."

"No, it's more than that. I've grown so tired of these sinister games. I've become so hardened." She balled her fist tightly, then unclenched her hand and looked at it, almost fearfully. "I sometimes have the impression that there's not a trace of femininity—or even humanity—left in me. And then I'm so afraid for my little sister, Yanita. Bejad, she's only seven years old. I can't allow my father and brother to do to her what they have done to me. I must get her away."

"Alright, I understand. Is that why I'm here?"

"Yes, the whole situation has become too dangerous. My father and brother no longer trust me. Just to vex me, and as a little parting gift towards the Resistance, they have given the order to target all suspected operatives before we leave and have them put to death. At this very moment your lodgings in Divestelan are probably being ransacked. I'm sure that, if you hadn't come, you probably wouldn't have survived the day. I'm certain they will attempt to catch me off guard with this information after we arrive in Tolares."

Bejad's face had grown pallid. "I see," he said hoarsely. "What of Sheletas?"

"Please, tell me no names. I can't betray what I don't know. I'm sorry, Bejad, but I'm afraid there's nothing more that I can do. I gave the alarm as soon as I discovered the plan. Our friends must fend for themselves now."

Bejad took a deep breath. "Alright, what do you wish me to do?"

"Her Eminence gave me your name in case anything like this should ever happen. You must go to her immediately. Please inform her that we are officially seeking asylum. She must organize an incident at the Conference of Tolares to get my sister and me away from my family. It might be difficult, because my brother won't let me out of his sight."

"Consider it done."

"Here," She pressed a slip of paper into his hand. "This is a plan I've compiled which describes the exact route you must take so that you can change your chyevi every few hours. The escape route has been ready for several weeks, but I couldn't inform you because I couldn't risk letting anyone else know about it. You may take one of our steeds. He is swift and reliable. You'll find him in the second stall on the right, already prepared and saddled. Stay to the north of the main roads and don't let yourself be seen."

"I will try, My Lady."

"Bejad, this will be the last time that one of my couriers travels this route. The farms along the way are in dire need. Tell the owners of the way stations you come to that they should keep the chyevi I have lent them, to do with as they see fit. They are excellent mounts, and the farmers will probably be able to sell them for a very good price. It is the least I can do for them after all they have done for me."

Bejad looked at her in awe, and his heart softened even more towards the extraordinary young woman before him. "That's very kind of you, My Lady."

"Now, after I leave, give me two minutes, and then go,"

she said, ignoring his remark.

She turned to leave, but Bejad held her.

"What is it, Bejad?" she asked impatiently, glancing back at him.

"I just wanted to tell you that it's been a pleasure meeting you, Lady Gevinesa."

She looked him in the eye. "When we meet again in Tolares and you address me in any other fashion than as Vinesa, I will slit your throat."

He smiled. "I don't think that will be necessary. Farewell, Vinesa."

"Farewell, Bejad."

She exited the bushes and casually took off her cloak, exposing the elegant dress beneath. He saw her toss the cloak into a stall before she disappeared around the corner. He waited two more minutes and then also left the shrubs in the direction of the stalls.

13. *The Sinaven*

The sound of children laughing and playing in the garden gradually penetrated Vilam's consciousness, and he blinked his eyes. The room had darkened, and from the quality of the light, he concluded that it was already late afternoon. He swung his legs over the couch and sat up.

Vilam reasoned that the abrupt movement must have quickened his pulse, sending a fresh flow of blood to his brain, for something triggered his memory. Sharp images of the past day's events came rushing back, and a sense of surrealism threatened to overwhelm him. He massaged his forehead and temples, breathing deeply several times to get a grip on himself. Then he went over to the window and drew open the curtains.

The view from the window was wonderful and allowed him to realize how refreshed he felt after his repose. A narrow path led from the garden to a tranquil pond at the edge of a little wood several hundred cubits away. The sparkling rays of the afternoon sun reflected like diamonds on the surface of the pond as waterfowl went carelessly about their business and reeds beckoned gently in the mild spring breeze.

In the garden one of the maidservants supervised a group of small children. She was teaching them a new game and evidently enjoying herself as much as the boys and girls giggling and frolicking around her. The setting seemed so perfect; everything was exactly as it should be. The scene radiated such joy and peace, a peace which, as he had been told, was now threatened.

He shook his head in exasperation. Why were people so ignorant and foolish? From what he had seen, they had a perfect society, a culture still innocent of the terror and violence he had experienced elsewhere. He felt anger rising inside him at such inanity.

He closed the window and walked towards the door. He opened it silently and noticed two maidservants standing in the corridor, talking quietly. They became aware of his presence almost immediately and curtsied. One of them hurried down the staircase while the other approached him.

"*Nolavelan mada,* good afternoon, my friend. Is there anything I can do for you?" she asked cheerfully.

"Yes, please. Is there a place where I could freshen up?"

"Yes, this door next to your room leads to a restroom. You are most welcome to use it."

"Thank you very much."

"Glad to be of service," she answered with a light bow.

As he entered, he saw a basin with a faucet on his left, so he assumed that the lodge was also connected to the town's water system. He tentatively turned the handle and was rewarded with a stream of clear, fresh water. After splashing his face several times, he stuck his head under the torrent and let the water run through his hair. The cool, prickling sensation felt good on his skin. Then he used his fingers in an attempt to manage his thick, black hair.

When he opened the door, Nova was waiting for him in the corridor. She suppressed a smile when she saw him.

"I'm sorry. We should have realized that you didn't have any personal items with you." She went over to the room he had rested in, where a maidservant was changing the quilts. "Tanola, could you please bring our guest a hairbrush from the sanitary supplies?"

The maidservant nodded. As she brushed passed Nova, the latter smiled at her and quickly squeezed her arm in thanks.

She then turned back to her guest. "Did you rest well?"

"Yes, very much so, thank you."

"I hope the children didn't disturb you?"

"Oh, no, not at all. On the contrary, I love children." His gaze turned inwards as some sad memories assailed him.

Nova must have seen it and gently touched his arm to get his attention. "A very dear friend of mine, the companion you saw me with in town this morning, will be coming by shortly. We were planning on going for a walk. Would you care to join us?"

"Yes, gladly. The fresh air and exercise would do me good."

Tanola returned and handed Vilam a brush with a smile and a bow of her head. He thanked her and returned to the restroom, where he used the brush to better effect on his unruly hair. When he was finished, Nova was still waiting for him.

"What would you like me to do with the brush? And the towel that I used, for that matter," he asked.

"Just leave them. Tanola will take care of it later."

"Alright, shall we go out front to wait for your friend? I would enjoy a bit of sunshine."

"Yes, of course, but maybe not out front. There are too many inquisitive eyes at the moment. Let's join Natilya in the garden."

She led the way down the stairs and then around and under the staircase to another double-winged door, but one with many windows, leading out to the garden. They strolled over to the maidservant who was supervising the children, and Nova introduced her.

"Vilam, this is Natilya of the House of Revan. She is a niece of the Lady Utalya."

Natilya curtsied cheerfully. "I'm very glad to meet you, Vilam."

"How is it going with the children?" Nova asked her.

"Oh, they're such darlings. I could play with them all day."

"I know," Nova answered with a smile. "Did the test for social competence go well?"

"Yes, they had a lot of fun with it. Two of them need a little polishing, but they'll do fine."

Vilam raised an eyebrow. "Social competence?"

Natilya turned towards him. "Why, yes, of course. You see, the people in town and from the surrounding farms send us their children for preliminary training. The children naturally believe they're just playing, but there's so much we can do with them while they're having fun. We evaluate and train them in fundamental aspects of our society: emotional and social competence, and especially perceptiveness. Their sensitivity for arts and sciences is heightened, their skills sharpened, and we can soon determine if they might be eligible for advanced instruction in spiritual matters."

"Ah, I see. So what we are seeing here before us are the future leaders of your society?"

Nova restrained a smile. "Well, in a sense you may be right. It makes it easier if we can begin their training at an early age. But many children don't have that chance to such a degree. Some children of less affluent parents live far out in the country, away from the townships, and their parents rely upon their presence to run their farms or businesses."

As she said that, her eyes took on a pained expression, but she immediately caught herself and continued.

"We would never make the calling of a person dependent upon whether they had preliminary training, or any training, for that matter. Each case must be evaluated for itself. Take my golden-haired friend here, for instance."

Her companion had just arrived and been shown to the garden by one of the maidservants. Nova fervently embraced her friend, then turned her around and presented her to Vilam.

"Vilam, this is Catyana of the House Faeren."

Catyana curtsied shyly and Nova turned back to her friend.

"I was just explaining to Vilam that the calling of a person isn't dependent upon whether they can participate in the children's preliminary training." She looked back at Vilam. "You see, Catyana is one of those girls that could only participate very sporadically in the children's training, because her family lives about an hour to the northeast, and her parents are very busy. It often just wasn't possible for her to attend. But she's now considering the possibility of also joining the Order."

The two women squeezed hands and smiled at each other.

"So, shall we go?" Nova asked.

They all agreed and took leave of Natilya, who returned to her task of supervising the children. Nova linked arms with Catyana, and they sauntered in the direction of the pond with Vilam at Nova's side.

Nova looked at her friend. "What do you think? Will your parents consent?"

"I'm sorry, but I just don't know," Catyana replied. "They're being very mysterious about it. They've asked me to invite you to the midday meal tomorrow. Will you come?"

"Of course. You know I will."

Catyana looked shyly over at Vilam. "May I invite you, too? I'm sure my parents would be delighted to meet you."

Vilam looked down. "Thank you, Catyana, I feel much honored by your invitation. But so many things have happened in such a short time. I might need some time to...sort things out. Do you need a definite reply immediately?"

Catyana's eyes revealed her disappointment, but she attempted to smile amiably. "No, of course not. It would suffice if you just showed up for the meal. We're a large family, and my mother is accustomed to throwing something together if unexpected guests turn up. Believe me, you would be more than welcome. My parents and siblings love visitors. We don't get them very often and can't always be leaving the farm because there's so much to do, so we're very happy when people bring the outside world to us."

"Well, anyway," said Nova, "let's hope that your parents have come to a decision, one way or the other. We'll be leaving for Tolares early the day after tomorrow and won't be able to wait any longer."

Catyana became starry-eyed. "Wouldn't it be wonderful, though, if they said yes?" she whispered. "Then I could go with you to Travis."

Nova smiled. "You know how much I would like that, Catyana."

"Yes, I know." She sighed and looked at her friend. "Nova, I don't mean to change the subject, but I'm worried about Sinara. Her nightmares seem to be getting worse."

"Oh? That's not good. Are they coming more frequently?"

Catyana nodded. "Yes, almost every night. She even had one this morning, just before she woke up. And I believe they're becoming more vivid, too."

"Alright, I'll talk to her when I come over tomorrow."

"That would be so kind of you, Nova."

Nova stopped suddenly. "Oh, look, a sinaven!"

They had arrived at the pond, and Nova pointed to a lovely, jet-black bird standing in the water near the edge of the pool. It raised its head on its long, slender neck to observe them for a moment and then returned to tending its feathers. The bird was of substantial size, reaching almost to Nova's waist, its dark plumage contrasted by white stripes along its wings and sides and white crescents behind its eyes. Its bill and webbed feet, which could be seen plainly in the clear water, were of a bright crimson color, and its eyes sparkled confidently from inside their snowy markings.

"Oh, he's so breathtaking!" Catyana whispered. "I wonder how many songs have been composed about this one single bird."

"I couldn't say. So many artists have been inspired by these graceful creatures. Although I must admit, I still feel that Vodana's composition, 'Sinavena,' is incontestable," Nova said, smiling to herself.

"Nova, that's not fair! Nobody can compete with her! She's in a league all her own. I'm surprised you could even bring her up. I wonder where his mate is, though. Oh, there she is, over by the reeds. Do you see her?"

"Yes, and look who she has with her."

"Oh, aren't they just adorable? How many are there? Let me see now, six little hatchlings, two males and four females."

Nova smiled at Catyana, then turned to Vilam. "You see, my friend, how perceptive she is?"

"Yes," Vilam agreed in amazement. "She really is, for one who seems so young and without any substantial training. I've never heard of distinguishing the gender of sinaveni just by looking at them."

"Exactly. But that is something I wish to speak to you about a little further on. There is something up ahead that I wish to show you."

Vilam glanced at her, but she wouldn't add anything to her previous statement.

"You've made me very curious," he said, hoping to coax her into betraying further details.

Nova only smiled and continued her walk.

"Alright, I see that you can't be moved to explain yourself and you'll bide your time. But there is something I've been meaning to ask you. Is it true that, on all of Piral, there is only one language?"

Nova looked at him. "Why, yes, of course. How could it be otherwise?"

"Hmmm...Have you never heard of the curse of the confusion of tongues?"

Nova studied the ground. "Yes, I see what you mean. But those are ancient prophecies and belong to the foundations of our faith."

"To what extent?"

"Well, the Selani s'Ulavan state that, when Anae created Piral and the Three Races, He..."

"The Three Races?"

"Yes. The Selani—being us—the Demantar, and the

Elinar. Although common people often refer to officials of the Order as 'Selani.'"

"Ah, I see." Vilam smiled to himself. So in this time the Selani hadn't yet learned the truth regarding the delicate ethereal balance on which their lives depended. "*Vot'ana,* please, excuse the interruption."

Nova shot him an inquisitive glance. "*Tezatal,* that's alright. As I was saying, when Anae created Piral and the Three Races, He also established a holy covenant with us, stating the terms and conditions, the promises connected with our obedience, and the consequences if we failed to comply. The terms were very simple: to love Him and each other with all our hearts. The consequences of unrepentant iniquity, though, were terrible and many." She smiled bitterly. "How soon we fell from our trust. Do you know the account of the Cataclysm?"

"Well, I have heard about it, but it was long ago and I can't remember the details."

"We were punished severely for allowing ourselves to be tempted by evil and for opening our hearts to the lure of darkness. Anae's judgment was severe: The age expectancy of the Selani was greatly reduced, and the Demantar and the Elinar vanished completely. But He admonished us through his prophets, stating that, should we fail again, the results would be even more terrible: the destruction of Piral and the confusion of tongues. But why do you ask about this curse?"

"I was just thinking. Can you imagine what the consequences of such a curse would be?"

Catyana stiffened.

"I would rather not imagine," Nova replied.

"It would definitely mean the end of your culture as you know it. Communication would become very problematic, if not even impossible. It would become arduous to promote cultural exchange, such as arts and sciences. Think of the setback for any kind of technological advance. You would be thrown back to your darkest beginnings."

Catyana shuddered.

"But then, imagine what the destruction of an entire world would imply: the annihilation of so many lives, your entire culture completely obliterated. It would be…"

"Vilam, please stop, if not for my sake, then at least for Catyana's," Nova declared firmly.

Vilam finally turned towards his companions, who were standing stock still. Nova had her arm around her friend. Catyana was trembling, and her face was a mask of horror.

14. Vicious Revenge

Keeping the hood of her dark brown cloak pulled low over her face, Dena elbowed her way through the vast crowd oppressing her on all sides, sick with the premonition of what she would see. The city was already overcrowded as it was, but since the attacks that had commenced at noon that day, the populace was in complete panic, making it almost impossible for her to get through. Just as she was gaining the front, a short, round grandmother in a simple frock tried to hold her back.

"No, young miss, you don't want to see that."

But even if Dena hadn't been obliged to ignore the warning, it would have been too late. She already had a good view of the thing lying in the street and stared at it determinedly with her teeth clenched, as she had in the past two instances. But this time it was too much, and her body revolted. She turned and bent over, gagging dryly, but only air would pass, and she coughed while tears gushed into her eyes.

The elderly woman stayed with her and supported her. "Are you alright?"

Dena nodded and held on to the woman's arm for a moment, clutching her aching stomach, before she straightened.

"Thank you," she managed weakly. She took a few deep breaths and then deliberately turned back and took another look.

As with the two cases she had already confirmed, this was undoubtedly no ordinary termination. The gory mess that the Black Guard had left behind was a premeditated display of vicious revenge, calculated to cause prolonged agony in the victim and meant as an object lesson for the Resistance. With an expert glance, she carefully scanned the crowd and buildings on all sides, but could detect nothing suspicious. It didn't seem as if the Black Guard had posted a counteragent to keep watch for an enemy operative like herself. She only observed the regular guards in their dark brown, black, and golden uniforms, who were keeping the crowd at bay, and the lamenting relatives and friends that surrounded the corpse.

Sick, weak, and trembling, she turned away from the dreadful scene and began moving through the packed multitude, but the elderly lady held on to her.

"You're from the Resistance, aren't you?" she whispered.

Dena just stared at her.

"You don't need to answer. I can see it in your eyes. He was a good man and he died bravely. Tell your friends that."

"Did you see it happen?" Dena asked in a low voice.

The woman nodded, her eyes bright but glistening with tears. "They appeared so suddenly, nobody could tell where they came from. They broke down the door of the building and threw him into the street from a third floor window. Then they…" A suppressed sob escaped her.

"It's alright. Did you see them leave?"

The woman nodded and pointed into a narrow alley. "It all happened so quickly. They were gone in an instant."

"I understand."

"Where are the law enforcement officers? And why hasn't the coroner come? He's been lying there like that for hours. The guards won't even let the relatives move the body."

"There have been attacks all over the city. It is difficult to get through and the authorities are understaffed. I assume a crew will arrive eventually."

"It's just horrible."

"Yes. Do you know who might have betrayed him?"

"Well, it was practically common knowledge in the neighborhood that he was working for the Resistance, although I couldn't imagine why anyone would give him away. We are all hoping that the Traveler will arrive soon to put an end to this dreadful state of affairs."

Dena squeezed her arm. "There is always hope. But please, kind ma'am, excuse me, I really must leave."

"Yes, of course. But never forget that we are praying for you. And you're so young, and such a pretty little thing, too. I marvel at your courage."

Dena bent down and gave the old woman a kiss on the cheek. "Anae bless you."

She soon lost herself in the crowd and headed towards the northern part of the city. She would have to hurry, but since she could now move more freely, she stuck to little used alleys and passages, which sped her progress. After half an hour, she walked into a shabby building, traversed its moldering, fetid corridor, and exited the structure by a broken-down door that was hardly hanging onto its hinges. As she stepped outside, she looked up, closed her eyes, and took a deep breath, enjoying the sun on her face and the gentle breeze that caressed her hair.

The public gardens of Divestelan that Dena had now entered were located just outside the north wall and had once been counted among the city's main attractions. They had originally been donated by several of the more noble families, who had meticulously kept up their maintenance for many generations, but in recent decades the gardens had been allowed to deteriorate beyond recognition. Even so, the extensive grounds still retained a unique and untamed loveliness, harboring little islands that seemed to radiate a kind of mystifying and sometimes melancholic tranquility.

In one of these alcoves, Dena sat down at the edge of what had once been a large fountain, but the statue in its center had long since crumbled, the walls were overgrown with weeds and thistles, and the silent, stagnant waters were choked with slimy green bands of rotting algae. The alcove was surrounded by trees, and since there was no one to clean them away, the ground was covered by layers of wilted leaves that had been left there as the spoilage of many unfeeling winters. To her left, a plot of struggling novantan had somehow managed to raise their snowy white and yellow blossoms above the leafy carpet, and little clusters of colorful venora decorated the scene in all directions.

Dena was glad for the silence of the moment, and hoped she could contain the terror of the past hours that still shook her delicate frame before her contact appeared. Everywhere around her, in the thickets amongst the trees, she could hear the whispering and muted sobs of others that had managed to flee the panic-stricken city to seek refuge beyond its walls. Would the terror never end? They had worked so hard these past years, but instead of getting better, things were only getting worse.

She was still lost deep in thought when she noticed a female figure step into the clearing and walk towards her. The woman was wrapped tightly in a simple, dark brown cloak like her own with the hood pulled far down into her face, leaving her countenance in deep shadow. Dena looked up when the figure sat down beside her.

"The prosperity of summer at last fulfills the anticipation of spring," the woman whispered.

"And winter's wisdom the perseverance of fall," Dena answered with a trembling voice. "Oh, Mirayla!" she cried and threw herself into the woman's arms.

Dena felt Mirayla stiffen at the sudden imposed closeness, but she didn't care. She felt a sense of relief as the woman mechanically rocked her back and forth, and she allowed herself to finally spend the pent-up tears that had constricted her chest all afternoon.

"There, there now, child. Why don't you take a moment to get your act together," Mirayla said. Her voice was frosty and Dena sensed contempt in her words.

She hastened to quiet herself and sat up, sniffing back a few straggling tears.

"Get a grip, Dena. Was it that bad?" Mirayla asked.

"It was horrible! No matter which post I visited, all I saw was the carnage of our operatives. It reminded me of..." Dena gagged and fell silent.

"Varan?" the woman coaxed, but her subtle smile was artificial and her eyes remained cold.

Dena nodded. "The whole city has gone mad! I could hardly get through because of the panic. Mirayla, how many of us are left?"

"I don't know exactly, but quite a few were able to get to safety. Thank you for reacting so promptly and relaying the alert," Mirayla replied curtly.

"I only passed on what my informant told me. Is...is Tuvel...?" Dena asked, fearful of the answer.

"I'm sorry, but I don't have any information regarding your brother. And I gather from what you just told me that you weren't able to contact the three missing operatives assigned to you."

"No, I confirm that all three operatives have been terminated," she answered, attempting to emulate Mirayla's crisp, professional attitude. Dena explained the details.

Mirayla took a deep breath. "Alright, Sheletas wants you to make another contact in the Skull Alley tonight at 28:00 hours. Do you know where that is?"

"Yes, it's behind the Gilder's Lane. Tuvel and I have often met there."

"Good. I'm sorry, child, but it's not safe for us to be here together like this. Will you be alright?"

Dena nodded.

"Farewell, Dena," the woman said, embracing her briefly. Then she quickly left the clearing.

"Farewell, Mirayla," Dena whispered hesitantly, following the woman's retreat with a troubled glance. Why had Mirayla been so distant? And just because she was now practically engaged to Sheletas didn't give her the right to be so patronizing. *Child* indeed!

Dena suppressed a shudder. As procedure required, she waited a few minutes, but was hardly able to control her anxiety. Was her brother safe? Would she ever see him again? She rose and returned to the city by a different route.

15. The One Law

It was difficult for Vilam to hide his embarrassment as he looked at his companions.

"I…I'm sorry. I got carried away," he said.

"Yes, it seems so," Nova replied. "My friend, what can be the matter with you that your mind is engaged by such dismal thoughts?"

Vilam looked at the ground, and the group remained silent until Catyana had regained her composure.

"Please, Nova, Catyana, I'm very sorry. I formally apologize to both of you. It won't happen again."

"I believe you, my friend," Nova replied. "Vilam, you mustn't forget that we are living in difficult times and people everywhere are tense. Referring to such calamities may raise images and sentiments that you weren't anticipating."

They continued their walk but nobody spoke.

Vilam broke the silence after several minutes. "Since we need to change the subject anyway, may I ask your ages? I hope my question doesn't seem disrespectful?"

"No, of course you may. We have no reason for keeping such information to ourselves. I am forty-three and Catyana is twenty-six."

"You're forty-three?"

"Yes. Why does that astonish you?"

"Well, from what I know, female acolytes usually take on the office of priestess at thirty-three, isn't that correct?"

"That is not quite correct," Nova said, her tone cautious. "Yes, a female acolyte can accept a commission as priestess at thirty-three. That is the usual guideline. But we take care to point out that it is and remains a guideline. There are very many exceptions. And sometimes, things don't turn out the way we might have wished," she added, almost whispering.

Vilam remained thoughtful. If Nova was forty-three, it was possible that she had been a member of the Order for over twenty years, which would explain the extraordinary level of her equanimity. The extent of self-control he sensed in her could only be the result of intense and long-term training. And judging from her last, whispered words, she might even have attempted to earn a commission as priestess at some point in the past and failed, although he couldn't understand how that could have happened. Compared to other priests and priestesses he had known in the past, Nova seemed easily capable of holding her own. But he didn't want to embarrass her and therefore decided not to pursue the subject.

"Alright, I can accept that," he replied. "But just for the record, let me see if I can get the facts straight. Acolytes are usually recruited at twenty-two."

"Yes, but there have been cases of hardship or exceptional circumstances where we have accepted apprentices as early as fifteen, or much, much later than twenty-two. There is no age limit upwards."

"Alright, by thirty-three, many female acolytes have usually decided where their interests and abilities lie and commission either for priestess or deaconess. With male acolytes, I believe the age is forty-four."

"Yes, the age in both cases coincides with the official Age of Maturity for men and women."

"Maybe I should become a deaconess," Catyana said dreamily.

"Why do you say that, dearest?" Nova asked.

"Well, a deaconess can specialize in a charge such as Protectoress of the Woods or Guardian of a certain rite. That sounds so romantic."

"But it's mainly a lot of hard work, even if you do find a trace of romanticism somewhere. I'm surprised, Catyana. I've always told you clearly what to expect."

"Yes, I know, and I'm very grateful to you for being so honest with me. But I've been hearing Mother's bedtime stories much longer than your sober descriptions of reality. All those wonderful tales of how the High Priestesses and High Priests were discovered and chosen and all the adventures they went through. Please, don't take all the romance away from me just yet. If my parents do allow me to join the Order, I'm sure everyday life will soon overtake my childish fantasies."

Nova gently squeezed Catyana's arm. "I understand what you mean. It's sometimes so brutal, being pulled out of a secure and ideal world so suddenly. But even if you were to become a deaconess, you can always change your track to priestess later." Turning to Vilam, she continued, "We're very flexible in the Order. If a deaconess takes on a commission as priestess, she may even keep her previous duties, if she so wishes and feels up to it, although the workload would probably be immense."

"Yes, I'm beginning to appreciate just how flexible you are," Vilam said. "But I've never really understood why women can commission so much earlier than men."

"It isn't really so much earlier; it's only eleven years. And besides, it's an accepted fact that men just naturally take longer."

"Oh? Why do you think so?"

"Well, the current hypothesis is that, during puberty, female hormones allow women to stay more in touch with their emotions than men, and well-trained perceptive abilities are an absolute prerequisite to the priesthood."

"And men?"

"We are taught that male hormones somehow seem to tear men's minds apart during puberty, condemning them to rely on their reason to somehow regain control of their emotions later, which is why it takes them longer to attain the social maturity required to handle the demands of a commission. But the process usually leaves them less vulnerable to emotional turmoil because they have then learned to deal with their emotions in a rational manner, which, for us women, isn't always quite so easy."

She considered for a moment before continuing. "I think we can be very grateful that our society is intact and young men and women are gently and wisely guided through this difficult stage of their growth. Imagine the chaos that would ensue if it were not so. I shudder to think of it."

"I agree," Vilam declared grimly. Nova's last words had again triggered some very dismal images in Vilam's mind. He sighed and asked, "Is that the reason why only men are chosen as elders?"

"I'm afraid that question is based upon a false presumption. There have been women on the Council of Elders."

"Ah, that's interesting. So this is not a strictly patriarchal society?"

"No, it's not. We do feel that men are generally better qualified to make abstract and legislative decisions. But for us, the affinity between men and women is more like the relationship between mind and heart. The mind must ultimately make the decisions, but the heart is the one that feels and cares. In our culture we look upon men as the mind and women as the heart. Priestesses therefore have mostly custodial or supervisory functions, just as deaconesses mostly assume roles of protection or guardianship. That is also why the High Priestess customarily officiates at conferences, and not the High Priest or an Elder."

"Alright, but how do you then actually reach any decision?"

"That's not so easy to explain. It's sometimes a very complex process. We feel that the head must learn to listen to its heart if a decision it makes is to be of any real value. For this reason the priestesses, and especially the High Priestess, are so prominent in the Advisory Council in Travis. I've never heard of the elders coming to any decision without the counsel of their women."

"So you try to reach decisions by forming a kind of symbiosis?"

"You might call it that, yes. Mind and heart must form a unity; they must be one."

"What happens if mind and heart disagree?"

"I'm sorry to say that such things have happened, but the result was usually catastrophic. We have learned from such experiences and now allow each other enough time to discover why each party thinks the way it does. It's a process of growing comprehension on both sides. In situations in which a decision must be reached quickly, though, it is sometimes necessary for the elders to come to their own conclusions."

"Interesting. So you actually do sometimes have women on the Council of Elders. I must say, I find such a system very reasonable. But I still don't understand why you are so lenient in the interpretation of your own laws and guidelines."

"Well, there are in fact two reasons for that. First of all, there can be no justice without mercy. Strict and unqualified asceticism leads to legalism, for instance if you attempt to enforce holiness without love. We feel that is the case with the Videsian Order."

"I understand. And what is the other reason?"

"Simply put, we don't want to be caught in the act of attempting to curb Anae's sovereignty. In our limited minds, we so often believe that our interpretation of the facts is the only possible explanation, which also quickly leads to legalism. Because we are aware of this constant danger, we hardly dare to stamp a mark of exclusivity upon our interpretations of spiritual matters, except of course in the case of the One Law, which Anae has shown us to be completely indisputable and must always constitute the basis for any further legislation."

"Which One Law are you referring to?"

"Why, the Law of Love, of course, as I mentioned earlier." She looked at him, astonished. "Is that not perfectly clear?"

He smiled bitterly. "I'm afraid it's not always clear to everyone."

Nova swallowed and continued in silence. "Yes, I see what you mean," she said after a moment.

"Anyway, is that the reason why you allow women on the Council of Elders?"

"Yes, if Anae deigns to bestow the necessary abilities and spiritual bearing for the office of elder upon a woman and she feels the calling, who are we to hinder Him?"

"Alright, but I still think eleven years can seem like a long time."

"Excuse me?"

"The eleven years' age difference between men and women gaining a commission as priest or priestess."

"Oh, yes, of course. But if you take into consideration that the current age expectancy is approximately 230, then eleven years really isn't that long."

"But you mentioned earlier that the age expectancy once was much higher."

"Well, that may be true, but we can't really tell how long the age expectancy was then, because before the Cataclysm, nobody actually died of natural causes."

"So what do you figure happened?"

"The current theory is that, when the asteroid fell from

heaven, it destroyed a large portion of the protective layer of water vapor surrounding Piral, therefore allowing various types of cosmic radiation to enter the atmosphere. The radiation may have impaired our biological capability for regeneration, consequently reducing our age expectancy."

"Ah, I see."

"Yes, we have even determined a workable method to calculate the age expectancy in relation to the thickness of the water layer in the atmosphere. If the layer were negligible, that is, somewhere between zero and five percent, our age expectancy would be about three times less. We calculate after our fifteenth year of age, because childhood and puberty have an enormous, dynamic effect on the physique, which must be taken into consideration. Age expectancy in that case would be about eighty-six years."

"Now that's interesting. You subtract fifteen years from 230 and divide by three, then again add the fifteen years. So, in that case, seen from a biological point of view, you would be about twenty-four and Catyana about eighteen, if we were living on a world with only very little water in the atmosphere."

Nova smiled. "An interesting way of putting it, but, yes, you could say that."

"Alright, but, if I may once again return to our original subject, men may attain the priesthood when they are forty-four."

"Yes, and it is another eleven years after the initial commission that a priest or priestess may generally be considered for the office of High Priestess or High Priest. The age guidelines for those offices are therefore set at forty-four and fifty-five, respectively. Elders are typically not chosen before the age of 111. We want them to have enough experience."

"Nova, do you by any chance know the current High Priestess?" Catyana asked.

"Well, a new High Priestess usually doesn't come out until she has been officially introduced at the first Selanian conference after her election, which, in this case, will be Tolares," she said carefully. "But I might know her."

"I heard that a very young High Priestess was elected shortly after that terrible accident in Divestelan, in which the late High Priestess perished five years ago. Why do you think the elders waited so long to call a conference?"

"They will have had their reasons," Nova observed quietly.

She seemed distracted as she kept her eyes on the path in front of her. Vilam felt that she might be looking out for something in the road ahead, and he noted the expectant smile that touched her lips.

16. *Sincerity and Hypocrisy*

"Hyelisa, could you please join me over here?" Natilya called, beckoning to the acolyte tending the herbs in the garden.

"Sure, I'll be right there," Hyelisa called back. Natilya watched her as she set down her hoe, shed her gloves and apron, and hurried over.

"Yes, Natilya, what can I do for you?"

Natilya put her hands on Hyelisa's shoulders and smiled at her. "I'm glad that you enjoy working in the garden so much. You're such a big help."

The young woman attempted to return the smile. "Thank you. I know you mean it; otherwise I would believe you're just trying to keep up morale when you say such kind things."

Natilya let go of her friend, astonished at her remark. "And what would be wrong with that?"

"Well, I'm concerned your praise might sound hollow if you allow it to become a mere habit."

"Oh?"

Hyelisa's smile faltered, and Natilya could see fear in her eyes. "Please, I don't mean to seem disrespectful, but my brother is in the west, and..." Hyelisa swallowed, but couldn't bring herself to continue.

"You mean Bejad?" Natilya coaxed, keeping her voice gentle.

Hyelisa nodded, her eyes cast downwards. She took a deep breath. "You know the things they're saying about our society in the western provinces. They make us out to be hypocrites. They say our manners, our social graces and etiquette are all just sham and pretense. And sometimes," she added, glancing up at Natilya, "I'm afraid they're right."

Natilya just stared at her, aghast.

"Oh, Natilya, sometimes I'm so frightened of what's coming," Hyelisa whispered. "I can feel a storm brewing. Our enemies in the west want to change everything. They claim that the world will be a better place. But what will it all lead to? And I'm so afraid for Bejad. If we, who are representatives of the Order, can't be sincere in our affections and protestations, how can we expect those that look to us for spiritual and moral guidance pretend to be anything else? I would like to believe that, in some small way, we are doing something to help my brother, even if it's only to be sincere in the things we do and say. I would like to believe it, but I sometimes don't know if I can."

Natilya shuddered. It seemed as if a cloud had passed before the sun and the air had turned cold, sending a chill down her spine. But when she looked up, Velana was still shining down upon her from a blue sky, as she had been all day, and Natilya relaxed when she felt the sun's pleasant warmth on her face. She turned back to Hyelisa.

"Don't you think you might be overreacting?"

Hyelisa solemnly returned Natilya's glance, but couldn't bring herself to answer. "I...I'm very sorry if I've been too blunt in the way I've expressed my opinions," she finally replied.

"No, that's alright. I do think that we need to be more careful of such subtle traps, and I'll be sure to put it on the agenda for the next staff meeting. Thank you for mentioning it."

"Glad to be of service."

"Listen, dearest, could you take over the children for me? I have an appointment with Aunt Utalya. I'm afraid we can't spare any of the other girls because we have two guests and several of the children staying for the meal. All you need to do is finish up with the children here, make sure the ones that aren't staying go home, and keep an eye on the ones that are until I get back. Do you think you'll manage alone?"

"Yes, of course. I'm not as good with the children as you are, but it'll be alright."

"Thank you. It shouldn't take that long."

"Alright, I wish you well," Hyelisa answered, but Natilya thought she detected a trace of sadness in her friend's voice.

Their embrace was somewhat hesitant, and Natilya hastened away, deliberately pushing the uncomfortable conversation from her mind. She had more immediate things to worry about. When she reached her aunt's parlor, she took a deep breath and then knocked.

"Come right on in," a voice called from inside.

She quietly opened the door. "Hi, aunty."

"Hi, dear. Why don't you have a seat? I just need to finish this up and I'll be right with you."

The Lady Utalya continued writing at her desk, and Natilya made herself comfortable on the couch. After a moment, Natilya saw her aunt put her quill away. When she came over, she gave her niece a kiss on the cheek and sat down in the armchair across from her.

"Did Nova instruct you on tomorrow's schedule?" the Lady Utalya asked.

"Yes, she asked Tanola and me to go into town for her in the morning. In the afternoon we'll be expanding on herbology. I was actually thinking of putting Hyelisa in charge of that. She knows more about plants than all of us put together. Tanola suggested that we combine the lesson with medical training. I believe that would…"

"Um, excuse me, honey, I'm certain Nova has an excellent program worked out for the day, but I sincerely doubt that's the reason you wanted to see me."

Natilya bit her lower lip and sighed. She folded her hands on her lap and looked at the carpet. She knew her aunt was waiting patiently for her to find the courage to say what she undoubtedly knew would be coming.

"Aunty, we're leaving for Tolares day after tomorrow, aren't we?"

"Yes," the Lady replied, her tone cautious.

"And we'll be staying at His Excellency's residence again."

"You know that we are."

Natilya finally looked up. "Don't you think it would be better if I stayed here?"

The Lady regarded her niece, and Natilya saw pity in her eyes. "Natilya, why can't you get over it?"

"I don't know," she whispered.

"What do you want?"

Natilya shook her head. Her eyes were moist.

The Lady got up and sat down next to her, taking her

hands in hers. She sighed. "Natilya, you mustn't forget that it's been over ten years since the Lord lost his wife. A man can feel very lonely under such circumstances. Maybe he was just seeking a bit of companionship. You must admit that your presence can be most diverting, and your natural cheerfulness is extremely contagious. It helps people take their minds off things. Just because he stood up with you for every dance four years ago doesn't necessarily mean anything."

"Aunty, you didn't see the look in his eyes."

"Alright, what look?"

Natilya thought about it for a moment, attempting to recall the experience. "His eyes were so deep, and so kind. They seemed to be pleading with me. I was afraid I would lose myself in them."

"Child, we've been over this so many times. Do you know how old he is?"

"That didn't stop you when you met your first husband."

"Touché, my dear. I wasn't quite as young as you are and he wasn't quite as old as Lord Tolares, but the age difference was still significant. But look at it this way, Natilya: you are now thirty-five. You could accept a commission as priestess anytime you wish. Do you really want to throw that away?"

"You didn't begin your career in the Order until your first husband died. You became an acolyte when you were 83, made priestess at 102, and were chosen as High Priestess when you were 133. Then you met Lord Revan and gave up the office at 148. That was fifteen years ago. I'm sorry that he passed away so soon, but those are the facts."

"Now you sound as if you're trying to justify yourself. Natilya, be honest. Let's assume he did care about you. Would you really want to marry him if he asked you?"

Natilya sighed. "Oh, aunty, I just don't know."

"Well then, come along to Tolares and find out."

Natilya shook her head. "I'm afraid."

"Of what?"

"I don't know. I'm afraid he really will ask me. But I'm also afraid that he won't."

"Oh, I see." The Lady sighed. "You know, things would be so much easier if you could just fall in love with someone else. What about the young Lord Tolares?"

"Oh, aunty, all he's interested in is science. Besides, Nova is attracted to him."

"What? Nova? I never noticed anything like that, and I know her better than any of you."

Natilya smiled. "Well, I'm glad to discover that you don't notice everything. Besides, you were both very busy when we were there four years ago. And I'm certain that the young Lord wasn't aware of Nova's preference. He was too busy with his science projects." She sighed deeply. "Believe me, I've tried falling in love with someone else. But I can't stop thinking about Lord Tolares."

"Alright, listen. Lord Tolares is an honorable man, and I'm sure he would never do anything to deliberately hurt you. If you come with us, I promise that I'll keep my eyes open. If things get difficult for you, I'll talk to him. Does that sound feasible?"

"That would be very kind of you."

"Is it a deal?"

Natilya looked at her for a moment and then nodded.

The Lady pulled her close and gave her a warm hug. "Come on, get out of here. Let Hyelisa get back to her garden, or you'll never hear the end of it."

They smiled at each other, and Natilya left the room. The Lady Utalya returned to her desk and picked up her quill, but she couldn't bring herself to do any more work. She stared out the window and watched her niece playing with the children, an expression of concern on her face. As Natilya had said, they would be leaving for Tolares on the day after tomorrow, and with the way things were developing, it seemed that they were heading directly for the center of the storm.

17. *The Artifact*

When the party came around a bend at the edge of the wood, a meadow opened up before them, and Nova glanced at Vilam with interest. She saw that he had slowed his pace and was staring in amazement at the artifact that dominated the scene with its enigmatic presence. Nova held Catyana back and motioned for her to be silent and watch carefully. Catyana nodded as Vilam moved towards the object, not taking his eyes from it.

The artifact looked like a very short but broad, tapered cylinder that had been sliced off diagonally, like an oversized ice cream cone that had landed top down in the grass and then been beheaded near its base. The cylinder had a diameter of about fifteen cubits, and the walls were approximately one cubit thick. The object had four vertical incisions at regular intervals. Guarding each incision was a rectangular post. The entire artifact shimmered darkly in the late afternoon air.

Vilam turned back to Nova. "It's a magnificent work of art, but there's something wrong with it."

Nova didn't answer but watched expectantly.

Vilam moved closer to the artifact. He stretched out his hand and let it glide along the object's smooth surface. This action prompted a smile.

"Ah, there we go! It's made of metal. It should have been made of stone."

Nova smiled and pulled Catyana forwards. "Excellent! There we have more proof of your natural perceptiveness for art. Folan told me about your reaction to Elder Yonatan's light sculpture this morning. Are you, in that case, familiar with the concept of Sensation and Induction?"

"Well, I have studied the concept, but only very sketchily. As you already stated this morning, I'm not trained. What I can sense, I sense intuitively."

"Intuition is always valuable. But, for Catyana's sake, would you mind if I explained the concept in more detail?"

"No, be my guest."

"Could you tell us first how you deduced that the artifact should be made of stone, and not metal?"

"From what I have heard, every object and every environment has a distinct pattern of harmony and dissonance which is initiated at the subquantum level. I believe the current subquantum kinetic theory states that the patterns are produced by the reaction processes of particles termed etherons, which compose the basis for all matter and energy in the universe. A perceptive person can sense this pattern, although it is dependent upon so many variables that the art of Sensation is usually placed in the realm of spirituality, and not science. It seems that the mind has an uncanny ability to distinguish patterns that can often not be qualified or quantified scientifically, because the patterns are too complex. A simple example of Sensation might be when you get the impression that someone is watching you in the dark."

"Well, I don't know what you mean by 'subquantum,'" Nova replied, "but the rest sounds fairly accurate. We do believe in an ethereal substrate which composes the basis for all matter and energy in the universe. But the scientific method that you have just described usually works bottom-up: You work upwards from the phenomenon that you study, formulating assumptions and theories regarding the underlying processes with which you attempt to explain what you have observed. You then perform experiments to prove or disprove your assumptions. The results are called scientific evidence.

"The spiritual method we use is more experiential and works top-down. We implicitly believe in the essence that we perceive and attempt to learn its qualities and characteristics empirically, by experience. We hope that, one day, the spiritual and scientific communities will achieve a comprehensive, holistic model which encompasses all these aspects."

"I understand. I'm sorry I got so carried away again."

"No, that's quite alright. You were attempting to explain the phenomenon from a scientific point of view, although I wasn't aware of the model you just presented. But let me explain more about the patterns we were discussing. We can often sense a pattern best when it has been disrupted."

"For instance, the way I sensed that there was something wrong with the artifact?" Vilam asked.

"Well, almost. The fundamental nature of the universe sometimes requires a particular textural pattern for various forms and vice versa. If an object is constructed in any way different from what its natural pattern calls for, the dissonant component becomes too intense and we sense that the object is no longer in tune with its environment."

"I suppose that is why I sensed that this artifact should be made of stone, and not metal."

"Yes, that is correct."

"What would happen if you made an object with only harmonic components and no dissonance?"

"Oh, that would be terrible. It would be like a ballad without a tragedy or a soup without any salt. I don't believe it's even possible."

"So is this the artifact that you wanted to show me, what you mentioned back at the pond regarding Catyana's abilities?"

"Yes, it is. As we have seen, Catyana's perception is very well developed, although she's had no formal training to speak of. That is the reason she could sense the gender of the six little sinaveni back at the pond without so much as even trying."

"Ah, I see. Is that why you would like to initiate her as an acolyte?"

Nova smiled. "No, we don't normally initiate someone into apprenticeship because of their abilities, although a certain degree of proficiency is required in particular areas in order to enter the priesthood. It is the attitude of a person's heart which is most essential in our evaluation."

Catyana shot her a grateful glance.

"Now, my friend, what do you know about Induction?" Nova asked Vilam.

"Well, I have read that you might define Induction as the inversion of Sensation. Sensation is passive, Induction is active. Induction is the process of not only sensing the pattern of an object, but actually affecting the pattern."

"Yes, exactly, you are very well informed, Vilam. A simple example of Induction would be a charismatic leader's ability to bend the people around him to his will. Not a very desirable ability, especially if that person has no compassion."

Vilam grimaced. "Now that is one statement I agree with."

"Anyway, the art of Induction has developed to a point where we first attempt to sense the pattern of an object or environment. Inside of this pattern, there is always the possibility of variance, and the induction process utilizes this fluctuation. We can attempt to reinforce or counteract certain characteristics of the pattern, as long as the influence remains inside of the parameters for that object. Let me give you a practical example."

She picked up a small piece of wood lying at her feet.

"Most objects have the natural capacity to burn, or

oxidize. This piece of wood here in my palm, for instance, could do that if we were to set fire to it. For that reason, I can induce it to believe that it is burning. Watch!"

She concentrated, and the piece of wood began to glow a bright, intense red.

"What I'm actually doing is inducing the photonic component of the oxidization process, which is inherent to the piece of wood I'm holding."

She let the glow fade and placed the piece of wood back on the ground.

"We've discovered that procedures involving hydro-, pneuma-, base- or pyro-oriented processes often function as an anchor for Induction, which is why these four process elements have become so important to us. As a matter of fact, they have become so essential that these components have even been integrated into the traditional wedding ceremony as water, wind, earth, and fire, respectively."

"*Hydro*, *pneuma*, and *pyro* I understand, but what exactly do you mean by *base*?" Vilam asked.

"Well, an example of a base process would be the act of grounding, for instance when connecting a lightning rod on a building with the earth. Further examples would be an architect's reckoning of the center of gravity in a structure or a warrior's assessment of the fulcrum of a sword. We attempt to sense the correct locations for these points, and if necessary, induce the material so that they are placed correctly."

"Ah, I see." Vilam nodded appreciatively. "Do you also use your abilities to read other people's minds or maybe even influence them?"

"It could be done," she admitted cautiously. "But we are very careful about such methods. They could quickly get out of hand, which would be a direct affront against the laws of personal freedom and choice. We do use Induction in training, though, to help others perceive what we are sensing, or for instance, in the Rite of Union, in which we join with the One."

Vilam nodded. "I understand."

"Another more futuristic example of Induction might be what Elder Yonatan is attempting with matter," Nova added. "He is striving to describe the qualities of all substances and how they react with and influence each other, either physically or chemically. I have heard that he has already differentiated many elements at an atomic level. If someday he were to learn how to change one element into another, he would be physically changing the pattern of the underlying ethereal substrate, which would be the scientific counterpart to Induction. We, on the other hand, would attempt to directly affect the underlying substrate, which, in the end, would also be changing one element into another, only on a different level. But that is, of course, a utopian fantasy at the moment."

"Science fiction."

"Excuse me?"

"Oh, sorry, never mind. Are you aware of where your inductive abilities come from? I could imagine that some people might consider them to be occult."

"Occult?" Nova exclaimed. "I don't understand how anyone could harbor such a far-fetched idea. In my opinion, occult powers are gained by contact with beings from the invisible, spiritual world around us. Our Holy Scriptures explicitly prohibit such practices. To us, Sensation and Induction are natural concepts that, like any other abilities, are enhanced by training. I can fathom that they may seem a bit cryptic to someone not accustomed to them," she added thoughtfully, "but we certainly have no need to resort to the deceitful tricks of the enemy. Why do you ask?"

"Just wondering," Vilam answered with a faint smile.

"You're an excellent teacher, Nova."

"Thank you," she said with an inquisitive glance in his direction. She had the feeling that Vilam knew more than he was letting on.

"Nova, you mentioned that you were going over all this for my benefit," Catyana said, "and I'm very grateful. I've really learned a lot and I believe I understand the underlying processes much better. But there is one question that I just can't get out of my mind."

"Yes, dearest, go ahead," Nova said.

"Would it be possible to change the pattern of the artifact to match its form?"

Nova looked at her in surprise. "Well, there have been attempts at that. A theory states that, if we bring an object into a certain form, we can change its pattern to match its form instead of its texture, thereby circumventing the object's natural resistance."

"May I try?"

"Well, yes, of course."

Catyana approached the artifact, and Nova could tell that she was attempting to sense a suitable entry point into the object's essence. She decided on one of the higher posts guarding the object. Her hands gently caressed both sides of the metal post, hardly touching it. Then she stopped and closed her eyes. A faint light radiated from where she held her hands over the object. The light expanded to include the entire artifact.

Nova held her breath and could see that Vilam was feeling as much suspense as she was. But she was surprised when she detected a slight fluctuation in the glow with which Catyana had surrounded the object. She was even more astonished to see that the artifact was changing. It lost its dark hue and shone brightly in the sun.

Catyana dropped her hands and exhaled slowly. "I'm sorry, but that's the best I can do. The essence of the metal's lattices was too resistant, so I changed the pattern to that of a more noble substance, platinum."

Nova just gaped at her. "Catyana, that's...amazing."

"Catyana, do you think you could try it again and enhance the iterative process you were using?" Vilam said.

Both women looked at him in surprise.

"What do you mean, Vilam?" Catyana asked, shading her eyes against the sun.

"I noticed a slight fluctuation in your inductive influence. I assume you were exploiting the force produced by bouncing back from the pattern's natural resistance. Now try it again, but concentrate more on the bounce effect. See if you can attain some kind of resonance from the artifact to create an inductive pulse. When you've done that, try to use your inductive powers to manipulate the force of the pulse instead of the pattern of the artifact. Do you think you can do that?"

"I can try."

She closed her eyes and raised her hands. The artifact began to glow again. Slowly, the glow became a throb, but it was apparent that the frequency was somehow off. It quickly fell in upon itself and collapsed.

Catyana dropped her hands and glanced over at Vilam, obviously disappointed at having let him down. "I'm sorry. It didn't work."

"Hey, that's alright. Travis wasn't built in a day, was it? But there was some pulsation, even if the frequency was off. Now try again, and this time, don't just sense the essence of the artifact, but try to get a feel for its heartbeat, just as if you were taking its pulse."

Catyana nodded and turned back to the object, closed her eyes, and raised her hands, breathing deeply. Once more the artifact began to glow, and then throb. Gradually and almost imperceptibly, the luminous, pulsating shimmer around the object changed. Suddenly she smiled.

"Yes, there it is. I can feel it."

She was no longer inducing the pattern of the object, but the pulse itself. When a continuous pulse had been established, she quickened its pace, and the artifact appeared to shift out of phase with reality. Catyana took control of the phase shift and steadily changed the texture of the artifact, like a skillful equestrian directing her mount with a gentle nudge here or slight pressure there. When the artifact's consistency had reached a subtle, roseate hue, she dropped the pulse and stepped back.

Vilam nodded, amazed at how quickly she had grasped the concept. He stepped up to the artifact and let his hand glide over its surface. His satisfied expression informed Nova that he was indeed feeling the smooth, cool grain of solid rock.

"That's it, Catyana. Perfect. The texture of the material now completely matches its form," he said.

Nova moved towards her friend. Could it be true? Were such things actually happening in her time, in her presence, even? Had she in reality experienced what she had just seen? The notion that had engaged her thoughts ever more often in the past months regarding her friend flashed once more through her mind.

Golden Messenger.

She cautiously reached out and touched Catyana's cheek. Then she took her friend's hands and squeezed them.

"Catyana, I don't know what to say. That…that was the most astonishing thing I've ever seen." Looking at both her companions, she added, "Would it be alright with you if we didn't tell anybody about this just yet? I'd like to discuss it with the Lady Utalya first. Catyana, you might not be aware of this, but you've just initiated a breakthrough in the art of Induction."

Nova tried to maintain an astonished yet joyful expression and hoped that Catyana didn't sense her apprehension. It was clear that her friend's powers by far exceeded what Nova had initially believed. As a matter of fact, she wasn't even near her full potential. How could Nova protect her against the sinister forces that were rallying all around them? Nova knew that if they discovered her friend's talent, they would undoubtedly attempt to either use her abilities to their own advantage, or ensure that she would never use them against her enemies. All she could do at the moment was pray that Catyana's parents would allow her to accompany Nova to Tolares. In the eye of the hurricane, they might find enough calm to prepare Catyana before the full force of the storm engulfed them.

18. Tracks in the Forest

Cetila took a deep breath, enjoying the fresh scents and tranquil sounds of the forest. Only the busy but ordered hum of the girls pitching camp nearby intruded upon her lazy thoughts as she rested against one of the countless majestic conifers that separated her from the brigade. Ever since they had left Navaresa and entered the seemingly endless expanse of the Northern Forests a week ago, Cetila had been in raptures. She couldn't explain it, but she had never felt so alive and simultaneously at peace with herself and everything around her. If it hadn't been for the recurrent conflicts with her captain, this would have been the happiest time of her life.

She stepped forwards and bent over the calm surface of the little pool at her feet. Yes, there was the same thin face that had always stared back at her from her reflection, although it now harbored an almost serene expression instead of the strained and apprehensive glance she was accustomed to seeing in the mirror of late. Even so, her thick, dark eyebrows, full lips, and prominent cheekbones made up for her otherwise too delicate features, and some even considered her pretty. Her outfit went well with the dark shade of her skin and the massive chignon that designated her as a princess of the Northern Covasins and the House Marusen. Of course, her hair was often veiled by the mask she wore during critical operations, but here in the Navaren such precautions were unnecessary.

When she had first donned the black and crimson uniform twelve years ago, she had been so proud. The crisp, flowing dress, chic cape, and black gloves shrouded her in an aura of elegance and authority, although she had to admit that her attire seemed strangely out of tune with her momentary surroundings. She wasn't as tall and stately as Captain Pira, but that didn't really matter. Tavita was even shorter than Cetila and had been promoted to Captain of the Crimson Brigade at the age of nineteen, when the Lady Gevinesa had stepped back five years ago.

Cetila smiled bitterly at the recollection of her sister. In an attempt to suppress her helpless anger, she pulled off her gloves and filled her hands several times with the clear water pouring into the pool from a little stream, drinking deeply of the pure, sweet liquid. She splashed some remaining water back into the pool in an impatient gesture, wishing she could ignore the pain and resentment that resurfaced every time she thought of Tavita. Would she ever be able to forgive her? Tavita didn't have any right to do that to her brother, regardless of the allegations she had brought up against him.

Cetila had been very close to Varan. She could still picture him with Dena Cemasena, who had almost become her sister-in-law. The two had been a perfect couple and had been so happy together. Poor Dena! The tragedy had naturally hit her even harder than Cetila, and she had become pale and distant in the past two years, shutting her pain inside herself. Although it was now almost certain that she was a member of the Resistance and therefore working for the enemy, Cetila couldn't find it in her heart to harbor any ill feelings towards the young Lady Cemasena. On the contrary, after the tragic event Cetila had finally turned her analytical capabilities towards the ideology of her own indoctrination and had discovered many discrepancies between the words and actions of her superiors. She could now better understand some of the views of their enemies in the east.

She immediately returned to her current situation when she registered hushed steps in the soft moss behind her. She drew on her gloves and turned towards her approaching comrade with her left hand on the hilt of the sword that was strapped around her waist, prepared to draw the weapon in an instant.

Dalina Novesta stood before her, eyeing her uneasily. She slapped her left fist to her breast and bowed in a brusque military salute. "Sorry to disturb you, Commander, but Pira has been asking for you. We've discovered some interesting tracks that she wishes you to examine."

Cetila sighed. "Alright, Lieutenant, lead the way."

As they marched towards the camp, Cetila scrutinized the girl walking ahead of her. Pira's sister wasn't quite twenty, almost fifteen years younger than both Cetila and Pira. She was slightly taller than Cetila but appeared much more delicate. She made up for her seeming fragility by an eagerness that was unrivalled in the Brigade, except of course by Tavita, which is why Dalina had risen through the ranks so quickly in the past four years. When Tavita left the Brigade indefinitely two weeks ago to assume responsibility of a clandestine operation in the eastern provinces, Dalina had been promoted to second lieutenant and taken Cetila's place as commander of the second company. Cetila herself had surprisingly been promoted to first lieutenant and was now the captain's first officer and commander of the Brigade. She still couldn't understand Pira's decision, unless it was a bit of sentimentality on their new captain's part, for old time's sake.

The thought brought back pleasant memories. In younger years, Dena Cemasena, Pira Novesta, and Cetila Marusen, who were born only days apart of each other, had been virtually inseparable and had spent as much time together as distance, and of course their parents, would allow. Later Tavita, Cetila's junior by ten years, had joined them and become an integral member of the small clique. The three girls had practically raised the child by themselves, and the group had often playfully been termed the Three Nursemaids by their friends.

Then, about twenty years ago, Gevinesa Divestelan secretly began recruiting eligible girls into the Crimson Brigade. Without knowing the cause, the friends registered that their acquaintances found less and less time for social engagements. After five years of observing this strange development, Pira had been the first to succumb to Gevinesa's subtle inducement, and Cetila followed several years later. Tavita was appointed to the Brigade two years after Cetila and, at the age of fourteen, had been the youngest member ever to be admitted. Of course Tavita was always amazingly adept, and her ascent was quick and steep. At the age of seventeen, she was promoted to first lieutenant and became Gevinesa's right hand.

Dena never joined. Either she wasn't approached, or, as Cetila rather believed, she declined to understand Gevinesa's devious insinuations. Interestingly enough, Dena and Cetila remained very close, despite the apparent differences in their world views, but Cetila and Pira had grown apart. The harsh indoctrination to western ideology, the fierce training, and incessant tactical operations had taken their toll on their relationship. Because of conflicting duty rosters, Pira and Cetila hardly saw each other, and she knew that Pira and Dena had seen each other even less. A little over two years ago, the three friends had met once more to celebrate their Coming of Age and Dena's quickly arriving nuptials. But the meeting had been awkward almost to the point of embarrassment, and several months later Cetila's brother had found his demise, to put it gently.

When Cetila and Dalina reached the camp, Cetila stopped and monitored the progress of her brigadiers for a moment. A satisfied smile touched her lips. They had only arrived half an hour ago, but everything seemed to be in place. The Crimson Brigade was a slick and efficient military machine and in Cetila's opinion the deadliest force the planet had ever seen. In earlier years she had held the Black Guard in awe and wanted to emulate their seemingly lethal efficiency. The past five years had taught her otherwise, and today she felt nothing but contempt for Corsen Divestelan's supposed elite legions.

Dalina urged her on, and as they traversed the camp, many of Cetila's sisters in arms flashed her respectful salutes. Dalina led her back into the forest, where they continued for approximately five minutes. They arrived in a clearing where Cetila saw Pira with a squad of the second company, investigating the little stream that flowed through it. Pira looked up as they approached.

"Ah, very good. Step back girls; I wish for Tavita's sister to examine the tracks," she said with a smug grin and a subtle trace of sarcasm. "We absolutely must consult our commander before we attempt to do anything."

The troop immediately obeyed their captain and made room for Cetila, who groaned inwardly. Pira was at it again. What had gotten into her these past two weeks?

"Tavita's sister still has a name of her own," she murmured towards Pira.

Pira only honored her with a wry smile and pointed towards the stream. Cetila stooped down and looked into the joyfully babbling water.

What she saw made her heart leap.

This had to be what they had come here to find, what her mother had commissioned them to search for! All her instincts told her that these prints must belong to the elusive creatures they were hunting. She could hardly contain her excitement and felt the skin of her cheeks flush. With her breath quickened, she looked up.

"The tracks are fresh, hardly an hour old. We must have disturbed the animals when we arrived as they were watering. Although they are very clever and attempted to erase their tracks by moving into the stream, they probably didn't realize that the ground in this area is partly composed of clay. The water therefore didn't wash the tracks away as soon as they might have wished. I predict that you will find the tracks leaving the water several hundred cubits upstream. I assume you have contained the area and traced the prints?"

Pira stared at her as if she was out of her mind. "Thank you, Commander. Your opinion and singular expertise are most welcome." Her voice was crisp and professional, but she shot Cetila a provocative glance, daring her to retaliate.

Cetila clenched her teeth and swallowed the anger that was again boiling up inside her. She didn't want to make a scene in front of the girls. Breathing deeply to calm herself, she deliberately surveyed the young woman that had been her best friend in her youth.

Captain Pirena Novesta, Pira for short, had the tall, aristocratic bearing and slender figure of a true patrician beauty. Her thick, dark hair was pinned back in a tucked braid, as was Dalina's, indicating that the two sisters were princesses of the House of Novesta. She had wonderfully fair and creamy skin, and decidedly marked yet somehow delicate features. Her countenance had once been supple, but had grown harsh during her fifteen years of service in the Crimson Brigade. Her dark eyes flashed dangerously as she returned Cetila's gaze.

"If First Lieutenant Marusen has finished her inspection of my person, maybe we can resume the task at hand?" she said, a cold smile embellished on her lips. She motioned for Dalina to continue.

"Commander, two squads of the second company are following the tracks. They lead in a north-easterly direction. From the number of prints, we assume that it must be a herd consisting of approximately fifty animals."

"Very good, Lieutenant," Cetila answered. "I advise that two squads from each company remain to supervise the camp and maintain security. The rest shall be dispatched to encircle the herd according to our prearranged strategy." She glanced at Pira.

Pira nodded her accord.

"You have your orders, Lieutenant. Ensure that your platoons maintain the required distance of at least a league from the herd until all the troops are in position."

Dalina slapped her fist to her heart and bowed, then ordered the squad back to the camp, leaving two guards as protection for the captain. Cetila watched her leave and then turned to Pira.

"Captain, I…" Her eyes pleaded.

"Is there anything you wish to add, Lieutenant?" Pira replied coldly.

Cetila sighed. "No. I will instruct the commanders of the other companies."

"Very good. It's going to be a long night. I have much paperwork to complete, and I don't wish to be disturbed. You are dismissed."

Cetila saluted and stalked back to the camp. She felt excited at the prospect of ensnaring one of the animals and was certain they were up to the task, even though they would be tracking the creatures in the darkness. But she still couldn't understand why her mother had been so insistent when she had ordered the search for these mythical creatures. What was going on? And why was Pira playing such antagonistic games with her? She could only hope that the next day would bring some answers. As Pira had mentioned, it was going to be a long night.

19. *Eastern Technology*

Nova shaded her eyes and checked the sun's position. "It's getting late. We need to think about getting back."

She linked arms with Catyana, and the threesome continued on their circuit, soon reaching the wood to the east of town, each of them diverted by the astonishing event they had just experienced. They turned south, ambling along the edge of the forest.

Nova glanced at Vilam. "May I ask you a personal question?"

"Well, you can always ask. Although I can't promise that I'll answer."

"I noticed the way you looked at me when we first met in the tavern, and also how you have been glancing at me now and again during our walk."

"Yes, that's true. I'm sorry, I didn't mean to be intrusive, but you remind me of someone."

"Oh, I see. I thought that might be the reason. May I ask who it is that I resemble?"

"Yes, you look very much like my wife."

Nova stopped, forcing Catyana to a sudden halt beside her. She was incapable of suppressing her astonishment.

"You...you are married? You somehow just don't seem like the type."

Vilam shook his head. "No, I'm afraid she passed away about twelve years ago."

"Oh." She looked down. "I see. I'm sorry."

Vilam smiled bitterly. "There isn't much that can be done about it. Would you mind if we changed the subject?"

Nova nodded discreetly and remained silent.

Vilam shaded his eyes against the sun and looked across the meadow on their right. "What are those fascinating structures in the field? They look almost like works of art."

"Well, it's not always easy to distinguish between a good work of art and a fine piece of technology. We need to go in that direction anyway. Why don't we go over and have a quick look?"

They soon arrived at the first of the structures. There were quite a few of them spread around in various locations on the field. The base of the object extended about two feet above Vilam's head and looked like a concave cone with a sphere set on top of it. Nova pressed against the base and half of the object smoothly opened outward. In the sphere they could see combustion modules that were spinning horizontally at immense speed.

"These are solar generators," Nova explained. "The light of the sun is bundled and used to stimulate four light amplification units, which produce the beams of light you see.

They heat the air in the combustion modules, thereby creating minute explosions and propelling them. The energy is translated to a magnetic turbine underground."

"For what purpose?" Vilam asked.

"For instance the hydraulic pumps needed for the town's water distribution pressure."

"Ah, I see. Brilliant! How do you pump the water at night, when there is no sun?"

"We have learned to bundle and focus even ambient light so well that we can use the light of the moons and stars at night, even if it is only at a reduced level. Nonetheless, we usually produce much more energy during the day than we actually need. It is stored by heating water in insulated containers underground and then utilized at night. Water is an excellent natural heat repository."

Vilam nodded, seeming impressed, and Nova closed the access to the generator. They resumed their walk.

"Is this technology used everywhere?" Vilam asked.

The question wasn't a very comfortable one, and Nova considered it for a moment before replying.

"I'm afraid not," she answered. "The technology currently doesn't extend much farther west than Cemasena. The plan was originally to make the expertise available everywhere, but the hostilities that began in the western provinces about thirty years ago brought all such notions to an abrupt stop. The elders wanted to see how things develop. That's one of the main allegations the western provinces have made against us, and it's led to quite a bit of tension on both sides."

"So the right to eastern technology has become a political issue?"

"Very much so, I'm afraid," Nova replied while glancing up at Vilam.

They continued on their path in silent contemplation and

had soon returned to the Lady's manse.

The meal was already served, so they quickly freshened up and joined the others at the dinner table. The table was very large and could accommodate at least two dozen people, although only a little over half of the seats were filled. The Lady Utalya officiated at the head of the table and had left two places empty on her left, which were taken by Nova and Catyana, and one on her right, to which she winked Vilam. All of the acolytes and even some of the children had joined in the meal. The atmosphere at the table was one of relaxed cheerfulness. The acolytes were chatting quietly amongst themselves or with the children, and Nova, Catyana, and the Lady were quickly involved in a conversation regarding the upcoming conference.

While talking with Utalya, Nova discreetly watched Vilam. He was a complete mystery to her. He seemed to know so much, and yet so little. Although she was grateful, she couldn't help wondering where he had come by the knowledge necessary to aid Catyana with her inductive abilities.

She could see Vilam's eyes wandering about the room, which was spacious and light. Various works of art adorned the walls, but his eyes lingered on the wall opposite the Lady, which contained the mandatory image of a sword. Nova was certain that Vilam had seen the sword's counterpart in Folan's tavern that morning, and from the contemplative expression on his face, she mused that he must be wondering at the lost artifact's vital role in their society. Was he aware of the part that the prophets assigned to him in this regard, if he truly was the Traveler?

As always, the food was strictly vegetarian, but Nova felt that such a diet wouldn't hurt their guest, and he certainly wasn't complaining. Nova smiled when she noticed how often he helped himself to the sautéed mushrooms in sour-fried bread.

Nova turned back to the Lady. "I promised Folan that I would get Vilam back to him before nightfall. We therefore need to be leaving soon. Will you be joining us?"

"No, dear, I'm very sorry. I would love to, but I still have so much to prepare for the conference. Please excuse me and give my love to Folan and Semanta. I do believe that Tanola and Natilya very much wanted to join you, though."

After the meal, they hurriedly prepared to leave. Nova had a private consultation with the Lady, which only lasted several minutes, after which she joined the group and led them into town.

20. *The Games of the Noble*

Gevinesa noticed Corsen leering over at her as she was reading a large, illustrated storybook to their youngest sibling, Yanita. Outside, the sun was going down and setting the forests around their coach ablaze in its fiery light. They had already traveled over forty leagues in the past nine hours. If they continued at this pace, they would reach Tolares in two days.

"Sister, I have a little surprise for you," Corsen declared coolly.

Gevinesa looked up at him. "Oh, and pray, what might that be?"

"We cracked down on a few cells of the opposition today. I am pleased to inform you that we caught about twenty of the accursed dissenters. They were all executed."

"Well good for you, brother. They do become a bit tiresome after a while, don't they?" she stated in a bored tone, returning his cold stare.

"I also thought you might want to know that your

personal handmaiden was among them."

"Oh." Gevinesa hesitated. Something in her face twitched, but she had herself under control again immediately.

Yanita gently squeezed Gevinesa's arm and looked up at her, concern in her eyes. But she remained silent, just as Gevinesa had taught her.

"Well, that's alright, brother dear," Gevinesa continued, certain that the slight tremor in her voice could hardly be detected. "I was planning on getting rid of her myself, but I guess you got around to it before I did. You always were so thoughtful. I suppose I know now why she was becoming such a nuisance. Next time, though, I would be grateful if you would let me in on the fun."

Corsen was noticeably disappointed. He had probably hoped for a more vehement reaction.

"Corsen, don't you think you could have waited with that specific piece of information until we reached Tolares?" Lord Divestelan asked calmly.

"Yes, sir, I'm sorry," Corsen replied, but Gevinesa sensed that he was simulating more respect than he probably felt.

"You're a gifted young man, Corsen, and what is more, you are my son. But you must learn to control your passion. Sometimes it is more efficient to wait. We all enjoy playing these little games, but the tools must be honed, and temperance is one of them. That seems to be a lesson your sister has learned quite well these past few years," he added, with a meaningful glance at his daughter. "But the game isn't over, and it yet remains to be seen who will win." His eyes appeared cold as he looked her over.

The coach slowed unexpectedly. The four inhabitants looked out the windows in surprise as the vehicle came to a full stop.

"Corsen, come with me," the Lord said. He opened the

door and stepped outside with his son following. "Guard, ensure that nobody enters or leaves this coach," he ordered.

One of the guards flanking the coach on their chyevi snapped to attention. "Yes, My Lord."

Gevinesa watched intently from behind the curtain as the Lord and his son approached the front of the coach, where a courier was talking quietly with the coachman. It was well that she had learned to read lips and could therefore follow most of the conversation, even if she couldn't hear all of it.

"Do we have a problem, Martan?" the Lord asked the courier.

"I'm sorry for the interruption, My Lord, but I have an urgent message for you," the courier replied, handing him a sealed envelope. The Lord accepted it and thanked the courier. He moved away with his son, broke the seal and opened the letter. After studying it for a moment, he took a deep breath.

"It is as we feared. Bejad has escaped," he stated in a composed voice.

"How could that happen?" Corsen fumed.

"Patience, my son, patience. It seems a steed from our stable is also missing."

Father and son exchanged a significant glance. They walked back to the courier.

"Are you aware of the contents of this message?" the Lord asked the courier.

"Yes, My Lord."

"Where do you think Bejad has disappeared to?"

"I would assume that he has gone to Tolares."

"Sharply observed, my friend. There is hope for you yet."

"Thank you, My Lord."

"Alright, Martan, alert our operatives in Tolares."

"What shall we do with him when we find him, My Lord?"

"Kill him."

The Lord turned his back on the courier and marched back to the vehicle.

As soon as the men approached, Gevinesa resumed reading to Yanita. Although both of the sister's faces were well hidden behind the book's large and colorful pages, Gevinesa could almost feel the intensity of her brother's glare. But she didn't care. Her heart ached for Zetara, the simple young woman that had been her personal handmaiden and her dearest friend for so many years, and who was now probably buried in a cold and anonymous grave somewhere on their estate near Divestelan. Neither of the men saw the tears that streamed silently down Gevinesa's cheeks or her little sister wiping them gently away with a handkerchief as Gevinesa attempted to read on in a firm voice.

21. *An Evening in the Tavern*

Semanta, the proprietor's wife, kept the promise she made to Nova to the letter. She told only one very dear friend, whom she trusted completely, about the events in the tavern that morning. That dear friend also told only one other dear friend about what she had heard from the tavern owner's wife. Before evening, the whole town knew every last detail of the mysterious incident.

The townspeople weren't blind, nor were they dim. Although Vilam never knew it, at least a dozen eyes watched him go into the tavern shortly after sunrise and remain there for the rest of the morning. Several of those witnesses were shrewd—and curious—enough to take their midmorning break in the tavern, making silent observations, coming to conclusions, and promptly relaying their findings to their neighbors. At noon, dozens of alert and probing eyes, foremost those of the potter's wife, Lutrisya, followed Folan as he ran into the street like some madman to apprehend the Lady Utalya's handmaiden and then proceeded to drag her into his tavern. When the handmaiden emerged a short while later with the stranger in tow, most of the town was informed in minutes.

But reliable information was not easy to come by, which made the mystery even more intriguing. After the handmaiden had returned to Her Excellency's lodge, it seemed as if every available resource had dried up. The handmaiden's companion, Catyana, was of absolutely no use, although she was one of their own. Her family had always been very close regarding town gossip, but since she had become friends with Nova it had gone from bad to worse. When Semanta's account therefore trickled out that afternoon, the new revelations were soaked up like fresh rain after a drought.

Consequently it was not surprising that many of the townspeople were on the street and heading towards the tavern when the group walked into town that evening. Natilya and Tanola were walking behind Catyana, Nova, and Vilam. The women had linked arms and were talking quietly, so Vilam was left to himself to take a closer look at his surroundings.

He was astonished at the many lights he perceived. He hadn't noticed them before because they blended so well into the environment. Ground lamps, which could hardly be distinguished from normal paving stones during the day, were installed at regular intervals near the edges of the lane, illuminating its boundaries. Set back from both sides of the road, waist-high lamps alternated with full-sized lanterns, creating a picturesque avenue of warm luminescence. Similar welcoming lights shimmered through the curtained windows and on the walls of the various buildings.

"Excuse me, Nova. I'm astonished to see that the entire town is illuminated. Do you have a network of electric power?"

"Electric? No, why should we use such a thing? Our culture is founded upon light. We employ an optical pulse system. In every lamp the pulse acts as a tiny flash tube for a small light amplification module. The amplifier ionizes the lamp, which is refocused by mirrors or crystals. The power comes from the solar generators we saw this afternoon. They're not only used to power the pumps for the water system, but also for the light pulse system we use for lighting and heating."

"Heating?"

"Yes. A light amplifier can be used to heat a substance to several thousand degrees, if necessary. I believe that, for this purpose, some simple amplification medium such as carbon dioxide is used. The heated water is then pumped through ceramic conduits, which are usually built into the floors of the buildings."

"Absolutely ingenious. How did you come by such a system?"

"Oh, it has been in use for decades now. Mainly thanks to Elder Yonatan and his mentor before him, Tilantes."

"Ah, yes. I should have known. Do you know how they came about these discoveries?"

"Well, from what I recall, when Tilantes was still very young—this must have been almost three hundred years ago—he became infatuated by natural but seldom occurring luminous phenomena, such as auroras, ball lightning, and earth lights. He studied them intensively and attempted to reproduce them in his workshop. An example of this might be the generation of luminescence by applying pressure to crystals. But his most brilliant innovations were most likely founded upon his work regarding the ionization of substances, and the possibility of using magnetic fields to control and stabilize the incandescent vapors that were produced in this manner. His most gifted student, Yonatan, continued and improved upon his work. The result of this research you see here everywhere around you."

"Very interesting. Is anyone continuing his work?"

"Yes. I've heard that Elder Yonatan has found one promising young student to whom he is passing on his art. Although he did initiate the one or other apprentice in the past, he stated that he's never found anyone as talented as this. I'm curious to meet this student myself, but I'm sorry to say that I haven't been able to discover who he is yet."

Vilam became thoughtful. He wondered if these people understood the implications of the knowledge they had acquired. Were they conscious of the fact that they stood upon the threshold to a completely new form of technology, a technology with possibly terrifying repercussions?

His musing was interrupted by a disturbance ahead. Several guards in the uniforms of the western houses were standing around a wagon that had stopped in the middle of the road, and were laughing at the spectacle that presented itself. One of their comrades, a corporal and by far the tallest and heaviest of them, was attempting to force the chyeves pulling the wagon to move on.

The chyeves wasn't a sleek pedigree like the ones ridden by cavaliers, but a simple draft beast. It had powerful hindquarters and massive fetlocks, well suited to pulling carts. Despite its designation as a beast of burden, its mane was full and well-groomed and its thick, curly pelt of a soft, creamy-brown texture. But its floppy ears weren't twitching playfully. They were laid back flat against its head, and its gentle, brown eyes, which should have been studying its surroundings in an intelligent and inquisitive manner, expressed agony. It lifted its head once more to give forth a pitiful bellow of pain from its short, rounded muzzle as the guard raised his arm and beat it with the flat of his sword. He wasn't being very tender about it, either. It was plain that he was putting his weight into each blow.

"Get on now, ya stupid beast." *Whack!* "Come on, hurry it up." *Whack!* "I haven't got all night, ya damn brute." *Whack!*

Laughter from his comrades followed each one of the beast's pained bawls.

"If you want to know what a man is really like, then observe the way he treats his wife or his animals," Nova whispered to her two companions. She gently let go of Catyana's arm and stepped determinedly up to the guard. "Excuse me, friend, but the chyeves is in pain. I must ask you to stop beating him."

The comrades' laughter ceased abruptly and they stepped back, astonished at the handmaiden's resolve while apprehensively eyeing her robes.

The corporal himself, though, looked her brashly in the eye. "Eh, what? And who do you think you are, its nanny?"

Laughter again poured forth from his comrades when they perceived that their comrade wasn't being intimidated by the handmaiden's resolute manner.

"Get outta here, this is none of your *coritan hi'tev!*" he retorted.

He raised his sword to strike the beast again, but Nova intervened once more by stepping between him and the tormented creature. She placed a hand gently on the chyeves's back, but her eyes were ablaze with an inner fire.

"I'm sorry, but I must insist. Please stop beating him immediately," she said, her voice stern.

"What the…? Will you get out o' my way?"

The corporal turned his sword and was going to shove her away with its pommel, but his arm was seized from behind in a viselike grip. Vilam turned the corporal around to face him using only the hand with which he had arrested the guard's arm.

"I suggest you do as the lady says," he said, his voice as cold as ice.

The corporal was almost a head taller than Vilam, but he cried out as Vilam casually applied more pressure, causing him to drop his sword. Vilam pulled him to the side, giving Nova room to work, and released his arm. Nova shot him a grateful glance, then turned towards the beast and tenderly fondled its neck.

"There, there, now, I'm not going to hurt you."

The chyeves rubbed its warm muzzle gratefully against her open palm. She stooped and lifted the beast's left front leg onto her lap, then examined its shank.

"There we go, just as I thought."

She pulled a splinter from the chyeves's limb, gently set its hoof back on the ground, and held the splinter to the light for all to see.

"The poor animal must have hurt itself about three days ago, and I fear the wound has become infected." She turned towards the guard. "If you don't want the injury to cause permanent damage, you will have to tend to it immediately."

The corporal was still holding his arm in pain and shot her an angry glance. He mumbled something into his beard and unhurriedly picked up his sword. Then he gestured to his men, and they unhitched the chyeves from the cart. When they had completed the task, Nova pointed them in the direction of the veterinary. Catyana had her eyes fixed on her in anticipation, but Nova shook her head and Catyana

dropped her gaze in disappointment. One of the guards took
hold of the animal while four of the others began pulling the
wagon, spurred on by the jeers of their comrades.

After Nova had ensured that her instructions were being
followed, the party continued on their route to the tavern.
When they reached it a minute later, Vilam recognized that
the front of the tavern was not flat but convex and tapered
slightly, so that the windows were leaning somewhat inward
towards the top. Such a construction would allow the sun to
shine in from sunrise to sunset, filling the tavern with light all
day long.

When they entered, the hall was already quite full, but
Folan saw them immediately and bustled towards them as
quickly as he was able to get through the crowd.

"My friends, how wonderful! Welcome, welcome!" he
cried over the din. "Look, my friend, I have reserved your
preferred table." He smiled at Vilam as he led them towards
the back of the left side of the hall where Vilam had been
sitting that morning.

The noise subsided substantially when they entered.
Vilam could hear whispers on all sides that were probably
variations of "Covatal." He felt embarrassed but was glad that
their table was in a back corner.

Folan pulled him aside. "Your quarters have been prepared
for you. May I show you to them?"

Vilam nodded, and Folan directed him through a door in
the back of the hall near his table. A corridor led to the back
of the building where they turned right.

Folan opened the first door on the left, switched on the
light, and ushered Vilam inside. "This is it. I hope it suits your
needs."

He walked over to the far side of the room and opened
two sections of a triple-winged, windowed door leading out

onto a veranda and the gardens, letting in some of the warm evening air.

Vilam was astonished. The room was wonderful and very spacious. The ceiling and walls were tiled with whitely glazed wooden panels, the furniture made of some type of oiled spruce. A large, comfortable-looking double bed adorned the left side of the room. The furniture was not only of excellent workmanship, but each piece was individually crafted and designed, every one of them a singular and organically structured work of art.

"The lavatory and bathrooms are in the hall, as you will remember from your visit in the morning," Folan said.

Vilam turned to his host. "This is absolutely luxurious. Thank you very much, my friend."

Folan was very pleased and beamed at his guest. "I'm glad you like it."

He bowed himself out of the room and shut the door, leaving his guest to himself.

Vilam walked out onto the veranda, which was raised slightly above the courtyard. Wooden benches adorned the scene. The cobbled walkways leading away from the court all converged upon the gardens. A sculptured fountain decorated the center of the court. He felt that he could really enjoy himself here. He turned from the peaceful scene and closed the doors.

When he returned to the hall, Catyana and the two maidservants were already seated comfortably at the table. Catyana smiled up at him and motioned to one of two empty chairs that faced the hall. The women had arranged themselves so that everyone could comfortably see the stage from where they sat. He took the seat further away from Catyana, leaving the empty chair next to her for Nova, whom he couldn't spot anywhere.

He finally discovered her on the other side of the hall near the stage, where several musicians were tuning their instruments. She was speaking to a man approximately twice her age. They held each other's arms near the elbows and looked deeply into each other's eyes. Whatever they were talking about, it seemed quite important.

The man had dark hair and a beard. He was dressed in a robe similar to Nova's, but more fitted to the forms of the male physique, which didn't pronounce the waist quite as much as the female dress and left more room for the upper torso. The man's robes also didn't flow down all the way to the ground, but only to a little below the knee. Under the robe the man wore long, comfortable trousers, and a black cloak covered his attire. The cloak's material seemed to be of a coarser and more robust material than the cloaks of the Lady's acolytes. He had moccasins similar to Nova's, but again of a more masculine form.

Vilam believed he could distinguish a platinum brooch with a golden border pinned to the man's breast. The brooch had the same shape as the solid golden ornament he had seen on the Lady Utalya: a circle, which represented the Selani, or the spirit, superimposed by the Triphyllon, the rounded, three-leafed symbol for eternity. The brooch had three tiered layers. The top two layers were platinum, but the third and lowest layer was made of gold, designating the man as the High Priest. Vilam was aware of the multifaceted symbolism inherent to this composite icon. Just thinking about it always left him bewildered, and he quickly diverted his gaze.

Standing next to the pair was an elderly man with gentle but wise features. The expression on his face was intent as he listened to their conversation. He had a robe and cloak similar to that of the younger man. His long hair and beard were completely white. Pinned to his breast was a solid platinum brooch.

In the meantime, Nova and the younger man had

completed their conversation and now touched cheeks in a light embrace that characterized mutual respect. She then turned to the older man who embraced her lovingly, like a daughter, and gave her a few whispered instructions. She nodded and planted a gentle kiss on his cheek, then turned and walked back to her table while the two men quickly left the tavern. Vilam watched them leave and noted that people made it a point to keep a respectful distance and bow to the pair as they passed.

On her way to their table, Nova was stopped once more by an authoritative, middle-aged gentleman in elegant clothes. Nova listened carefully to what he had to say. It seemed, though, that her answer didn't turn out quite as he had wished, for his face expressed annoyance. She nodded coolly and continued on her way to the back of the hall. When she arrived at the table, she unhooked her cloak and draped it over her seat, then sat down between Catyana and Vilam.

"So, how did you like your quarters?" she asked pleasantly.

"They're absolutely exquisite. By the way, I noticed the two men you were talking to near the stage. Was my eyesight accurate? Did I actually see a platinum brooch with a golden border pinned to the younger man's breast?"

"Yes, you observed correctly. He is Vordalin, the High Priest. The man next to him was Elder Yonatan."

"Ah, I see. I'm very sorry if I appear to be prying, but it seemed to me that you know them well."

Nova turned towards him. "Yes, as a matter of fact, I do. I have been with the Lady Utalya for many years and so it is almost impossible for me not to know them. The Lady asked me to bring them a message, since she wasn't coming herself. Does that satisfy your curiosity?" she asked with a playful smile.

"Yes, of course. *Votalaran,* I'm sorry, I didn't mean to be so obtrusive."

"*Tezatal,* that's alright."

"Although I really would be eager to get to know Elder Yonatan, if that were somehow possible."

"Well, that might actually be possible, for he will be coming to the conference. If you decide to come also, you might be able to make his acquaintance. He regretted that he could not stay for leisure tonight because he will be leaving for Tolares early tomorrow morning and still has an important matter to settle this evening. The High Priest, though, will not be attending the conference. He stated that he has urgent business farther west and needs to depart immediately." Her last words were marked with quiet concern.

"May I ask who the other gentleman was that stopped you on your way back to the table?"

"My, you are an inquisitive one, aren't you?" she teased. "But it is no secret. It was Menirel, the Mayor of Nadil. And to forestall your next question, he asked me whether the Order has come to any official conclusions yet regarding your person."

"Oh, he did? What did you tell him?" Vilam asked anxiously.

"I told him to mind his own business and to consult with his Videsian friends if he wanted further information."

Vilam gaped at her. "You told him that?"

She returned his stare with a smile. "Of course not, Vilam. At least not in so many words," she added mischievously. "He might have received a different answer if he hadn't attempted to threaten Folan."

"He threatened Folan? In what way?"

"It doesn't matter. It is an old feud. Menirel has never particularly cherished Folan. Another good reason to distrust our dear mayor."

"Well, what did you tell him, then?"

Nova didn't reply, but only smiled to herself. From his experience that afternoon he knew that it would be impossible to coax further information from her.

Folan soon arrived at their table with refreshments: clear water for Vilam and a light, sweet cider for the others. In the meantime, the hall had become quiet. Vilam leaned towards Nova.

"It seems as if everyone is waiting for something," he whispered to her.

"Yes," she whispered in return. "Evenings in a tavern of this class traditionally commence with a song or some unique piece of instrumental music, and everyone is wondering what Folan has come up with."

They didn't have to wait long. A few minutes later Folan stepped onto the stage, and the silence became conspicuous.

"My dear friends and patrons," the proprietor said. "It is with the utmost pleasure that I may present a very special guest here tonight. The renowned vocalist and musician, Vodana, has graced us with her presence."

A surprised murmur went through the crowd.

"Since her name is already introduction enough, I will say no more and leave the stage to her. My friends, I give you— Vodana."

He bowed to the applause of the audience and extended his hand to the side, then quickly removed himself from the scene. As the lights in the hall were dimmed, a noble figure walked onto the stage and faced the audience. Catyana turned and squeezed Nova's hands, her face flushed with excitement. Then she leaned over and whispered something to Tanola and Natilya. The three young women were radiant with anticipation.

The artist was slightly taller than Nova, but it was difficult to judge her age. Her face appeared young, yet seemed wizened with experience. She made a stately impression in her cream and scarlet colored gown. Her thick, dark hair was alternately braided, giving her an elegant look.

Everything was now perfectly still. The singer stood alone, highlighted on the stage, her eyes far away, contemplating. In the background, a flute took up a single, soft note, rising on a mellow crescendo. A harp subtly joined it, outlining the harmony and providing substance to the flute's tone. The other instruments delicately joined in, taking up the theme in different voices, luring the audience into the rising and falling harmonies.

Softly, the artist's voice joined the instruments, entering into the intertwined strains of melody almost unnoticeably. But soon her clear voice rose gently above the polyphonic themes and subtly dominated the flowing musical structure.

Vilam was completely entranced. He had never heard anything so beautiful. He sat back in his chair, closed his eyes, and gave himself up to the song.

Alin
Peniranu
Camar nevilas lacemitarae madan?
Coni dineval lalovanirae vosal?
Cadan mitalen lavetenarae vilas?
Alin ten'alin
Selanae netarae lu tenari
Sutani saratae l'adanisai
Satulen tesira l'ambarena
Alin vor alin
Isanai tenarata
I'ulavan tenevarae
Imala t'ulavara
Alin cel alin
Pesatas corata se linosa

Porodi miratae se velana
Piralai cosira se nimata
Alin set'alin
Cadan Demantar ataer pilavaratae?
Coni Elinar Adaer sitavaratae?
Camar Selanae anur enavimarae?
Peniranu
Alin

Again
We ask
How could darkness slay goodness?
Where could evil obscure love?
When could hate consume light?
Time after time
The wind blows through the reeds
Doves sail through the heavens
Emptiness was filled
By and by
All joy went away
And eternity held its breath
Kindness ceased
Here and there
Little things become important
Golden squirrels rejoice in the sun
All the earth sings of life
To and fro
When will their Dragons breathe fire?
Where will His Angels take wing?
How will our Spirit be revived?
We ask
Again

Even after the final notes had long diminished into silence, the hall remained completely still, as if the audience had been enchanted. Vodana stepped to the very front of the stage and bowed, breaking the spell. The audience erupted into violent applause. Vodana bowed once more, then turned and moved off to the back of the hall.

Order gradually returned to the tavern, the musicians began playing some simpler pieces of background music, and the crowd resumed their various activities. Vilam noticed that Nova was watching two groups of guards near the stage with concern. One of them was the same group of western guards they had encountered earlier that evening. The other was dressed in the forest green attire of the eastern provinces. Listening intently, Vilam caught snatches of the taunting remarks they were throwing at each other over the din.

"...better things you can do with an Angel," one of the western guards sneered. This must have been followed by an obscene gesture, for there was a burst of coarse laughter from his colleagues.

"You better watch your mouth, you dirty..." The rest of the eastern guard's retort was lost in the general commotion.

"Oh, yeah? I'll show you where you can stick your Dragons!" a western guard scoffed.

It was apparent that the rude allusions to Angels and Dragons were a deliberate reference to Vodana's song. Vilam turned his attention back to his companions, but he felt that it was unfortunate that the two groups were sitting so close together. It could become a problem.

Catyana was still in raptures. "I've never heard anything so lovely. How can a single person bring an art to such perfection?"

"Yes, it is marvelous, isn't it?" Natilya answered. "From what I've heard, she composes every song herself."

"I've heard that she can play almost any instrument and generally practices six to eight hours a day," Tanola said. "Oh, it's just a silly dream of mine, but wouldn't it be wonderful if we could meet... *Tev'anar!*"

Folan had suddenly appeared at their table, and with him was—Vodana. The three young women just sat there with their mouths open, Tanola with her hands over her lips, embarrassed by the traitorous expletive that had just escaped them. Folan nodded to the party with a wink and a smile and disappeared again as quickly as he had come.

Nova rose from her seat, quietly radiant. She gently kissed the newcomer and then embraced her in a fervent but tender hug.

Vodana held her back at arm's length, her smile as radiant as Nova's. "Well, little sister, what a surprise to see you here."

"Or maybe not such a surprise. Oh, Vodana, why didn't you inform us that you were coming?"

"Because then it wouldn't have been quite such a surprise."

"Well, you've certainly succeeded." Nova hugged her once more. "Dearest sister, it's so good to see you again." Then she turned to the young women, who were still sitting at the table in stunned silence. "But I think there are some admirers of yours here that are also very eager to meet you."

Vodana moved around the table and embraced each of the three younger women, who had regained their senses enough to rise from their seats.

Nova then introduced her to Vilam, who had immediately risen from his seat when Vodana had appeared. "Sister, I would like you to meet a friend of ours, Vilam."

Vodana's deep eyes locked with his, searching. "I'm very pleased to meet you, Vilam."

"No, it's my pleasure. I'm honored to meet the artist who performed that beautiful catoptric inversion. I will never forget it," Vilam answered.

Her eyes grew wide with astonishment and she almost blushed, but then she bowed her head. "Glad to be of service. It is the greatest compliment for an artist to learn that her work was genuinely recognized and appreciated."

They sat down again, Vodana taking a seat which had been placed between Nova and Catyana. The three young women were gradually losing their shyness and began asking the famous artist various questions. Vilam again noticed Nova looking over to the other side of the hall, where the smirking and taunting between the two camps of guards was growing louder. She seemed apprehensive, but rejoined the conversation between her sister and the younger women.

"Vodana, may I invite you to stay with us at the Lady Utalya's manse? I'm sure you'd be more than welcome."

Tanola and Natilya held their breath.

"Why, yes, Tinasa, I was hoping that would be possible," the artist replied.

While the two acolytes attempted to contain their rapture, Vilam smiled to himself at the pet name Vodana had used for her younger sister. So that was what Nova was called at home: Tinasa, 'Little Blossom.' It reminded him of the pet name his foster parents had given him after he had been found. A silent shudder went through him as memories resurfaced of the Time Before. That was what he called it, the Time Before, with capital letters.

Vilam was suddenly torn from his reflections by the escalating clamor on the far side of the hall.

"You take that back, ya slimy newt!" an eastern guard shouted, jumping to his feet.

"On the day hell freezes over, ya stinkin' toad!" a western guard snapped, pushing his red, angry face towards his adversary.

"Go eat yer mother's britches! No wonder your friends have to watch their backs around ya!"

At this, the western corporal, whom they had dealt with earlier and whose expression had become more and more livid during this exchange, leaped to his comrade's aid.

"Eh, what? You're gonna eat your words!" he roared, and landed his enormous fist squarely on the transgressor's jaw, sending him flying backwards into a table.

The two groups were now on their feet, wreaking havoc. Any attempt at order in the hall had ceased and almost everyone was standing. Vilam saw that Nova had also risen from her seat and was inching forward, trying to get through to see if she could be of assistance, but there was not enough room, with the tavern packed as it was and everyone trying to get a look at what was going on. She gave up and scrutinized the situation sharply as it developed.

Folan then made one of the biggest mistakes of his life. He apparently hadn't realized that the quarrel had already exceeded the boiling point and was just on the verge of erupting into something really ugly. In an attempt to restore order, he bustled right between the quarreling parties, his hands waving in the air.

Nova saw it, attempted once more to press forwards, and Vilam could just hear her whispering to herself, "No, Folan, please don't do this."

"My dear friends, please, get a grip on yourselves," Folan exclaimed. "Can't we settle this like grown men?"

The corporal, who seemed to be leading the rabble, grabbed Folan by the front of his shirt. "Eh, what? Who the *s'nevilas* do you think you are? Get the *cost'corvos'* out o' my way!"

Several people gasped at the guard's vicious rape of their beautiful language as he pushed Folan to the side and started back at his rivals.

Folan really was a very courageous little man. He stepped

right back in front of the guard. Vilam could see that Nova no longer had any hope. She closed her eyes, helpless to stop what she knew must follow.

"Please, my friend. You'll damage the fixtures," Folan cried.

"Oh, yeah? Here, I'll give you some real damage to worry about."

The corporal pulled his sword and raised his arm to strike.

There was a swish and a dull, wooden thump, then the loud clatter of metal on the tiled floor as the corporal's sword fell unchecked to the ground. The guard had been violently wrenched backwards and his arm pinned to the wooden column behind him. In the ensuing silence, the corporal attempted to get back on his feet. He looked up to see who was holding him, but cried out in shock.

The end of a silvery arrow protruded ominously from his forearm.

22. *The Way Station*

Bejad leaned into the wind, almost touching his mare's neck with his head as he raced through the bright night. Vinesa's escape route had been well thought out, and he had received outstanding pedigreed chyevi at each stop. He had therefore made excellent time, covering close to ten leagues every hour. By midafternoon the blue waters of Lake Divestelan, which had been visible between gaps in the forest to the south, had been left behind. Towards evening he had passed Novesta, the fervent gleam of the setting sun at his back reflecting from the roofs and windows of the noble town. He had seen the dim lights of Pitaren on his right about twenty minutes ago. If he could keep this pace, he would reach Cemasena in the early hours of the morning and Tolares shortly after sunrise.

Had he been in the eastern provinces, the lights of the townships and farms he now passed would have been much brighter, but the technology being advanced by the Selanian Order did not yet extend so far west. He supposed it was a slow process, training the necessary personnel to produce and maintain the equipment. The population of the secluded western regions therefore often used very primitive forms of lighting, sometimes even falling back on torches, oil lamps, or archaic methods to produce phosphorescence.

His mare was beginning to froth at the mouth. She had been his most energetic mount yet and had needed hardly any coaxing, enjoying the feel of the wind in her mane as she sped forwards. But even she was now beginning to tire. He was grateful that the next way station lay just ahead.

He had hardly formed the thought when he rounded a bend and saw lights before him shining from the windows and porch of a small farmhouse. His mare bawled gleefully, sensing that her journey was over and that a cozy stall and fresh oats awaited her.

As Bejad galloped into the farmyard and reined his mount, the door of the house opened and a very young woman in a worn and patched dress stood silhouetted in the entrance.

"Who's there?" she called fearfully, staring out into the darkness.

"A courier of the Lady Gevinesa," Bejad answered as he dismounted.

The young woman exhaled in relief. She turned and spoke some reassuring words which Bejad couldn't hear. Then she gently closed the door, took down the lantern hanging on the wall and stepped out into the night to take his mare.

"*Ulavelan mada, vil'anar.* Good evening, my friend. It is not often that the Lady sends us a courier these days," she said softly.

"Yes, and I fear that I will be the last. These are difficult times, and until they are abated, the Lady has found it necessary to go into hiding."

The young woman was dismayed at his words. "Then let us hope that the Covatal arrives soon," she replied.

He looked into her pallid face. "There is always hope," he said.

She sighed and turned back to his mare. "Let me tend to your mount, and then I will get you some refreshments."

"*Sin', votal, tsemires ana la jevar esa.* No, please, allow me to help you."

She looked at him in surprise. "Alright, follow me," she replied, then turned and led the mare towards the stable.

They crossed the yard, and Bejad opened the door for her, allowing her to enter with the chyeves. She hung the lantern on a post and proceeded to undo the saddle. Bejad helped her.

When they were putting away the harness, he noticed that there were eight stalls, six of them occupied. Two of them contained excellent steeds, similar to the mare he had been riding for the past few hours. Four stalls held simple farm beasts.

What especially caught Bejad's attention was a massive, cast-iron semblance of the Sword of Selanae, which was attached to the main supporting beam in the center of the stable. He knew that very pious families living in the country sometimes did this, because they hoped for Anae's blessing and guidance at all times.

He took a brush and began to curry the mare's reddish-brown pelt, pulling gently through the many whirls in her coat. The young woman pitched fresh straw into one of the empty stalls. When she had finished she turned and watched him for a moment.

"Where did you learn to care for a chyeves?" she asked shyly.

He smiled at her. "I grew up on a farm. I've been around animals all my life."

"Oh. How is it then that you became such an important official?"

He laughed. "I am no important official. I'm just a simple deacon of the Selanian Order."

"Oh, you are in the Order?"

"Yes. Why does that astonish you?"

"Well, it's been a long time since someone from the Order has visited us. Nowadays all we see are those ominous Videsian priests who seem to be lurking everywhere. It was difficult enough, hiding the Lady's chyevi from them and the guards that patrol the area regularly. Why aren't you wearing your robes?"

"I've been a liaison officer for Her Eminence during the

past five years, doing intelligence work in Divestelan. But I suppose that time is now over. I'm on my way to Tolares and am not planning on returning."

She stared at him with round eyes. "You know the High Priestess?"

"Yes, although it's been several years since I've seen her."

"What is she like?"

"I don't know what to tell you. Kind, gentle, determined. She even has a sense of humor. I think she's the best thing that has happened to us for many years."

She sighed. "I wish so much that I could join the Order."

"Why don't you?"

"My four brothers have all been drafted into the guard. I'm the only one left to help my parents work the farm."

Bejad shook his head. "I don't understand why so many men are being drafted. That's one of the mysteries we haven't been able to solve," he said quietly. "The men disappear into the mountains and are never seen or heard of again."

The young woman paled. "Do you think my brothers might be dead?"

Bejad looked at her somberly. "I'm sorry, I just don't know." He considered her for a moment. "May I know your name?" he asked carefully.

"Yes. I am Netira."

"And I am Bejad. Your parents are devout followers of Anae's Golden Path, aren't they?"

"Why do you ask?"

He nodded in the direction of the symbol of the Holy Sword.

She smiled. "You're very observant. Yes, it's true. My parents were always very meticulous in their instruction. As a matter of fact, it was their love and kindness that first aroused my desire to join the Order."

"I see. But tell me, Netira, why do your parents let you

tend to the Lady's couriers?"

"I'm sorry. I hope you weren't offended by their behavior. My parents are both in bad health and don't care for the night air. Actually, we all prefer to stay inside after it gets dark."

"I understand," he answered.

He had finished currying the mare and led her into the newly prepared stall. Netira filled the trough with fresh water and the manger with oats. The mare bawled her gratitude and drank deeply. Then she buried her muzzle in the crib.

Bejad and Netira smiled at each other.

"Chyevi are so easy to please," Netira said. "All they need is a warm and cozy stall and some fresh oats. I just love caring for them."

"Yes, I see that you do." He looked at her more closely. Netira was no extraordinary beauty, but her features were pleasant and her expression kind and gentle. She was quite short, hardly rising to his chin, with delicate features contrasted by dark eyebrows, full lips, and prominent cheekbones. She wore her thick, black hair unbound so that it streamed down her back, as did the priestesses of the Selanian Order.

She regarded him with a questioning gaze. "Is something wrong?"

"No, I was just wondering what kind of priestess you would make."

Her smile lighted her dark eyes and brightened her features. Bejad caught his breath. Maybe there was more beauty here than he had anticipated.

"Listen, Netira, the Lady Gevinesa wishes to make a gift to you and your parents. She wants you to keep the two chyevi that you've been holding for her. You may do with them whatever you like. The Lady herself suggests that you sell them."

Netira gasped. "Why, those chyevi are worth a fortune. We would be well-off to the end of our days."

"As I said, they're yours to keep. Think of them as a gesture of the Lady's kindness."

Netira shook her head. There were tears in her eyes. "That's more than just kindness, Bejad. That's a miracle. Have you forgotten that she used to be known as the Demoness of Divestelan? But we never stopped praying for her. I can hardly believe that Anae has answered our prayers so completely."

It was now Bejad's turn to stare in awe. "Netira, you don't care about the money, do you?"

"Of course I care about the money. Who wouldn't? I want my parents to be provided for. But isn't such a phenomenal change of heart more precious than all the money in the world?"

"Yes, you're right, of course."

Netira stood pondering for a moment. "Oh, Bejad, this changes everything. I know I'm asking far too much, but would you please take me with you?" she pleaded.

"Take you with me?" he echoed in astonishment.

"Yes, please take me with you. If we may keep the chyevi, then my parents could sell them and the farm and buy a simple home in Pitaren. They would be safe there."

"I don't know, Netira."

"Oh, please, Bejad. You don't know what it's like, living out here. So many of the farms around us have been attacked, the inhabitants butchered like cattle, and you know what they do to the women. I don't know how much longer we can take it, constantly living in fear. The only reason we stayed on was to serve the Lady and her couriers. And even so we were hardly getting by. We would never have survived if it hadn't been for the additional income we were receiving from the Lady. Believe me, my parents would be so relieved if they knew I was in a safe place. I promise I won't be a burden to you. And as soon as we get to Tolares, you can turn me over to the priestesses. I know they'll take good care of me. Maybe they'll even let me join the Order."

Bejad regarded her solemnly for a moment. "You're really serious about this, aren't you?"

She nodded, not once taking her eyes from his face.

"Netira, how old are you?"

"I am twenty-four."

He sighed. "Well, there won't be a problem if you wish to join the Order."

Her face brightened again. "Do you really think so?"

"I'm sure of it. But it will slow down my journey considerably, with an additional person on my mount."

Netira shook her head. "No, Bejad, we'll take a second mount. My parents can sell the one remaining, and I'll sell mine in Tolares. I'm sure to get an even better price for it there, and I can send the proceeds to my parents later."

Bejad smiled. "You have a very quick and practical mind, Netira."

She returned the smile. "It's very kind of you to say so. But what do you expect of a farm girl that had to learn to survive under such circumstances?"

Bejad knew what the High Priestess required of him. He took a deep breath. "Alright, let's get our chyevi ready."

"Oh, Bejad, thank you." She took one of his hands and raised it to her lips. Her eyes were moist. "I'll never forget you for this," she whispered.

They quickly saddled the two steeds, led them into the farmyard, and tied them to the porch. Netira entered the house to inform her parents. A moment later she came back.

"Bejad, I just want to pack a few personal things," she said. "I'll be with you in a minute."

"What about your parents?"

"I'm sorry, Bejad. Please don't be angry with them, but they would rather remain in the house."

"That's alright. I'll come in with you." He moved towards the door.

She gently took his arm to stop him. "No, Bejad, please. They're very frightened. Let them say their good-byes to me in private." Her eyes pleaded with him.

Bejad sighed. "I understand. It's tragic that conditions have grown so desolate that simple farmers can no longer greet their guests."

"Thank you, Bejad. You're so kind," she said gently.

She squeezed his arm in gratitude and slipped back into the house. Bejad untied their chyevi and mounted his steed, holding the reins of the second animal for his new companion.

Netira returned quickly. She only had a small purse with her, which she strapped behind her saddle. Then she swung herself nimbly onto her mount, and the two riders galloped into the moonlit night.

23. *Prophecy*

The guest hall was completely silent. Nova turned with everybody else in the direction from which the arrow had come. For just an instant, her eyes opened wide, and she forgot to breathe.

The Prophet's Bow glistened menacingly in the dimly lit tavern.

Vilam stood on his chair, motionless, his right foot braced against the table for support. He held the bow and a second arrow firmly in his slightly bent, outstretched right arm, while his left hand hovered stationary behind his left ear from where he had released the bowstring just seconds before. Slowly, he lowered his arms and walked over to where the guard was pinned against the column, stepping boldly over the table and through the stunned crowd which parted before him like a wave. The corporal quailed before his smoldering gaze. Vilam turned to the guards that had participated in the quarrel.

"You fools!" he said quietly, suppressed fury evident in his voice, but in the shocked silence his words could be heard in every corner of the great hall. "Don't you realize what you are doing? Until now, your civilization has been characterized by love, wisdom, and righteousness, and you have been blessed for it. You have enjoyed peace and prosperity, your thriving culture has produced such wonderful works of artistry and beauty. You stand as yet united, with one mind and one tongue. There is no confusion of speech that would hinder an unfettered exchange of knowledge so that you could become greater still. You have truly created a society that others could only dream of, and yet you go and throw it all away with your petty squabbling over wealth and power!

"If only you had seen what I have seen. So much pain and suffering because people refused to recognize the growing darkness and narrowness of their own hearts. The chaos unleashed when a race was cursed with the confusion of tongues and could no longer understand each other's speech. The desolation of a world after all the fountains of the deep and the floodgates of the heavens burst open to utterly destroy everything that anyone had ever lived and fought for.

"'For so speaks the High and Exalted One, who inhabits eternity and whose name is Holy: I dwell in the High and Holy Place, and also with those who are contrite and humble in spirit, to revive the spirit of the humble, and to revive the heart of the contrite.

"'But the wicked are like the tossing sea that cannot keep

still; its waters toss up mire and mud. There is no peace, says the Lord, for the wicked.'

"Beware, for you have been warned."

There were tears of pain and anger in his eyes as he turned his back upon the men he had rebuked and walked towards his table.

Nova watched the events silently from where she stood and noted the reaction of the overwhelmed crowd around her. When Vilam returned, she gazed at him with lips compressed in contained passion, a fire burning in her eyes.

"Well, my friend, no matter how little you wanted anything to do with the title that seemed to be such a burden to you, I fear you are stuck with it now."

She turned, picked up her cloak, and beckoned for her sister and her companions, who were all a bit shaken but had collected themselves, to follow. She took the amazed Vilam by the arm and pulled him towards the stunned proprietor while the whispering crowd withdrew from their path, awe and reverence mirrored in their eyes.

Folan was standing in front of the pinned guard, scratching the back of his head and not knowing what to do. Pain had replaced shock and the corporal was beginning to moan, but he pulled himself together when he saw Vilam returning. Blood was soaking through the fabric around the location where the arrow had penetrated his forearm. Nova took a sharp scalpel from a pocketbook that Tanola handed her.

She fixed the guard with a penetrating gaze. "Will you allow me to inspect your injury?"

The corporal eyed her apprehensively but nodded. Nova cut through the fabric with several skillful movements and examined the wound.

"Vilam, could you please remove the arrow from the

column? I need to examine the exit wound."

Vilam nodded and took a small cloth from the left side of the bow, which he was still holding. He held the bow out to Folan. "Thank you, my friend."

Folan took the deadly instrument, staring at it as if he were seeing a ghost.

Vilam turned back to the guard with the cloth, which seemed to be made of vulcanized rubber. He looked the corporal in the eye, and Nova could sense the fear coming from the corporal's sweat and stench.

"Brace yourself; this is going to hurt," Vilam said.

The corporal nodded and clenched his teeth. Vilam steadied the guard's arm near the wound with his right hand and gripped the arrow with the cloth. He began to move the arrow in tight circles while pulling steadily. The impact of the arrow must have been immense, for although Vilam seemed strong, it took all his strength to loosen it.

The corporal's breath was now coming in short gasps. After a few more circular motions, Vilam was finally able to withdraw the arrow from the wood. He relaxed his grip, placed his right hand behind the pinned arm, and eased the guard's arm away from the column together with the arrow.

They settled the corporal, who was growing faint from shock, in a chair and placed his injured arm on the table. Nova sat in a chair next to him. She removed the remaining fabric, felt the corporal's pulse, and inspected the wound once more, giving particular attention to the side that had been hidden from view while he was pinned to the column.

"It was a clean shot, no broken bones." She shot a meaningful glance up at Vilam. "The arrow penetrated exactly between ulna and radius." Turning back to the corporal, she said, "You are fortunate. The ulno-radial arteries were not injured. The wound will heal tolerably as soon as the arrow has been removed." Then she stood and spoke to the corporal's comrades. "Take your friend to the infirmary, and let us hope that no further trips will be necessary."

"Why are you doing this for me?" the corporal asked weakly, looking up at her.

Nova gazed down at him with a soft glow in her eyes. "Because it is our duty as servants of the Highest to love each other," she replied gently.

She helped him to rise from his chair. The other guards then supported their comrade and slunk from the tavern. Nova watched them carefully until they had left, then turned to Vilam.

"Come, my friend. I think it is time to renew our conversation regarding certain matters."

She whispered to Folan, suggesting that he clear the hall. He nodded but was white as a sheet, and Nova couldn't determine if he had really heard. She gestured to her sister and their three companions, who had been watching silently, and they quickly left the tavern, with Vilam in tow.

Once they were outside, Nova spoke softly to her friends. Tanola and Natilya agreed to take Catyana home, since Nova was engaged elsewhere. Vodana informed her that she wouldn't repair to the manse until later that evening, since she had some unfinished business in the tavern. Nova then said good-bye to the three women and her sister, embracing each in turn. The young women left in the direction of the Lady Utalya's manse, and Vodana returned to the chaos that was now audible from the tavern. Nova took Vilam's arm and pulled him around the corner of the building, disappearing towards the north end of town in order to quickly withdraw from any inquisitive eyes that might have wanted to track them.

The path Nova and Vilam followed soon led them

through a wide and open meadow. The night air was mild and pleasant. Vilatanas was shining brightly, highlighting stray cumulus clouds sailing by above, while countless stars glinted down at them from the dark sky. In the distance, to the east, the Tyenar Range was barely visible as an outline of jagged and sometimes snow-capped peaks above the darker mass of the woods. Somewhere near, a stream could be heard rushing by.

They walked briskly for a while, but Nova slowed the pace as soon as they left the last cottages behind. When she felt that they had put enough distance between themselves and the town, she broke the silence.

"I brought you here so that we could talk without being disturbed. Is that alright with you?"

"Yes, I think that might be a good idea."

They walked on for another minute while she collected her thoughts. Then she glanced at him. "Thank you, Vilam, for intervening. I really feared for Folan's life."

"I'm glad that I could be of some help."

"Your aim with the bow was outstanding."

"No, it was pure chance."

She looked up at him, astonished. Then she smiled, a playful twinkle lighting her eyes. "Well, now, if that wasn't the most pitiful attempt at modesty I've ever encountered."

"No, really, you can't draw an unfamiliar bow and expect to hit your mark on your first try. You don't know how the bow is tuned, you're not accustomed to the weight of the arrows, you don't know how the fletch was designed. It's almost impossible. There are just too many variables."

"Look, Vilam, I may not be a master at arms, but I'm not quite ignorant, either. You can't hit a mark you're aiming for dead center by chance. That would be too much of a coincidence. As you said, there are too many variables. That was either a perfect shot, or you were aiming for something else and missed, which is highly unlikely, given where the arrow ended up."

Vilam hesitated. "Well, the bow did feel pretty good in my hands, almost as if it had been made for me," he admitted. "It was excellently tuned and completely silent. I can't understand how it could remain so after all this time."

Nova glanced at him, her expression once again serious. "Thank you for being honest with me, my friend. It makes it easier for me to do what I feel we should have done all along."

"And what would that be?"

"I believe that we should have been completely frank with you from the beginning. No secrets, no mysteries, no—how would you say?—skeletons in the cupboard. At least on our part," she added, almost as an afterthought. "We decided to keep further prophecies from you, because we felt you had experienced enough for one day. I'll attempt to correct that mistake now."

He took a deep breath and nodded. "Alright, I'm ready."

"What do you know about the bow you used?"

"Well, Folan told me it was called the Prophet's Bow and was made over five hundred years ago."

"Yes, that is true. The Prophet's name was Nevacad. He foretold that the only person after him who would be able to utilize the bow as it was intended would be Covatalae, the Traveler. And so it has come to pass. Nobody since Nevacad has ever been able to handle the bow properly. Tonight was the first time in over five hundred years."

"I almost feared as much. The way everybody looked at me...But I don't understand. Why couldn't anybody else draw the bow?"

"Well, for one thing, the weight on that bowstring is absolutely enormous. I even tried it once myself, of course to no avail. I therefore first assumed that you must have some kind of superhuman strength, until I noticed how you struggled to pull the arrow from the column. You are very strong, but not that strong. How did you do it?"

"It's not really that difficult. The bow is a compound."

"Excuse me?"

"A compound bow. Weren't you aware of the pulley mechanism on the end of each limb? When you attempt to draw the bow, you must first overcome the initial drawing weight. For most compound bows, you hardly find one that draws over seventy or eighty pounds. For this bow, I might guess that the weight is almost twice that. But as soon as you get past the initial resistance, the pulley mechanism kicks in and reduces the actual holding weight to something between sixty-five and eighty percent less than the drawing weight. The Prophet's Bow has such a superb mechanism that I estimate a let-off greater than eighty percent, so the holding weight would be significantly less than thirty pounds. But when you release the bowstring, the arrow is launched with a force closer to the initial drawing weight, which is why it was so difficult to get it out of the column."

Nova stared at him, incredulous. "I can hardly believe it. So many experts have examined the bow, but nobody was able to discover the purpose of that mechanism, as if Anae had confused our senses." She shook her head. "But that might explain why nobody could draw the bow," she said, more to herself. "First of all, a person would have to be very strong to even try. Then, after the initial attempt, most people just gave up, not realizing that there would be a decline in the drawing weight. Their reverence for the weapon most likely added to the dilemma, so I assume the problem was more an enigma of the mind." She turned back to Vilam. "What is even more astonishing, though, is that you seemed to be able to discern the mechanism's function immediately."

"Even that is not such a mystery. I've worked with such bows before. I therefore knew how it must be handled from the first moment I set eyes on it."

Nova shook her head again. "Well, no matter. I do hope that you understand, though, how staggering this event is for all of us. There can hardly be a doubt anymore…"

She stopped and turned towards him, looked into his eyes. Then she cautiously squeezed his arm in several places. Finally, she lowered her gaze.

"I'm sorry. I know; it's childish, but I just wanted to be sure." She turned forwards again and they continued their walk. "You really are just an ordinary person, aren't you? Although my training has helped to prepare me, a certain sense of awe still remains. In my mind, I seem to be just as mesmerized as everyone else. I know that, when prophecies are fulfilled, they're always fulfilled by normal people, like you and me. It somehow seems so strange, though, that such a thing is possible. How could prophets predict something so far ahead? How could people, who are described in such detail so many centuries in advance, be just regular individuals? It all sounds fine in theory, but when you're suddenly confronted with reality, it seems so bizarre, almost impossible. Yet, here we are."

"Really? How can you be so sure? Couldn't your prophets have been mistaken?"

She slowly shook her head. "No, that's impossible."

"Why impossible? Because you don't wish to believe it? Would that be too much of a blow to your precious faith?"

Nova turned her eyes back to his, surprised and concerned at the sarcasm and bitterness that had surfaced so suddenly. "No, Vilam, you can't be serious."

"Well then, how can you be so certain?"

She studied the ground in front of her before she replied.

"Well, let me put it this way: the probability of anyone fulfilling the prophecies is almost overwhelmingly low. Oh, there have been some that have tried, of course. Every now and then somebody turned up that wanted the attention or was eager for power and influence. But it's always been easy to expose them. Nevacad's Bow, for instance, didn't turn up again until about five decades ago, so nobody could have fulfilled that prophecy until then. At that time Elder Yonatan presented it to Folan, believing Nadil would be the right place to keep it. He wanted it in a location in which he knew that the proprietors were trustworthy and dedicated to the cause. You see, Nevacad was mentor to Eluset, who was mentor to Yadez, who was mentor to Tilantes. Each passed the bow on to his successor, without anybody else's knowledge. Tilantes also kept it to himself, later passing it on to Yonatan, who ultimately gave it to Folan. That's an interesting question in itself, by the way. There are three taverns in Nadil. Why did you choose Folan's tavern?"

"Well, it was the first tavern I came to when I got into town. It appealed to me, and I needed information."

"So you came from the east?"

"Yes."

"From Travis?"

"No."

She fell silent, sensing that he didn't wish to continue the subject. After a moment, she continued.

"Vilam, don't you see, just the fact that you entered Folan's tavern, and not one of the others, is already astonishing in itself. In this difficult time, it's not always easy to come by somebody you can fully trust. But Folan is such a person. He and his wife might not possess the gift of Sensation, but they have such wide and open hearts and a wisdom all their own. You can sense it immediately when you enter their tavern. It's filled with light and song and, well, yes, even with magic, if you will. Elder Yonatan always goes out of his way to stop off in Nadil, if possible, just to keep Folan's company."

"Yes, I must admit, I do take to him myself. He has a very engaging and pleasant personality. Which house is he from?"

"He is of the House Revan." Nova smiled. "As a matter of fact, he's the Lady Utalya's cousin."

"Ah, I see. But still, might it not be possible for the prophets to have been at fault? How can you know that everything they foretold will really come to pass?"

Nova again thought carefully, knowing how important her reply would be to her companion. Then she looked up at him once more.

"Vilam, I truly believe that you're being sincere and that your questions are candid, but I also sense the pain that you've buried so deeply in your heart. I respect your wish not to discuss this, but it makes it difficult for me to answer your questions appropriately because I don't understand the motives behind your doubt of Anae. Please bear with me, and I'll attempt to give you an answer worthy of your sincerity."

Vilam nodded for her to continue.

"Personally, I believe that, in the end, the question of prophecy will always remain a question of faith. Nobody can really prove that a prophecy will be fulfilled until it actually comes to pass. And even then one could always argue that it was just coincidence. But as I said before, the prospect of someone actually fulfilling prophecy is very, very slim. The more prophecies there are regarding a certain person or event, the more difficult it becomes for anyone to fulfill them all by chance. And believe me, there are quite a few prophecies regarding the Traveler.

"On the other hand, we must also examine the prophet himself. One of the key factors in discerning a legitimate calling is a person's life and background. I don't know of any person claiming to be a servant of Anae whose life hasn't been marked by the intense trials which refine and purify their faith and character. If they haven't been through Anae's School, the school of life, they probably don't have a valid calling. For prophets, the test is even more meticulous. Anae allows many or even most of a prophet's revelations to be fulfilled within his or her lifetime, so that His people may gain the necessary trust. If only one prophecy were to go awry, the prophet would be completely discredited."

"Hmmm…What you're saying is very interesting. But isn't it still quite dangerous? Imagine the power that a so-called prophet would exercise over normal people. Couldn't he somehow fabricate a few self-fulfilling prophecies and use the people's growing trust to control them? In my experience, one of the main characteristics of the many cults and sects that are always forming is the pressure placed upon members to blindly follow their spiritual leaders wherever they go. Maybe like that Videsian Order you told me about."

"Well, yes, that is true. And your assessment of the Videsian Order is probably quite accurate. But from what I know of Anae, I don't believe that He wants us to follow anyone blindly, without the possibility of thoroughly testing divine claims or without freedom of choice. Although I believe in the importance of competent leadership, I, for one, would never just do as anyone says, without first exercising my right to question the legitimacy of their statement. By the way, that's one of the most important principles taught in the Order. It is written in the Selani s'Ulavan: 'Anae is the Spirit, and where the Spirit of Anae is, there is freedom.'

Nova hesitated. "I believe that Anae wants us to love and to trust Him, but I also believe that He doesn't use pressure or force to accomplish this. If I sense that a person is using unwarranted pressure, I become suspicious. Anae teaches us, but He's also very patient and gives us much time to learn our lessons, even if it means that we make many painful mistakes in the process. I know it might just be a leap of faith, but for my part, I've learned to love Anae and to trust that He watches over His Word."

Vilam sighed. "Yes, Nova, I understand what you're trying to say. And deep down in my heart, I believe you. In a way, I also love Anae, but sometimes, I just hate Him."

Nova took a deep breath. "I can empathize with that. Not everything we experience is always easy to digest. And sometimes, it might even become too much." Her last words were almost inaudible.

Vilam must have heard the tone of her voice, for he looked up, directly into her eyes.

She hadn't meant for it to happen, but she had allowed the pain buried so deeply in her own soul to surface momentarily, and Vilam was sensitive enough to perceive it. She immediately shoved the horrible memories far down inside of herself and slammed the lid back in place.

"Nova, I'm so sorry."

She diverted her gaze and shook her head.

"Was it very difficult?"

She swallowed and her voice was weak. "Yes, it almost cost me my life and just as nearly my faith. If it hadn't been for the Lady Utalya, I probably wouldn't be here today."

Vilam remained silent. Nova was grateful that he had enough tact not to intrude upon her with further questions.

"Do you think that I will ever learn to trust Anae as much as you do?" he asked after a while.

She raised her eyes again, sensing his momentary vulnerability. "Oh, my dear friend, do you really know how much I trust Him? And are you sure that my trust is so much greater than yours?" She sighed. "I believe that, in the end, trusting Anae might just be as simple as being prepared to pass on the love we have received, in the hope that some wounded heart may catch a glimpse of a love far greater than ours. Sometimes, though, we are so injured and deprived of love ourselves that we feel we will forever want of any love to give."

Vilam glanced at her. "And what do you do then?"

She returned his glance. "Can we ever do very much? I know that there is always hope, though, even if we can no longer believe in it ourselves. And I have also experienced that, sometimes, Anae might inspire some unsuspecting soul to utter a word that strikes deeply into our hearts and may bring healing, if we care to listen."

Vilam nodded. "Yes, you may be right. I can only pray that I'll have the prudence to recognize such a word when I hear it."

"Wisely spoken, my friend."

"So, what else did the prophets say about...the Traveler?"

She looked at him and attempted an encouraging smile, although she was feeling the fatigue of a long and eventful day.

"Well, you've already heard about Nevacad's prophecy regarding the bow. But there are so many prophecies that I think it would be best to advise you regarding the four most prominent ones which you still aren't aware of. If you wish, I can show you the others in the Scriptures by and by."

He nodded for her to continue.

She took a deep breath. "There is one prophecy that I regard as particularly significant. It states that the Traveler will be a master and teacher of the martial sciences, come in a time of turmoil to prepare our people for conflict. You demonstrated tonight that you certainly know something about archery. And the way you dealt with the guard earlier this evening makes me suspect that you're not ignorant of combat situations.

"But the most important prophecies have yet to be

fulfilled. They concern the Demantar, the Elinar, and the Sword of Selanae. All three were lost to us a millennium ago, but they will be restored when the Covatal arrives."

Vilam regarded her calmly. "Dragons, Angels, and the Sword. Interesting. So, how am I supposed to do that? Stumble over them here in the dark?"

Nova sighed wearily. This wasn't going to be easy. "Vilam, so much has already happened today. Maybe we should just give it a little more time."

They had completed a whole circuit during their conversation and were now standing in the garden behind the Lady's manse. Most of the acolytes must have retired, for many of the windows were dark, but a bit of light could be seen penetrating the moonlit night from behind a few curtains.

"Will you be accepting Catyana's invitation to join her family for the midday meal tomorrow?" Nova asked. "I know it would mean very much to her if you did."

He nodded. "Yes, I think I would like that."

"Good, I'm glad." She smiled and squeezed his hand. "Could you be here tomorrow an hour before noon?"

"Yes, that would be fine."

"It's been a very…eventful day. Please don't be angry, but I really need to retire." She shuddered at the thought of all the paperwork that still awaited her.

He gave her a wry smile and nodded.

"You will find your way back to the tavern by yourself, won't you?" she asked.

"Yes, that won't be a problem."

She reached up and planted a gentle kiss on his cheek. "*Nevelan mada,* good night, my friend. Sleep well."

Then she deliberately turned and disappeared into the manse, leaving her companion to fare for himself.

24. *Meeting in Skull Alley*

Dena was leaning against a grubby wall, and although the night was warm, she was shivering and had her cloak wrapped tightly around herself. She had spent most of the evening wandering about the city, and the constant activity had helped her to suppress the dreadful images and distressing thoughts that were stalking her. But when the time approached for her rendezvous, she had repaired to the alley and, with nothing to do but to wait for her contact to show up, the emotional impact of the day had again caught up with her.

A movement at one end of the passage made her look up. Her nerves were raw, and she apprehensively followed the darkly cloaked figure with her eyes as it came towards her. When the approaching person perceived her, he reached up and threw back his hood.

"Tuvel!" she cried and flew into her brother's arms.

It was so good to feel his comforting warmth, the pressure of his arms around her, and she let her tears flow freely. Her brother was quiet and just held her until she could control herself again. She rubbed her face on his cloak to rid herself of her tears and looked up.

"Oh, Tuvel, I was so afraid that you…" She stopped when she saw the grave expression on his face. "What's wrong?"

"Dena, I'm so sorry."

"What is it?"

"Zetara is dead."

Her heart almost stopped. "No. No, it can't be, I saw her myself just this morning. She told me she was going east and that she…"

But her brother's eyes didn't waver, and she knew instinctively that it was true.

"No!" she wailed, as inexpressible pain and anger welled up inside her. "No, no, no!" she cried while beating her fists against Tuvel's chest. He didn't move as she pounded him, but he embraced her tightly when her legs gave out and she almost collapsed. She hardly knew what she was doing as she sobbed her hurt and sorrow into her brother's garment. She felt like a rag doll in the relentless clutches of her own waxing emotions. But her brother waited patiently until she was finally able to hang on to his cloak and support herself. It took quite a while before she had quieted and was able to contain her trembling. She deliberately kept her ear against her brother's heart.

"How did she die?" she whispered, not looking up.

"It was a quick death, Dena, not like the others. For some reason she returned to the residence after she left you. They were probably afraid that she might slip away again and killed her at least an hour before the actual operation commenced. The entire estate was in an uproar, which is how we found out about it. A minor informant was able to sneak the news out."

Dena took a deep, shuddering breath. "When will it end, Tuvel?" she said, looking up at him. "Zetara was such a kind and gentle person. And I wasn't even particularly nice to her this morning." She wiped her nose and some straggling tears on her sleeve.

"Why was that?"

"I…I told her that I was also planning on going east, and she tried to dissuade me."

"It seems that she was a very wise person. So you are determined?"

Dena clenched her teeth. "Yes, now more than ever."

"Dena, I really think…"

"Don't even try, brother." Her eyes blazed in anger.

"Alright, alright, simmer down," he answered, raising his hands in a defensive motion. "Besides, after what happened here today, someone must go to Tolares to inform the High Priestess. Will you join me?"

Dena glanced up at him. She dearly loved and respected her brother. In the dim light of the torches that lit both ends of the alley, she could see the resemblance to his father and his grandfather. He had a tall, robust frame, expressive features, a square jaw, and dark, wavy hair. Even in the simple dark brown cloak in which he stood before her, he was yet capable of imparting an air of authoritative proficiency. She knew that he would one day make a very good Lord Cemasena and head of state of one of the richest and most progressive cities in the western provinces.

"Come, brother, let's not argue. You know that I would be more than glad to join you. Do you know a safe place where we can stay?"

"Yes. Sheletas has called a meeting at exactly midmorning tomorrow. That is actually the reason you were asked to meet me here. But we can stay together now, so I'll show you where it is." He glanced at her and must have noticed how worn out she was. "Dena, you've done more than your share today. You need to get some rest. Why did you take that last assignment?"

"Someone had to find out what happened to our missing operatives. There were only ten agents available at the time, and more than thirty had still not reported in, so we split the number in equal shares and I took my three, just like everyone else."

Tuvel studied her quietly for a moment. "Sister, you're amazing."

"I do what I can." She slipped her arm through his. "Come now, let's go."

25. *The Second Shot*

Vilam stood indecisively on the illuminated road that would have taken him back into town. Instead of moving forwards, though, he turned and spotted the crescent of a waxing Vilanevos rising on the eastern horizon. The night was so pleasant and peaceful. Although he was tired, he felt he couldn't go back to the tavern yet. There was so much he needed to think about. He therefore strode east, away from the town, and took the next road south along the edge of the woods he had emerged from that morning. After about an hour, the trail took him back into town, but this time he arrived from the west.

He reached the tavern ten minutes later. It was now empty, except for Folan, Semanta, and Vodana, who were waiting for him when he entered. Folan must have cleared the tavern after what had happened earlier that night. He immediately jumped up from the table where they had been talking, ran up, and grabbed Vilam's hands.

"Vilam, my dear friend! I'm so sorry. I wasn't able to thank you. I was stunned by what happened. I only realized after you left that you probably saved my life." His words came out in torrents, almost stumbling over themselves.

Semanta also came up to him and shyly took his hand in both of hers. Tears were running down her cheeks. "Please forgive me that I was so distant today. I'll try to be a better hostess tomorrow. I just don't know what I would have done if anything had happened to my husband."

Vilam smiled at them. "What I did, I did gladly. There's no need to thank me. I'm happy to know that I was of some help to my friends."

"Oh, I almost forgot." Folan bustled back to the table where they had been sitting, picked up the Prophet's Bow and the quiver, and presented them to Vilam. "These belong to you now."

Vilam stared at him, aghast. "But I can't accept these."

"My friend, you must. They are rightfully yours. You have proven that beyond a doubt to everyone here tonight. Oh, and by the way, the physician brought this around from the infirmary a while ago."

He held up the arrow which Vilam had put to such competent use a few hours before. Vilam accepted the lethal projectile with a wry smile and placed it carefully in the quiver.

In the meantime Vodana had risen from her seat and carefully approached the group, but stopped at a respectful distance.

Folan saw her and beckoned for her to come closer. "Please, my friend, don't be angry. Vodana asked if she could stay after closing to speak with you."

She cautiously moved towards him. "I'm very sorry," she said. "I don't wish to intrude upon your privacy."

"No, it's alright. You're Nova's sister."

She looked into his eyes, searching, the way she had when they first met after her song. She seemed tense. "I can hardly believe that Anae has deemed me worthy of witnessing the fulfillment of such a renowned prophecy before my very own eyes. And now I stand before the legendary Covatal himself."

Vilam fidgeted uncomfortably. "No, please. I'm not what you think I am. I'm just a normal person. Please don't treat me any other way."

Vodana's eyes grew soft as he said this. She relaxed visibly and smiled at him. "If I hadn't witnessed your reaction to my friends' distress just a few minutes ago, I would have known it now. Anae does not choose conceited tools to accomplish holy tasks. I'm very sorry if I made you feel uncomfortable, but I'm glad to see that there is no arrogance or conceit in you. I would be very happy to call you my friend."

"I don't understand. Why are you testing me? Are you a priestess?"

"No, my friend, we don't all have the same calling. But a true artist must also be one with everything beautiful and harmonious, and consequently requires many of the talents and skills that a priest or priestess may need. We therefore work very closely with our spiritual leaders."

"Ah, I see."

"On the other hand, I probably am a bit overprotective of my little sister. I wanted to be sure of the kind of man she's dealing with. Please, forgive me, but she is the only sister remaining to me."

"Excuse me, did you say 'remaining to you'?"

"Yes, we were once six sisters. But please, let us not ponder such sorrowful memories on this bright night."

Folan had been attempting to gain his attention. "My friend, I have a favor to ask." He walked over to the wooden column which had received the arrow. A dark hole at approximately face level marked the spot. "Could you put another arrow in exactly the same place?"

Vilam smiled tiredly. "I can try."

He moved back to the corner from which he had released the first arrow. He then proceeded to remove two arrows from the quiver and smoothly nocked one of them into the correct position on the bowstring. He raised the bow, breathing in, then slowly breathed out through his mouth while pulling the bowstring back behind his left ear, his left index finger above, his middle and ring finger below the nock of the arrow, but not touching it. He then held his breath and took aim. His audience, which was also holding its breath, heard a swish and a dull thump. The black hole in the column disappeared, replaced by a silvery shaft protruding from the wooden post.

They applauded in astonishment.

Vodana shot him an appreciative glance. "You've just proven once again what I have always maintained, that despite all their violence, martial sciences can be just as much a form of art as music. But tell me, my friend, why did you remove two arrows from the quiver?"

"Oh, yes, sorry. That's just an old habit of mine, one that has probably saved my life many times. Always be prepared to fire a second shot."

Vodana stared at him in dismay. "Wherever did you live to make such a habit necessary?"

"I'd...rather not talk about it, if you don't mind."

He removed the vulcanized rubber he had used before from the bow and proceeded towards the column to withdraw the arrow.

"Oh, no, my friend, please, would it be possible for you to leave the arrow in the column?" Folan asked bashfully.

Something clicked in Vilam's head, and he almost laughed. "Ah, now I understand. Yes, of course. By all means, keep the arrow. But if you don't mind, I need to get some rest. Would you be very offended if I retired?"

"No, of course not. *Nevelan mada,* my good friend. And once again, thank you."

Vilam shook hands with each in turn.

"I am very glad to have made your acquaintance, Vilam," Vodana stated when she took his hand in both of hers. "I hope very much that we shall meet again soon. As a matter of fact, I will make a point of it."

She left the tavern soon afterwards in the direction of the Lady Utalya's manse, and he retreated to his room. He opened one of the windows to let in the fresh night air, and then pulled the curtains closed. He didn't bother to take off his clothes but fell on the bed just the way he was and soon drifted off to sleep.

26. *The Message*

A vague bell-like tone of finality entered the dismal fantasies churning in the priest's mind as he tossed uneasily in his sleep. The bell sounded once more, tearing him from his disturbing dreams. He sat up and switched on the light, glancing at the clock on the mantle beside his bed. It showed five o'clock in the morning. The sun would be rising soon, but he had only been in bed for a few hours. He rubbed his eyes and his temples. Downstairs one of his acolytes was negotiating with a courier.

Talenon had left Nadil shortly after noon. The journey in his proud and heavy coach had been slow in the thick traffic flowing towards Tolares and had taken almost sixteen hours. It would have taken them longer if the flood of carriages had not abated after sunset. By the time they had reached the Videsian Order's main headquarters in Tolares, it had been nearly midnight.

He rose and pulled on his robe, then tied the sash neatly around his waist. He was straightening his clothing in front of the mirror when there was a knock on his door.

"Come in, it's open," he called.

An acolyte apprehensively stuck his head in. "A message by courier, Your Grace," he said hoarsely.

"Yes, Fichyal, give it here."

The acolyte presented the envelope to him with his head bowed, not daring to raise his eyes to his superior.

"That will be all," Talenon said as he took the envelope from the acolyte's outstretched hand.

The acolyte bowed his way out of the room and quietly closed the door.

The priest sat down at his desk. The envelope carried the seal of his operative in Nadil. He felt his stomach knot. Only the worst of intelligence could have compelled Menirel to have the operative send a courier at this time of night. He broke the seal and took out a small slip of paper. He stared at it for a few minutes. Then he let himself fall back into his chair with a deep sigh.

He couldn't believe it. The fact that they had retained western guards to ensure that the Prophet's Bow would not be handled had resulted in exactly what they had hoped to prevent. Then again, how could they have known that guards of the eastern provinces would be in the tavern that evening? The commotion induced by the two opposing parties had been so tumultuous that his operative had found it impossible to avert the dreaded event.

He pounded his fist on the desk. Confounded! How had the accursed foreigner managed it? That smug, clean-shaven man in his light gray uniform! Ever since the Prophet's Bow had resurfaced, they had been attempting to place their own "Traveler." But no matter what they did, their coverts were always denounced as imposters. If they had succeeded, it would have given them leverage and probably put them a long way towards attaining seats in the Advisory Council in Travis. Maybe they would even have been able to commission their own High Priest. As it was, the Advisory Council was still completely in the hands of the Selanian Order, and it didn't seem as if the status quo would be changing anytime soon.

He sighed again. There was nothing anyone could do now. They would have to terminate their operations regarding the Traveler and concentrate their efforts on infiltration and aggression. They had hoped to plant a mole in the Advisory

Council long before the Conference of Tolares to discover the identity of the High Priestess and have her assassinated. The plan had been successful, but too late. The mole was finally in place, but any information they retrieved now regarding the High Priestess would be useless. They would have to wait for the conference, during and after which their assault plans would be activated. She would probably not survive that phase of the plan. He hoped that they would now find a competent agent to lead operations in Travis. The work there had been proceeding far too slowly.

Talenon turned and stared out the window. He could see a faint glow in the east. It would be a long day, trying to sort through the mess that had been created inside of a few minutes yesterday evening. He picked up his quill and got to work.

27. *Practice*

Although Vilam's previous day had been very demanding, he rose early, shortly before sunrise, feeling the urge to take up his training again. It had been several days since he had enjoyed a good workout, and he wasn't planning on getting out of shape. Besides, he needed to get some personal items if he intended to make the journey to Tolares. He was surprised to realize how much he had come to value the people he had so recently met. Most of them were going to the conference, and he hoped to join them.

It was going to be another warm, beautiful day. The Tyenar Range was visible as a black chain of jagged peaks against the reddish-yellow glow of dawn in the east. Since he had no appropriate clothing, he began with a light run which would produce no perspiration. He headed north along the route Nova had taken with him last night, then east towards the pond, which he reached just as the sun rose. The inhabitants of the manse also seemed to be early risers, for they were already practicing some form of calisthenics in the garden. He raced on, hoping nobody had noticed him, and continued to the forest that bordered the town in the east. There he turned south, passing the field with the solar generators, and kept going until he hit the paved road which he knew would take him to Travis, the "City of Light," as it was called, if he continued far enough to the east. But he didn't intend to travel quite so far. At the point where he had emerged from among the trees yesterday, he disappeared from the road.

He was soon deep in the woods and speeding almost soundlessly through the underbrush. His razor-sharp instincts allowed him to reach the spot where his ship was buried in five minutes. He was fairly sure that nobody would be able to find it. He had used what was left of the ship's telatian field to slice into the earth, hiding it from any prying eyes. With part of the field, he had carved a tunnel to the ship's entrance. Even if the ship were found, nobody would be able to enter it, since he had activated the security system.

Once inside the ship, he quickly replicated more gold and a few clothes. When he was finished, he looked around the cockpit one last time and shook his head. He still couldn't understand what had caused the ship to buckle the way it did when he had entered Piral's atmosphere. He'd hardly gotten her down in one piece. The field stabilizers had overloaded and were completely shot. The computer had gently informed him that the telatian reactor had suffered severe damage and the hull was breached in several places. He had repaired the stabilizers and reactor as well as he could with the small replicator at his disposal, but he couldn't think of any way to repair the hull. He wasn't even sure he could ever completely assess the damage his ship had sustained with the tools available to him, but he did know that he wasn't going anywhere anytime soon.

After his emergency landing, he had asked the computer what the hell had happened. The computer had responded that feedback in the field stabilizers had caused them to overload. But that was impossible. Only a very strong telatian field, focused as a directional weapon, could have caused such feedback. His sensors would have picked up any technology capable of producing such a field. But there was no such technology here. Nothing even comparable would be invented on this planet for at least another thousand years. He shrugged and packed his gear. He couldn't do anything about it now, but he made a mental note to look into it in more detail later.

He reappeared on the road about half an hour after leaving it, wearing clothes more appropriate for running. Since his outfit now allowed it, he picked up his pace and cleared the forest in several minutes, then turned south, then west again. He circled the entire town, staying clear of the frequented paths, and reached the tavern from the north about a half hour later, having worked up a good sweat.

He opened the door to the veranda, letting in some fresh air, and began his stretching exercises: neck, arms, torso, and legs. He was very thorough and systematic, a routine that he had developed over many years and which worked for him. When he had completed this phase, he took a short break. He sat on a bench in the garden and watched the sun rise higher over the trees in the east, highlighting the wispy, high-altitude cirrus clouds that the clear morning had produced.

Then he strolled back to his room and over to the main door, which he opened a crack to listen into the corridor. Yes, his hosts were up, getting things ready for the day. He walked to the large guest hall, which was filled with rays from the morning sun shining in through the tall windows.

Folan saw him immediately and smiled cheerfully, only to have his expression change to one of dismay. "My friend, what has happened to you? Are you not well?"

Vilam at first didn't realize what kind of impression his appearance must have made upon his host, but he quickly caught on. "Oh, no. Sorry to worry you, Folan. I was only exercising."

"Exercising? Oh, yes, of course. I suppose a warrior like you must do that," he winked. "What can I do for you, my friend?"

"Please excuse me for intruding upon you, but may I borrow one of your swords to practice with?"

"Borrow one of my swords? Why yes, of course. My goodness, what an honor! The Cova…I'm sorry…my good friend Vilam, practicing with one of my swords. Take your pick, my friend."

"Thank you, Folan."

Vilam examined the various swords hanging on the walls and decided on one with a distinct watering. He hoped that the design wasn't faked, but distinguished a genuine Tesalian blade. Steel didn't have to be pretty in order to be strong and flexible or to produce a robust and resilient weapon, but the Tesalian swordsmiths on the western slopes of the Covasins had a solid reputation and were known to manufacture only reliable killing tools. When he took the sword from the wall, he was immediately gratified. It was well balanced, with the percussion point near the tip of the blade to facilitate both thrusting and cutting. Its weight was about three pounds, which was comfortable for a two-hander of its size.

Folan winked at him. "You do know your weapons, my friend."

Vilam smiled and took the sword back to his room, then stepped out into the garden. He had been more accustomed to other weapons lately, but given the circumstances, he felt boning up on his swordsmanship wouldn't be completely out of place. He spent the next hour vigorously practicing the various positions, attacks, defenses, and footwork, conscious of the fact that he was being observed from several windows. Then he stepped back into his room and gently placed the weapon on the table. It had proved itself to be an excellent tool. Its true test would, of course, be an actual duel, for which he hoped there would be no need at the moment.

After he had freshened up and changed his clothes, he returned to the guest hall with the sword, which he returned to its owner. "Thank you, my friend. It's a truly exceptional weapon."

Folan smiled gratefully at his guest for the compliment, carefully wiped the hilt and cross without touching the blade, and returned it to its place on the wall.

Then he turned back to Vilam. "Now, my friend. What else can I do for you? Are you ready for breakfast?"

"Yes, indeed, that would be very kind. I'm starving."

"Starving? Excellent, my friend! Let's see if we can't come up with a suitable remedy for your unpleasant condition."

Semanta now also came out and greeted him most cordially, wishing him a very good morning. She then helped her husband to set the table and bring out all the victuals, which was accomplished quickly and efficiently. They worked very well together as a team. When the ceremony had been completed, Vilam wondered how many people had actually been invited to the feast.

"Uh, Semanta, excuse me, but is this supposed to be for me?" he asked, gesturing at the heavily laden table.

"Why, yes, of course. But don't worry, dear, there's more if you want it," she shouted over her shoulder as she bustled back to the kitchen.

He sat back, an exasperated smile on his face at their overwhelming hospitality.

"Well, I hope I don't disappoint you," he murmured under his breath.

He helped himself, and soon found that he really was very hungry. His hosts were delighted over the way he dug in.

After breakfast, he returned to his room and brought out the Prophet's Bow in order to examine it more closely. He placed it carefully on the table and inspected it from all angles. It shone bright silver in the early morning light. The pulley mechanism was really superb. It didn't resemble any normal single or twin cam system that he knew of. The limbs and riser seemed to be made of one solid piece, but the whole bow didn't weigh much over five pounds, a weight which he felt much at ease with. The bowstring was comfortable to draw, although he didn't have a tab to protect his fingers.

Situated directly in the front center of the bow, above the grip, a crystalline half-sphere protruded from the riser, with several smaller crystals positioned symmetrically above and below it. At first he felt they must be some form of decoration, but their appearance reminded him of something. He was examining them more closely when a thought occurred to him. He went looking for Folan and found him bustling about the kitchen.

"Folan, I'm sorry to bother you, but could you help me?"

"Yes, of course. Gladly. What can I do for you?" he said, wiping his hands on his apron.

"Were you given any other object that was supposed to go along with the Prophet's Bow when you originally received it from Elder Yonatan?"

Folan was visibly startled. "Why, yes, of course. I'm so

sorry, my friend, but it's been such a long time, and I never had any use for it since I displayed the bow on the wall. I will get it for you immediately."

He rushed off to some obscure part of the tavern, but soon returned with a type of rack.

"There you go, my friend. Is this what you were looking for?"

"Yes, that's it exactly."

"May I ask what it is?"

"Yes, it's an invertible double pull bow press."

"Excuse me?"

"It's an instrument used to relieve the pressure on a compound bow for maintenance purposes."

"Ah, I see." The expression on his face made it plain that he didn't.

"Thank you very much, my friend. You have been a very big help."

Folan smiled. "Glad to be of service."

Vilam took the bow press back to his room and placed it on the table. The press wasn't as heavy as one might have expected, but very robust and constructed of an unfamiliar type of metal that exhibited a black, matted finish. The rounded, massive base was more complex than the ones he was accustomed to, but he would discover soon enough whether he had correctly deduced the reason. The wheels that held the bow in place were of a semiopaque crystalline texture.

He turned the bow press over. There was a small compartment in the bottom of the base, directly in the center, covered by another craftily designed piece of metal. The cover and the compartment were of the same form and size as the Selanian brooches he had seen on the Lady Utalya, the High Priest Vordalin, and Elder Yonatan, but the compartment was empty. Was it supposed to contain some kind of power source?

Would the construction work as he expected without it? He shrugged. There was only one way to find out.

He again set the bow press upright on the table. He mounted the bow into the press, inverting the bow so that the crystals on the front of the riser faced the ceiling, and applied only enough pressure to the limbs to ensure that the bow was fastened securely. Then he tapped the base of the press.

"Brilliant!" he said, smiling to himself at the result.

28. Aftermath

The smell of decay was all-pervading. Cobwebs adorned the corners and entries to the corridors. The rooms themselves were moist; mildew covered the walls, and rodents scampered across neglected and rotting floors. Despite the building's appalling condition, the housing situation in Divestelan was so desolate that every available spot was occupied by some wretched soul seeking shelter and the comfort of anonymous numbers.

The site had deliberately been chosen because of its repugnant and undistinguished nature. As expected, the small group that huddled together in a musty corner on the third floor didn't attract any attention. The somber, cloaked individuals stirred every now and then, but no words were spoken.

Sheletas stood at the entrance and carefully probed the room. It passed his inspection, and he walked across to join his friends. When he had taken his place in the circle, he glanced at the participants. Mirayla was sitting at his side, and his older brother, Picanas, had taken a place across from him. Next to Picanas were Tuvel and Dena. Having ascertained that the principal operatives were present, he acknowledged the other eight agents in the group. Then he looked at his brother.

"How many?" he asked curtly.

"We haven't heard from all our operatives yet, but the number seems to have leveled off at twenty. I'm sorry, Sheletas."

Sheletas buried his head in his hands and massaged his face. Then he dropped his hands and sighed. "So many good people."

Mirayla caressed his arm. "How was such a thing possible?"

"It seems that we have greatly underestimated our enemy's capability to undermine our organization. They must have been observing us closely for a long time without our knowledge. There might even be a traitor in our midst."

The others looked at each other, visibly shocked.

"What disturbs me most is how swift and widespread this offensive was," Sheletas continued. "The warning barely reached me in time. I observed the Guard entering the building just after I made my escape."

"Yes, Corsen's Black Guard seems to have grown immensely," Picanas remarked.

"That isn't so surprising, since Varan discovered that Lady Gevinesa's Crimson Brigade and Lord Corsen's Black Guard have merged," Miralya answered.

Sheletas shot a glance over at Dena, whose face was grim and ashen. He shook his head at Mirayla.

Mirayla was clearly embarrassed at her obvious lapse of diplomacy. "We haven't noted any independent activity of the Lady's Brigade in the past three or four years," she continued quietly. "They really do seem to have fused with the Guard."

"On the other hand, it worries me that no female brigades were spotted during this offensive," Picanas interjected. "It's possible that they've been pulled off for another assignment.

Besides, I believe the growth of the Black Guard is due to other factors. Although I completely trust Varan's intelligence, Anae rest his soul," he said, bowing respectfully towards Dena, "the Lady's single battalion of Brigades doesn't account for the large number of Black Guards we've been observing."

"That's true," Sheletas answered. "But it's also disquieting that the Black Guard is showing itself in broad daylight. They usually operate only after dusk."

"Was Bejad able to make his escape?" Mirayla asked.

"Yes, he did, although I must admit that I'm almost glad he's gone. Of all the inept..." He took a deep breath. "Anyway, I doubt that he will be able to inform Her Eminence of the desolate condition in which the Resistance has been left. Picanas, we need to get another courier to her while she is in Tolares."

"I agree," the elderly man replied. "Besides, I would very much like to get a message to our sister while we're at it. I'm very relieved that she has made it safely to Tolares."

"Alright, how about it, Tuvel?" Sheletas asked, looking over at the young man.

"I think we can manage it," Tuvel declared soberly. "Would you like me to notify Her Eminence regarding our surveillance of the patrols and mercenaries heading for Navaresa and the Northern Forests?" he asked.

"We still have absolutely no information regarding their objectives, only speculation. But you might as well bring her any intelligence we have." Sheletas looked contemplative for a moment. "Tuvel, I know your sister has a personal debt to settle," he continued, glancing at the young woman sitting quietly beside Tuvel. "I trust you won't let it interfere with your mission."

"You can rely on us to do what is necessary," Tuvel replied.

Sheletas sighed. "It's going to take quite a while to

reestablish our links. After what's happened, many of our informants may no longer trust us. As for the rest of you, lie low until we're back up to speed. Are there any more questions or comments?"

There were none.

"Good. I'll be in touch. Meeting adjourned."

Tuvel shot a questioning glance at his sister, who hadn't said a word during the short conclave. Dena nodded, and the siblings rose to follow their comrades into the hall.

29. The Bow

After Vilam had completed his preparations for his visit to the manse, he lay down to take a short midmorning nap. He must have been more tired than he imagined, though, for it was already three hours to noon when he woke up. He quickly packed his things and went to bid farewell to his host, promising to return sometime in the evening. When he reached the pond behind the Lady's manse, he could see the acolytes at work around the house. Nova was giving Tanola and Natilya instructions for the day and was very surprised to see him.

"*Setavelan mada, Vilam.* It's a pleasure to see you again, albeit somewhat earlier than arranged and with such an unexpected cargo."

"*Setavelan mada,* my friends. Yes, I'm sorry to intrude upon you like this, Nova, but I have something here that I think you and the Lady Utalya should see."

"Oh." She shot him an inquisitive glance and eyed the bow he was carrying with a playful twinkle. "Alright, then let's go find her. She expressed a wish to speak with you before we left for the Faeren farm, anyway. Come along," she said, leaving her friends to their work and pulling him into the house. "I'm certain we'll find the Lady in her study with Vodana. I hope you don't mind, but my sister said she would like to accompany us to the Faeren farm. Is that alright with you?"

"Yes, of course. Catyana will probably be thrilled."

"By the way, was it you we saw, running by the pond at sunrise?"

"Oh, you did notice." He felt a bit embarrassed.

Nova flashed him a teasing smile and knocked on the last door in the hall before entering. The Lady Utalya and Vodana were sitting on the sofa, talking quietly. Both looked up in expectation.

"My Lady." Nova bowed lightly. "Vilam has come and asked to speak with you in a matter of some importance."

Vodana and the Lady both rose, and the Lady rushed over and took Vilam's hand in both of hers.

"Vilam, what a pleasant surprise! Come in and make yourself comfortable. Is it alright if Vodana stays?"

Vilam bowed his head. "Thank you, My Lady, for such a warm welcome. Yes, Vodana is most welcome to stay."

He nodded in her direction, and Vodana smiled back, a mischievous twinkle in her eyes. "*Setavelan mada,* my friend. I promised you that I would make it a point to see you again soon," she teased.

"That you did, and I see you are a woman of your word," he replied, smiling at her banter and bowing his respect.

"What is it that you would like to speak to me about, Vilam?" the Lady asked, coming to the point.

"Well, it's not so much that I wish to say something, but rather show you something. Could I please use a table? I need to set something up."

"Yes, by all means," she answered, showing him to a table near the bookcases.

Vilam set up the bow press on the table and mounted the bow, just as he had done in his room in the tavern.

The Lady marveled at the silvery instrument. "What a wonderful weapon."

"Yes, it is. But do you see these crystals here on the riser?"

The women now crowded around the table to get a closer look.

"Yes, they're very beautiful," the Lady remarked. "The Prophet was quite an artist."

"That may be. I also first thought that they were just decorations, maybe even functional adornments to help balance the bow. But then I remembered Elder Yonatan's light sculpture, which Folan keeps displayed in the guest hall of his tavern. Do you remember the one?"

"Yes, of course. How could anyone ever forget it?"

"Well then, watch."

Vilam gently touched the base of the bow press. An image appeared above the bow, silently filling most of the space between the bow and the ceiling. The women stepped back in surprise. Vilam grinned.

"This...this is amazing," the Lady said.

"Yes, but, what is it?" Nova asked.

"It looks like some form of map," Vodana replied, "but of no kind that I've ever seen."

"It's called a topographic relief, but very detailed and holographic," Vilam explained. "I didn't realize they had this kind of technology five hundred years ago."

"They didn't," Nova said, gazing at the map in awe.

"No, but everybody always insisted that Nevacad was a man beyond his time. And this seems to prove it," Vodana added.

"Vilam, would it be possible to show a larger section of the area indicated by the map?" Nova asked.

"I don't know, but it's a good question. Let me see." He studied the bow and the press for a moment. "Hmmm…this might be a possibility."

He lightly turned the wrench of the press, which decreased the distance between the top and bottom wheels applying pressure to the limbs of the bow. The map zoomed in.

"Ah, that's it. But I turned it in the wrong direction." He turned the wrench the other way. The map zoomed out. "This is brilliant. The information for the image must be stored in the limbs of the bow. The wheels of the press must act as some kind of sensor or scanning device," he observed excitedly.

"Yes, but look. I can see what it's displaying now," Nova remarked. "The map is facing south, instead of north. The chain of mountains on the left is the Tyenar Range, the center portrays the Desert of Vortelan, and what we see on the right are the Covasin Mountains. The blue smudge on the very right, beyond the Covasin Range, must be part of the Sea of Ventara. I…I've never been out that far west. It would be so wonderful to just once see Piral's largest body of water," she whispered dreamily. "I've heard that you can't see to the other side when you stand on the shore, and if it storms, the waves are so enormous they might even sweep you off your feet."

Vilam glanced at her with a soft glow in his eyes. "Be glad that they can't do more than that."

She eyed him curiously. "What do you mean, Vilam?"

He shook his head and smiled sadly. "Better not get into that. But let's see where this map takes us."

He turned the wrench slowly and let the map zoom in. It centered on an outcrop of the Tyenar Range which grew out into the Vortelian Desert almost exactly between the eastern and western mountain ranges.

The three women looked at each other. "Malentisa," they said in unison.

"Ah, so that's the famed Malentisa I've heard so much about," Vilam said.

"You know of it?" the Lady asked him.

"Yes. It's supposedly the home of the Elinar."

"Well, it was their home. They disappeared a thousand years ago. But Malentisa's location was never a secret. We've always known where it was. It is said, though, that during the height of its power, it supposedly harbored a beautiful underground city of light. Even in that time it was a legend unto itself because our people were hardly ever invited into it. It is rumored that the Elinar were very close. But today it's nothing more than an enormous pile of ruins. Nobody ever goes there anymore. Some people even believe it's haunted because of the terrible things that happened there."

"Oh," Vilam said, sounding a bit disappointed. "I was hoping I was onto something."

"Maybe you are," Vodana cut in. "What are those two symbols over there?"

Everybody looked back at the map. Near the end of the outcropping and leading west into the desert, there was a very small icon. A second icon was placed at almost the exact center of the map. Vilam cranked the wrench a bit more and zoomed in even further.

"Why, that's the ancient Elinian symbol for the Demantar!" Nova exclaimed, pointing to the symbol on the right. She turned to Vilam to clarify. "Even in the days of the Three Races, there was only one language on all of Piral, although our writing developed along completely different lines. We developed an alphabetic form of written communication, as you well know, but the Elinar preferred a symbolic script, usually employing one symbol for each word or phrase. In order to decipher even a simple text, it was necessary to discern almost ten thousand characters, which accommodated the Elinar's preference for intricacy. This symbol on the map was their sign for the Demantar. Interestingly enough, though, there are no records of the Demantar using any form of verbal or written communication. Many people therefore felt they were just brainless, fire-breathing beasts, a theory which I, personally, can't support."

"Interesting," the Lady said.

"What's interesting?" Vilam asked.

"Well, one of Nevacad's prophecies states that his bow will lead the Covatal to the Demantar. But I never imagined that the prophecy should be interpreted quite so literally."

"Could it be true?" Vodana whispered. She was still staring at the map, but at the other symbol at its very center.

The Lady also glanced back at the map and examined the second symbol more closely. "Yes, it's possible."

Vilam looked from one to the other. "I don't mean to pry, but I would be very interested in knowing what you've discovered."

Nova turned towards him, her eyes bright. "The Fountains of Malentisa. It was believed that, deep below the caverns of the city, the Elinar retained magical fountains that possessed the most magnificent regenerative properties. They are only rumors, though. No prophecy has ever mentioned them. It's remarkable that Nevacad included them on his map."

"Well, if he put them there, he probably knew something we didn't. Is it alright with all of you if I switch the map off?"

They all nodded and Vilam tapped the base of the press. The map disappeared instantly.

"Would you mind if I leave these instruments here until we return this evening?"

"No, of course not," the Lady replied.

"I wonder," Nova said, her eyes out of focus. "If it was intended for the prophecy regarding the Bow leading the Covatal to the Demantar to be interpreted so literally, what about the prophecies regarding the Sword, or the Admonition, for that matter?"

"That's a very interesting idea, Nova. But maybe we shouldn't be speculating quite so much at this point," the Lady conjectured. "We have neither the Sword nor the Admonition."

"What's this about the Sword and an Admonition?" Vilam asked.

"I'm very sorry, Vilam," Nova said. "I keep forgetting that there are points in our history which you might not be familiar with. The Admonition was also an artifact which was lost to us at approximately the same time as the Sword of Selanae. After the Cataclysm, Anae commanded our artists and smiths through His Prophets to create the Sword and the Admonition from the material of the asteroid that had fallen from the heavens. Both were forged in the crater, which lies south of the Sea of Ventara, in the Plains of Tesalin. The Admonition must have been huge, as large as this manse, from what is written of it. They were transporting it to Travis when the earth trembled and an area hundreds of cubits around the Admonition began to sink. Everybody was so terrified that they ran off, fearing for their lives, leaving the Admonition to itself. The earth continued to tremble for months and the landscape changed. The war against darkness was still raging, so nobody had any time to look for it. When they finally got around to it several years later, everything in an area of thousands of square leagues had somehow become so overgrown with vegetation that it was impossible to search for it. It is believed to be somewhere on the western slopes of the Covasin Range."

"Hmmm...the quakes must have been a result of the tension which developed in Piral's crust after the asteroid's impact. How large do you believe the asteroid to have been?"

"I believe it was estimated to have been fifteen hundred cubits long and five hundred wide. Of course, it could have been substantially larger. Much of it was pulverized by the impact."

"And what was its effect?"

"The effect was devastating. Much dust was thrown into the atmosphere. Velana, the sun, was red and dim for many weeks, and it rained very much. The Chronicles of Cades in the Selani s'Ulavan report that all of Piral used to be one marvelous paradise. But the climate changed after the Cataclysm, giving us extreme seasons, as we have now, and a diversified troposphere, resulting in hot, dry deserts on the one hand, icy wastelands on the other, and many variations in between. I'm grateful that our climate here is still quite mild."

"Thank you for filling me in. You were very fortunate that the asteroid didn't do more damage than that. It could easily have turned into an extinction-level event. But what did you mean by a literal interpretation of the prophecies regarding these artifacts?"

"Well, the prophets have stated that, even if Anae was to one day punish us again and totally obliterate Piral because of our continued iniquity, He will not completely destroy His people. He will lay open the paths of the cosmos, and the Sword of Selanae and the Admonition will show us the way to our new home, Chyoradan, the 'Heavenly Paradise.' I have always believed that these prophecies were meant metaphorically, but now..."

"Ah, I see. You believe that Chyoradan might be shown to you in a similar manner as the Prophet's Bow is supposed to show me the way to the Demantar?"

"Maybe."

The three women exchanged significant looks.

Vilam noticed their glances. "What? What did I do now?"

The Lady smiled at him. "You said that the bow would show you the way to the Demantar. But I believe the prophecy states that it will show the Covatal the way."

"Um, well, yes, I'm sorry."

"Oh, no, it's perfectly alright. For us, the situation is quite clear. After the events of last night, which have been recounted to me in great detail by various parties, there can no longer be any doubt. We are just very grateful that you are becoming accustomed to the situation."

"Well, I wouldn't put it quite..." Suddenly, a thought occurred to him, and his features turned grim. "Just a moment. I know you're expecting me to find the Demantar, the Elinar, and the Sword of Selanae. But please don't tell me you also want me to find this...this Admonition?"

Nova turned towards him and smiled sweetly. "No, of course not."

Vilam exhaled deeply, much relieved. "Anae be thanked for that."

"First of all, the prophets say nothing about your finding the Demantar, the Elinar, or the Sword," Nova explained. "They only maintain that they will be restored to us when you arrive, or, in the case of the Demantar, that you will be led to them. Also, the prophets say nothing about your finding the Admonition." Then she added in a soft voice, "They state that that particular task will be accomplished by the Covasatal, the Traveleress, your wife."

Vilam stared at her with his mouth agape. "My...wife."

At the sight of his face, the three women could no longer hold themselves and burst into merry laughter.

Nova touched his arm, but was almost bending over with

mirth. "Oh, Vilam, I'm so sorry," she said between gasps. "We really didn't mean to laugh at you. But you should have seen the expression on your face."

As Vilam slowly came out of his daze, his expression changed to one of annoyance. "Alright, I admit, I must have looked pretty, uh, ridiculous. But, please, tell me, what's all this about a wife?"

The three women were still wiping their eyes but were getting a hold on themselves.

Nova was at last able to look him in the eye. "The Prophets state that you and your wife will both exhibit a distinct sign, which will distinguish you as being one with the Three Races. That is why your union will mark the beginning of a long and lasting peace between the Three, even though there will still be discord among the Selani for a very long time."

"Hold on. I thought you said the turmoil would end after the Covatal arrived."

"Yes, but first of all, it doesn't state how soon the turmoil would end. And then, turmoil is not necessarily the same thing as discord."

"Ah, I see."

"Come, my friend," said the Lady. "Why don't we have a seat?"

They all moved over to the other end of the parlor. The Lady chose the chair, with Nova once again sitting at her feet, while Vilam and Vodana took the sofa.

"We're very grateful that you brought the bow with you, Vilam," the Lady continued. "Thank you for showing us what you've discovered."

"You're most welcome. I was very glad for your expertise in interpreting the map."

"Thank you for the compliment. But if you don't mind,

we need to discuss another very serious issue: the artifact. Nova, thank you again for informing me about the incident before you left for the tavern yesterday evening. It gave me some time to think the matter over. I was delighted when I discovered this morning that Vodana was staying with us. I immediately took advantage of her presence and asked her to join me to get an artist's expert opinion. We set out right after breakfast to have a good look at the artifact in the early morning light. It's needless to say that we were both completely astonished. It's just as you described, Nova. I never would have believed it if I hadn't seen it with my own eyes."

"Yes, as an artist, I must say that the artifact is now completely in tune with itself and its environment," Vodana said. "That horrible, metal contraption always did bother me so. But now it has been transformed into a thing of exquisite beauty. Like Utalya said: It's amazing!"

"The question is: What are the consequences? What do you think, Nova? Will Catyana's parents allow her to join the Order?"

"I'm absolutely sure that Catyana's parents want what is best for her," Nova replied. "They're such dear people. I'm quite confident they will let her join. As a matter of fact, I'm almost certain that's the reason her parents invited me for the midday meal today."

"Well, we'll discuss that point when you know more. It's apparent that Catyana's abilities are absolutely extraordinary. With her gentle frame of mind and her tender heart, she would be a valuable asset to the Selanian Order. On the other hand, this event signifies an absolute breakthrough in the induction sciences, with or without Catyana. And it seems that you, Vilam, played a key role in its advent. Would you be so kind as to explain again the iterative technique you described to Catyana?"

"Me? Well, I, um, what shall I say?"

"Nova already gave me a very detailed report this morning on what transpired yesterday and what you said to her and Catyana. Could you please just describe in your own words what you meant and why you said what you did?"

"Well, the way I understand it, it's always been a problem to actually transform objects from one pattern to another because of the internal resistance inherent to the pattern itself, similar to the cohesive forces that particles of an atomic nucleus exhibit, only on a lower, subquantum level. The resistance can be circumvented by using alternating inductive processes, almost like an alternating electric current. You utilize the effect produced by bouncing off its inherent resistance and then sort of attack it from the other side. I guess you kind of outwit it. When the alternating inductive sequence reaches the correct frequency, it creates a transdimensional telatian field. It's almost like the plasmatic state of matter, in which all atomic particles are in abeyance; only in this state, it's not atomic particles, but time, space, energy, and matter that are diverted, allowing the object's ethereal pattern to be changed. It isn't really that difficult, once you've grasped the basic principle."

The room had become very quiet, and the three women stared at him in utter astonishment.

"Why, Vilam, I never realized what an expert you are in the sciences," Vodana finally proclaimed.

"Well, I wouldn't call myself an expert. I'm more the engineering type. I employ the underlying theories to create practical applications. But that implies a good working knowledge of the fundamental concepts."

"Vilam, there are quite a few terms you used that we don't understand," the Lady Utalya said. "Could you, for instance, explain to us what you mean by a 'subquantum level' or a 'transdimensional telatian field'? We've never heard of such concepts."

For the first time, Vilam wondered if he had done the wrong thing by helping Catyana. Had he violated the Temporal Displacement Directive by disclosing such information? Why hadn't he thought of this before? But it was too late and he would have to cover up as best he could.

"Oh, I'm sorry," he replied, attempting to sound casual, but his voice was cautious. "I guess those are just names I've come up with to put a tag on something I couldn't quite define."

The women looked at each other.

"I'm also sorry, Vilam, because this time, you're not being quite candid with us. Is there anything you would like to add to your previous statement?" the Lady asked.

Vilam took a deep breath. "No, I'm afraid I can't do that."

"Can't? Or won't?"

"Both."

"Alright, I take it that you were attempting to be diplomatic, and as always, we will not press you further in this matter. But would you be prepared to instruct us in the basic concepts of this new technique, as you did Catyana?"

Vilam hesitated. If he thought about it, any damage he might have inflicted was probably done already. Besides, Catyana's ability was so far advanced that it would only have been a matter of time before she discovered the technique herself. She had used the inductive bounce effect to change the artifact's corten steel to platinum without his help. As a matter of fact, if he wasn't mistaken, the Selanian Order's discovery of the inductive pulse dated from approximately this time. Could Anae actually be using him to speed these things along? Might there even be some truth to these people's belief that he was the Traveler?

He recoiled from the thought. He didn't want that kind of responsibility.

He realized that the silence was becoming awkward. The women were watching him curiously.

He took a deep breath. "Alright, if I can be of any help to you in that way, I'll be glad to do it."

"That's very kind of you, Vilam, and we're very grateful."

"You're most welcome."

"Vilam, excuse me for interrupting, but the concept is absolutely fascinating," Nova said. "When you explained to Catyana what to do yesterday, you mentioned that she must feel for the object's heartbeat when inducing the pulse. Does that mean that every object has its own pulse, or frequency? Almost like every object has its own pattern? It seemed that way when Catyana attempted it."

"Yes, exactly. As a matter of fact, it has great similarity with resonance phenomenon. You know, when you pluck one string of a harp, the other strings swing along with it, depending on their various harmonics?"

Vodana nodded in agreement.

"So all we really need to do is find each object's underlying inductive harmonic," Nova continued. "It sounds simple."

"Well, as I said, it really isn't that difficult. Although I was amazed at how quickly Catyana grasped the concept. I hardly had to tell her what to do. The tricky part is using the pulse field once it has been induced and turning it upon the object to change the pattern of the ethereal substrate. Catyana mastered it brilliantly."

"I suppose I'll need to write another report and send it on to Travis with the next courier," the Lady sighed. "The elders have asked me to keep them up to date and get any new information to them as quickly as possible. Again, let me express how immensely grateful we are to you, Vilam. But

now I have another matter that I would like to place before
you. Do you have any plans for the next few weeks?"

"Not really," he answered carefully.

"Good. We would like to ask you if there is any way we
could persuade you to join our delegation to Tolares and then,
after that, maybe to come back with us to Travis. We believe
that, after everything that has happened, it would be…wise, if
we could remain together for a while longer."

"Well, actually, I had already planned to ask if I could join
you, that is, if you felt that I wasn't too much of a burden."

The three women again looked at each other, but this time
their glances expressed relief.

Nova turned towards him. "Vilam, you've just taken a very
large weight off of our shoulders. You know that we would
never compel you to do anything you didn't want to. On the
other hand, we really feel that you should come with us.
Thank you."

"No, thank *you*. I'm honored that you wish to have me
with you."

"I wouldn't be, if I were you," Vodana said, a merry
twinkle in her eyes. "You don't know what horrific ideas we
had to keep you with us if you had declined. We would have
tried anything, from drugging you to seducing you to marry
one of us."

"Vodana, that's not true!" Nova exclaimed. "Well, almost
not true," she added bashfully. "We were getting rather
anxious there for a while."

"Anxious? We were terrified! Since none of us exhibit any
kind of sign that we are one with the Three Races, we felt that
the one that had to marry you would probably soon be struck
down by the Almighty in order to make room for the one He
has ordained for you."

"Vodana!"

"Oh, alright, I confess, I am exaggerating. But you must admit that some words along that line were dropped."

"Yes, but not nearly as seriously as you have made them out to be."

Vilam had been watching the exchange grimly. "I can't believe I'm hearing this. Most women I've known would rather have died than say anything like that with a man present."

"And I'm very sorry you had to listen, Vilam," Nova answered, sensing his distress. "Believe me, this isn't our usual conduct." She shot Vodana a deliberate glance.

"Alright, little sister, I promise to behave. But I really think you need to loosen up."

"Vodana, I feel quite at ease. You know that I am..."

"Yes, I know exactly who and what you are," Vodana interjected, cutting off her sister's words. "I'm your sister, aren't I? But that doesn't mean you have to lock yourself up in a cage of solemnity."

"Well, I'm not you, Vodana. Please stop trying to turn me into something I'm not."

"Nova, I can't believe that, after all these years, you still..."

"Stop it, Vodana, just stop it!" Nova shouted. "*Te'linos,* sister, what do you want? Would you rather it had been you? Would you rather have been at home with Momma and Tisala and Para when it happened?" Tears glistened in her eyes. "Would you rather have seen Cosina and Lita, when they were...?" She turned her head and covered her face with her hands.

Vodana looked at her sister in alarm and swallowed. "Oh, Nova, I'm so sorry. I didn't mean to..."

"Well then, what exactly did you mean?" Nova asked through her tears, suppressed anger evident in her voice.

"Please, Nova, believe me. I really am sorry. It's just that...sometimes when I look at you I feel so...helpless."

Nova's glance softened. "Vodana, it's been over twenty years. Don't you think I've had to learn to live with it, one way or another? I'm not a child anymore."

Vodana looked at her sister tenderly. "I'm not always so sure. Somehow you'll always just be my little baby sister. And it seems that there's always so much pain…"

"Yes, sister, there still is very much pain. There's no getting around it. I just have to deal with it when the memories come. But, Vodana, there's also so much joy, and beauty, and wonder. Please, don't keep picking on me because I'm not as perfectly beautiful and full of joy as your artistic sagacity might wish. Can't you just accept me for what I am?"

Vodana knelt down in front of her sister and took her hands in hers.

"Dearest Tinasa, I am trying. Please believe how much I'm trying. Maybe we just need to learn to be more patient with each other. And, Nova, you are beautiful." She caressed her sister's cheek and then took out a handkerchief with which she wiped away her sister's tears. They looked into each other's eyes.

The Lady Utalya, who had been watching the scene carefully while keeping her arm around her protégée, spoke up. "Well, I'm glad you two have finally gotten that out of your systems. It's been worrying the other girls all morning. Natilya even came to see me because of it."

The two sisters looked up at the Lady in surprise.

"Well, what did you expect?" the Lady responded. "We aren't training you girls for nothing, are we? If they hadn't sensed what was going on between you two battle hens, I would have thrown the whole lot out and started over with someone worth the effort."

Vodana could appreciate the Lady's humor and smiled up at her. "Thank you for your forbearance, Utalya, with two such cantankerous fiends as us."

"Yes, two very young, cantankerous fiends."

"Why, Utalya, I'm sixty-seven!"

"So I've got almost one hundred years on you. We'll resume this topic when you've reached a round hundred. I would advise you two to spend more time together, though. I believe there's still a lot you need to work out—even if some things are already a few years in the past," she added discreetly.

Vodana nodded and rose to her feet, pulling her sister with her. The Lady and Vilam also rose. Vilam had been absorbing everything and now shot an inquisitive glance at Nova.

Vodana saw it and responded. "Not this time, Vilam. I'm very sorry that you heard even as much as you did, and it's all upon my head. Sometimes, I really am an obtuse old cetesa."

"Now, now, my dear, don't go overrating yourself," the Lady Utalya chided playfully.

Vodana looked at her, abashed, but when she saw her teasing smile, she returned it. "Why, Utalya, I didn't think you had it in you."

"You should know me better by now," the Lady replied gently. "Anyway, I do believe you need to prepare for your departure," she added, glancing at the timepiece on her desk. "Catyana would be very disappointed if you were late."

She dismissed them graciously from her presence. The two younger women went up to their room, while Vilam waited in the garden. The women soon returned wearing their summer cloaks, and the three of them left for their rendezvous.

30. *The Market*

The market in Tolares was well known for its opulence and diversity. Tolares was a most prosperous city of almost sixty thousand inhabitants, and its market was a typical example of its abounding affluence. Although Travis was the designated legislative capital of the world, Tolares was undoubtedly the economic center. The city was within a comfortable day's journey of the western border and constituted a crossroad between Navaresa in the Northern Forests and Lake Elinas in the south, with the Suviltan Highway passing directly through the market. The city's dignitaries had taken advantage of its illustrious location and gradually transformed it into the progressive metropolis it was today.

Netira's amazement amused Bejad, for she had obviously never seen a market this size. He could see that her senses were completely overwhelmed by the sheer volume of merchandise on display as she led her chyeves through the dense multitude. The people around them eyed the couple curiously, for although it was not unusual to see members of the Order leading a valuable mount, the nobility of this steed far surpassed the norm.

They had arrived in Tolares around six o'clock, shortly after sunrise, just as Bejad had predicted. Their first stop had been the Selanian Order's headquarters south of the city, which was located near the new conference building. The priestess in charge of the women's division had taken an immediate liking to the practical-minded Netira. She had been more than happy to aid a young maiden in distress by helping her escape the rumored poverty and horror of the western provinces, especially since she displayed such a fervent desire to join the Order.

Netira had been registered and instated as an initiate, the

three-month trial period that preceded the status of full acolyte. This gave the Order enough time to check her background, and the initiate some time to reconsider. Since Netira was still well below the Age of Maturity and could not produce a sanctioned guardian to vouch for her, a letter to her parents was immediately dispatched by courier, asking for their written consent. Then she had been assigned quarters with another acolyte, where she was allowed to freshen up after her arduous journey and change into her new robes.

Bejad had received quarters in the men's division where he had washed and changed and then taken a nap. His first and foremost duty had then been to contact the High Priestess's liaison officer in Tolares. The officer informed him that the High Priestess should be arriving in Tolares by tomorrow evening. Since his message was urgent and concerned an extraction, she would definitely see him almost immediately. He would be notified regarding the time of the audience as soon as possible.

About an hour ago he had met with Netira again and taken her into the city to help her find a reputable merchant who would give her a fair price for her chyeves. They were therefore now both clothed in the cream-colored robes and black cloaks of the Selanian Order, although Bejad had a bronze brooch pinned to his robe, designating him as a deacon.

They had reached the quarter of the market dedicated to pets, domestic animals, and livestock. Although the noise and smell couldn't possibly compare to what Bejad had experienced in Divestelan—the market in Tolares was actually quite orderly and serene—Netira appeared tense but enthusiastic.

"Oh, Bejad, look! What are those beautiful birds over there? They have such vivid colors!"

Bejad glanced in the direction his companion was pointing and smiled. "Those are jitesi. They are originally found in the forests south and east of the Plains of Tesalin."

"Where the porodi are from?"

"Yes, as a matter of fact, there is a booth selling them, right over there," he remarked, pointing at cages containing the peculiar squirrels with the golden pelt.

"Oh, aren't they just adorable? I've always wished I could have one."

"They cost a small fortune. There are farms, though, around the Sea of Ventara that have taken up breeding them. If they are successful, the prices will probably be dropping."

Netira was dismayed. "Breeding porodi? But then they would have to lock them up, the poor things. Such animals belong in the wild, and not in cages. People will do anything for money."

"Well, that depends on the person doing it. I've heard there are breeders who build huge cages so that the animals feel comfortable."

"Still, it's somehow unnatural. I don't think it's right."

She walked by the booths looking straight ahead, deliberately ignoring them. Bejad grinned at her vehemence. He led her towards the area where the chyeves merchants had their stalls. Just before they reached them, Netira stopped and pressed her fingers against her temple.

"Are you alright, Netira?" Bejad asked in concern.

She smiled up at him, but her expression appeared strained. "Yes, I'm fine. Everything's so different from what I expected." She sighed. "I suppose in the end it's just all the noise and the people. I'm not used to it."

"I understand. Look, here are the chyevi. Let's get this over with so we can leave."

She nodded, and Bejad steered her towards the stall of a merchant he knew well. The businessman had his back turned towards them and was brushing down one of his animals. Even seen from behind, it was evident that he was a giant of a man with broad shoulders, muscular arms, wild, wavy hair and a full, unkempt beard.

"You call that old nag a chyeves?" Bejad called with a smile.

The merchant turned around. When he saw who had addressed him, his face lit up.

"Bejad, you old scoundrel!"

The two men flung themselves at each other, embracing, slapping each other's backs and laughing.

Bejad held his friend out at arm's length. "Hyumosen, it's so good to see you. How long has it been?"

"You tell me. But it must be two years, at the least. When did you get in?"

"Just this morning."

"Will you be staying?"

"Well, certainly for a few days. I might be going back to Travis then."

"I see. How about a round at Rotesil's tavern?"

"We can do better than that. It's almost noon. How about I invite you to the midday meal? It's on me."

"That's a word, my friend."

Bejad noted that Netira had been watching the reunion with a demure smile and now heard her discreetly clear her throat.

"Who is this charming companion of yours?" Hyumosen asked, glancing in Netira's direction. His smile faded when he saw the steed she was holding. *"Tev'anar!"*

"Yes, my friend. That is exactly the reason we have come to you," Bejad answered. "Hyumosen, this is Netira. She has just joined the Order and would like to sell this chyeves so she can send the money to her parents. Are you interested?"

"I'm pleased to meet you, Netira. But you can't be serious. Where did you get this extraordinary animal?"

"It was a gift to Netira's family from a very high official," Bejad explained. "I'm afraid I can't tell you more than that."

Hyumosen circled the chyeves and examined it carefully from all sides. "I can't believe my eyes—a Sumelian steed. I have seldom seen its like. If it had been anyone but you, Bejad, I would have said that foul play was involved." He glanced at his friend. "I take it everything is in order?"

"Yes, believe me. Nobody will come looking for this chyeves. The transaction would be legitimate."

Hyumosen gazed over at Netira, assessing her carefully. She returned his glance innocently enough. It was apparent that he couldn't imagine having any problems with such an inexperienced young maiden.

"Alright, I could let you have twenty ayjeni for this steed, my dear. You must agree that that is a reasonable price," he offered, commencing the negotiations.

"Yes," she answered. "It is a reasonable price. But I'm afraid I can't let you have him for less than thirty-five."

"Thirty-five ayjeni! Girl, are you out of your mind? Your father would be fortunate to earn that much in as many years! Twenty-five."

"That may be true, my friend. But you know as well as I that Lord Tolares just purchased two thoroughbred Tesalian mares a week ago. Lord Vetena doesn't want his stables rivaled and will easily pay you fifty for a Sumelian steed. You'll still be making a most generous profit. Thirty."

Hyumosen sighed and looked over at Bejad. "That's what you get for underestimating your opponent. Alright, thirty it is," he declared, turning back to Netira. "You drive a hard bargain, my friend. Where did you learn to barter like that?"

The young woman didn't flinch when Hyumosen took her

delicate hand firmly into his huge paw to confirm the transaction. She held his gaze without wavering. "You learn much when you grow up on a farm. And I keep my eyes and ears open," she answered.

"I didn't realize that the inhabitants of the Northern Covasins were into farming," Hyumosen countered.

"Northern Covasins? She's from Pitaren," Bejad replied.

"Oh? Then what about her skin?" Hyumosen asked, letting go of Netira's hand.

Bejad looked at her more closely. "You're right. I'm sorry, Netira. I've been riding with you all night and never saw it. It's difficult to judge skin color if you're not in the sunlight. Besides, I must have grown accustomed to the darker shade during my time in Divestelan, so it didn't catch my attention."

"Please, my friends, don't quarrel. You're both right," Netira explained. She was clearly embarrassed. "You mustn't justify yourself, Bejad. You couldn't know. My parents are originally from the mountains, but moved to Pitaren before I was born. I'm afraid, though, that to the locals, we always remained foreigners," she added sullenly.

"Well, that explains it then," Hyumosen replied with a smile that didn't quite touch his eyes. "Listen, my friends, I truly appreciate your business, but you must understand that I don't carry such assets around with me. If you accompany me to the municipal treasury before we go to Rotesil's, I'll be glad to withdraw the amount for you. Then we can go and celebrate the conclusion of a successful transaction."

"That's very kind of you, Hyumosen," Netira answered, "but I have some very pressing matters to attend to. Would it be possible for you to advance a small amount? You can pay over the rest to Bejad. I trust him implicitly."

Bejad rewarded her with a smile for the compliment.

"Alright, how much do you need?" Hyumosen asked. "I

could advance as much as three ayjeni, if you like."

"Oh, no, that would be far too much. Five hundred domani would be more than enough."

"That shouldn't be a problem. My equerry keeps the loose change around here. Let me bring him his new charge, and I'll fetch the brass."

Netira smiled at Hyumosen's words and handed him the reins. Hyumosen fondled the fiery steed's neck, stroking the soft, curly black pelt and long, thick mane that almost completely covered the back of its neck. He turned towards the stalls.

"Hey, Ludanes, get over here," he yelled. "I want you to tend to this steed for me. And you'd better take good care of him, because he's worth more than you'll ever be, you no-good piece of *ate'felen!*"

Netira turned towards Bejad as the tall and strongly built Hyumosen walked off with the steed in tow.

"Does he always use such coarse language?" she whispered.

"Depends on who he's talking to," Bejad replied with a smile. "But it's never meant as seriously as it sounds. You get used to it after a while. By the way, how did you know about Lord Tolares? That's not common knowledge, is it?"

"As I said, I keep my eyes and ears open. Listen, Bejad, I'm very sorry, but I really do need to leave. I can hardly begin to tell you how grateful I am for everything you've done for me so far."

"Don't mention it, Netira. I did it gladly. There is something I would like in return, though."

"Oh? And what would that be?" She eyed him curiously.

"I would like to see you again. And I don't mean just to bring you the recompense for the steed."

"Oh." She almost blushed and glanced shyly up at him. "Well, alright."

"Look, tomorrow is Velavides, the Holy Sabbath, and our schedules will probably be overloaded as it is. But the day after would be a good time. Could I pick you up about midafternoon?"

"Won't that be a problem with the head priestess? I'm not even an acolyte yet."

"No, don't worry, I know her well. I'll talk to her. Besides, with the conference and all, they usually tend to be less strict."

She nodded. "Alright. But shouldn't you be trying to get in touch with the High Priestess?"

"I've already contacted her officer here in Tolares. I'll be hearing from her as soon as she arrives. All I can do until then is wait."

"Oh, I see."

"Are you sure you'll manage alone in town? Tolares is quite a large city."

"No, I'll be fine. I've always been good at finding my way around."

"Alright, then I look forward to seeing you later."

"Good-bye, Bejad."

Hyumosen returned and handed her the sum they had agreed on. She placed the coins in the small purse that she kept in her robe. Then she thanked him, bade him farewell, and turned away. Bejad and Hyumosen watched the confident young woman disappear into the crowd, then turned and walked in the other direction with their arms around each other's shoulders, gossiping cheerfully.

31. Confessions

Nova, Vodana and Vilam started out towards the pond and then turned northeast. When they reached the woods, they turned north onto infrequently traveled farm roads. Vodana immediately took possession of her companions by linking arms with both of them, Nova on her left, Vilam on her right. Nova had taken her basket with her, which contained several items she believed Catyana's family would enjoy. It also contained a package which she was very secretive about.

"Well, my friend, you mustn't forget, they did almost marry us off," Vodana replied teasingly to Vilam's inquisitive glance when she linked arms with him.

"Don't mind her, Vilam," Nova remarked. "She's been engaged for years now. And she's very devoted to her fiancé."

"Oh? Who's the lucky man?" Vilam asked, raising an eyebrow.

"Just keep your eyes open when we get to Tolares, and you'll see soon enough," Nova replied with a smile. "Although you may have to wait a few days into the conference," she added as an afterthought.

"Now, Nova, since when do we go revealing family secrets? I thought I could trust you," Vodana declared affably.

"Well, I'm not the one that called myself an old cetesa and was chided for it by the Lady Utalya, now was I?"

"That's not true! I said I was an *obtuse* old cetesa." The sisters smiled at each other. "Anyway, I consider Vilam just as good as family, after everything that's happened." She tightened her hold on his arm and looked up at him. "I don't know, Vilam. Somehow, a woman can feel very...secure in your presence."

"Yes, sister, that's the word I've been looking for: secure."

Vilam looked at his two companions. "Well, I feel much honored by your confidence. I just hope you won't be too badly disappointed."

"Not to worry, my friend," Vodana replied. "We are always disappointed and disillusioned. It's one of the basic facts of life. Anae wants us to trust mainly Him, and not ourselves or someone else. If someone or something becomes too important to us, disappointment is sure to follow."

"Does that include disappointment in Him?" he asked, bitterness evident in his voice.

Nova looked at him with wide eyes. "Yes, sometimes," she answered.

They walked on mutely for a moment, Vodana glancing inquisitively from the one to the other.

"Oh, it's no use!" he exclaimed.

"What's no use, my friend?" Nova asked gently.

"I know all the arguments. I've even used them myself so many times."

"Which arguments?"

"That Anae gives us freedom of choice because he loves us and doesn't want marionettes as His servants. In other words, He wants genuine relationships with beings that can think for themselves. He wants us to make our own choices and love Him of our own accord. But it's sometimes awfully hard to make the right choices."

"Yes," Nova whispered.

"Make a wrong choice and your sister dies. Make a wrong choice and your wife dies. Or someone else makes a wrong choice, maybe even deliberately, and you suffer the consequences. Now I ask you, is that truly a God of love and mercy, who never intervenes, no matter what happens and how bad the situation becomes?"

Vodana shot a questioning glance at her sister.

Nova silently shook her head and then replied. "Vilam, are you sure He never intervenes?"

They were again silent for a moment.

"Well, I wouldn't say He *never* intervenes," he answered. "But if He does, it's only when He damn well pleases."

Vilam felt Vodana stiffen, but chose to ignore it.

"Have you ever tried praying?" Nova asked.

"Praying? Well, what do you think? Of course I prayed. And believe me, it wasn't just a short intercession of a few hours or days or weeks. No, I was down on my knees for months, but His ears were deaf to my pleas."

"Vilam, you know that I can't give you the answer you'd like to hear."

"Oh, yes, I know: Anae's sovereignty. 'Who is this that darkens counsel by words without knowledge?' Or 'indeed, O man, who are you to reply against God?' Those are the only answers we ever get."

"Excuse me, you two. Would you mind if I just disengage myself for a moment?" Vodana asked her companions, releasing their arms and standing back.

They both turned and looked at her in surprise.

"Why, what's wrong, Vodana?" Nova asked.

"Well, do you really think I enjoy playing the part of an undefended country between two battling nations? Is this all you do on your long, rambling walks together, argue theological points of view so that Vilam can rationalize his bitterness?" She looked directly at Vilam. "What's eating you, anyway?"

Vilam took a deep breath, opened his mouth to speak, then closed it again and looked at the ground.

"Well, if you don't want to answer, let me do it for you," Vodana exclaimed, her eyes flashing. "It seems you've lost a wife. Alright, that hurts. But you aren't the first person that ever happened to and you won't be the last. My father lost his wife, and I never heard him whining about it. I'm absolutely certain your wife didn't want you moping over her grave after she was gone, if she was a woman with any sense whatsoever. She would have wanted you to reach out and get on with your life. If it really took her all those months you spent howling on your knees to finally kick the bucket, then I'm sure she had time to express some kind of opinion. What did she say?"

Vilam just stared at her and swallowed.

"I thought so," Vodana said. "So what exactly is your problem?"

Vilam remained silent, while Nova watched her sister in amazement.

"Alright, I'll tell you what your problem is. Nova told you today that the Lord God possibly has a new wife in store for you, and now you're just plain petrified, aren't you? Afraid to fall in love again, afraid she'll be struck down again, afraid to feel the pain again, am I right?"

Vilam looked at her silently for a moment, but then nodded. "Yes," he answered hoarsely.

"Good. At least you have the guts to admit it. Tell me, Vilam, did your poor wife really have to listen to your whimpering all those months before she passed away? Or were you man enough to provide a bit of support during her last, difficult journey?"

Vilam gazed into her blazing eyes. "I tried," he answered weakly.

Vodana sighed, and the fire in her eyes went out as quickly as it had come. "My friend, your life really must have been one hell of a mess," she stated calmly.

"Well, I'm sorry that I've disappointed you, and I'm sorry that you must now despise me for it," he replied despondently, his bitterness momentarily consumed by Vodana's fervor.

"Despise you?" Nova exclaimed. "Vilam, the only people that receive such passionate treatment from my sister are the ones she cares very deeply about. If she despised you, she would either ignore you completely, or, even worse, acknowledge her loathing by being sweetness itself."

"Oh, really?" he asked resignedly.

"Yes, my friend, I'm afraid my little sister knows me a bit too well," Vodana admitted. "So, for better or worse, I fear that you must get used to the fact that I really do care about you. As a brother, mind you. And I'm truly sorry that you've been through so much, but please, Vilam, do try to get a grip on yourself. I sense so much potential inside of you, and I do so much want to be proud of the people I care about."

Vodana again linked arms with her companions, pulling them forwards.

Nova leaned over to look at Vilam. "Is it really true, what Vodana said? That my words regarding your future wife have made you…apprehensive?"

Vilam nodded. "Yes, I'm afraid it is true."

"That's so sad. And we even laughed at you. I'm so sorry, Vilam."

"Do you think Anae will really force me to marry someone?"

Vodana again stopped dead in her tracks. "For heaven's sake, Vilam, that's not how such things work." She looked at him in exasperation. "What kind of strange notions do you carry around with yourself regarding Anae's inspiration?"

He looked at her, uncertain of himself. "I guess I really don't know."

Vodana began walking again. "Well, inspiration and prophecy can be challenging subjects, but I always look at them from an artist's point of view. When a prophecy is uttered, the prophet has usually been inspired by a momentary picture of how the situation will be at the time the prophecy is fulfilled. He then attempts to paint the picture he has seen with words, but the picture usually doesn't contain the events leading up to it. The picture therefore stands by itself and must be interpreted. Often we can't understand everything about it until it has actually happened. As a result, a prophet might state that you will have a wife, but he doesn't assert how that will come to pass. It stands to reason, though, that you will probably fall in love and want to marry like everybody else. You see, Anae doesn't need to force you to do anything. He just uses the feelings He has already planted inside of you, like a virtuoso playing a finely tuned musical instrument."

"But what if I fall in love with the wrong woman?"

"Goodness, Vilam, fall in love as often and as violently as you like. As a matter of fact, I'm beginning to believe that would probably be the best treatment for your condition. Find some pretty girl and court her ardently and passionately. It certainly won't have any effect on the prophecy's fulfillment."

"How can you be so sure? How do I know that Anae is guiding me? What do I need to do?"

"Look, Vilam," Vodana explained impatiently. "Have you ever tried to maneuver a heavy wagon that was standing still?"

"No, of course not. That would be pretty foolish."

"Well, what would you do?"

"Hitch a chyeves to it and get it moving."

"Well then, get moving! How do you expect Anae to guide you if you just stand there doing nothing?"

"Yes, but how do I know that it's Anae's voice or hand that is guiding me?"

"One very simple word, my friend: experience. And you won't get any of that just by moping around and licking your wounds."

Vilam's mouth worked silently for a moment.

"Come on, Vilam, spit it out. Or don't you have the backbone for such a confession?"

He stared at her. "I guess I'm afraid of making more mistakes and being hurt again, or hurting others," he admitted reluctantly.

"Well then, I suppose you'll just have to grow up and take responsibility for your actions, like everyone else. There's never a guarantee that you won't make any more mistakes, no matter how much experience you have. The difference between an adolescent and a mature individual is not that they no longer make any mistakes, but how they cope with the mistakes they do make. Do they cringe and whimper and crawl into some dark hole, or do they deal with the situation, learn what they can, and then get on with their lives?"

"Vodana is right, Vilam," Nova intervened. "You must learn to listen to your heart and do what you feel is the right thing to do. There never will be a guarantee that things will develop the way you plan them. But if you really wish to do Anae's bidding and your heart remains at peace, then you should proceed, even if the result turns out to be very painful. That's a risk we all have to take. In your case, though, your pain and fear seem to center very much around your first wife. May I ask how you felt when you met her?"

Vilam considered the question for a moment. "Well, pretty confused," he answered.

"How so? Didn't you love her?"

"Yes, I did, very much. But I just didn't see it for a long time. There were…too many other things in the way," he said, his voice low.

"That can be a problem," Vodana replied. "I often compare it to a sculpture. The artifact is there, but you have to chip away at the stone surrounding it until it becomes visible. I believe that's what Anae does with us. We're His works of art, and he chisels and hones away at us until we're beautifully polished artifacts, glowing in His light, every one of us completely unique. But it takes time, and there's often much pain involved in the process."

"I'll say," Vilam responded bitterly.

Vodana squeezed his arm. "Come now, Vilam, stop sniveling and carry your share of the burden with dignity, just like the rest of us. I doubt He's given you more than you can handle, unless, of course, you're deliberately attempting to evade your destiny. Then you would be getting what you deserved."

"Well, I guess I was running away for a while, but not anymore. At least I don't think so. Although I do believe the load I was asked to carry was somewhat heavier than most."

"Heavier than that of my little sister?"

Vilam fell silent and looked at the ground while Nova glanced up at her sister and tightened her hold on her arm.

"Even going on the little I've heard, I don't think I'd ever want to be the judge of that," he declared somberly. "Although I really wonder why some people have to carry such overwhelming burdens, and others don't."

"My goodness, Vilam, isn't that clear? First of all, there are so many different types of people. You wouldn't give a five-year-old child a thirty pound bag to haul, would you? There are some very sensitive souls out there. You could use a very fine and delicate tool on them and even so you might cause irreparable damage. And then there are some on which you could pound away with a sledgehammer and you would hardly scratch their surface. On the other hand, there is also the question of your personal calling. I believe a serviceable sword would need to be honed until it was a very keenly tuned instrument, but how much honing do you need for a simple anvil?"

"Thank you, Vodana, you really have a point there. Why is it that you can explain things so well, even though it's your sister who is in the Order?"

"My sister's alright, Vilam. It's just that Nova is probably more rational than I am, and more gentle in her approach. I am usually more direct, as you've undoubtedly noticed, at least with my friends, and as an artist, I use a lot of intuition and must see things from an artist's perspective. As a priestess, or should I say a potential priestess, Nova must think clearly and logically and formulate accurately. She's more of a scientist than an artist—at least that's my personal opinion."

"Well, I never!" Nova exclaimed playfully. "Thank you, dearest sister, for telling me who I am."

"I believe I stated that it is my personal opinion."

"Vodana, you know that your opinion has always been very important to me," Nova replied, turning serious.

"Yes, dearest, and you can't believe how sorry I am that I've been away so often. Utalya was quite right; there's a lot that I've been repressing. I confess that I have been keeping you at a distance all these years. I guess that's the real reason I was away on so many extended tours or kept myself busy practicing until I dropped half dead. I just couldn't cope with the situation, especially when I saw you in such agony. I'm so sorry, Tinasa. But believe me, things will not go on the way they have."

"Oh, dearest Vodana, don't you think I know why you stayed away? But look what Anae has made of it: He's given us one of the greatest artists the world has ever seen. Knowing that has been such a consolation to me."

"A consolation? Little sister, you're so magnanimous. But a consolation is and remains a meager substitute. It can never replace the real thing." She sighed. "I sometimes wonder if it was all really worth it."

Nova leaned her head against her sister's shoulder. "I love you, my darling sister, and that will never change, no matter what has happened in the past or will happen in the future."

"Damn, I'm such a jerk," Vilam mumbled to himself.

"Why do you say that, Vilam?" Vodana asked.

"Listening to you, I realize how much pain and anguish there must be around me, but all I ever do is to indulge in my own misfortune. Why am I so self-centered?"

"That, my friend, you will have to answer for yourself. If I may give you some advice, though: Stop torturing yourself with self-doubt and open yourself to your surroundings. We often don't find the answers to our innermost questions until we look beyond ourselves. As a matter of fact, let's begin right now. We still have a way to go, and I don't want to waste this beautiful day groveling over such somber matters."

"I agree," Nova said. "It's such a marvelously clear day. Look, isn't that Mount Vaduras over there? Travis would be right under its western slope. By the way, Vodana, did you see Natilya and Tanola last night when you came home?"

"Yes, as a matter of fact, I did. They came in just after me. They took Catyana all the way home, one hour each way, in the middle of the night. They're such dear hearts."

"I would have gladly taken her myself, but it wasn't possible."

"Oh, yes, I forgot. Another long, rambling walk with Vilam, right?"

"Oh, Vodana, you're impossible. But, please, tell me. What do you think of Catyana?"

"She's an absolute darling with a very gentle and vulnerable heart. I would advise you to take extremely good care of her," Vodana replied, giving her sister a significant glance.

Nova was silent for a moment. "Yes, she does have a very gentle and vulnerable heart. But I think you will soon find that there is much more to her than meets the eye," she said softly.

32. The Debt

The two riders trotted steadily southwards along the western shore of Lake Divestelan. It was almost noon, and the sun glared down upon the dark blue waters, transforming the waves into sparkling sapphires. The riders were both wearing simple dark brown cloaks. Had it not been for the young woman's long dark hair, it might have been difficult to tell the two travelers apart from a distance.

Dena raised her head, closed her eyes, and took a long, deep breath.

"Oh, it's just so wonderful," she declared joyfully. "The fragrance of the conifers blends so well with the scent of the sea. Thank you, dearest brother. I bow to your superior judgment and admit that you made the right choice—for once," she added teasingly.

Tuvel smiled at his sister. It had been long since he had seen her so cheerful. "I thought you'd enjoy it, although it won't be easy getting the stench of the city out of our clothes. And I still believe there was no other choice. The highway would have been impossible, and the roads to the north have just become too dangerous."

"Yes, but it will take us at least twice as long to get to Tolares by the southern route. And since we won't be able to change our chyevi, we will need to spare their strength. When do you think we will get there?"

"I estimate roughly four days. When we reach the southern boundary of the lake, we'll cut across and head directly east for Elinas. From there we can take the normal route north into Tolares. I doubt we'll have any problems at that point, since we'll already be in the eastern provinces. We will most likely arrive there on the second day of the conference."

"I wish we could speed things up somehow."

"Please, Dena, don't be so impatient. I would rather get there late than not at all."

"I'm trying, brother. You know me well enough to understand. I need to feel as if I'm really doing something, and not just sitting around."

"But sister, you've already done so much. You were the one with the deepest ties to His Excellency's family. And you were the one who passed on the alarm when Zetara gave it, Anae rest her soul. By the way, who do you think was the source of her information? You should be able to tell me, now that the entire network has practically fallen apart."

Dena looked grave at the recollection. Tuvel sensed that it would take a while before his sister would be able to resign herself to the fact that Zetara was dead.

"Well, as the Lady's personal handmaiden, she never could tell me very much. But from the many hints I gathered along the way, I'm fairly certain that her information must have come from the Lady Gevinesa herself. Some fundamental change must have taken place in that woman's life, although I can still hardly believe it, after all the atrocities she committed. But it's the only explanation that fits the facts."

"Then it is as Mirayla stated this morning: the Lady dissolved her Crimson Brigade after her transformation," Tuvel said.

"Yes, definitely. But the members of her Brigade couldn't understand it. They had been hand-picked and trained by the Lady herself. They were completely loyal to her and must have felt betrayed when she dissolved the group. I still can't believe that Tavita was actually once her right hand and later even captain of the Brigade. But she is the one who regrouped and merged them into Corsen's Black Guard."

Tuvel didn't like the direction this conversation was going. He only had to look at his sister's face to know what she was thinking.

Dena gazed into the distance, hardly seeing. "How could

someone we once knew so well, someone we once loved and cared about, revel in such gruesome deeds? It seems she can't get enough of it, as if the scent and taste of her enemy's blood were the essence of her life. She's become a monster, Tuvel."

Tuvel shot his sister a troubled glance. Her face had become grim and pale.

Varan's death had come two months before he and Dena would have been married. In addition to the obvious political advantages of a union between the Houses Marusen and Cemasena, Tuvel knew that it would not just have been a marriage born of practicality. Varan had meant everything to his sister. Dena had helped Varan infiltrate the Black Guard, and through his work, they had finally proven that the Black Guard was connected directly to His Excellency's family. But Varan's cover had been compromised. When his sister Tavita discovered his betrayal, she cut out his tongue, slit him open, and left him to die in agony. He had barely been alive when Dena found him. Since he couldn't talk, he wrote down as much as he could on a piece of paper, the section of parchment with rusty brown smudges that Dena was holding. Varan had died in her arms.

"Dena, why do you torture yourself by keeping that parchment?"

She looked at the paper in her hand. "No, brother, it's not like that. It helps me to focus on my task and to remember why I'm doing all this."

Tuvel sighed. "So you really believe she has gone east?"

"Yes, we are sure of it. Just last week we received reliable intelligence that she has initiated a covert operation. Lord Divestelan's intelligence network in Travis seems to be in poor shape since the High Priestess hit them so hard five years ago, and they want to get someone in there with hands-on experience. I must admit, Tavita is an excellent choice. I'm afraid, though, that we have no idea where she is now. All I can do is go east and attempt to track her down."

"And what will you do if you find her?"

"I'm going to make her wish she had never murdered my love. Believe me, she will pay her debt."

"Dena, she's a trained killer. Please, promise me you won't go after her by yourself."

She looked at him. "Why so concerned, brother?"

"We've already lost enough good people. And for goodness' sake, Dena, you're my sister! I love you and I don't want to lose you."

Her expression softened. "I know, and I love you too, Tuvel. I promise you I'll try to be careful. But you must admit we do make a good team, don't we? I mean, the way we raided His Excellency's stables to get these two chyevi was just splendid."

Tuvel smiled. "Well, it wasn't really so difficult. With Lord Divestelan and most of his family gone, the security has become a bit slack. And besides, it's the last thing they expected after their assault yesterday. By the way, do you know why Lady Divestelan didn't go to Tolares with the rest of the family?"

"Well, I'm not quite sure, but from what Zetara told me, it seems that Lord and Lady Divestelan have been living their own lives for years. She has a handsome residence up in the mountains and doesn't really come to the city very often anymore."

"Hmmm…Has anyone ever tried recruiting her?" Tuvel asked.

"That's an interesting thought. Why don't you run it by Sheletas when you get back?"

"I might just do that."

Dena chewed on her lower lip. "Tuvel, what was Sheletas talking about this morning, regarding patrols in the Navaren, the Northern Forests?"

"That's just the problem: We don't know. All we know is that Lord Divestelan has been sending patrols and hired mercenaries to Navaresa. It seems that they're looking for something up there."

"But Sheletas did mention that there was some conjecture."

"Yes."

"Does it have anything to do with the ancient legends, the Tinavar?"

Tuvel sighed. "It's possible. For some reason, a few of the Great Houses in the west have been delving into ancient lore, but we have no idea what they're up to."

"I thought that might be it. I've also been hearing some rumors along those lines." She took a deep breath. When she raised her head, she gasped. "Oh, Tuvel, look. Isn't that a mivelin?"

He turned west, in the direction his sister was pointing. "Yes, it is. What a magnificent bird! I believe their wing span can reach fifteen cubits. But look, it's sailing back in the direction of Mt. Toradeh. What a wonderful view!"

"It's breathtaking! Oh, Tuvel, I'm so glad we can be together like this. It really does feel good not to be under any pressure for a change." She smiled at him.

He returned her smile. He was grateful that her desolate mood had passed and she seemed almost cheerful again. She had earned a break after everything she'd been through in the past two years. It was the main reason he had chosen the southern route, and he hoped a slow and peaceful journey might help to heal her pining spirit. But he hoped even more that the High Priestess could help her to see reason. If not, he would probably never see his sister alive again.

33. *Waiting*

"Caty, would you please lift me up?"

"Well then, come, my little poroda."

Catyana lifted her eight-year-old sister onto her lap and placed a kiss on her cheek, while brushing her sister's golden locks out of her face. Then she looked up from her task of chopping vegetables and glanced at her mother, who was supervising the contents of various pots on the stove.

"Mother, do you think she'll be arriving soon?"

Her mother glanced at her eldest daughter with a tender smile. "Yes, my dear heart. I'm sure she's at least five minutes closer than the last time you asked."

Catyana slipped with her knife and cut her finger. She dropped the instrument in agitation. "Oh, Mother, I'm sorry to be hassling you so. Whatever can be wrong with me?"

She put her bleeding finger to her mouth and licked it, then placed her free hand over it. The hand glimmered for a few seconds, and she removed it again. Her finger had been completely restored. The process itself had been entirely routine; Catyana hardly realized what she was doing. To her, it was a simple procedure, regenerating a disrupted ethereal pattern. Neither her mother nor her sister had taken note of what had happened, but even if they had, they would not have thought that anything out of the ordinary had occurred.

Her mother put down the ladle with which she had been stirring the gravy, wiped her hands on her apron, walked over to her daughter, and gently stroked her hair. Catyana looked up at her.

"Well, for one thing, your dearest friend is coming to visit," her mother said, replying to her daughter's previous query.

"Yes, I know."

"And then, I gather that you're preoccupied with several very essential questions." She smiled at her daughter. "Catya, why don't you go outside and wait? I can finish in here."

"Are you sure?"

Yes. There isn't much left to do, anyway. And take Sinara with you."

Catyana returned her mother's smile, picked up her sister, who straddled her waist and put her head on her shoulder, and walked out of the kitchen into the bright spring day with her precious, golden-haired cargo. She looked up into the intensely blue sky and took a deep breath of fresh air while gently swaying her sister back and forth.

"Are you tired, my little one?"

Sinara nodded.

"Don't you want to see Nova?"

Sinara vehemently shook her head.

"Well, why not?"

Sinara raised her head and looked at her while letting her finger glide gently down her eldest sister's nose. "Nova's going to take you away, and I don't want that to happen."

Catyana looked into her sister's bright blue eyes in astonishment. She hadn't realized how aware her sister had been of all the various discussions that had taken place in the family in the last weeks. She should have known better.

"Oh, Sinara, I'm so sorry." She hugged her sister tightly to herself. "I love you very much, little one, and nothing is ever going to change that, no matter how far away I am."

Sinara plucked gently at her sister's shoulder in an unconscious gesture. "Caty, will you write to me?"

"Why, yes, of course, every day, my little poroda, if you want me to. Will you promise to write back?"

Sinara nodded. "As often as mommy lets me. You know

how she is about paper."

Catyana sighed. "Yes, dearest, I know. I hope that, one day, you'll have all the paper you could ever want." She rubbed noses with her, and Sinara giggled. "If you keep practicing the trick I showed you this morning, you probably will. Just take a pile of leaves and change it into anything you want."

They smiled at each other. Catyana hadn't kept what she had learned during her walk yesterday with Nova and Vilam to herself. Although she would never have told anyone else, she always shared everything with her family. Her siblings weren't quite as gifted as she was in that regard, but they got along quite well and had grasped the concept rather quickly. It would still take quite a bit of practice, though, before they began changing large artifacts from metal to stone.

Her expression became solemn as she thought about the episode yesterday afternoon. She had of course sensed Nova's apprehension after the event, but she had no idea what had caused her friend's anxiety. And then there was that incident with the chyeves yesterday evening as they were walking into town. That poor animal! Catyana had wanted to heal it. She knew that Nova understood her hopeful gaze, but Nova shook her head. Catyana was still very disappointed. Why was her friend acting so strange lately? She would have to ask her about that. Maybe they would get a chance to talk about such things on their journey to Tolares. Just thinking about it sent a surge of excitement and anticipation through her. Would her parents allow her to go? Would they permit her to join the Order?

"Caty, they're coming!"

Her brother Torvos came tearing down the road towards the house, with her sister Minora following not far behind. No surprise there. Wherever Torvos went, tomboy Mina was sure to follow.

They had been helping their father load the wagons for a

log shipment that was going into town early the day after tomorrow, but were given some free time just before noon and had immediately taken up position at the bend in the road to watch for their guests. Both of them were barefoot and dusty, and Mina's skirt was torn in several places. Torvos ran up to Catyana and stopped, bending over and supporting himself on her free shoulder, gasping for breath. When Mina caught up, she continued to skip around them, jumping up and down with excitement like a rubber ball gone out of control.

"My goodness, look at you two!" Catyana exclaimed in dismay.

"But, Caty, there are three of them!" Mina cried.

"What? Three?"

Torvos had caught his breath and stood up straight, nodding. "Yes, two women and one man."

"A man? Oh, how wonderful! Vilam has accepted the invitation! But who could the other woman be? Oh, no, it can't be possible. That would be too much! I must inform Mother immediately. I want you two in the house cleaning yourselves up, right now! No, I won't take any of your insolence, Mina. Get inside, at once! They mustn't see you like this. I'm sorry, honey, but I'm going to have to put you down."

The sudden activity around the house became even more pronounced when everybody heard who Catyana believed was coming. Catyana's second oldest sister, Zetavira, appeared from the family room, where she had been preparing the flax, and her father came in from behind the house, wiping the dirt from his chores on his overalls. But they were accustomed to working quickly and were soon ready with the family completely assembled in front of the house to greet their guests.

34. *The Grave*

Vordalin stooped into a crouch and picked up a charred piece of wood resting at his feet. It was still warm. All around him the blackened, smoldering ruins of what had once been a small farm cried out to the heavens, silently denouncing the terrible injustice that had been committed there. The scene was eerily quiet. In the distance he could hear a zicises, the black herald of death, cawing its somber message from the tip of a conifer.

He stared at the mound before him. His friends had told him that the grave contained the remains of an elderly male, an elderly female and a girl. He shook his head. It was so often the same heart-breaking pattern. The young men were drafted and were either recruited into the guard or more frequently just disappeared without a trace. The rest of the family was left without protection and hardly enough hands to run the farm. At some point the farm was attacked and the men slaughtered. Then the women were ravished and also slain. Sometimes, as in this case, the farm was burned to the ground.

But somehow this situation didn't quite fit the pattern. Here there was a grave, and the grave was already several days old. Usually an attack lasted only a few hours or a night at the most, and the carnage of the victims was left as a feast for the birds and wild animals. This family had been murdered two or three days ago and then buried behind the stable. But the fire had not been set until around midnight last night. That had been about sixteen hours ago, for it was now noon of the following day.

His friends, who were neighbors of the murdered family, had not been asleep at that time and had seen the glow of the flames over the trees. The heat must have been immense, and the fire had been visible for leagues around. When they had arrived at the scene, some of their neighbors were already there and more had come as they waited, but there was nothing any of them had been able to do. Now all that was left of the four buildings were the charred skeletons of some of the more solid beams, and here in the center of the stable a blackened, cast-iron semblance of the Sword of Selanae fixed to what must have once been a very solid supporting column.

There could be several explanations for what had happened here, but his intuition, based upon the experience of twelve years as High Priest, told him that something was very much amiss. He wished he had the time to better appraise the situation, but his mission was urgent and he could not linger. He had left Nadil yesterday evening after talking with Nova and Elder Yonatan, and had made fairly good progress, averaging about eight leagues an hour, although he hadn't been able to change his chyevi very often. He was now just northeast of Pitaren and had another 110 leagues to go to Divestelan, then on into the mountains.

Vordalin sighed. He rose and strolled back to his chyeves, where he unstrapped his bag and took out several pieces of parchment. He sketched a quick outline of the premises and jotted down a few notes so that he could compile a report when he returned to Travis. He had already recorded the names of the victims, which his friends had given him, and now added his own observations. When he had finished, he neatly replaced the parchment and firmly secured the bag behind his saddle. He ensured that his sword was still strapped safely to his side and then nimbly swung himself up on his mount and galloped towards the dark chain of the Covasins looming in the distance.

35. *Moment of Truth*

When Nova, Vodana, and Vilam rounded a bend in the road, they saw a typical farmhouse: a whitewashed structure with a red tiled roof constructed in the form of a square with rounded corners and built around a courtyard. A gallery rose up over the courtyard, so that the court could be used as a closed herbarium. Two solar generators of the type Vilam had seen yesterday were visible near the barns and sheds in the background. Vilam and Vodana were still several dozen cubits away when they both noted with surprise that all members of the Faeren family had golden hair and bright blue eyes.

Nova immediately rushed forward and ardently embraced her friend. "Oh, Catyana, it's so wonderful to see you again!"

As soon as Vilam and Vodana arrived, the entire family, except for Catyana and her father, dropped down on one knee and bowed their heads. Catyana's father stepped forward and bowed to Vilam.

"Your Holiness, we are greatly honored that you should visit our modest home. Please forgive the plainness of our situation, but we are simple people."

Vilam just stood there with his mouth agape, not knowing what to say. Catyana's father quickly realized that something was amiss, but it was Vodana who graciously came to their rescue by stepping forward and taking his hand in both of hers.

"Thank you so much for your warm and well-meant welcome, but I believe our friend here is just as simple a man as you are and not accustomed to such formal introductions. Please, just call him Vilam and treat him as an equal. My own name is Vodana, and I am Nova's sister."

A relieved smile spread over the man's face as he clasped

Vodana's hands in his and shook them heartily.

"Thank you, Vodana, for making things so easy for us. I am Lotis, Catya's father. Your name, of course, is not unknown to our house, although we never realized you were Nova's sister. She could have mentioned it, since she has become almost like a daughter to our family, but she has always been a close one," he said, smiling over at the handmaiden, whose eyes twinkled back at him. He then stepped over to Vilam and firmly took his hand.

"Vilam, I'm very pleased to meet you, and I hope that you'll feel at home in our humble abode."

Lotis's words put Vilam at ease, and he smiled broadly at his host. "Thank you, Lotis. I'm sure I will."

Lotis now turned and introduced his family, who had risen again after realizing with relief that no formality would be necessary to entertain these particular guests.

"This is my wife, Matila; my son, Torvos; and my daughters Mina, Vira, and Sinara. Catya you already know."

Greetings were said all around, and the family began to disperse.

Nova presented her basket to Matila after stowing the other package she had brought under her cloak. "Matila, here are a few things I thought you might be able to use."

"Why Nova, that's so kind of you. Let me put them in the kitchen and I'll get your basket right back to you."

Vodana followed Matila into the kitchen to see if she could help, but everything had pretty much been taken care of.

"Matila, I don't want to embarrass you, but you and Lotis do make a very handsome couple, although a bit young for a family of this size," Vodana said carefully.

Matila smiled at her. It was true. She was very attractive, with her thick, golden hair cascading down her back to her waist and her bright blue eyes. She usually wore her hair bound together in a ponytail but now had it open because of the special occasion. Like the rest of her family, she was dressed in attire that was simple and a bit worn but clean and well tended.

"Thank you for the compliment. Yes, Lotis and I married very young, even before our Age of Maturity. We therefore needed our parents' consent, but they knew us both well enough and agreed. I, for one, have never regretted it."

She was going to take the basket and return it to Nova, who had entered the dining room where the rest of the family was gathering, but Vodana stepped in front of her and touched her arm.

"I just wanted to tell you, Matila, before we get back to the others, what a wonderful daughter you have. I was only able to get to know her briefly yesterday, but she made a very deep impression on me. Even if you are a hard-working family and probably must exert yourself immensely to get by, I know that your hearts are in the right place and would like to thank you for it. It's no longer such a matter of course in these difficult and increasingly unstable times for a family to follow Anae's Golden Path as you do. I admire you greatly for it."

Matila looked at her guest, her eyes shining. "Thank you, Vodana. You don't know what it means to a mother's heart to hear something like that."

They smiled at each other, and Vodana, in a compassionate impulse, embraced the younger woman, who clung to her motherly counterpart with spontaneous affection. They parted and Matila hastily exited the kitchen with Vodana behind her. The family was already seated about the table as Matila returned Nova's basket.

"Thank you, Matila," Nova said as she rose to store the basket with her cloak.

"No, thank *you*, Nova," Matila replied, while squeezing her guest's arm in gratitude.

Lotis was presiding at the head of the table, with Vilam at the other end as guest of honor. Matila took the seat at Lotis's left, as usual, while Vodana sat at his right. Nova, Catyana and Sinara made up the rest of the group on Matila's side of the table. Sitting next to Vodana were Vira, Mina, and then Torvos.

"Shall we sing a song before we commence with the meal?" Matila asked cheerfully.

"Oh, that would be wonderful," Vodana replied. "What shall we sing?"

"Anae Pirae cel Pesati Mada," Sinara quickly called out, reciting her favorite chorus. The other children immediately agreed.

"Alright, 'The Lord Provides All Good Things' it is. Who will lead us?" Matila asked, looking hopefully in Vodana's direction.

Nova also glanced over at her sister, her eyes pleading. Vodana took the hint.

"I will, if you like," she replied.

Everybody smiled, and Vodana began the song. It was a simple children's tune, which even Vilam, who didn't know the words, could follow easily. Vodana didn't draw on her training, but deliberately let her voice blend in with the family. They sang the short chorus once, and then began the song again as a canon, splitting the party at the table into four groups. It was obvious that the family sang often and well. When they had completed several rounds, Vodana signaled that they would close and they all stopped at the end of their verse, filling the dining room with one last, ringing chord. When it had died away, everybody laughed and clapped.

"My, that was so lovely," Vodana exclaimed, her eyes shining.

"Yes, and may Anae bless this meal and our fellowship at this table," Lotis added firmly, turning his head towards a representation of the Sword of Selanae that adorned one wall of the room.

"Amen to that," Nova replied under her breath, also paying obeisance to the memory of the Sword and what it represented.

The rest of the family followed suit and complied with the custom by bowing their heads. After Lotis signaled that a minute's silence had been observed, everybody began talking quietly while passing the bowls of victuals around and filling their plates with as much or as little of the appealing dishes as they liked.

In the meantime, most members of the family had realized that Vodana didn't put on any airs regarding her talent. Although she was by far one of the world's most celebrated musicians, she blended in naturally and enjoyed being around the children. She had especially taken the shy but industrious Vira into her heart, who was sitting next to her and was about eighteen years old.

"Vira, could you please pass the fetara?" she asked.

"Yes, of course. One moment, please. There you go."

"Thank you. You have a very beautiful voice, do you know that?"

Vira put down her spoon and looked at her neighbor, her eyes wide. "Please, don't say that. You're only being kind, aren't you?"

"No, Vira, I really mean it. I'm the kind of person who says what she thinks, nothing more, and nothing less."

Vira swallowed. "Oh, please, don't raise my hopes. You must realize that, coming from you, such a statement would mean so much more than if it had come from anybody else. I've always dreamed of becoming a musician."

Vodana also put down her silverware and turned towards her neighbor, searching in her eyes. "Do you really mean that, Vira?"

The girl nodded.

"Do you know what it takes to become a good musician?"

Vira shook her head and looked at Vodana, holding her breath.

"Well, it's really quite simple," Vodana explained. "It takes a lot of hard, demanding work and grueling hours of never-ending practice. You push yourself to the limit, and then you push yourself beyond that, until you wished you had never started. Imagine your father loading logs for eight hours every day of the week, every month of the year, for years without end; then imagine yourself doing the same with your music. And if, after years of intense training and nerve-wracking rehearsals, you discover that you might possibly have a spark of talent, you may even become a great musician, instead of just a good one."

Vira sighed in relief. "Thank you so much for telling me that. You've given me hope. If what it takes is mostly just plain, hard work, then I believe I might stand a chance."

Vodana looked at her with a peculiar expression on her face and caressed Vira's cheek. "You dear child, you really would be prepared to work that hard, wouldn't you?"

"Yes, ma'am. Hard work is nothing unusual if you grow up on a farm."

"Oh, don't *ma'am* me, please. Just call me Vodana."

"Yes, ma...Yes, Vodana."

Vodana reflected for a moment. "Listen, Vira, do you think your parents would allow you to practice here, at home, in your spare time?"

"Well, what little spare time we do have, we can usually employ as we wish."

"I'll tell you what, when we're finished with the meal, I'll ask your mother if she will allow me to test you. All we need is a room to ourselves, and if it turns out at all the way I expect, then I promise you that I will visit you as often as I can and help you with your studies."

Vira's jaw dropped. "Oh, Vodana! Why would you do something like that for me?"

"For a very simple reason: I hate to see good material go to waste. From the little I've heard, I do believe that you have the necessary talent. And if you're as willing to work at it as you say you are, then I don't see why you shouldn't be given your chance."

They were interrupted by a disturbance at the other end of the table.

"Mommy, tell Mina to stop making faces at me," Sinara cried.

"Yes, but Sinara keeps kicking me under the table," Mina retorted.

"Alright, that's enough, both of you!" Catyana exclaimed. They both dropped their eyes at their sister's intent glare. "Sinara, did you really kick Mina?"

"Not on purpose," she replied huskily. "I was practicing the new dance steps you taught me yesterday, and I guess it got a little out of control."

Catyana suppressed a smile. "Alright, then maybe it would be a good idea if you practiced after the meal. And apologize to your sister."

Sinara looked shyly across the table. *"Votalaran, Mina."*

Mina bristled at her sister, her lips pressed into a thin line and her eyes flashing defiantly.

"Mina." Catyana looked directly into her sister's eyes.

Mina flinched as if she had been struck and dropped her gaze. She finally looked over at Sinara, her expression softer.

"*Tezatal, Sinara.* I believe you if you say you didn't do it on purpose."

Everybody at the table had followed the exchange with interest. Now that things had returned to normal, they continued with their meal.

Vodana looked at Lotis and Matila in astonishment. "That was most enlightening. I never would have believed Catyana had it in her."

Nova smiled at her sister. "I told you that there is more to her than meets the eye. But then, I've had a lot of time to get to know her in her accustomed environment."

She squeezed Catyana's hand, who smiled back at her friend.

Matila was also smiling. "Yes, she's quite the housemother. I always know that I can rely on her to take care of anything that needs to be done, from dealing with squabbling children to organizing the household. The children all unconditionally bow to her authority, even Torvos, although he's already twenty-two. It is kind of amazing, if you think about it."

Lotis took his wife's hand and looked at her, his eyes searching. Matila nodded and smiled at him encouragingly.

"Yes, we're going to miss her very much," he declared loud enough for everyone to hear.

All activity stopped, and the room became so quiet you could hear a pin drop.

"Father?" Catyana whispered, not daring to believe that her moment of truth had finally arrived.

Lotis gazed tenderly at his daughter and nodded. "Yes, dearest Catya. Your mother and I have talked about it at length, and we both believe that you should have your chance, although we'll be very sorry to see you go. If it's truly what you wish, then we would be very proud to have a daughter in the Order."

"Oh, Father!" Catyana rose quickly, dashed around the table, and put her arms around her father's neck, kissing him on the cheek and hugging him tightly. Then she turned, dropping down on one knee, and embraced her mother passionately. Tears were in her eyes. "I don't know what to say. I don't know if I should rejoice that you've allowed me to go, or if I should cry because I'm leaving you."

"Caty!" A heart-wrenching wail sent Catyana rushing down to the other end of the table, where she took Sinara in her arms. Tears were already streaming down her cheeks in torrents. "Caty."

"Oh, my poor little darling."

While Catyana comforted her youngest sister, Nova turned to Catyana's parents.

"Lotis, Matila, I would like to thank you with all my heart that you are giving Catyana this chance. I know what a great sacrifice it is for you, but I'm sure that your daughter will one day make you very proud."

"Oh, no, Nova, we already are very proud," Matila replied.

Nova smiled at her. "Yes, I believe you are. But there's another matter that I need to speak to you about. Did you realize that we're leaving for Tolares tomorrow morning?"

"Yes, we did," Lotis answered. "It's unfortunate that you'll be traveling on Velavides, the Holy Sabbath, but that can't be helped. On the other hand, you'll have much less traffic, which will speed your journey. Matila and I have discussed this point as well and we believe it would be more efficient if Catya returns with you to the Lady's manse tonight. It might make things…easier."

"And we're also much honored that you have come today and brought your sister and Vilam with you," Matila added. "We hope that it will help to make this parting a very memorable one, for all of us."

Nova smiled. "Well, we will hopefully be returning this way after the conference. I promise that we'll stop by on our way back to Travis, so we should be seeing you again soon enough. But, if it's alright with you, we'll stay until later this evening, so we still have a little time."

"You're more than welcome to stay as long as you wish," Lotis replied. "I'm afraid that I'll have to return to the woods to finish loading the wagons, though, and that will take most of the afternoon. We usually don't work on Velavides, so I must finish today if we're to complete our delivery for the coming Velanav."

"Excuse me, Lotis," Vilam said, "but may I come with you and offer my assistance? It might expedite things a little."

Lotis looked at him in surprise. "Well, yes, gladly. But it's very hard work. Are you sure you feel up to it?"

Vilam smiled. "Don't worry. I'd be most obliged if you had another pair of working gloves and some overalls for me, though."

"Yes, of course. We always have more than enough of those. I wouldn't want to be doing this kind of work without them."

Nova put her hand on Matila's arm. "I've brought a little surprise with me for Catyana. Would you like to see her in her new robes before she leaves?"

"Oh, Nova, you're such a dear. Yes, I'm sure everybody would like that very much."

The meal had been disrupted through these various events, so everyone turned their attention back to their plates, except for Catyana, who was still comforting Sinara.

Torvos resumed his lively discussion with Vilam. "I've heard that the Tesalian steel forged on the western slopes of the Covasin Mountains is so resilient, it will even split stone."

"You mustn't believe every rumor you hear, my friend,"

Vilam replied. "Yes, Tesalian steel has a distinguished reputation, but you must never forget that a sword blade has a very specific function. It is used to cut flesh and bone, not wood and stone, and it is honed for exactly that purpose and no other. Even though the carbon content of the alloy is much higher in Tesalian blades than in most others, over 2 percent I believe, and the blade itself is therefore very hard, I would never use it on material it was not intended for. If you do, you could easily chip the blade, unless you were very fortunate."

Torvos looked disappointed. "I always thought you could cut down trees with a blade like that."

Vilam's expression was solemn. "When you're facing your opponent in battle, believe me, you'd rather that your tool fulfilled its intended function well and saved your life. Knowing that you could cut down a tree with it wouldn't be much of a help to you in such a situation."

Torvos nodded slowly. "I see that I still have a lot to learn."

"Let's hope that you never have any need to learn it," Vilam replied soberly.

"I do," Mina cut in. "It sounds exciting, what you said about cutting through flesh and bone. Whoosh! Whoosh!" She made a gesture of slicing through the air with a two-hander.

"Mina, come on! You're a girl. When will you finally grow up and act like one?" Torvos exclaimed indignantly.

"Torvos, I'm only thirteen, so I can still act like a child if I want to. And besides, Caty will be learning to use a sword now that she's going into the Order. Why can't I? Whoosh! Whoosh!"

Vilam regarded her with a wry smile. "Alright, Mina, does your father have any swords?"

Mina stared at him, her eyes wide. "Why, would you teach me?"

"I could give you and your brother a short lesson, if you wish."

She cast down her eyes, her expression crestfallen. "We don't have any swords," she muttered.

"Mina, we still have the wooden imitations we made last winter," her brother offered. "Maybe we could begin with those."

Mina looked hopefully up at Vilam, who smiled at the dissimilar pair.

"Alright, I'll tell you what," he said. "When we get back from the woods, I'll take a look at your swords, and we'll see what we can do."

Mina jumped eagerly up and down in her seat. "Oh, how exciting!"

"Mina, calm down," Catyana warned sternly. She was sitting in her chair across from Mina and was eating again, but she kept her left arm around Sinara, who was still weeping quietly while leaning against her older sister.

"Oh, alright. But I really can't help feeling excited," Mina mumbled to herself, while listlessly pushing her food around on her plate.

Shortly after that, Lotis rose from his seat. "I'm very sorry, but I need to get back to work. Those of you who are staying are welcome to continue the meal. My beautiful wife has once again outdone herself and made such wonderful delicacies that I'm actually tempted to stay myself."

The couple smiled at each other. Vilam and Torvos also rose from their seats to join Lotis.

Mina looked up at her father. "Daddy, may I please come with you? I'm not very hungry, anyway."

Lotis winked at her. "You really were a big help to me this morning. Nobody can swing an axe like you, my little shield maiden. If you still feel like coming and your mother has no other plans for you, you're welcome to join us."

When Matila nodded her accord, Mina jumped from her seat and rushed to her father's side, throwing her arms around him. He gently stroked her silky golden hair, and she looked up into his eyes, smiling eagerly.

"Thank you, Daddy," she whispered.

The party soon left, and the women cleared the table and carried the dishes into the kitchen. When things were pretty well cleaned up, Vodana took Matila aside and told her about her conversation with Vira.

Matila smiled. "Yes, I know. Vira just loves music. I'm afraid, though, that we never could have done for her what you might be able to do. We have a music room in the back of the house that you can use. Vira will show you where it is."

She embraced Vodana, not knowing how else to express her gratitude. Vodana returned the smile, delighted that she had found a way to benefit this family she had come to admire so much in so short a time.

When she heard that her mother had agreed, Vira eagerly took Vodana's hand and pulled her into the corridor that completely surrounded the herbarium. Catyana and Nova had overheard the conversation and smiled at the departing pair. They weren't aware of Sinara's concerned expression as she followed her sister's retreat with her eyes.

36. *Dispute in the Navaren*

The forest around them was filled with the quiet sounds of the wilderness. From above, Velana shone brightly down upon the dense branches that sheltered them, casting the scene in a hushed, emerald glow. Everywhere Cetila looked she saw islands of fern and moss covering the rocks that surrounded them, as if her eyes were drowning in green.

The little brook beside her gurgled with subdued amusement at the young woman's astonishment. She leaned back against the immense trunk behind her and stared up into the mammoth tree's branches as she reclined luxuriously in a soft carpet of pine needles. The air was filled with the fresh scent of resin. A sense of awe befell her. When her eyes returned to the earth, the aggressive black and crimson design of her uniform seemed like a rude intrusion into this peaceful sanctuary.

"I don't think we should be here," she remarked in a soft voice. "I feel as if we're trespassing."

"Well, then I suppose it's best that it's not your decision to make."

She looked up at her companion, who was leaning against a tree across from her. "No need to rub it in, Pira," she said, annoyed at the renewed provocation.

Her companion gazed pointedly back at her. "Interesting."

"What's interesting?"

"That wasn't quite the point I was trying to make. I wonder that you took it that way."

Cetila sat up and pressed her lips together. She would have glowered, but that seemed just as childish as the silly game Pira was playing. Instead, she closed her eyes, took a few deep breaths, and allowed the soothing atmosphere of the forest to calm her.

She opened her eyes. "Pira, believe me, just because I'm Tavita's sister doesn't mean I'm looking for exclusive treatment. She had a good reason for leaving you in charge, and I'm perfectly happy with the status quo."

Pira glanced at her, doubt in her eyes. "Cetila, we've known each other for a long time, and I still am fond of you. I really want to trust you, but so much has happened, and I somehow can't seem to place you anymore."

"And I beg you not to try. I don't enjoy being categorized."

"And I thought you didn't want to be reminded of your rank. But you are now second in command. You therefore have certain responsibilities towards your sisters in arms, and as your superior, I must know where your loyalties lie. You're not making things very easy for me. Why won't you play along?"

Cetila sighed. "I don't want to always be weighing every word everyone says. Can't we just have a normal conversation and say what we mean?"

"Tavita felt that mind games help us to stay sharp."

"Tavita is Tavita. I feel there are better ways of sharpening our minds than learning how to drop veiled hints or seeing through ambiguous speech."

"And then there's still the question of your brother," Pira said.

Cetila paled. "I really don't feel like having that particular subject brought up again," she said with cold deliberation. She struggled to contain the pain and anger building up inside her.

Pira eyed her warily. "Your reaction isn't very comforting."

"Well then, Lady Novesta, tell me truthfully. How would you feel if your younger sister killed a brother you had been very close to?"

"I would rein my emotions and set my mind to what is best for…"

Cetila's long, black dress fluttered as she lunged at her companion, coming almost face-to-face with her. "How dare you use such trivial, indoctrinated propaganda on me?" Her left hand tightly gripped the hilt of her sword.

Pira almost cringed at the intensity of the attack, but then raised her head and took a deep breath. "Alright, Cetila, if you're so eager to know what's on my mind, then why don't you tell me honestly if I need to watch my back around you."

Cetila sucked in her breath and stared at her comrade, clenching her teeth to suppress the tears she could feel burning just below the surface.

"Pira, that really hurts. Why do you doubt my loyalty?"

"Varan was working for the enemy, and I'm almost certain that Dena is, too," Pira countered. "Why do you continue to defend them?"

Cetila looked into her friend's eyes. How could she explain to this devoted warrior the reasons why she still respected and cherished Varan and Dena without seeming like a traitor?

"There's an immense difference between defending someone and hurting for them," she finally answered. "I would never betray our cause, Pira. I'm fighting for a free world just as much as you are."

"You have a strange way of showing it. Must I rebuke you for insubordination?"

"No, of course not. I will do whatever you ask, My Leader," she replied, snapping to attention and bowing her head. "Although I was hoping very much that we could be friends again," she added meekly, looking up at Pira through her lashes.

"So was I," Pira said, regarding Cetila evenly. "As you were, Brigadiess."

Cetila stood at ease, but kept her hand leisurely on the pommel of her sword.

"Cetila, despite my rank and service to the Brigade, I haven't grown as cold-hearted as you might believe," Pira said, softening her voice. "I've never lost a brother, and I can hardly imagine the pain you endured. I suppose that my approach might not have been appropriate for your particular situation. Why don't we start over again?"

"I would like that very much."

Pira let herself slide down and rested her head wearily against the trunk of the immense conifer behind her. Cetila sat down beside her, a bit tentatively.

"When did Tavita leave?" Pira asked.

"Tomorrow will be a fortnight."

Pira sighed. "I really would be grateful for your help, Cetila. I suddenly have an entire battalion of energetic young women to supervise. Neither of us has Tavita's vigor or prowess, and I fear it will take our combined effort to handle them. I must admit that the Lady's request was a godsend. It gives us something to do."

"Yes, my mother has been very adamant about such things lately. I wonder why she's suddenly become so interested in the Tinavar. Wouldn't it be wonderful, though, if we really caught one?"

"A Unicorn? Are you seriously implying that such creatures exist?"

Cetila stared at her, astonished. "Why yes, of course. Just look at this forest. It's like a presence all around us, as if it were some enchanted, sentient being. Don't you feel it?"

"You've always been a bit odd in that way, Cetila. And what's worse, you're beginning to sound like a Selanian priestess. What's next, Sensation and Induction?"

"I wouldn't underestimate the powers of the Selani if I were you."

"I suppose you're right."

"How much longer do you think we will need to wait?" Cetila asked.

"As long as necessary, but with the entire battalion enclosing the area, I'm certain we'll hear some report within the hour, so we'll see soon enough if we're chasing a phantom or not. The tracks we found did seem very promising, though. I've never seen anything like those hoofprints. Who knows, maybe you'll get your Tinavar after all."

"I wish I had traveled to the Navaren earlier in my life," Cetila remarked, filling her lungs with fresh air and looking around. "I never knew the Northern Forests were so breathtaking. It's exciting, being at the heart of ancient lore. It makes me wish Mother would send someone to the Sea of Ventara to look for Mermaids."

"Oh, didn't you know? She did."

"What? I can't believe this! Why wasn't I informed?"

"I suppose it was on a need-to-know basis."

Cetila fell into sullen silence. It was bad enough that Tavita didn't seem to trust her anymore. Why her mother, too?

"Are you grateful that the Lady has reassigned us away from Corsen and his Black Guard?" Pira asked.

"Yes, absolutely."

"Don't you think it was a good idea for Tavita to merge the Brigade with the Guard?"

"No, and I believe Tavita knows it, too. She just did it to be closer to Corsen. But in the end, even she had to recognize that it was a grave mistake."

"Our sisters insist that it was…invigorating."

"That's what they've been taught to say, but it's just more indoctrinated propaganda. It's Brigade Policy, so it must be true, no matter how they feel about it. But those men only saw us as objects of gratification to satisfy their own perverse cravings, or maybe even as a chance to prepare for the attacks on the farms. I felt violated just by the way they looked at me." Cetila shuddered.

Pira shot her a sidelong glance, obviously shocked. "You've become a very outspoken person, Cetila. That could be dangerous."

"Why? I haven't done anything wrong. Besides, what could they do to me?"

"Look what Tavita did to your brother."

"Well, I'm not planning on giving her a reason. Besides, how are they going to fight a war with an army of pregnant women?"

"You have a point there. I'm certain that's why Tavita and Corsen finally put a stop to it."

"Corsen is a fool."

"Cetila!"

"It's true. If your Uncle Citenes wasn't still captain of the Black Guard, I doubt there would be a glint of common sense left in them. Corsen thinks of this whole campaign as a game, and we are the pieces he plays with. He is but a spoiled brat who uses others to accomplish his vain notions. Tavita would see it, too, if she wasn't so infatuated with him."

"Why don't you talk to her?"

"Tavita hasn't listened to me since…well, you know, since the Three Nursemaids. Besides, I'm certain she's aware of the problem. That's why she allowed Mother to have the Crimson Brigade reinstated for this assignment. As a matter of fact, I think she even went on this covert operation of hers to get away from Corsen, although she probably would never admit it, even to herself."

"Well, at least it will be interesting, working with you again on such close terms."

"Why did you choose me as your right hand, Pira? I still can't quite understand it. You could have promoted any of the other Brigade leaders when Tavita left. I mean, it's not as if we were very close anymore."

Pira eyed her solemnly. "Yes, I know, and you can't imagine how much I regret that. I can't really tell you why I chose you, Cetila. Maybe it was just a feeling. To tell you the truth, I was getting a little tired of the other girls' exaggerated submissiveness. You're probably right about all the indoctrination. Hardly anyone dares to formulate their own thoughts or ideas anymore."

"Yes, I sometimes can't understand why it's necessary to brainwash people who are supposedly fighting for a free world."

"I was taught that it's an essential means to an end, like the attacks on the farms, and that everything will change when we emerge victorious."

"Exactly: You were taught. More indoctrination!"

"I see what you mean. How is it that you've become so…unconventional?"

"Well, I wasn't, really. I was just like the other girls, eager to serve towards this noble ideal that had been drummed into us. Please, understand me correctly, I still completely agree with the ideology. I mean, who needs the bigoted laws and hypocritical concepts of the Selanian Order? It's just our methods that I'm sometimes in conflict with. Anyway, Tavita ensured that I quickly came up through the ranks. But then Varan…died. That really shook me up, and I started thinking."

Pira turned towards her. "Cetila, will you promise me to always tell me what's on your mind, no matter how unorthodox your thoughts are?"

Cetila looked at her, astonished. "Well, yes, of course, if that's what you want."

"It is. It'll be just like old times." Pira grasped Cetila's hands, and the two women smiled uncertainly at each other, then lapsed into uncomfortable silence. There were still too many unanswered questions regarding their relationship, and Cetila realized that renewing their friendship would probably take more than just a little effort on both sides.

37. The Audition

Vira had lived in the house all her life and knew it like the contents of her apron's pocket. The front side of the house contained the dining room and the family room. She and Vodana also passed several bedrooms on the left side of the house, then the study in the back, at last coming to the music room. The right side of the house contained the kitchen, which was connected to the dining room, a pantry, and a storage room. A wooden spiral staircase on one side towards the back of the herbarium would have taken them up to the gallery where the children usually did their schooling or enjoyed reading and painting on lonely winter evenings.

Vira could tell that Vodana admired the herbarium as they went around it. The entire corridor was windowed so that the view was completely unobstructed. It was well cared for and had a beautiful fountain in the center. Vira was proud of the substantial variety of plants they grew. Large skylights in the roof surrounding the gallery allowed generous quantities of light to illuminate the room.

The music room was just as large as the dining room. It also had sizeable windows, which faced north. Every member of the family was musical, and there were therefore several instruments lying or standing around. Torvos had even constructed a glass organ, which stood dormant on one side of the room.

Vodana seated herself in front of the harp and let her hands fly gracefully over the strings. She smiled her approval, for the harp was well tuned.

"Alright, come and stand here, Vira, right next to me," Vodana said. "No, don't look at the harp, look at me. I'm going to see how far along you are in aural comprehension first. Now, tell me which interval I'm playing." Vodana plucked two strings.

"A perfect fifth."

"Very good. How about this?"

"Major seventh."

"And this?"

"Minor third."

"Alright, what about this?"

"That's not an interval."

"Well, what is it?"

"A major triad in its second inversion."

"And this?"

"A diminished ninth."

"I see you're solid on your chords."

"Yes, I'm sorry, I should have told you. Mother taught us all that when we were little."

"And a very good job she's done of it, too. Now, can you tell me which tones these are?" Vodana plucked a short progression of strings.

Vira's eyes opened wide. For some reason, the theme brought disturbing images to her mind, and for the first time since her discussion with Vodana at the dining table, she faltered in her eagerness. She looked down.

Vodana must have mistaken Vira's hesitation for embarrassment. "What's wrong, dear? I sense that you're holding back. Just open up and let yourself go."

Vira shook her head. "I'm sorry, Vodana, I don't have

absolute pitch," she answered untruthfully, staring at the ground in sudden confusion.

"Not to worry, my dear. Many people that do often don't have a very good feeling for harmony and dissonance, and their ability to understand melodic patterns is sometimes severely impeded. It can be very aggravating having to work with them. Can you at least make an educated guess?"

"I would say it's approximately D, A, B-flat and F, all in the fifth octave."

"Not just approximately, but exactly. Very good, Vira. Did you reach that conclusion by working from a familiar reference tone?"

Vira nodded. She knew that Vodana was correct in her assessment regarding individuals with absolute pitch. She had accrued similar experiences during the few times that someone with that particular talent had visited them. But she also knew that the impairment didn't apply to her. She couldn't understand why she felt so reluctant to reveal herself to her new friend.

"Alright, now we'll try some rhythmic exercises," Vodana continued. "How do you usually acquire your reference tempo?"

Vira felt for her pulse.

"Excellent! I always do it that way, too. Now, I'm going to clap a fairly lengthy rhythm. I want you to close your eyes, and when I'm finished, I want you to try to repeat it."

Vira continued and didn't miss a beat, although her heart somehow was no longer in it.

38. A Tinavar's Choice

Itinales raised his head and sniffed the air. His herd was in danger. He nervously pawed the ground and then sniffed once more. The noose was tightening. He was still undisputed Prince of the Forest, yet who would respect him if he allowed his herd to be entrapped? From the realms north of the Sea of Ventara to the regions north of the Chyenesar, the forest was his. He still had not found his Tinasal and therefore could not mate; he had not yet fought the Becintas in the far north and was therefore not yet King of the Navaren; but he had always believed that there was still time. Now, time was running out. And if he couldn't even protect his own herd, he didn't deserve the title.

Through the dense foliage he cautiously eyed the two women leaning against the trunk of a mammoth pine in the clearing. There was evil brewing. The two women themselves were not necessarily malevolent, nor were the many women who were hunting down his herd. But the purpose that had brought them here was born of malice, and behind that purpose, he could feel an even darker power. The shorter woman, who was called Cetila by her friend, had already partaken of the refining pain that led to purification and might some day make a good Tinasal. He could even sense the beginnings of the process in the taller of the two young women, but alas, all of the women had been poisoned. He perceived the shadow of darkness in their auras.

He raised his head and sniffed the air once more. The women were slowly surrounding his herd, and he knew that there was no escape. In the past years they had encountered more and more men who had wandered into the forest, looking for them. It had usually been easy to evade them, but this time there were just too many. He had counted over five hundred. Why hadn't he listened to his instincts and traveled further north? It would have been the safe thing to do.

On the other hand, where there were no people, there were no Tinasal, and without the Tinasal, the mares would remain barren, there would be no young, and his race would die. In this sense the past millennium had been good to them. There had been peace, evil had been held at bay, and there had always been maidens with a pure heart that could be found wandering in the forests, drawn by a burning desire they could not quite define. Of course it was necessary for the steeds to leave their beloved Navaren to search for a Tinasal, but until a few decades ago, the forests in the south had been safe for the Tinavar to travel in.

All that was changing quickly. Evil was lurking everywhere. What would happen if they were forced to bond with an impure Tinasal? Itinales shuddered and tossed his thick, silvery mane. The consequences of such an act would be horrendous. And yet the possibility of such a thing happening was drawing nearer. The safeguard that the One had put in place to shield the precious balance of life on the planet was slowly melting away with each day in which the Millennial Peace was undermined by the forces of darkness.

The Elinar would have known what to do. They had been the Divine Heralds of Wisdom and the Guardians of Passage. With their singular insight, they could have distinguished the subtle currents of ethereal space that ensured equilibrium. They would have taken the necessary steps.

But the Elinar were long gone, and his herd was now in immediate danger. There was really only one thing he could do. He stood still and called silently to his herd, informing them of his plan. They mutely cried out in anguish, pleading with him to reconsider. He didn't respond. He knew they would obey.

He looked once more at the two women sitting at the base

of the tree. They were the leaders. If they recalled their troops, his plan might work. His thoughts wandered back to his hopes and dreams and conjured up the image of the Golden Messenger that had been the longing of his heart for so many years. What a Tinasal she would make! But it was probably just a meager fantasy, born of false pride. Not his hopes and dreams were important at this moment, but the safety of his herd. He shook the thoughts from his mind and steeled himself to the task ahead. He had made his choice, and he knew what he had to do.

39. *Empty Assurances*

Catyana and Nova went outside with Sinara while Matila completed some minor tasks in the kitchen, promising to join them before long. They sat on one of the benches in front of the house, enjoying the afternoon sun.

Nova took Sinara and lifted her onto her lap. "Sinara, are you very angry with me?"

Sinara looked up at her and shook her head. "No, I'm not angry, Nova, just dreadfully sad. I do like you, very much even, and if Caty has to leave, then I'm glad it's with you and not anybody else. But it still hurts so much in here," she said, pressing her hands against her heart while another tear slipped down her cheek.

"Oh, you poor thing," Nova exclaimed, hugging the little girl to herself and rocking her back and forth. "I do promise you, though, that I'll take very good care of her."

Sinara looked up at Nova and nodded, then cuddled up against her again, brushing another tear from her eye.

"Sinara, your sister told me that you've been having nightmares again. Is that true?"

Sinara nodded.

"Would you like to talk about it?"

The girl sighed. "I don't know. I don't really like talking about them. They're scary."

"I understand, honey. Could you tell me what's so scary about them?"

"Well, it's not so much the fire and the black men. But then I hear the song and there's suddenly blood all over and a big, black hole opens up and I feel like I'm being swallowed by…" Sinara shuddered.

"By what, dear?"

"By her," Sinara whispered as another shiver went through her.

Nova and Catyana looked at each other in concern.

"She calls her *'Tevasala se Nemata,'* the Goddess of Death," Catyana said.

Nova gazed out across the fields, contemplating the words her friend had just revealed to her. Then she turned back. "Yes, it's an ancient prophecy, foretold by Cades himself, and one of the first prophecies regarding the Traveler: 'Let the accursed beware, for he will awaken the Goddess of Death when he comes and the song of the siren will unleash the Goddess's wrath upon his enemies,' 1 Cades 24:16. Passages like that have been known to induce anxiety in tender individuals, which is why we are very careful with them. You haven't been reading such accounts to her, have you?"

Catyana thought about it for a moment but then shook her head. "No, not that I'm aware of. Mother has been concentrating more on the Latter Prophets of late."

"Could this be another prophecy that must be taken literally?" Nova asked somberly. She sighed. "Everything I've been taught seems to be falling apart." She looked down upon her young charge and discovered that Sinara was trembling.

"Please, Nova, don't let him wake her up," she whispered.

Nova hugged the little girl tightly to herself. "It's alright, Sinara, it's alright."

Nova couldn't think of any other way to comfort her, although she realized that her assurances must sound empty, for she couldn't even believe them herself.

40. *The Sacrifice*

Cetila caught her breath. She could feel the blood draining from her face. Pira looked at her and almost jumped.

"Cetila, what's wrong?"

"*Te'linos*, it's so beautiful," Cetila whispered.

Cetila heard her friend gasp, as if her breath had been forced from her.

They were both staring at the most beautiful animal they had ever seen. The Tinavar's translucent horn gleamed dully in the soft light of the forest. Its silky coat shone like silver, and its thick mane and luxurious tail rekindled dreams that the little girls still buried somewhere inside of them must once have had.

Cetila's heart reached out. Was this what she had been yearning for all her life? Was this what had called to her on moonlit nights when she tossed restlessly in her sleep? Had its alluring voice drawn her outside to wander in the forests, seeking her desire, searching for that which had been lost in the depths of her soul?

"Pira, where's your horn?" She could hardly breathe.

"No, Cetila, it might be trying to trick us."

"I don't think so. It's as if I could almost feel its thoughts. I believe it wants to be caught."

"Why?"

"It's going to sacrifice itself for its herd."

As she spoke, the Tinavar turned and walked leisurely back into the forest.

"Do you see? It's walking right back into our trap," Cetila insisted.

Pira swallowed. "Alright, let's try it. At the worst, we'll lose a day. My horn's in my bag."

Cetila reached for her friend's bag and pulled out the horn. Then she stood and blew a short burst of isolated notes. They soon heard the theme being repeated from different locations in the distance. The two women took up their gear and followed the clearly visible tracks the Tinavar had left. From its stride, it was apparent that the animal wasn't moving very quickly.

"How's your brother?" Cetila asked in a hushed voice.

"Talenon?"

"Yes."

"I haven't really heard very much from him since Lord Divestelan made him head of his intelligence organization."

"It seems like an interesting idea, though, using a religious order as a cover."

"An interesting idea? I thought you didn't like ambiguity."

Cetila smiled. "Alright, interesting, but ineffective. From what I've heard, the new High Priestess is very devious. I'm certain she's long since discovered that the Videsian Order is just a front for covert activities."

"Is it really just a front? I'm sure that many of the followers are true believers and have no idea what's going on behind the scenes. Cetila, what's really bothering you?"

"It just seems that your house is…highly involved. Your brother is head of intelligence, your uncle is captain of the Black Guard, and your father is practically Lord Divestelan's right hand."

"Are you saying House Marusen isn't involved?"

"My house is a known variable."

"I see. And I'm an unknown?"

"Maybe."

"Look, Cetila, I oppose these methods as much as you do, which is probably why I chose you as commander of the brigade. I promise you, if you watch my back, I'll watch yours, alright?"

Cetila took a deep breath. "Alright, I really do want to trust you, and I've wanted to renew our friendship for quite a while now. I was somehow hoping you might understand. But it does seem as if my sister has quite a bit of power over you. You were her first officer after Lady Gevinesa stepped back. It would hurt me very much if someone wanted to get close to me for the sole purpose of reporting back to my sister."

"No, please, believe me, it's not like that. You know for yourself how confused we all were when that bitch of a Gevinesa betrayed us. Tavita was the one who held us together and gave us the moral support we needed during that difficult time. I pledged to be faithful to her and her cause, and I intend to honor that pledge. But Tavita's gone, and I really could use a good friend by my side right now."

Cetila cringed. "I don't feel very comfortable when you talk about Gevinesa like that. The Crimson Brigade wouldn't even exist if it hadn't been for her. Besides, she might have had some very good reasons for leaving us."

"Then why didn't she talk to us? We practically worshipped her. We would have followed her anywhere or done anything for her."

"Things change."

They fell silent and concentrated on the tracks before them, both of them hesitant to resume the conversation.

Cetila finally looked over and spontaneously took Pira's hand, dragging her to a stop. "Pira, I really do want us to be friends again."

Pira gazed at her in astonishment. "So do I, very much. Will you promise to watch my back?"

Cetila nodded. "Yes, I promise, I'll watch your back."

They beamed at each other in relief, falling into each other's arms, and Cetila felt a surge of joy wash over her. When they finally parted and looked at each other, Cetila was surprised at the elated glow in Pira's expression, which highlighted her friend's almost divine loveliness in a way she hadn't seen in many years. Then Pira turned, and grasping Cetila's hand tightly in her own, she pulled her forwards to continue their search. Cetila felt as if a terrible weight had fallen from her, and with the newfound lightness in her heart, they made good progress.

After half an hour they again saw the enthralling creature grazing quietly in a good-sized clearing. As she watched, Cetila saw her sisters signaling from all sides, completely surrounding the animal. She took the net out of her bag, stepped out of her hiding place, and walked towards the Unicorn.

"Cetila, wait," Pira called after her.

But she couldn't. Something inside of her lured her towards the enchanting beast.

The clearing was completely silent. She couldn't hear a sound of her sisters in the underbrush, who were most likely watching her outrageous behavior intently. As she approached the Tinavar, it stopped grazing and eyed her cautiously.

She reached out and carefully stroked its sleek neck. "You're beautiful, do you know that?"

The Tinavar whinnied softly.

"I suppose you do." She stepped back. "I'm very sorry, but I have to do this."

In an abrupt motion she threw the net and let it glide out of her hands. It draped itself over the Tinavar, which snorted anxiously, but otherwise remained calm.

Suddenly the underbrush around her came alive as her sisters jumped out, cheering her for her supposed courageous performance. The net was quickly fastened to the ground. She turned and found Pira standing behind her.

"You couldn't help yourself, could you?" Pira asked.

Cetila shook her head.

"I understand. I won't tell the others that it didn't take as much courage as it seemed."

They smiled at each other. Cetila walked over to Dalina to discuss methods of transport.

Pira stepped towards the entrapped animal and turned to the leader of the first company, who had just entered the clearing with her brigadiers. "Lieutenant, you have your orders. Begin the treatment."

The lieutenant bowed and gestured towards two of her sisters. They took out their whips, but hesitated when they saw the beast gazing calmly at them from inside its latticed prison. They turned back to their superior. The lieutenant swallowed. Then she closed her eyes, took a deep breath, and nodded for them to begin. The two women raised their whips and struck out viciously at the animal, which no longer had any way of defending itself. The beast's cries sounded like the screams of a woman in the throes of profound anguish.

Cetila jerked around at the noise and paled when she saw what was happening. "Pira, are you out of your mind? What are you doing?"

Pira turned towards her. "I'm sorry Cetila, but those are the Lady's explicit orders. The Tinavar must be near death when we deliver it to her in Tolares. I really am sorry," she reiterated when she saw Cetila's anguished expression. "I have no idea what your mother is up to."

Cetila pressed her lips together to keep them from trembling. She turned back to Dalina. "Prepare the crate. We will begin transport immediately."

Then she walked stiffly out of the clearing and back towards the camp with her head held high, but bitter tears stinging in her eyes.

41. *Golden Gifts*

Matila soon joined her two daughters and Nova for a short walk around the farm. The farm itself was quite diversified; the family not only owned many different types of livestock and poultry, but had also sown various forms of grain and vegetables. It clearly took a lot of work to tend to everything.

Nova smiled when she saw the little cetesi, which reminded her of her sister's remark earlier that day. The colorful creatures came scampering hopefully up to the women, butting against them with their little horns to get their attention and blatting disappointedly when they discovered that no supplementary fodder was forthcoming.

The women returned to the house after about an hour, where they found Vodana sitting in the family room, conversing quietly with a radiant Vira. They all looked at Vodana expectantly.

"Don't look at me, look at Matila," she told them. "She's the one that instructed this young musical genius here. And I must confess that she's done an excellent job. I've started Vira on a few advanced breathing techniques and shown her some exercises and drills that will help her to develop volume and intensity in her head voice. I hope those will keep her busy until I can stop by again, although I doubt it. If only I had brought some advanced training manuals with me."

Matila quickly vanished into the kitchen, obviously embarrassed by the emotions that were overpowering her. Nova and Catyana sat down facing Vodana and Vira, with

Sinara again on Catyana's lap.

"Come now, sister, tell us exactly what happened," Nova urged.

"Well, it was actually quite amazing. Vira had no problems whatsoever with basic musical comprehension. Then when we got to the vocal exercises, she just closed her eyes and felt herself into the songs and techniques. The moment I explained something to her, she had already grasped it. Her perception for music is absolutely astonishing. I still feel you're holding back, though, Vira. I'm certain you could have done even better." She looked at Catyana. "It reminds me of what Nova told me about you and the art of Induction, Catyana. It seems to be the same domestic trait, only Vira's ability focuses on musical instead of ethereal patterns."

Nova nodded. "Yes, I've been reasoning along the same lines myself. Every one of the children exhibits some remarkable form of perception, although I haven't been able to completely categorize them yet. It's especially difficult with Mina. Sinara's talent is quite clear. Her domain is emotional and social perception. Torvos seems to revel in any form of practical, scientific application, just like his father. I believe Vilam calls it 'engineering.' Vira, you have inherited your mother's musical abilities. And your talent, Catyana, is Induction. But Mina is completely mystifying. She seems to be the most aggressive one of the family, although I have no idea what that will lead up to."

"Do you believe it has to do with their golden hair and blue eyes?" Vodana asked. "Those specific physical characteristics only surface very rarely. Maybe they are somehow related to their perceptive abilities?"

"Yes," Catyana answered, "that could be possible. I've heard that other members of our house back west have also exhibited such remarkable talents."

Nova was watching Sinara and saw that the girl had been glancing over at Vira. The sisters' eyes met. Despite Vira's apparent delight, her joy seemed subdued and Sinara's expression was troubled. Nova wondered what the problem was.

Matila returned to the room with a tray filled with cups and plates for the traditional, postmeal deventas, a drink that was customarily brewed from roasted cereals. Nova rose from her seat and followed Matila back to the kitchen, where she helped her bring out more trays loaded with pastries and drinks. Then they all sat around the deventas table, partaking of the various refreshments and talking pleasantly. Catyana browsed through a colorful book with Sinara, portraying the flora and fauna indigenous to their homeland west of the Covasin Mountains. Sinara especially dwelt on the pictures of the porodi, the golden squirrels that inhabited the forests east of the Plains of Tesalin and were popular as pets in those houses that could afford such luxuries.

After half an hour of friendly conversation, they were surprised to hear the party returning from the woods.

Matila rushed to the window. "Goodness, they can't be back so early. Has something happened?"

It didn't seem so, for the arriving party appeared quite cheerful. They had soon washed and changed clothes, then joined the women in the family room.

"Dearest, what happened? Couldn't you finish loading the wagons?" Matila asked her husband, concern in her voice.

"On the contrary," Lotis replied while taking a seat. "Although I would hardly believe it myself if I hadn't seen it with my own eyes. The way Vilam launched into the job, it was incredible. Nobody could keep up with him. He worked like an automaton. He also showed us a few tricks which helped speed things up considerably. I've already asked him if he's for hire, but he politely declined," Lotis added teasingly. "We even got the wagons hitched up and deposited them in the barn, so we won't have to worry about the dew in the morning."

"Oh, it was nothing," Vilam answered. "If you and Torvos hadn't caught on so quickly, it would have taken twice as long. And Mina, of course, was unbelievable. She seems to be a real bundle of energy."

"Why, that's wonderful, darling," Matila exclaimed. "Now we can spend the afternoon together."

"There's still some work for *Tevasala se Nimata*, the Goddess of Life, though," Mina declared playfully.

Catyana looked up from the book. "Why, what's wrong?"

"Oh, nothing serious," Lotis answered. "One of the logs slipped sideways and grazed me. It's just a minor flesh wound, though."

"That's not quite accurate," Torvos said. "The log would have pinned me if Father hadn't intervened. He probably saved my life."

While Catyana examined the wound, Vodana looked inquisitively over at Nova.

"Goddess of Life?" she asked.

Nova smiled. "It's a kind of family hoax. Catyana's capacity for restoring disrupted ethereal patterns is so pronounced that most wounds or illnesses in the family are usually treated by her. The other family members can do it, too, but it takes longer. The children therefore often refer to her teasingly as *Tevasala se Nimata*, the 'Goddess of Life.'"

Catyana had, in the meantime, finished her inspection of the deep, ugly gash in her father's thigh and looked at him reproachfully.

"This is not just a minor flesh wound, Father," she admonished him gently. "I can't understand how you could have continued working like this. It must have been quite painful. Why didn't you come to me as soon as you got back?"

"You know how I feel about such things, Catya. Besides, I knew you'd be there for me as soon as I needed you."

She gazed into the proud, careworn face she knew so well. "I won't be here much longer," she whispered. "You need to be more careful. But I love you for being so gallant and coming to Torvos's rescue."

Nova had seen this procedure often before, but Vodana and Vilam watched in fascination as Catyana placed her hands over the injured area and closed her eyes. Nova knew that she was feeling for her father's ethereal pattern in her spirit, unconsciously crossing the boundaries of space and time in doing so. As Catyana knitted the disrupted pattern in her mind, a bright glow emanated from her hands. The sides of the ugly wound seemed to phase out, dissolving into each other and becoming clean, unscathed skin. Only the excess blood around the wound betrayed that there had been a rift in his leg. The task completed, Catyana rolled down her father's trouser leg, placed a kiss on his cheek, and returned to her seat, where she again lifted Sinara onto her lap and continued reading as if nothing out of the ordinary had occurred.

42. A Goblet Together

It was well past noon, which coincided perfectly with the amount of wine Bejad and Hyumosen had consumed, for it was well past their limit. They were sitting at a table in Rotesil's tavern, each of them tightly clutching the goblet in front of him in fear of sliding under the table if he loosened his grip, seeing as the room was twisting so dangerously.

"I'm in your debt once again, my friend," Hyumosen breathed into Bejad's face.

Bejad carelessly waved the stench away. "Think so?" he mumbled.

"Oh, yeah, certainly. How much of my fortune do you think comes from you bringing me customers?"

"I never thought of it that way." Bejad waved away another cloud of alcohol. "Um, don't you think we should slow down on the drink?" he slurred.

"Well, you know what they say: A goblet alone no one can condone. But a goblet together goes down so much better."

"Oh, yeah." Bejad grinned stupidly.

Hyumosen stared at the table, attempting to concentrate. "Bejad."

"Yeah?"

"You plannin' on gettin' hooked up?"

"Nuh uh. Not 'nough time. Career's been more important lately, ya know?"

"Well, listen, 'bout that little companion of yours."

"Oh, yeah? You mean Netira? She's cute, isn't she?"

"What? Yeah, guess she is. Listen, I don' wanna get too personal."

"Well, then don't."

"Yeah, but you're my friend."

"I am? Aw, shucks, Hyumosen. What a nice thing to see, uh, say," he babbled, blearily eyeing one of the waitresses as she went by.

"Yeah, anyway," Hyumosen continued.

"What?"

"Maybe you should keep your eyes open."

"'Bout what?"

"'Bout your companion."

"What companion?"

"That girl. Uh, Netira."

"Oh, yeah?"

"Yeah."

"Why?"

"'Dunno. Just think you should. You know, she might be the one that finally gets ya."

Bejad beamed deliriously. "Oh? Alright." His head banged onto the table.

Hyumosen looked over at his friend, trying desperately to focus. He then attempted to rise from his seat. With a little more effort, he might even have succeeded, if the room hadn't tilted precariously at exactly that moment.

The waitress that strolled by a while later stopped and put her hands on her hips, shaking her head at the two men slumped over the table. She went to fetch a pail of nice, cold water.

43. *Mina's Lesson*

Mina sidled up to Vilam and carefully plucked his sleeve.

"Please, excuse me, but you did promise," she coaxed.

"Aren't you tired, Mina? You've worked hard for almost two hours, collecting and chopping up all of our leftovers," he replied.

"But I'm not tired, really I'm not."

"Mina, why don't you let Vilam rest for a while," her mother gently reprimanded her.

"No, that's alright," Vilam answered. "If she's willing and up to it, I'll take her on. Torvos, would you like to join us?"

Torvos shook his head. "No, why don't you go ahead. I wouldn't mind sitting for a moment. I'll join you later."

Vilam stood, and Mina raced to her room. She returned almost instantly with two wooden swords.

Nova glanced at Vodana and Catyana. "This should prove

to be very informative. Vilam, do you mind if we watch from the window?" she asked.

"No, I'm getting used to that," he grinned, recalling his training that morning. "What do you say, Mina?"

"Well, I guess it's alright," she replied, although she didn't sound very enthusiastic. "I'm not accustomed to having an audience. Please don't ridicule me if I make any mistakes."

Catyana looked at her sister tenderly. "I promise, Mina, that if anyone should say or do anything even slightly resembling any form of mockery, I will rebuke them myself most severely."

Mina went over to her and squeezed her hand. "Thank you, Caty," she whispered.

Then she took Vilam's sleeve and pulled him into the corridor and outside, eager to begin. They stepped into the sunshine, and Vilam walked away from the house, assessing the distance to give them enough room to maneuver comfortably.

"Alright, Mina, now show me one of your swords," he said.

Mina handed him one.

Vilam gripped it firmly in both hands and nodded. "Not bad. Good, solid workmanship for a wooden imitation, all the way down to the leather grip and the steel pommel. I must say, your brother does have a gift."

Mina smiled at him.

"I watched you swinging that axe of yours earlier, Mina. That wasn't bad, really. Now, do you know what to look for in a sword?"

Mina shook her head.

"Well, it's actually quite diverse and depends completely upon the weapon. Different blades will respond differently, depending on whether they are long or short, straight or curved, thick or thin, wide or slender. You test them subjectively by hefting them or striking and thrusting with them. Sometimes you might even flex them.

He glanced at Mina to see if she was following before he continued.

"When you grip the sword and swing it, you can feel immediately whether the sword resists or facilitates your swing. A good sword can be honed to facilitate thrusting, cutting, or both."

He demonstrated each of these details as he explained them. Then he asked Mina to try it. She did, and proved to Vilam that she understood everything he told her.

"Very good, Mina. Now, as you heard at the dining table, the making of a good sword is a science in itself. I won't tell you about the different types of steel that are used and what to look for, but I do want you to be aware of the fact that it is a very delicate art. If your swordsmith is a quack, you're in big trouble. A good sword can mean *etino*, the difference between life and death."

Mina nodded, her eyes wide, not missing a single, precious word.

"Alright, now we'll get down to the real thing. Swordsmanship, like most other physical arts, relies on four basic principles, which I call the pneumatic, static, dynamic, and rhythmic components. The pneumatic component is air. If you can't breathe, you can't fight. The static component deals with your stance and your posture. If your stance or posture is off, you will overbalance and fall. End of story. The dynamic component involves your movements, which must be accurate or you will lose momentum and energy. If your attack or ward carries too far, your opponent will ruthlessly exploit your weakness. That leaves the rhythmic component, which deals with timing and cadence. Even if all of your movements were absolutely perfect, you wouldn't want to be too late to ward a thrust, now would you?"

Mina vehemently shook her head.

"Now, grip your sword firmly in both hands, close your eyes, and just breathe, while being aware of yourself, your sword, and your surroundings."

Vilam instructed her in basic breathing techniques, stances, positions, and footwork, taking his time without rushing her. He was soon amazed at how adept she was and found that she was actually pushing him. She just soaked everything up like a sponge absorbing water. After half an hour, Torvos joined them, and Vilam patiently explained everything again while simultaneously continuing Mina's lesson. She smoothly listened in on Torvos's class without once missing a beat of her own exercises.

An hour later, Vilam was already dueling with her, something he wouldn't have attempted with any other student unless they had been through at least a week of extensive training. He soon dropped the swords and taught her basic hand-to-hand combat procedures, explaining the different uses of each extremity as a deadly weapon and how to discern various targets on her opponent in regard to their lethality. When they resumed sword practice, he found that her wards and attacks had profited immensely, focusing her attention on essential objectives.

Vilam was more than just astonished. Who was this young girl, who seemed to be the most talented, but also the deadliest, student he had ever encountered? Only time would tell, and he concentrated on imparting as much knowledge as this seemingly insatiable vessel could hold.

44. The Operative

Talenon sat back and sighed in relief. He had been writing all day, had even skipped the midday meal, and his fingers were sore. The doorbell had been ringing continually, and countless couriers had been in and out since he had commenced his dismal work just before sunrise. Despite the many messages that had gone back and forth, this was the first decent piece of news he had received all day.

He took another look at the page on his desk. Their new operative had finally arrived in Tolares and would soon be continuing on to Travis. The girl had an excellent track record, and he had to admit that the report on her skills was unprecedented. He was astonished at the amount of experience she had accumulated despite her young years. It was general knowledge, though, that the members of Lady Gevinesa's personal guard were usually recruited at the age of sixteen. In this case, it had even been fourteen. The Lady had then trained them herself as ruthless and efficient killers, and Tavita had been her most talented apprentice. She had soon become the Lady's personal aid, had risen to the rank of captain and led the Crimson Brigade in countless assignments. Every task had been completed competently and resourcefully.

For some reason, though, the Lady must have grown tired of her guard. Corsen had been more than happy to merge her Brigade into his own guard, and Tavita had continued her steep climb, quickly earning Corsen's complete trust. He was the one who had recommended her for this assignment.

Her full name was Tavita of the House of Marusen. Talenon knew Lord Marusen personally. The man was quite competent and belonged to a noble family that had its residence in the mountains north of Divestelan. And of course

Talenon also knew Tavita well enough. She had been the charge of the renowned Three Nursemaids, of which his sister Pira had been a member. He snickered at the notion. Who would have thought that the sweet, innocent little girl that he had seen so often playing at their residence in Novesta would one day become such a competent and formidable operative?

Talenon smiled to himself. He could imagine how it must have happened. The Lady Gevinesa was, of course, acquainted with all the daughters of the more distinguished houses. None of the lords and ladies realized how she had gradually spun her webs, biding her time, evaluating the girls and then recruiting the most promising of them into her Brigade. After all these years, many of the families still didn't know what their daughters were up to when they visited Divestelan. Some of the young women had even persuaded their parents to allow them to take up permanent residence near the city, so that they could be closer to their comrades.

Well, it was no matter of his. He was grateful that he could now begin coordinating the plans for Tavita's transfer, ensuring that she would be assigned to the mole they had placed in the Advisory Council. He bent back over his desk and continued writing.

45. The Ballad

In the family room, Vira was sewing. She saw Nova, Vodana, and Catyana exchange significant glances as they observed the speed with which Mina was assimilating the deadly skills of swordsmanship.

"Is her progress really so remarkable?" she asked Nova.

"Yes, I must admit it is. I've never seen anything like it. But I also marvel at Vilam's expertise. It reminds me of the prophecy which characterizes the Traveler as a master and teacher of the martial sciences."

"So you really think he is…"

"Well, we'll see."

Vira remained thoughtful for the rest of the afternoon.

At some point, her mother rose to prepare the evening meal. Vodana and Vira joined her. Lotis also stood and collected Torvos to attend to various chores. Mina, who seemed indefatigable, would rather have continued her instruction, but Vilam decided to lend the two men a hand, so Mina tagged along.

The evening meal was simple, consisting of bread, cold meat, vegetables, and milk. After everything had been cleared away, they all returned to the family room and made themselves comfortable. Nobody realized that Nova and Catyana had disappeared until they suddenly stood before them, Catyana wearing the same cream-colored robe that designated Nova's affiliation with the Selanian Order. She had her black cloak draped over her arm.

They were all astonished at how stunning she looked. Her thick, golden hair was freshly brushed and cascaded elegantly down her back to her waist. She looked like some kind of heavenly messenger, illuminated by the light of the setting sun. The robe itself was high-necked and long-sleeved, coming together to accentuate the waist, then slipping smoothly over the hips and draping gracefully to the ground. The material and workmanship looked very soft and comfortable, allowing full freedom of movement.

The whole family crowded around her, touching her and her new robe, realizing that the time of her departure was drawing near.

Matila covered her mouth with her hands. "Oh, Catya, you're so beautiful," she whispered, blinking back the tears that glistened in her eyes.

Catyana embraced her. "Mother, I love you so much, I hardly know how to express it. And I'm so grateful for everything you've done for me."

"Oh, dearest child, nothing we ever could have done for you will ever amount to what you have already given us."

They looked at each other and embraced again.

Sinara tugged at her mother's skirt while leaning against Catyana. "Mommy, could we please sing something?"

"Why yes, that's a very good idea," she replied, while brushing her tears away. "What would you like to sing?"

"*Cozatenae se Malentisa,* the Destruction of Malentisa."

"Alright, we all know that one. Why don't those of you that would like to accompany the ballad go get your instruments? Vodana, would you like to lead us again?"

"I have a better idea," Vodana replied. "Why don't you let Vira lead, and I'll support her."

Vira blushed at the compliment. But she also noted that Vilam seemed very expectant.

"Is this a favorite piece of yours, Vilam?" she asked shyly.

"No, I've actually never heard it before. But I am grateful that Sinara chose it. It gives me an opportunity to finally hear an account of the events surrounding the Cataclysm."

"Oh. Well, since you're not participating, you might as well just sit back and enjoy the recital."

He smiled at her. "Thank you, I believe I will."

The family was soon assembled again. Since they had performed this particular ballad often in the past, everybody knew what to do, and they took their positions without being told. At Vodana's signal, the instruments began the introduction, after which Vira closed her eyes and commenced the song. Nobody could deny that her voice really was uncommonly clear and beautiful as she skillfully and delicately accentuated the finer nuances of the piece. Vodana

soon joined her, assuming a lower voice to subtly underscore
Vira's solo.

Hear now this tale that transpired long ago
In an era long past and hardly remembered
Ancient scribes have recorded this tragic account
So we all may tremble and forever recall
The Destruction of Malentisa

A world had been born, a paradise unrivaled
Where Elinar persisted in gathering wisdom
And Demantar peacefully grazed in the plains
Not perceiving the evil that soon would yield
The Destruction of Malentisa

Caverns of light harbored the diligent Elinar
As they grew in knowledge and sophistication
But their unbalanced eagerness before long brought forth
A pride so immense that no soul could prevent
The Destruction of Malentisa

Vilasan was his name, the Bright One his distinction
His understanding and insight of unrivaled perfection
The sole power on Piral he deemed to become
An Elinar so conceited he at last conceived
The Destruction of Malentisa

There was no relief when Elinar and Selani
Perceived his deception and feebly resisted his designs
The Selani he seduced to forsake their ways
Binding many to darkness so they might achieve
The Destruction of Malentisa

In the fated year four ninety six
His dark army of slaves smote the unwary Elinar
He showed no mercy but slew them all in their homes
His Selanian bondmen cruelly carrying out
The Destruction of Malentisa

Nevilan was his name, the Dark One his distinction
No longer did light shine upon the former Bright One's
    face
He continued his devices of Piral's systematic subjugation
His lust for power yet unquenched by
The Destruction of Malentisa

The Lord of Light, Anae Himself, no longer could endure
The agony and suffering this malicious being had
    produced
Down He came in glory and supreme sovereignty
To call to account the one who had realized
The Destruction of Malentisa

The Asteroid fell in a great Cataclysm
From the heavens it came to chastise us all
For in our conceit and proud complacency
We stood not against darkness but passively allowed
The Destruction of Malentisa

Yet Anae had discovered that not all had complied
In the anguish and pain He even now found a spark
Of love and righteousness that one day could restore
The wisdom and knowledge that was consumed in
The Destruction of Malentisa

Anae showed mercy in His righteous Judgment
And did not allow Piral to utterly perish
But His punishment was severe on the day He descended
And His heart was grieved as He perceived
The Destruction of Malentisa

His people stood up to reprimand evil
No longer did they permit darkness to prevail
In the twilight the Cataclysm had spared of the sun
The Selani waged war in the shadow of
The Destruction of Malentisa

Anae bestowed wisdom upon artists and smiths
To forge the metal of the Rock from the Heavens
A symbol was born of vast strength and great hope
The Sword of Selanae that at last would revenge
The Destruction of Malentisa

Lord Pival Tolares bore the Sword into battle
A High Priest to repel the dark forces of evil
His army of light converged upon his rival
While tears were wept and memories evoked
The Destruction of Malentisa

In one last battle upon the eastern slopes
Of the Covasin Range was the foe overthrown
No longer did darkness obscure the light
Nor wickedness revel in the tragedy of
The Destruction of Malentisa

The Evil Lord fled through the Desert of Vortelan
While Lord Tolares pursued through the night to
    his doom

In the Ruins of Malentisa the two rivals met
Adding one further loss to the fatalities acquired in
The Destruction of Malentisa

Lord Tolares's remains were in the Ruins discovered
But no sign of the Dark Lord could ever be found
And the Sword of Selanae had utterly vanished
Leaving a mere silent hope to commemorate
The Destruction of Malentisa

The tale is now told and peace long been restored
But in the silence of wreckage and ghostly remains
An injustice cries out and beckons to be heard
So that through all time we shall never forget
The Destruction of Malentisa

After the last subtle notes had dissipated, everyone began to stir.

"My, that was beautiful. You all did an excellent job," Vodana praised them. "But you, my dear, were magnificent," she added, turning to Vira and touching her arm.

Vira could only glance back at her. She managed to collect herself and turned, not knowing how to thank her newly found benefactress. "Well, what shall we sing next?" she asked, attempting to sound cheerful in order to conceal her distress.

They decided on several simpler tunes, many of which Vilam was able to join in, and continued singing for another hour, not wanting their time together to come to an end.

Alas, the evening had advanced, and they could no longer postpone the inevitable moment when Catyana had to depart with her friends. Nova, Vodana, and Vilam said their farewells, and Vodana gave Vira a few last-minute instructions, embracing her lovingly when she had finished.

Vira felt uncomfortable, knowing that she had held back on her new friend. She was not accustomed to concealment and could hardly suppress the uproar of her emotions. She therefore removed herself to a quiet and unobserved corner until she had composed herself, but the sadness and confusion in her heart remained, together with an indistinct feeling of some impending doom.

46. *An Approaching Storm*

"I'm sorry, Culisa, but I just can't do this any longer, not after everything that's happened." Semanta gazed pleadingly at her friend.

"I understand, and I'm not angry. As a matter of fact, I'm thinking of quitting myself."

"You are?" Semanta asked in astonishment.

"Yes. Don't get me wrong, it was fun while it lasted. I've always been a hopeless romantic, and an adventurous lifestyle does appeal to me. But currently I've been getting this strange feeling that we're working for the wrong side."

"I know what you mean, and I feel the same way. Besides, I think Folan is getting suspicious. I could hardly get your message to Talenon out last night."

"Oh? What are you going to do?"

"I really would like to come clean. I'm probably going to tell him everything."

"Won't that be a problem?"

Semanta bit her lip. "Well, I've tried to be a good wife to him all these years. I'm sure he'll understand. What about you?"

"Oh, you know how it is. In the end Menirel will always do as I say."

Semanta sighed and attempted a smile. It was an open

secret who the real mayor of Nadil was. She looked nervously over her shoulder. The evening rush hadn't quite begun, and Semanta was taking a short break to exchange a few words with her friend in the little room that adjoined the side entrance of the tavern. She would need to return to work soon, or Folan would probably come looking for her.

"Semanta, are you alright?"

Semanta looked back at her friend and noticed her worried glance. "Yes, yes, I'm fine. Culisa, do you sometimes feel worn out?"

"No, not really. What's wrong?"

Semanta bit her lip again. "I don't know. Sometimes I feel as if I could sleep for a week."

"You haven't seemed quite yourself lately. You should take better care of yourself, dearest."

"It's not that easy, with the tavern and all."

"Yes, your tavern is very successful. Folan is quite proficient, and he employs as little personnel as possible in order to save costs, doesn't he?"

Semanta shot her a bittersweet smile.

"When are you going to tell him?" Culisa asked.

"Tomorrow being Velavides, it will be a full day. I'll wait until the morning after. We hardly have any business on Velanav morning."

"Semanta, where are you?" they heard Folan calling from down the hall. "Come quickly, woman, we have guests."

The two women glanced at each other, and their eyes expressed their unvoiced thoughts.

"I need to go," Semanta declared. "Thank you for stopping by."

The mayor's wife embraced her. "I was glad to. Please remember, if you ever need anything, my door is always open."

They parted and Semanta turned hastily towards the guest

hall, biting her lip. Disheartened by her constant fatigue, she couldn't rid herself of the sense of a swiftly approaching storm, nor of the feeling that their small and secure world would soon be viciously disrupted and forever torn apart.

47. *Taking Leave*

Catyana took only a few personal belongings because everything else would be provided by the Order. When she was ready to leave, her mother touched her arm.

"Are you alright, Catya?"

Catyana shook her head. "I don't know, Mother. I feel an urge to be off, as if a completely new life full of mystery and wonder were about to begin. You know, like the bedtime stories you told us at night before you tucked us in. On the other hand, I feel so reluctant to leave you all behind. You're all I've ever known, and I love you so much. Oh, Mother, will I ever see you again?"

Her mother attempted a smile. "We never know what Anae has planned for us, dear heart. But I hope we'll see each other again when you return from the conference."

Catyana looked into her mother's eyes for a moment, incapable of expressing the sadness and puzzling anxiety in her heart, before finally tearing herself away.

Sinara stayed close to her as Catyana embraced and kissed each of her siblings and then her mother and her father. In the end, though, Sinara gently caressed her oldest sister's cheek one last time and kissed her ardently while Catyana knelt in front of her. Then Sinara deliberately let her go and stood next to her mother, holding on to her tightly as if fearful that she would drown if she released her grip.

Surprisingly, it was Mina's last, simple words which

echoed in Catyana's mind long after she left. When Mina embraced her, she looked deeply into her sister's eyes and spoke in an uncommonly serious voice.

"Dearest Caty, I know I wasn't always very good or very obedient, but I want you to know that, no matter what happens, I love you very much. Please don't ever forget that."

At length they took leave of the family. Before they disappeared around the corner of the wood, they turned and waved. Catyana saw them one last time, standing in front of the house, illuminated by the warm light falling through the windows, but somewhere in her heart she knew that she would never see them together like this again.

END OF PART ONE

The Traveler: Appendices

TABLE OF CONTENTS

Appendix A: The Traveler's *Excerpts on History*
Appendix B: The Selanian Calendar
Appendix C: Selanian Units of Measure and Currency
Appendix D: Introduction to the Selanian Language
Appendix E: Selanian - English Dictionary
Appendix F: Index of Persons (First Name)
Appendix G: Index of Persons (Family Name or House)
Appendix H: Index of Places

AUTHOR'S NOTE

The following articles were originally written by experts in the various disciplines. Because of the extent and complexity of these articles, I have taken the liberty to shorten and abridge them into appendices to give readers a better overview of the history and culture of the Selani and therefore a better understanding of the events portrayed in *The Traveler*.

I would like to thank the scholars of the Selanian Order on Chyoradan, and especially Philip Brannon of Bend, Oregon, for their assistance, insights and valuable contributions during the compilation of these appendices.

A peculiarity of the text of *The Traveler* may be the extensive usage of *alright*. I have decided to use *alright* to denote the difference between our use of *all right, okay,* or *fine* in the English language, and the use of *tezatal* or *desar* in the Selanian tongue. So if Philip uses the word, he might say *okay* or *all right*. But Silana or Nova would say *alright*.

For more information on the Selani and the Selanian culture, including examples of the Selanian script and full color maps of Piral, please see the author's website:

www.PeterKrausche.com

Appendix A:
The Traveler's Excerpts on History

INTRODUCTION

Because of the Traveler's unique insights into the history and culture of the various ethnic groups indigenous to Piral, and later of the seceded factions that were scattered across the galaxy after the Galactic Diaspora, his *Excerpts on History* have become the basis for any historic research attempted by the Selanian Order. It is rumored that, with a little incentive from the High Priestess presiding at that time, he began to compile his knowledge and experiences into this academic epic soon after his arrival on Piral.

What sometimes makes scientific examinations tedious when employing the *Excerpts* as a source for academic research is the Traveler's reluctance to admit his own connection to any of the occurrences described in his work. Many scholars have attributed the Covatal's unwillingness to focus on his personal involvement in central historic events to his unusually demure nature, although wicked tongues have been known to accuse him of deliberate chicanery. Because of such obstacles, the *Excerpts* have been meticulously cross-referenced with the records of the Traveler's contemporaries, beginning with the memoirs of the renowned Lady Novantina Tolares, and ending with the Covasatal's *Reflections of the Soul*. A study group is currently attempting to cross-reference the *Excerpts* with the *Selani s'Ulavan*.

Despite the various difficulties involved in studying the *Excerpts*, they remain the most prominent source of information in regard to Selanian history. Acquiring a general working knowledge of the composition's structure is therefore mandatory to any students of the chronological sciences.

Although most computer systems today are distributed with a complete copy of this classic opus, it is always prudent to verify on occasion that a particular system retains the latest update. The Traveler's *Excerpts* can be accessed or downloaded in their entirety at any time and from any terminal with a transdimensional field link to the scholastic library's computer of the Selanian Order on Chyoradan.

OVERVIEW

This section is devoted to imparting an outline of the Traveler's *Excerpts* to students not yet accustomed to the composition's intricate structure. The proposed framework is this author's personal attempt to interpret the anatomy of the *Excerpts* and does not necessarily coincide with the Traveler's actual intent. It is this author's desire that the overview will aid students of the chronological sciences in their endeavor to become acquainted with a most extraordinary document, so that prospective graduates and scholars may initially come to appreciate the value of the Traveler's contribution to the academic community.

ERA	From	To
Short Description		
Singular Events	Date	
PARADISE	1 TC	450 TC
Rise of the various cultures on Piral. Emergence of the first townships and cities. The Traveler especially directs our attention to the relationships between the various races, which in many cases were not discovered until after the Millennial Peace. Since the Traveler did not experience the events of the Eras termed "Paradise," "The Cataclysm," and "The Millennial Peace" himself, it is assumed that he collected his data from scholars of the various races, while also leaning heavily on the *Selani s'Ulavan*.		
Lord Pival Tolares establishes the City of Tolares.	289 TC	
Cades, a simple quarryman, is called to be a prophet of Anae.	314 TC	
The Prophet Cades establishes Travis, the "City of Light," at the site of his first encounter with Anae.	376 TC	
THE CATACLYSM	450 TC	550 TC
This section examines the conditions that lead to the rise and fall of the High Elinian Scholar Vilasan, thereafter known as Nevilan. The Traveler also scrutinizes the consequences that these devastating events have upon subsequent eras.		
Nevilan commits genocide on his own people, the Elinar, simultaneously slaughtering the Demantar that coexist with them.	496 TC	
A large asteroid crashes in the Plains of	521 TC	

ERA	From	To
Short Description		
Singular Events	**Date**	
Tesalin.		
The Sword of Selanae and the Admonition are constructed from the metal of the asteroid. The work is supervised by the Prophet Cades.	524 TC	526 TC
The Admonition is lost on the western slopes of the Covasin Massive while being transported to Travis.	527 TC	
Last battle against Nevilan on the eastern slopes of the Covasin Massive. Death of Lord Pival Tolares. Loss of the Sword of Selanae. Nevilan disappears.	534 TC	
THE MILLENNIAL PEACE	**550 TC**	**1550 TC**
In this time of peace and affluence, the Great Houses are first recognized and begin to strengthen their influence. Although most historians terminate the Era of the Millennial Peace with the Conference of Tolares in 1524 TC and the beginning of the Selanian Civil War, this author believes that a more global view of the subject must be taken.		
Establishment of the Selanian Order and the Advisory Council during the first Synod of Travis.	572 TC	
Death of the Prophet Cades.	737 TC	
Various Holy Scriptures are collected and appraised by the Advisory Council and formed into the *Selani s'Ulavan* during the third Synod of Travis.	816 TC	
First Conference of Travis.	861 TC	
The Prophet Nevacad constructs the Prophet's Bow.	1009 TC	
Conference of Divestelan and assassination of the High Priestess Halita Penates.	1519 TC	

ERA	From	To
Short Description		
Singular Events	**Date**	
Conference of Tolares.	1524 TC	
Selanian Civil War. Reemergence of the Demantar and the Elinar. The Sword of Selanae is retrieved.	1524 TC	1525 TC
Quadrilateral Concord.	1533 TC	
The High Priestess Catyana Faeren initiates the Vetenian Non-Violence Act, prohibiting the use of technology in any form to aid in the design of weapons.	1545 TC	
THE SWORDMASTERS	1550 TC	2250 TC
After the events of the Selanian Civil War, the Great Houses begin to assemble armed forces strong enough to protect the population and enforce the laws of the provinces. Swordmasters are usually hired to supervise these functions. The Swordmasters are almost always priests of the Selanian Order. Their status becomes nearly as important as that of the lords to whom they have sworn their allegiance. Because of the widespread fear of the use of technology to advance weaponry (i.e. the *sitanem* developed by Lord Chyardal Tolares), the main responsibility of the Swordmasters is to suppress such attempts in compliance with the Vetenian Non-Violence Act. One of the chief characteristics of this era is therefore the almost non-existent advance of technology. A beneficial side effect of this form of government is the expansion of the provinces and the urge to control as yet new and unsettled territories. Tighter bonds are formed with the Elinar.		

ERA	From	To
Short Description		
Singular Events	**Date**	
The High Priestess, Lady Yanita Divestelan, emulates the initiative of her friend, the Lady Novantina Tolares, and engages the services of the former High Priest Vordalin Penates as official Swordmaster of the House Divestelan. Many of the other Great Houses quickly follow suit.	1581 TC	
The Covasatal discovers the Admonition while en route to Travis with Sevana Faeren.	2096 TC	
Riots in the streets of several major cities. The High Priestess Sevana Faeren annuls the Vetenian Non-Violence Act.	2136 TC	
THE TECHNOCRATS	**2250 TC**	**2850 TC**
Despite the annulment of the Vetenian Non-Violence Act, the constant censorship of technological progress by the Great Houses finally leads to incessant civil commotions. Technical experts independent of the houses gain influence. Since the effective operation of the Advisory Council in Travis is based upon the symbiosis between the Selanian Order and the leaders of the Great Houses, the Council's authority declines. The Technocrats develop their own honor codex and a refined form of the *sitanem* becomes the preferred method of dueling.		
Telates Catanin elected as first Technical Advisor of the City of Divestelan.	2292 TC	
Comprehensive time warp model advanced by Telates Catanin.	2364 TC	
First inductive pulse produced by technical means. The resulting inductive	2587 TC	

ERA	From	To
Short Description		
Singular Events	Date	
field is termed *telatian* field, in honor of Telates Catanin, who anticipated the formation of the field in his time warp model.		
FEDERALISM	2850 TC	3350 TC
The society's need for greater independence yet efficient structure leads to federalism. Church and state are separated. Travis remains the legislative capital of Piral, but is now governed by the Selanian Assembly, whose members are elected by the populace of the various provinces. The Federal Council is elected by the assembly and the president by the Council. The Technocrats retain judicial sovereignty and form the Federal Congress of Provinces, which appoints the Federal Court.		
Establishment of the Selanian Federal Assembly in Travis.	2932 TC	
Flight of the *Mivelin*, the first space vessel to employ telatian technology.	3176 TC	
PLURALISM	3350 TC	3850 TC
The provinces become more independent. The Technocrats have long since lost control of the Federal Congress of Provinces, which is in the meantime also designated by the populace, although actual domination over the corrupt politicians is retained by powerful industrialists. Various forms of religion are now acceptable. The members of the Selanian Order have become but a minority. Only a small number of citizens therefore heed		

ERA	From	To
Short Description		
Singular Events	Date	
the quiet voices that advise caution.		
In order to satisfy the growing energy demands on Piral, construction commences of the first telatian reactor to orbit Velana.	3492 TC	
THE GALACTIC DIASPORA	3850 TC	50 SV
Although the exact reasons for the devastating events leading to the Galactic Diaspora are unknown, many scholars believe that the telatian reactors built in orbit around Velana led to an imbalance in Piral's sun, triggering a supernova of unprecedented proportions.		
Piral's sun, Velana, goes supernova. All life on Piral is annihilated.	3983 TC	
SOLITARY WORLDS	50 SV	650 SV
During the first six centuries following the Galactic Diaspora, most of the newly populated worlds just struggle to survive. Because of the confusion of tongues, which must have been the result of some unidentified form of radiation before the supernova, there is little or no communication between the solitary worlds. Only the Advisory Council on Chyoradan is capable of establishing an efficient government.		
Development of the Mitelian Decryption Algorithm on Chyoradan, which functions as a universal translation method and facilitates communication with the civilizations of nearby stellar systems.	533 SV	

ERA	From	To
Short Description		
Singular Events	**Date**	
THE ALLIANCE OF CHYORADAN	650 SV	850 SV
During the six centuries of near isolation, a loose bond is established between Chyoradan and some of the nearby stellar systems. This finally leads to the Alliance of Chyoradan.		
Alliance of Chyoradan	722 SV	
Temporal Displacement Directive prohibiting any unauthorized computerized temporal synchronization facilities.	834 SV	
THE COLONIAL LORDS	850 SV	1250 SV
Many stellar systems comprehend the advantages of the Alliance. Since the Alliance can not handle so many new affiliates at once, a peculiar form of colonialism develops. Representatives of the Alliance are stationed on worlds requesting admittance as members. Each candidate world with an Alliance presence retains a status as a *Protectorate of the Alliance*. Since the representatives are more or less independent and almost completely responsible for the admission process, they soon receive a significance never intended by the Advisory Council and often rule over the colony worlds as lords while lining their own pockets. For a while, the Alliance almost descends into chaos. This is the time of hot-headed space pilots and gun-slinging tradesmen.		
Horasen Cevanis is dispatched to the Caldarian stellar system, one of the most isolated systems of the galaxy. He is the first representative of the Alliance to	871 SV	

ERA	From	To
Short Description		
Singular Events	Date	
supervise an admission process.		
After almost three centuries of constant delays and temporizing on the part of Alliance representatives, the Caldarians, who have still not been admitted, break away in disappointment and frustration. They return to their lives of seclusion and religious obscurity.	1143 SV	
ENLIGHTENMENT	1250 SV	1650 SV
The immense expansion of the Alliance and the changes to society wrought by the Era of Colonialism have led to a certain measure of insecurity in the population. In their quest for answers, a renewed interest in history is awakened by the Selanian Order and the Advisory Council. A progressive form of Renaissance, termed the Age of Enlightenment, sweeps the worlds of the Alliance, yielding new forms of art, music, and literature.		
The Galactic Intelligence Division (Sevon Costenan Velitra; SCV), a branch of the Selanian Order that manages the official intelligence network of the Alliance, discovers first traces of a shadowy coalition termed the *Order of the Novantan*.	1278 SV	
Torvolan Novesta composes the inspired opera *The Swordmaster*, which recounts the moving love story which unfolded between Sevana Faeren and Perganes Cemasena during the Era of the Swordmasters on Piral.	1323 SV	
The SCV uncovers a conspiracy to gain control of the Advisory Council. The members of the conspiracy, who all	1592 SV	

ERA	From	To
Short Description		
Singular Events	Date	
commit suicide, are rumored to have belonged to the Order of the Novantan.		
MODERNISM	1650 SV	present
After the turbulent events of the past millennium, the Advisory Council decides that it is time for an honest and deep retrospection of its choices and actions. The worlds of the Alliance also acknowledge the need for more stability in their various ideologies. A new form of thought supplants the principles which governed the Age of Enlightenment. This contemporary philosophy attempts a self-conscious break with the past while searching for new forms of expression. Traditional teaching is accommodated to present-day concepts, and the exuberant metaphysical views of the Age of Enlightenment are toned down to a more moderate position. This endeavor to balance various academic disciplines with a call for more tolerance terms itself *Modernism*.		
Members of the SCV discover remnants of an abandoned military training camp of immense proportions in an isolated and unpopulated stellar system.	1734 SV	
The Free Trade Association reports an alarming increase in lost transports.	1887 SV	
The Advisory Council counters an Alliance initiative which strives to drastically enhance the size of the military forces.	1934 SV	

Appendix B:
The Selanian Calendar

Epochs

The Selani divide the calendar into two main epochs: the time after creation (*Tena Corasetal*; TC), which coincides with the approximately 4000 years of history up to and including the annihilation of Piral, and the time after the Galactic Diaspora (*Sevaten Velitra*; SV). The new calendar (SV) was introduced because the temporal units needed to be adjusted to the situation on Chyoradan, although several puritan factions (e.g. the Caldarians) insist on the continuous use of the old calendar (TC).

Selanian Epoch	English	From	To
Tena Corasetal	After Creation	3984 B.C.	2 B.C.
Sevaten Velitra	Galactic Diaspora	2 B.C.	Present

It is assumed that the light of Velana, the now dwarfed sun which the lifeless Piral still circles, takes approximately 56 years to reach Halena Yazoral (The Forbidden Planet, Terra, or Earth). Although Velana went supernova some 56 years earlier, the light of this devastating galactic phenomenon did not reach Halena Yazoral until August 30th in 2 B.C. (by Yazorian calculation). The time warp model advanced by the technocrat Telates Catanin—the propagator of the telatian field—in 2364 TC accounts for the contradictory flow of time in different sections of the universe.

Although, objectively seen, more time passed on Piral during the 4000 years of its history than on Halena Yazoral, the relative and warped structure of the universe allows for an astonishing concurrence of historic dates. Seen from a Yazorian point of view, 1 TC would correspond to 3984 B.C. and the year of the destruction of Piral, which is 3983 TC, would correspond to 2 B.C. in the Yazorian calculation. The new Selanian calendar (SV) corresponds almost seamlessly with the current Yazorian era (Anno Domini; AD).

A day in the old calendar was divided into 32 hours. High noon was therefore at 16 o'clock, Selanian time. One Selanian hour was slightly shorter than a Yazorian hour, approximately 52 minutes. A Selanian year had 480 days and was accordingly about 1_ times longer than a Yazorian year. The 4000 years of Piralian history would have objectively taken about 6000 years of Yazorian time, but this is accounted for in the Telatian time warp model.

A day in the new calendar is divided into 24 hours, and the hours correspond almost exactly to Yazorian hours. The 360 day year of the new calendar therefore takes about as much time as the Yazorian 365/366 day year.

Days of the Week

A Selanian week naturally corresponds to the 7 day creationistic model described in the *Selani s'Ulavan*. Yazorians reading this article may be uncomfortable with the fact that Sunday corresponds to Velanav, the first day of the week. Such readers are requested to remember that, in the original Yazorian model, Sunday also corresponds to the first day of the week, and that Saturday is actually the Holy Sabbath. Only after Christ's resurrection on the morning of the first day of the week (Sunday) did the custom change, in remembrance of Anae's act of hope for all mankind. The Selani on Chyoradan were not aware of such customs until the Traveler made contact with Philip Brannon and a tentative exchange of information between the two planets commenced.

Selanian Name	Yazorian Counterpart	English	Abbreviation
Velanav	Sunday	First Day	Van
Velamayav	Monday	Second	Vmy

Selanian Name	Yazorian Counterpart	English	Abbreviation
		Day	
Velabenav	Tuesday	Third Day	Vbn
Velapilav	Wednesday	Fourth Day	Vpl
Velanetav	Thursday	Fifth Day	Vnt
Velavedav	Friday	Sixth Day	Vvd
Velavides	Saturday	Holy Day	Vds

Months of the Year

In both calendars, the old and the new, a Selanian year begins at the vernal equinox, which corresponds to the first official day of spring, even on Halena Yazoral. In the old calendar, a month was divided into 40 days, which coincided approximately with the cycle of the larger moon, Velanevos. Each season therefore consisted of 3 months. Summer began 3 months after the vernal equinox, at the summer solstice, fall again 3 months later at the autumnal equinox and winter at the winter solstice. In the new calendar, a month has only 30 days, which corresponds roughly to the cycle of Chyoradan's largest moon.

Season	Selanian Month	English	Abbreviation
Spring			
	Anasetani	Early Spring	Ast
	Setanimata	Spring	Stn
	Ulanaseta	Late Spring	Ust
Summer			
	Anamadani	Early Summer	Amd
	Madanimata	Summer	Mdn
	Ulanamada	Late Summer	Umd

Season	Selanian Month	English	Abbreviation
Fall			
	Anatinani	Early Fall	Atn
	Tinanimata	Fall	Tnm
	Ulanatina	Late Fall	Utn
Winter			
	Ananelani	Early Winter	Anl
	Nelanimata	Winter	Nln
	Ulananela	Late Winter	Unl

Peter Krausche

Appendix C: Selanian Units of Measure and Currency

Linear Units

During the first decades of the Millennial Peace, the Selanian Order saw the necessity of synchronizing units of measure. Legend has it that the Advisory Council asked the Prophet Cades to find a satisfactory model for a cubit. Cades was inspired to use the forearm of his great-granddaughter Vitela at the time of her Affirmation, which is usually performed at the age of seven. A cubit is the length of the forearm measured from the elbow to the tip of the middle finger.

Selanian Unit	English	Consists of	US Equivalent	Metric Equiv.
Fires	Thread		0.09 inches	2.3 mm
Runam	Finger	5 Firesi	0.45 inches	1.15 cm
Bemar	Hand	5 Runami	2.24 inches	5.74 cm
Vitel	Cubit	5 Bemari	11.2 inches	28.7 cm
Norven	League	5000 Viteli	0.88 miles	1.435 km

Examples

The distance from Divestelan to Travis is 500 leagues (see the chapter *Dead Drop*). That is 440 miles, or approximately the size of the state of Oregon from east to west.

Mount Vaduras (the highest peak of the Tyenar Mountains) has been measured at 32,175 cubits, which is 30,071 feet (9,238 m).

348

Mount Toradeh (highest peak of the Covasins) is 44,325 cubits, or 41,425 feet (12,726 m). In comparison, Mt. Everest, the highest peak on Earth, measures approx. 28,760 feet (8,850 m), Mt. McKinley in Alaska measures 20,320 feet (6,242 m) and Mt. Hood in Oregon measures 11,239 feet (3,452 m).

Because Piral and Chyoradan are slightly larger than Earth, and their masses are therefore greater, people from these planets are generally slightly smaller and lighter than people on Earth. As demonstrated in the examples above, mountain ranges on Piral are also usually larger than Earth ranges. Since the curvature of Piral is not as pronounced, mountain ranges can be seen from a farther distance than they can on Earth. The Tyenar Range is therefore still visible from Nadil. Both mountain ranges (Covasin and Tyenar) can be seen from the top of a multi-story building in Tolares, or, of course, from almost anywhere in the Desert of Vortelan.

Currency

Just before and during the time of the Selanian Civil War, which followed the Millennial Peace, the owner of a small farm in the western provinces would often earn an average of only two domani a day, which was just barely enough to survive. For this reason, Hyumosen tells Netira that her father would be fortunate to earn thirty-five ayjeni in as many years (Chapter "The Market"). If a farmer earns two domani a day, that would make 960 domani a year (one Selanian year has 480 days), or just short of one ayjen.

Selanian Currency	Consists of
Tseval	(approx. 1 cent)
Doman	100 Tsevali
Ayjen	1000 Domani

Appendix D: Introduction to the Selanian Language

Overview

Before the Galactic Diaspora, the Selanian language was the only language spoken by the races indigenous to the planet Piral. It is therefore profitable for any students of the chronological sciences to study this language in more detail. What is even more fascinating is that the language endured the Galactic Diaspora, was in use on Chyoradan for many centuries and has today once again become the language most widely employed to communicate throughout the galaxy. Scholars assume that the language was able to survive because of its significant connection to the spiritual origins of the Selanian Order and its application in the *Selani s'Ulavan*.

A characteristic aspect of the Selanian language is that new words are often formed through association and combination of existing words. Because the Selani are very conscious of the flow of the tongue, the word combinations are often abbreviated to facilitate pronunciation, thereby sacrificing semantics for aesthetics.

Script

The Selanian script is alphabetic (contrary to the symbolic script of the Elinar) and is written from right to left, like Semitic scripts on Halena Yazoral such as Hebrew or Arabic. This seems reasonable, since the Selani are generally left-handed. When compared to Yazorian scripts, the written Selanian script would appear as a cross between Arabic and the Tengwar. Of the vowels, only yamel actually has its own representation. The other vowels are usually implicated by markings above or below the consonant carrying (preceding) the vowel. In cases where this is not possible (for instance at the beginning of a word or in a diphthong), the vocalic symbol is used. Another noteworthy attribute of the Selanian script is the use of a prolonged stem to depict a voiced consonant. The Selanian script does not recognize capitalization.

Pronunciation

Generally, the Selanian language is a very soft-spoken tongue. Harsh sounds are foreign to it. All consonants that sound harsh or hard in the English language must be toned down. The following examples describe only the differences between the English and the Selanian languages.

Vowels

Vowels are all pronounced in the European form, as in *do, re, mi, fa*. The vowel *u* is pronounced as in *Luna*, or like the two o's in *boot*.

Consonants

C is always pronounced as in *cake*, even if it comes before *i* or *e*, but not as harshly as a *k*. It is never pronounced like an *s*, as in the word *celebrate*.

G is always pronounced as in *garden*, even if it comes before *i* or *e*. It is never pronounced like a *j* as in the word *germ*.

J is always pronounced softly, as in the French *jardin* or *je*, but never as in *judge*. The English language tends to pronounce *j* as *dge*, such as in the word *grudge*. To pronounce the Selanian *j* correctly, just leave out the *d*.

R is rolled softly on the tip of the tongue. It may be compared to the voiced purring of a cat.

CH is a soft, vibrant and unvoiced sound produced by letting air pass between the back of the tongue and the roof of the mouth. It is pronounced softly as in the German word *Licht*, but never harshly as in the German *Bach* or the English *church*.

Alphabet

The following table portrays all 25 letters of the Selanian alphabet in their correct order. The name of each letter is given, and a short example of its pronunciation.

Letter	Name	Pronunciation
A	ana	European pronunciation, *fa*, as in do, re, mi, fa.
M	mayen	M as in *mother*.
B	benu	B as in *bat*.
P	pilas	P as in *pilot*.
E	eti	European pronunciation, *re*, as in do, re, mi, fa.
V	vedan	V as in *value*.
F	fola	F as in *fast*.
I	ino	European pronunciation, *mi*, as in do, re, mi, fa.
T	tulas	T as in *table*.
D	domay	D as in *dive*.
N	navin	N as in *nothing*.
L	lode	L as in *large*.
S	sina	S as in *Santa*.
J	jevis	French pronunciation, as in *jardin*.
SH	shoval	SH as in *shovel*.
Z	zedi	Z as in *zebra*.
TS	tsutal	TS as in *whatsup* or as the Z in the German word *Zimmer*.
R	retu	R is rolled softly on the tip of the tongue.
O	onay	European pronunciation, *do*, as in do, re, mi, fa.
CH	chyadas	CH is pronounced softly as in the German word *Licht*.

Letter	Name	Pronunciation
C	ceta	C as in *cake*.
G	guvin	G as in *garden*.
Y	yamel	Y as in *yellow*.
H	hesot	H as in *hurricane*.
U	ulan	European pronunciation, as in *Luna*.

Numbers

The letters of the alphabet are generally employed as numbers, although a stylized version of the corresponding letter is used in the written form. Since the Selani use the decimal system, the first nine letters are generally used. The exception is the number zero, for which the Selanian word *nel* is used.

The dashes used in the table below are not written, but are only employed to demonstrate how the number is assembled.

Selanian	English
nel	zero
ana	one
mayen	two
benu	three
pilas	four
eti	five
vedan	six
fola	seven
ino	eight
tulas	nine
ana-nel	ten
an-ana	eleven
a-mayen	twelve
a-benu	thirteen

Selanian	English
a-pilas	fourteen
an-eti	fifteen
a-vedan	sixteen
a-fola	seventeen
an-ino	eighteen
a-tulas	nineteen
mayen-nel	twenty
may-ana	twenty-one
ma-mayen	twenty-two
ma-benu	twenty-three
ma-pilas	twenty-four
may-eti	twenty-five
ma-vedan	twenty-six
ma-fola	twenty-seven
may-ino	twenty-eight
ma-tulas	twenty-nine
benu-nel	thirty
pila-nel	forty
eti-nel	fifty
veda-nel	sixty
fola-nel	seventy
ino-nel	eighty
tula-nel	ninety
domay	hundred
a-domay	one hundred
ma-domay	two hundred
be-domay	three hundred
pi-domay	four hundred
e-domay	five hundred
ve-domay	six hundred
fo-domay	seven hundred
i-domay	eight hundred
tu-domay	nine hundred

Selanian	English
navin	thousand
a-navin	one thousand
adomay navin	one hundred thousand
adomay mayana	one hundred twenty-one
lode	million
sina	billion
jevis	trillion
ulana	infinity

Cardinality

Cardinality is achieved by placing the suffix *-av* after a number.

Selanian	English
anav	first, beginning
mayav	second
benav	third
pilav	fourth
etav	fifth
vedav	sixth
folav	seventh
inav	eighth
tulav	ninth
anelav	tenth
ananav	eleventh
amayav	twelfth
abenav	thirteenth
apilav	fourteenth

Selanian	English
anetav	fifteenth
manelav	twentieth
benelav	thirtieth
pinelav	fortieth
enelav	fiftieth
venelav	sixtieth
fonelav	seventieth
inelav	eightieth
tunelav	ninetieth
domayav	hundredth
adomayav	one hundredth
anavinav	one thousandth

Gender and Articles

The Selanian language recognizes two substantive genders: masculine and feminine. If a noun requires a definite or plural article, the article is placed at the end of the word as a suffix. There is no singular indefinite article in the Selanian language. The masculine singular definite article rhymes with the English word *hay*. The plural definite articles are both pronounced exactly the same, as in the English word *eye*.

Gender	Singular Definite	Plural Definite	Plural Indefinite
masculine	-ae	-ei	-i
feminine	-a	-ai	-i

Examples

The formal address of the Selanian godhead is *The One*. *One* in Selanian is *ana*. *The One* is therefore written as *Anae*, since the godhead is recognized as a masculine entity in the Selanian faith.

The word for wind or spirit in the Selanian language is *selan*. The word is masculine, so *the wind* or *the spirit* would be *selanae*. The Sword of Selanae must therefore be translated as *The Sword of the Spirit*.

The word for *fire* is *pilan* in the Selanian language and is also masculine. *The fire* is translated as *pilanae*. The plural form, *the fires*, would be written as *pilanei*.

In English, one sometimes refers to *Mother Earth*. This metaphor receives its own significance in the Selanian language, since *piral*, or *earth*, is feminine. *The Earth* is therefore written as *pirala*.

Water is *osal* in Selanian and is feminine. *The Great Waters* of Halena Yazoral are referred to by the Selani as *osalai linos*.

Velan is the Selanian term for *sun* and is also feminine. The sun of Piral is therefore referred to as *Velana*.

The concept of gender is used profoundly in the Selanian marriage ritual. The male symbols of fire (light) and wind (spirit) are placed in the left and right hands (respectively) of the groom during the ceremony, and are complemented by the female symbols of water and earth in the left and right hands of the bride. As the ritual progresses, fire and earth, spirit and water are joined, converging into a new form of life.

Pronouns

Personal Pronouns

Subject personal pronouns usually aren't required in combination with verbs. They are only used when denoting emphasis. The Selanian language does not differentiate between subject and object personal pronouns.

Person	Selanian	English
Singular		
	ana	I / me
	esa	you
	adae, ada	he / him, she / her
Plural		
	anu	we / us
	esta	you
	atae	they

Possessive Adjectives

Because possessive pronouns are constructed from possessive adjectives in the Selanian language, the possessive adjectives are shown here first. Possessive adjectives are constructed by adding the suffix –r to the personal pronoun.

Person	Selanian	English
Singular		
	anar	my
	esar	your
	adaer, adar	his, her

Person	Selanian	English
Plural		
	anur	our
	estar	your
	ataer	their

Possessive Pronouns

Possessive pronouns are built from the possessive adjectives by adding the suffix *–ae*.

Person	Selanian	English
Singular		
	anarae	mine
	esarae	yours
	adaerae, adarae	his, hers
Plural		
	anurae	ours
	estarae	yours
	ataerae	theirs

Verbs

Verbs in the Selanian language usually end in *–ar* or *–ir*. Conjugation and tenses are quite simple, since there don't seem to be any exceptions to the rules.

Conjugation

Normally, the Selanian language doesn't use personal pronouns in combination with a verb. The pronoun is implied by conjugation, as in Spanish or Italian. Selanian verbs are conjugated by adding the corresponding suffix to the end of the verb.

Person	Selanian	English
Singular		
first person	-an	I
second person	-es	you
third person	-ae, -a	he, she
Plural		
first person	-anu	we
second person	-esta	you
third person	-atae	they
Examples		
	sir	to be
	siran	I am
	sires	you are
	sirae, sira	he is, she is
	siranu	we are
	siresta	you are

Person	Selanian	English
	siratae	they are
	votalar	**to be sorry**
	votalaran	I am sorry
	votalares	you are sorry
	votalarae, votalara	he is sorry, she is sorry
	votalaranu	we are sorry
	votalaresta	you are sorry
	votalaratae	they are sorry

Voice, mood and tense

Voice, mood and tense are expressed by prefixes joined to the root of the verb, or, in the case of the future tense, an affix inserted directly into the verb itself. If mixed forms are used, the correct sequence is voice, mood, and then tense.

Form	Selanian	English
Simple Past Tense	te-	
Present Perfect Tense	ta-	
Past Perfect Tense	to-	
Future Tense	-av-	
Passive Voice	a-	
Subjunctive Mood	la-	
Examples		
Simple Past Tense	tesiranu	we were

Form	Selanian	English
	temilantarae	he took
	tevaran	I went
Present Perfect Tense	tamilantaran	I have taken
	tasirae	he has been
	tacunatiratae	they have acted
Past Perfect Tense	tomilantarae	he had taken
	tojevaranu	we had helped
	tocosiresta	you had sung (pl.)
Future Tense	saviran	I will be
	enaviranu	we will return
	milavantarae	he will take
Passive Voice	amilantarae	it is taken
	alicosar	to be praised
	atecozatalarae	it was destroyed
Subjunctive Mood	latilares	you would/could tell
	lasiranu	we would be
	lamilantaran	I would take

Appendix E: Selanian - English Dictionary

The following dictionary is only a short excerpt of the official Selanian dictionary stored in the scholastic library of the Selanian Order on Chyoradan. The official dictionary itself contains over 600,000 entries. The excerpt should assist any parties interested in studying the accounts portrayed in the work titled *The Traveler* to better understand the culture of Piral during the time before and during the Selanian Civil War. The work was compiled by a good friend of Philip Brannon and has been appraised by linguistic experts of the Selanian Order. The Advisory Council wishes to extend its gratitude to the author for the time, effort, and affinity to detail apparent in his research.

The entries portrayed in this excerpt were placed in the alphabetic order of the English language to facilitate any queries regarding Selanian vocabulary.

Selanian	English	Function
a, al	to	preposition
-a	the	suffix definite article feminine
ada, adae	she/her, he/him	personal pronoun
adanis	heaven	noun; feminine
adar, adaer	her, his	possessive adjective
-ae	the	suffix definite article masculine
alin	again	adverb
alin cel alin	here and there	adverbial phrase
alin set'alin	to and fro	adverbial phrase
alin ten'alin	time after time	adverbial phrase
alin vor alin	by and by	adverbial phrase
A'mada	Good Lord! (Anae + mada)	expletive

Selanian	English	Function
ambaren	fullness	noun; feminine
ana	one	adjective
ana	I, me	personal pronoun
Anae	The One	noun; masculine
anam	once	adverb
anar	my	possessive adjective
anarae	mine	possessive pronoun
anavae	the beginning, the first	noun; masculine
anavelan	sunrise (beginning or first sun)	noun; feminine
anemar	ashes	noun; feminine
anu	we, us	personal pronoun
anur	our	possessive adjective
-as	little (as in talas, little man, or porodas, little squirrel)	diminutive suffix
atae	they, them	personal pronoun
ataer	their	possessive adjective
aten	behind	preposition
ates	buttocks	noun; masculine
atezat	anus	noun; masculine
ayjen	Selanian currency	noun; feminine
bemar	hand	noun; masculine
cadan	when	adverb
camar	how, as, like	adverb
cel	for	preposition
cemitar	to kill	verb
cena	who	pronoun
cetesa	goat-like creature	noun; feminine
chyeves	horse-like creature	noun; masculine
Chyoradan	Heavenly Paradise	noun; feminine
chyoras	paradise	noun; feminine
cita	why	adverb
civar	which	adverb; pronoun
coni	where	adverb
cor	to make, to become, to do	verb

Selanian	English	Function
coritan	business	noun: masculine
corasetal	creation	noun; feminine
corasetar	to make new, to create	verb
corvosar	to make love	verb
cosir	to sing	verb
costar	to penetrate	verb
costenan	intelligence	adjective; noun; masculine
cover	to travel	verb
covasatal	traveleress (traveling woman)	noun; feminine
covasin	impassable	adjective
covatal	traveler (traveling man)	noun; masculine
cozatalar	to make to nothing, destroy	verb
cozaten	destruction	noun; feminine
culen	what	adverb; pronoun
cunatir	to act	verb
desar	okay, fine, alright	adjective; adverb
deventas	drink brewed from roasted cereals, something like coffee	noun; masculine
dima, dimalen, dimalis	bad, worse, worst	adjective
dineval	evil	noun; masculine
dinevel	evil	adjective
doman	Selanian currency	noun; masculine
ela	there	adverb, pronoun
eli	here	adverb
enimar	to revive	verb
enir	to return	verb
esa	you	personal pronoun; singular
esar	your	possessive adjective
esarae	yours	possessive pronoun
esta	you (pl.)	personal pronoun; plural

Selanian	English	Function
estar	your (pl)	possessive adjective; plural
etino	The difference between life and death (the Selanian words for life and death, nemata and nimata, are only distinguished by the second vowel).	adverbial phrase; idiom
felen	dirt	noun; masculine
feles	dirty	adjective
fetara	dish of something similar to beans	noun; feminine
fires	thread	noun; masculine
gedashol	ratlike rodent	noun; masculine
halen	planet	noun; feminine
hitar	to damn, to condemn	verb
hites	damned, blasted	adjective
hi'tev	goddamn	adjective, expletive
imala	kindness	noun; feminine
imalan	kind	adjective
isan	joy	noun; feminine
jeval	help	noun; feminine
jevar	to help	verb
jites	colorful bird native to the Southern Covasins	noun; masculine
licosar	to praise	verb
linos	large, big, important	adjective; adverb
lovanir	to obscure	verb
lu	in, through	preposition
mada, madalen, madalis	good, better, best	adjective

Selanian	English	Function
madan	good, goodness	noun; feminine
madanimata	summer (good life)	noun; masculine
milantar	to take	verb
milusir	to learn	verb
mir	to celebrate	verb
mitalen	hate, anger n.	noun; masculine
miter	to hate	verb
mivelin	bird similar to an eagle	noun; masculine
nar	to walk, to wander	verb
ne	not	adverb
nel	none, zero	pronoun; adverb
nelanimata	winter (no life)	noun; masculine
nemar	to die	verb
nemata	death	noun; masculine
netar	to blow	verb
nevar	to stand still, hold ones breathe	verb
nevelan	night (no sun)	noun; feminine
nevilas	darkness (no light)	noun; masculine
nimar	to live	verb
nimata	life	noun; feminine
nola, nolasen, nolasin	low, lower, lowest	adjective
nolad	servant, priest	noun; masculine
Noladen Tina	High Priest	noun; masculine
Nolasa Tina	High Priestess	noun; feminine
nolasad	priestess	noun; feminine
nolavelan	afternoon (low sun)	noun; feminine
norven	league	noun; masculine
novantan	flower	noun; feminine
osal	water	noun; feminine
panar	to beg	verb
par	to speak	verb
paren	language	noun; feminine
penir	to ask	verb
pesan	thing	noun; masculine

Selanian	English	Function
pesat	things	noun; feminine
pesatas	little things	noun; feminine
petar	to stop	verb
pilan	fire	noun; masculine
pilar	to make fire, to breathe fire	verb
pir	to give	verb
pir cel	to provide	verb
piral	earth	noun; feminine
pora	golden	adjective
porodas	small golden squirrel	noun; masculine
runam	finger	noun; masculine
sar	to sail	verb
satal	woman	noun; feminine
satulen	emptiness	noun; feminine
se, te	from, of	preposition
selan	wind, spirit	noun; masculine
seta	fresh, new, young	adjective
setanal	child	noun; masculine
setanimata	spring (fresh or new life)	noun; feminine
setavelan	morning (fresh sun)	noun; masculine
seten	before	preposition
sevonatar	to scatter	verb
sevaten	the scattering, Diaspora	noun; feminine
sevon	division	noun; masculine
sina te nevilas	place of darkness, hell	noun; masculine
sinas	place	noun; masculine
sinaven	swanlike water fowl	noun; feminine
sine	no	adverb
sir	to be	verb
sirae	he is	verb; third person singular
siran	I am	verb; first person singular
sires	you are	verb; second person singular
sitanem	Winged death (weapon	noun; masculine

Selanian	English	Function
	developed by Lord Chyardal Tolares)	
sitar	to fly, to take wing	verb
sutan	dovelike bird	noun; feminine
tal	man	noun; masculine
talas	little man (diminutive)	noun; masculine
tanas	small	adjective
tani	this	pronoun; adjective
tavasin	stranger	noun; masculine
te, se	from, of	preposition
te'linos!	best translated as 'My god!' or 'Great god!'	expletive
teman	dust	noun; masculine
tena	after	adverb
Tena Corasetal	After Creation	adverb
tenar	reeds	noun; feminine
tev'anar!	best translated as 'Oh, my god!'	expletive
teval	god	noun; masculine
tevasal	goddess	noun; feminine
tezatal	no matter, you're welcome, that's alright (of nothing)	adverb
ti	yes	adverb
tilar	to tell	verb
tina	high, old, ripe, mature	adjective
tinanimata	fall (old life)	noun; feminine
tinar	to mature, grow up	verb
tinatalir	to be grateful, thankful	verb
tinatar	to thank	verb
tinavelan	noon (high sun)	noun; feminine
tivanar	to circle	verb
tivanes	circle, year	noun; feminine
tratan	house	noun; masculine
trates	town, city	noun; feminine
tsemir	to allow	verb
tseval	Selanian currency	noun; masculine
tusat	difference	noun; masculine

Selanian	English	Function
tyenares	majestic	adjective
ulanav	end, last, goal	noun; masculine
ulanavae	the last, the end	noun; masculine
ulavan	eternity	noun; feminine
ulavar	to cease, stop	verb
ulavelan	evening (last or end sun; sunset)	noun; feminine
vamir	to know	verb
var	to go	verb
vatalas	little wanderer	noun; masculine
Velabenav	Third Day; Tuesday	noun; masculine
Velamayav	Second Day; Monday	noun; masculine
velan	sun; f. , day	noun; feminine
Velanav	First Day; Sunday	noun; masculine
Velanetav	Fifth Day; Thursday	noun; masculine
velanitras	galaxy	noun; feminine
Velapilav	Fourth Day; Wednesday	noun; masculine
Velavedav	Sixth Day; Friday	noun; masculine
Velavides	Holy Day; Saturday	noun; masculine
velitra	galactic	adjective
venir	to come	verb
vetanar	to swallow, consume	verb
viden	messenger	noun; masculine
vides	pure, holy	adjective
Videsa Pora	Golden Messenger (used as a name)	noun; feminine
Videsan Pora	Golden Messenger (used as a title)	noun; feminine
vilanevel, vilanev, vinev	moon (light of night)	noun; masculine
Vilanevos	Luna Major	noun; masculine
vilas	light	noun; masculine
vilasenim	friend (light of life)	noun; masculine
Vilatanas	Luna Minor	noun; masculine
vinev	moon, month	noun; masculine
vital	wanderer (walking man)	noun; masculine
vitel	forearm, cubit	noun; feminine

Selanian	English	Function
vonal	name	noun; feminine
vonar	to name	verb
vor	by, near	preposition
vosal	love	noun; feminine
vosar	to love	verb
votal	please	adverb
votalar	to be sorry	verb
votar	to excuse	verb
yazoral	forbidden	adjective
zat	hole	noun; masculine
zatal	nothing	noun; masculine
zatulavan	void (eternal hole)	noun; masculine
zicises	bird similar to a raven	noun; masculine

Appendix F: Index of Persons (First Name)

Name	Description
Amendel Marusen	Lord Marusen, father of Tavita.
Bejad Tsimerel	Liaison officer of the High Priestess in Divestelan. Brother of Hyelisa.
Bill Marten	Husband of Carol Marten. Best friend of Philip Brannon.
Carol Marten	Wife of Bill Marten and friend of Silana Tolares Brannon.
Caty	Catyana Faeren
Catya	Catyana Faeren
Catyana Faeren	Daughter of Lotis and Matila. Sister of Torvos, Vira, Mina, and Sinara. Best friend of Novantina Satural. The family is characterized by golden hair and blue eyes.
Cetila Marusen	Daughter of Amendel and Lusina. Sister of Tavita and Varan.
Citenes Novesta	Uncle of Pirena and captain of the Black Guard.
Corsen Divestelan	Son of Vechiles and Ilanya. Brother of Gevinesa and Yanita.
Covasatal	Selanian: Traveleress. Wife of the divine emissary of the Selani.
Covatal	Selanian: Traveler. The divine emissary of the Selani.
Culisa Sitenan	Wife of Mayor Menirel of Nadil. Best friend of Semanta Revan.
Dalina Novesta	Daughter of Lord Novesta, younger sister of Pirena.
Dena	Denatila Cemasena
Denatila Cemasena	Usually referred to as Dena. Sister of Tuvel. Operative for the Resistance in

Name	Description
	Divestelan.
Eluset	Elder of the Advisory Council. Protégé of the Prophet Nevacad and patron of Elder Yadez.
Eratis Rotasen	Brother of Zetara. Steward of the estate of Lord Tolares.
Fatasa	Acolyte in the entourage of the Lady Utalya.
Folan Revan	Cousin of Utalya, husband of Semanta. Owner of a first-rate tavern in Nadil.
Gevinesa Divestelan	Daughter of Vechiles and Ilanya. Sister of Corsen and Yanita.
Gregg Bailey	Pastor who married Philip and Silana.
Halita Penates	Sister of Vordalin and Tanola. High Priestess until her assassination during the Conference of Divestelan in 1519 TC.
Hyelisa Tsimerel	Acolyte in the entourage of the Lady Utalya. Sister of Bejad.
Hyumosen	Friend of Bejad and a merchant of chyevi in Tolares.
Lotis Faeren	Husband of Matila, father of Catyana. The family is characterized by golden hair and blue eyes.
Ludanes	Equerry of the chyeves merchant Hyumosen.
Lusina Marusen	Lady Marusen; wife of Amendel; mother of Varan, Cetila, and Tavita.
Lutrisya Cemasena	Wife of an important member of the town parliament in Nadil.
Martan	Courier of Lord Vechiles Divestelan.
Matila Faeren	Wife of Lotis, Mother of Catyana. The family is characterized by golden hair and blue eyes.
Melina Tolares	Sister of Silana Tolares Brannon.
Menirel Sitenan	Mayor of Nadil and husband of Culisa.
Mina	Minora Faeren
Minora Faeren	Daughter of Lotis and Matila. Sister of Catyana. Usually called Mina. The family is characterized by golden hair and blue eyes.

Name	Description
Mirayla	Operative of the Resistance in Divestelan.
Natilya Revan	Niece of Lady Utalya Revan and acolyte in her entourage.
Netira Cilenas	Young girl on a farm near Pitaren. Companion of Bejad Tsemirel.
Nevacad	Prophet of the Selani who constructed the Prophet's Bow. Patron of Elder Eluset of the Advisory Council.
Nevilan	Selanian: Dark One. The Dark Lord of the Elinar.
Nova	Novantina Satural
Novantina Satural	Acolyte in the entourage of the Lady Utalya Revan. Best friend of Catyana Faeren.
Philip Brannon	Husband of Silana Tolares. Friend of Bill and Carol Marten.
Picanas Catanin	Operative of the Resistance in Divestelan. Brother of Sheletas.
Pira	Pirena Novesta
Pirena Novesta	Daughter of Lord Novesta, Sister of Talenon and Dalina, niece of Citenes. Captain of the Crimson Brigade.
Pival Tolares	Lord and High Priest. Leads last attack upon Nevilan's army but perishes in a duel with the Dark Lord at Malentisa in 534 TC.
Redina	Acolyte in the entourage of the Lady Utalya.
Semanta Vetena Revan	Wife of Folan Revan.
Sheletas Catanin	Leader of the Resistance in Divestelan. Brother of Picanas.
Silana Tolares Brannon	First wife of Philip, sister of Melina.
Sinara Faeren	Youngest daughter of Lotis and Matila. Sister of Catyana. The family is characterized by golden hair and blue eyes.
Sitenayla	Acolyte in the entourage of the Lady Utalya.
Sutanay	Eldest of the Demantar.
Tal	Vatal Penates
Talas	Vatal Penates

Name	Description
Talenon Novesta	Brother of Pirena. Priest of the Videsian Order and head of Lord Divestelan's intelligence network.
Tamenisa Seralotes	Protégée of the High Priestess Silana Tolares.
Tanola Penates	Sister of the High Priest Vordalin and the assassinated High Priestess Halita.
Tavita Marusen	Daughter of Lord Amendel Marusen. Former captain of the Crimson Brigade. Covert operative for the western provinces.
Tilantes	Elder of the Advisory Council. Protégé of Elder Yadez and patron of Elder Yonatan.
Torvos Faeren	Son of Lotis and Matila. Brother of Catyana. The family is characterized by golden hair and blue eyes.
Traveler	Also called Vilam or Vilamadan. Divine Emissary of the Selanian Order.
Tuvel Cemasena	Brother of Dena. Operative of the Resistance in Divestelan.
Utalya Revan	Lady Utalya Revan, one of the last High Priestesses during the decline of the Millennial Peace and patroness to Novantina Satural. Maiden Name was Utalya Bevelas. Sister of Lord Tolin Bevelas, Ilanya, and Renestal.
Varan Marusen	Covert operative of the Resistance in Divestelan. Fiancé of Dena Cemasena. Killed by his sister Tavita Marusen after his cover was compromised.
Vatal Penates	Adopted son of Regas and Novisya. Also known as Vatalas, Talas or Tal.
Vechiles Divestelan	Lord Divestelan; husband of Ilanya; and father of Corsen, Gevinesa, and Yanita.
Vilam	Assumed name of the Traveler on Piral. Short for Vilamadan.
Vilamadan	Name given to the Traveler by Novantina Satural. Shortened to Vilam.
Vilasan	Bright One. High Scholar of the Elinar. Later known as Nevilan.
Vinesa	Gevinesa Divestelan

Name	Description
Vira	Zetavira Faeren
Vodana Satural	Sister of Nova. A very renowned musician during her time.
Vordalin Penates	High Priest before and during the Selanian Civil War.
Yadez	Elder of the Advisory Council. Protégé of Elder Eluset and patron of Elder Tilantes.
Yanita Divestelan	Daughter of Vechiles and Ilanya. Sister of Gevinesa and Corsen.
Yonatan	Elder of the Selanian Order. Protégé of Elder Tilantes.
Zetara Rotasen	Personal handmaiden of Gevinesa Divestelan. Sister of Eratis. Killed during a retaliatory strike by the Black Guard in the spring of 1524 TC.
Zetavira Faeren	Daughter of Lotis and Matila. Sister of Catyana. Usually called Vira. The family is characterized by golden hair and blue eyes.

Appendix G: Index of Persons (Family Name or House)

Name	Description
Bailey, Gregg	Pastor who married Philip and Silana.
Brannon, Philip	Husband of Silana.
Brannon, Silana Tolares	First wife of Philip. Sister of Melina.
Catanin, Picanas	Operative of the Resistance in Divestelan. Brother of Sheletas.
Catanin, Sheletas	Leader of the Resistance in Divestelan. Brother of Picanas.
Cemasena, Denatila	Usually referred to as Dena. Sister of Tuvel. Operative for the Resistance in Divestelan.
Cemasena, Lutrisya	Wife of an important member of the town parliament in Nadil.
Cemasena, Tuvel	Brother of Dena. Operative of the Resistance in Divestelan.
Cilenas, Netira	Young girl on a farm near Pitaren. Companion of Bejad Tsemirel.
Divestelan, Corsen	Son of Vechiles and Ilanya. Brother of Gevinesa and Yanita.
Divestelan, Gevinesa	Daughter of Vechiles and Ilanya. Sister of Corsen and Yanita.
Divestelan, Vechiles	Lord Divestelan; husband of Ilanya; and father of Corsen, Gevinesa, and Yanita.
Divestelan, Yanita	Daughter of Vechiles and Ilanya. Sister of Gevinesa and Corsen.
Faeren, Catyana	Daughter of Lotis and Matila. Best friend of Novantina Satural. The family is characterized by golden hair and blue eyes.
Faeren, Lotis	Husband of Matila. Father of Catyana. The family is characterized by golden hair

Name	Description
	and blue eyes.
Faeren, Matila	Wife of Lotis. Mother of Catyana. The family is characterized by golden hair and blue eyes.
Faeren, Minora	Daughter of Lotis and Matila. Sister of Catyana. Usually called Mina. The family is characterized by golden hair and blue eyes.
Faeren, Sinara	Youngest daughter of Lotis and Matila. Sister of Catyana. The family is characterized by golden hair and blue eyes.
Faeren, Torvos	Son of Lotis and Matila. Brother of Catyana. The family is characterized by golden hair and blue eyes.
Faeren, Zetavira	Daughter of Lotis and Matila. Sister of Catyana. Usually called Vira. The family is characterized by golden hair and blue eyes.
Marten, Bill	Husband of Carol Marten. Best friend of Philip Brannon.
Marten, Carol	Wife of Bill Marten. Friend of Silana Brannon.
Marusen, Amendel	Lord Marusen, father of Tavita.
Marusen, Cetila	Daughter of Amendel and Lusina. Sister of Tavita and Varan. First Lieutenant of the Crimson Brigade. Friend of Captain Pirena Novesta.
Marusen, Lusina	Lady Marusen; wife of Amendel; mother of Varan, Cetila, and Tavita.
Marusen, Tavita	Daughter of Amendel Marusen. Former captain of the Crimson Brigade. Covert operative for the western provinces.
Marusen, Varan	Covert operative of the Resistance in Divestelan. Fiancé of Dena Cemasena. Killed by his sister Tavita Marusen after his cover was compromised.
Novesta, Citenes	Uncle of Pirena and captain of the Black Guard.
Novesta, Dalina	Daughter of Lord Novesta, younger sister of Pirena.
Novesta, Pirena	Daughter of Lord Novesta, Sister of

Name	Description
	Talenon and Dalina, niece of Citenes. Captain of the Crimson Brigade.
Novesta, Talenon	Brother of Pirena. Priest of the Videsian Order and head of Lord Divestelan's intelligence network.
Penates, Halita	Sister of Vordalin and Tanola. High Priestess until her assassination during the Conference of Divestelan in 1519 TC.
Tolares, Melina	Sister of Silana Tolares Brannon.
Penates, Tanola	Sister of the High Priest Vordalin and the assassinated High Priestess Halita.
Penates, Vatal	Adopted son of Regas and Novisya. Also known as Vatalas, Talas, or Tal.
Penates, Vordalin	High Priest before and during the Civil War.
Revan, Folan	Cousin of Utalya, husband of Semanta. Owner of a first-rate tavern in Nadil.
Revan, Natilya	Niece of Utalya and acolyte in her entourage.
Revan, Semanta Vetena	Wife of Folan.
Revan, Utalya	Lady Utalya Revan, one of the last High Priestesses during the decline of the Millennial Peace and patroness to Novantina Satural. Maiden Name was Utalya Bevelas. Sister of Lord Tolin Bevelas, Ilanya and Renestal.
Rotasen, Eratis	Brother of Zetara. Steward of the estate of Lord Tolares.
Rotasen, Zetara	Personal handmaiden of Gevinesa Divestelan. Sister of Eratis. Killed during a retaliatory strike by the Black Guard in the spring of 1524 TC.
Satural, Novantina	Acolyte in the entourage of the Lady Utalya Revan. Best friend of Catyana Faeren.
Satural, Vodana	Sister of Nova. A very renowned musician during her time.
Seralotes, Tamenisa	Protégée of the High Priestess Silana Tolares.
Sitenan, Culisa	Wife of Mayor Menirel of Nadil. Best

Name	Description
	friend of Semanta Revan.
Sitenan, Menirel	Mayor of Nadil and husband of Culisa.
Tolares, Pival	Lord and High Priest. Leads last attack upon Nevilan's army but perishes in a duel with the Dark Lord at Malentisa in 534 TC.
Tsimerel, Bejad	Liaison officer of the High Priestess in Divestelan. Brother of Hyelisa.
Tsimerel, Hyelisa	Acolyte in the entourage of the Lady Utalya. Sister of Bejad.

Appendix H: Index of Places

Name	Description
Bevelas	Town in the eastern provinces and on the Suviltan Highway. It is under direct rule of a lordship of one of the Great Houses.
Cemasena	Town in the western provinces and on the Suviltan Highway. It is under direct rule of a lordship of one of the Great Houses.
Chyenesar	Lake, swamp, and moor region east of the Tyenar Mountains.
Chyoradan	Selanian: Heavenly Paradise. A new world promised to the Selani in case Piral was ever destroyed.
Covasin Mountains	The Covasins (Selanian for "Impassable") are a very long and broad range of extremely high mountains and mark the western border of the Suviltan Plateau. The highest peak is Mt. Toradeh.
Divestelan	City at the feet of the Covasin Mountains. Capital of the Western Suviltan Provinces.
Elinas	Little town situated on the lake of the same name. It is under the political rule of Tolares and is governed by a mayor, who is the direct representative of Lord Tolares. Last major civilized stop before going into the southern wilderness or the Desert of Vortelan.
Faeren	Little town at the feet of the Southern Covasins in the Plains of Tesalin. It is under the political rule of a lordship of one of the minor houses.
Gisatena	Little town under the rule of a Lordship at the southern edge of the Suviltan Plateau.
Halena Yazoral	Selanian: The Forbidden Planet. Earth,

Name	Description
	which constitutes the center of the universe for the Selani, has been placed out of bounds by the prophets.
Malentisa	Former capital of the Elinian provinces before the Cataclysm. Now lies in an outcrop of the Tyenar Mountains in the Desert of Vortelan.
Marusen	Town nestled on the eastern slopes of the Covasin Mountains and under direct rule of a lordship of one of the Great Houses.
Nadil	Little town between Tolares and Vetena on the Suviltan Highway. It is under the political rule of Tolares and is governed by a mayor, who is the direct representative of Lord Tolares.
Navaren	The Northern Forests, which spread out from north of the Sea of Ventara to north of the Chyenesar. Legend has it that the Navaren is the home of the Tinavar, the Unicorns.
Navaresa	Town on the border of the Eastern Suviltan Provinces and gateway to the Navaren, the Northern Forests.
Novesta	Town of the Western Suviltan Provinces on the Suviltan Highway. It is directly controlled by a lordship of one of the Great Houses.
Peladin	Province west of the Sea of Ventara. Famous for its breeding farms of porodi (golden squirrels).
Penates	Little town in the Eastern Suviltan Provinces. It is under the political rule of a lordship of one of the minor houses.
Pitaren	Little town in the Western Suviltan Provinces, which is controlled by Lord Novesta and therefore has a mayor.
Revan	Town in the eastern provinces, which is under direct rule of a lordship of one of the Great Houses.
Satural	Little town in the Eastern Suviltan

Name	Description
	Provinces. It is under the political rule of a lordship of one of the minor houses.
Sumelan	Prairie south of the Tonisian Plateau.
Suvilta	City on the Suviltan Plateau between Elinas and Revan.
Suviltan Plateau	Large, fertile plateau ledged between the Covasin Mountains in the west, the Tyenar Mountains in the east, the Navaren (Northern Forests) in the north, and the Desert of Vortelan in the south.
Suviltan River	River that flows out of the Covasin Mountains, into Lake Divestelan, and then on to Lake Elinas.
Tesalin, Plains of	Plains west of the Covasin Mountains and south of the Sea of Ventara. Houses the crater of the asteroid that fell during the Cataclysm. Famous for its Tesalian steel and distinct breed of chyevi.
Tonisia	City on the Tonisian Plateau.
Tonisian Plateau	Large, fertile plateau (similar to the Suviltan) ledged between the Covasin Mountains in the west, the Tyenar Mountains in the east, the Sumelan (Prairie) in the south, and the Desert of Vortelan in the north.
Tolares	Main economic center of Piral. Largest city of the Eastern Suviltan Provinces. Under direct rule of the lordship of one of the Great Houses.
Toradeh, Mount	Highest peak of the Covasin Mountains. Measured at 41,425 ft. (12,726 m). Its stones were used to build the City of Divestelan.
Travis	City of Light. Legislative Capital of Piral located at the foot of Mt. Vaduras (Tyenar Mountains). Seat of the Advisory Council of the Selanian Order.
Tyenar Mountains	Mountain Range that is not quite as high and broad as the Covasins, but has very majestic peaks (Tyenar is Selanian for

Name	Description
	majestic). The highest peak is Mt. Vaduras.
Vaduras, Mount	Highest peak of the Tyenar Mountains. Measured at 30,071 ft. (9,238 m).
Ventara, Sea of	Largest body of water on the planet Piral. Legend has it that it is the home of the Ventaren, the Mermaids.
Vetena	Town in the eastern provinces, which is under direct rule of a lordship of one of the Great Houses.
Vortelan	Desert region south of the Suviltan Plateau. Once a very fertile region which contained the Elinian capital, Malentisa.